TOMORROW THE SUN MIGHT COME OUT

MIGHT | No one could be sure. Some years the sun didn't break through until as late as June or July.

Jeremiah Fronterhouse Cody remembered one childhood year when the sun had never really broken through at all. Of course, some of the few remaining Oldtimers like to talk about the days when they claimed there had been blue skies every month.

Sometimes Oldtimers were more trouble than they were worth, as though they always wanted to go back to the days before Shudderday, before the tectonic plates had moved, when the ground had been solid and didn't tremble under your feet every now and again. There weren't lots of things left anymore like the Oldtimers remembered them. But every month there were fewer and fewer Oldtimers to remember the way their world had been, so eventually it wouldn't make any difference. They'd just fade to memories as strange as the stories in the history books, and pretty soon be just another row of sunken graves to be tended on God Remember Day.

Cody tried not to think too much about things like that. Still, there wasn't a day that something didn't happen to remind him of time and history. But if he ever found Ann and his baby, he'd make sure the past didn't look so Oldtimer-different to his child.

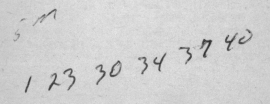

SHUDDERCHILD

WARREN C. NORWOOD

BANTAM BOOKS

TORONTO • NEW YORK • LONDON • SYDNEY • AUCKLAND

All characters and events in this story are entirely fictitious and any resemblance to actual persons living or dead, and actual incidents or events, is purely coincidental.

SHUDDERCHILD
A Bantam Spectra Book / May 1987

Bantam Books are published by Bantam Books, Inc. Its trademark, consisting of the words "Bantam Books" and the portrayal of a rooster, is registered in U.S. Patent and Trademark Office and in other countries. Marca Registrada. Bantam Books, Inc., 666 Fifth Avenue, New York, New York 10103.

For my parents with love, a book they can both read.
In tribute to
Alfred Wegener
whose insight into the dynamics of our changing earth
led to a revolution of understanding.

SPECIAL ACKNOWLEDGMENT

The MUST-Kit knife used in this story is an original Jack W. Crain design, and the trademarks MUST'KIT and MUST-Kit are his, and are used here with his permission. The prototype knife (marked "O X," "Prototype," and "MUST'KIT" on the back, and "CRAIN" with the crane symbol on the front) and its sheath were made for this book and presented to me. I altered the name slightly for reasons obvious in the text. My special thanks to Jack for his enthusiasm, generosity, and especially his superb craftsmanship. Anyone interested in more information about Crain Knives should write directly to Jack W. Crain, Rt. 2, Box 221-F, Weatherford, TX 76086.

HISTORICAL NOTE

A constitution for the State of West Texas was written in 1868 by a group of scalawags too cowardly to sign their names to the document. It proposed the political and physical division of Texas into two separate states during Reconstruction. Nothing came of that effort, as we hope nothing came of the scalawags.

The 1868 constitution was not used as a model for the Constitution of the Republic of West Texas. However, those wishing to examine the 1868 constitution may do so in the Rare Book Room of the North Texas State University Library in Denton.

SHUDDERCHILD

CHAPTER 1

IN THE BEGINNING | March. West Texas. The Republic of West Texas.

Wind. Cool wind from the north. Yesterday, warmer wind from the south. But always the wind.

The wind and survival—gust and breath—cling to the land, their majesty man-made, their new forms part of the new rhythms of life after Shudderday.

Flowers, the first ones to open their swollen buds, mark the near landscape with color—an early clump of bluebonnets, a few indian paintbrushes, red-orange mostly, but here and there yellow or pale peach-colored ones, a bit of bright pink phlox, a stray lavender spiderwort bouncing in the tall grass, and the odd dark red firewheels scattered amongst the black-eyed green-thread.

Later there would be mallows, orange and purple, or little fuchsia winecups, and the tiny white and purple fog-fruit, and blooming cactus, yellow cholla and prickly pear with its red fruit, and purple clumps of milk-vetch, and of course, cotton, most of it this far north growing wild amidst the mesquite—part of the history of change. When the heat of summer came there would be wild indigo and horsemint, and thistles—always the pink and purple thistles nodding stiffly in the constant Texas wind, along with deceptive star thistles soft to the touch.

Today under the grey skies there were only muted shadows of spring color daubed on the flat plain—and the grey-green line of a militia squad moving in single file well below the edge of the caprock, guarding their country against invasion from the Indian Nation, protecting the reliable supply of water that Shudderday had brought to the once dry West Texas land.

Today if the Texas militiamen made contact with the rumored patrol from the Indian Nation, red would blossom briefly on the tan uniforms of the Nates. But the red would dry quickly and darken to ruddy brown like the dark earth under the wildflowers.

Tomorrow the sun might come out. Might. No one could be

sure. Some years the sun didn't break through until as late as June or July.

Jeremiah Fronterhouse Cody remembered one childhood year when the sun had never really broken through at all. Oh, it had peeked through an occasional hole in the sky every once in a while surrounded by a patch of blue—just enough blue, like his grandmother used to say, to make a pair of pants for a sailor. But there was no real sunshine that year, not the kind that cast sharp dark shadows on the ground and made you feel like you could reach to the heavens—not that rare and special kind of sunshine that everyone waited for in the heat of summer.

Of course, some of the few remaining Oldtimers liked to talk about the days when they claimed there had been blue skies every month. Blue skies, mind you, hard crystal blue, not the pale milky-blue skies that made everyone so happy when the clouds opened now.

But the Oldtimers talked about a lot of things like sunshine and population and the old U.S. of A. and the different world they had been born into. Sometimes they held pictures in front of their grandchildren's faces—pictures of bright days with people standing almost naked beside boats, pictures of cars and Christmas trees and forgotten relatives on tractors in rows of cotton, and pictures of crowded cities lit with the light of another time when power weren't near so precious.

The Oldtimers liked to show the movies, too. Lots of movies. "Full of history," they said, and full of things that they laughed at, but their children didn't, and things they cried over that made their children and grandchildren stare at them with worried eyes.

Cody thought the movies were probably the worst thing for the Oldtimers because he had heard about too many Oldtimers found dead of old age or giving up. Like it was a tradition or a ceremony or something, another one would be found sitting dead in front of a sparking old teevee with some movie running on automatic, the screen filled with the faded colors they loved so much. And all the while that teevee was sucking electricity from the Co-op lines.

Sometimes Oldtimers were more trouble then they were worth, like they always wanted—even the best of them—to go back to the days before Shudderday, before the tectonic plates had moved, when the ground had been solid and didn't tremble under your feet every now and again.

Like Old Man Larkin—a hundred and five years old and he still wanted to go to some place called Houston on the old maps. Didn't matter to him that years before Bono Davis had taken him all the way down through Commanche to a town called Walnut Springs and he had stood on the edge of the Mexican Sea and they had told him there weren't no Houston no more—Old Man Larkin kept talking about how much he wanted to go there.

That was the problem, of course. There weren't lots of things left anymore like the Oldtimers remembered them. But every month there were fewer and fewer Oldtimers to remember the way their world had been, so eventually it wouldn't make no difference. They'd just fade to memories as strange as the stories in the history books, and pretty soon be just another row of sunken graves to be tended on God Remember Day.

Least ways, that's how it always seemed to Cody whenever he thought much about it. But he tried not to think too much about things like that. Except no matter how much he tried not to, it seemed like there weren't a day that something didn't happen to make him think about time and history. But if he ever found Ann and his baby, he'd make sure the past didn't look so Oldtimer-different to his child.

TWO | Healer Lucy Ilseng followed the militia patrol carefully and silently, a brown shadow on a plain with no sun. The smell of their unwashed bodies drifted downwind to her and she knew that one of those militiamen was suffering from a bad case of guilt. Even through the scents of the wildflowers she detected that singular odor from one who was marked. But which one? Which one? If the chance came for her to get back to them, would she really be able to tell which one of them needed her help?

CHAPTER 2

ONE | "I read it," Morgan said, staring into the fire with quiet determination.

Cody listened to the argument with only half an ear as he sopped up the last of his stew with the rough wheat bread he had baked for the squad earlier. Morgan was barely sixteen years old and seemed to have spent most of his life reading books and listening to Oldtimers. Cody respected Morgan's knowledge, but he had heard all these arguments too many times before to care much one way or the other.

"They had regular flights all across the old United States," Morgan continued, "even from New York to California."

Azle laughed. "Readin' it don't make it so. You believe everything you read, boy, and you'll be in sludge past your ass and over your ears."

She paused as though waiting for Morgan to say something else, or for someone else to speak. Her eyes glinted darkly in the firelight and Cody thought it made her wrinkles look deeper than they were, and her face much older than her forty years. But they all looked old to him, except Morgan.

"Don't mean to make you angry, boy," Azle continued more softly. "I'm not sayin' that there weren't such flights, not even sayin' that they didn't have the planes to make 'em with." She stirred at the edge of the fire with the butt of her mesquite walking stick, and sparks chased each other up into the darkness.

"But you got to remember that the folks who wrote them history books built up everything before Shudderday to look bigger than it probably was. That's just human nature. But if there was regular flights like they said, how come they built all the I-roads? Wouldn't have needed Forty and Twenty, much less all the US-Eighty-roads if folks could have flied anywheres they wanted, now would they?"

"There were a lot more folks then," Morgan said just as stubbornly as always. "Couldn't all fly. They had to have those roads to move 'em all."

"That's just what I been tryin' to tell you, Morgan." Azle smiled like she'd won the argument. "They had the I-roads and the US-roads to move people. Don't seem they would've needed all those roads if folks could have just flied wherever they damn well pleased. I'm tellin' you, boy, flyin' was for the rich folks, and the government, and the military, of course."

"Yes, but—"

"Just listen to me, boy. There are things you got to understand about the past and you got to accept them."

Cody stood up and turned away from the fire, blotting out the sound of Azle's voice, suddenly tired of all this talk about the past. His grandfather had been born ten years before Shudderday. His father had been born thirty-five years later, and Cody eighteen years after him. Shudderday was seventy-one hard years past. Almost everyone who was old enough to remember what the world had really been like before Shudderday was long dead and buried or recycled—except folks like Old Man Larkin who didn't seem to know how to die, and he sometimes said a nuclear war would have been better because everyone would have died.

As Cody walked into the cold darkness away from the fire, his thoughts were on the more recent past, on Ann and the baby she was carrying, and how he had joined the militia to try to find her—even though there was no evidence the Nates had gotten her that day when she went out for a walk and never came home—and how he felt guilty, and angry, and full of pity for himself and her, and how stupid it was at his age to be running off to hunt for Nates when Ann had probably run off with Kendrick Johnson anyway.

Following the rutted path, Cody easily found the large old mesquite tree whose thorny bark he had skinned away earlier to prepare for this private moment. He didn't mind being the squad's Extra, at least not to Azle, because he respected her. There were times, though, when he just had to get away from all of them, away from the responsibilities, and steal some time for himself where he could shut them out of his life for an hour or two. But as he sat down and made himself comfortable under the high overcast clouds that hinted at a bright moon, Morgan's words echoed in the back of his mind.

There were a lot more folks back then.

Back then, he thought. *Back then.* Cody laid his carbine across his thighs and turned up the collar of his jacket against the wind. Then he leaned back and stared up at the sky, hoping that the moon might find a crack to peek through.

His teachers had said that *back then* the things they called the tectonic plates had been fairly stable and people had counted on the ground being solid, and the air being free of volcanic dust. *Back then* had been another world—a world Cody had never known—a world of difference before the old earth had shuddered and readjusted its crust sending earthquakes shivering around the world, and volcanoes spewing hot death into the air.

His teachers had shown them the old maps and said that back then there had been different mountains from the ones now, mountains that had fallen and risen again, and different rivers, too, rivers that had changed their courses on Shudderday, or disappeared into the ground, or spread into shallow lakes that swallowed up the countryside leaving only tops of things showing above the waterline even now.

Cody knew that Morgan was right. There had been more people back then—maybe more people than the old earth could bear up under, enough people to make its skin itch with the shifting presence of them all. So the old earth had just shuddered a couple of dozen times—no one was really sure how many times—just shivered against the itch and shrugged its skin a little like it was trying to shake off part of the crowd.

Best as anyone could tell, the old earth had shaken off the majority of the crowd. There weren't many people now, least ways not that anybody knew of by comparison to the numbers they always used when they talked about population back then.

The Republic of West Texas claimed a population of almost a hundred thousand now. That seemed like an awful lot to Cody, but the books claimed that before Shudderday the old state of Texas had a population of close to twenty million people. That meant that nearly one hundred ninety-nine out of every two hundred people in Texas had died since Shudderday.

Or something like that. Cody couldn't really cope with those numbers, and he couldn't really imagine that many people, much less that many dying. Those numbers weren't his.

His numbers made more sense. Twelve people in his family—fourteen if he counted Ann and the baby—except he couldn't count Ann and the baby because they were gone now and so was Kendrick Johnson. Maybe two hundred people in New Delwin. A hundred or so in Chalk. About sixty in Grow

City, sixty more over in Matador, and maybe three hundred in Paducah. Altogether he had probably never seen more than a total of a thousand people in his whole life, and never more than a couple of hundred together at one time.

There were lots more, he knew, in Lubbock and Armadillo and Midessa, and last year he had heard an old Scavenger tell his father that there were forty or fifty thousand people living in Dallas and Fort Worth in the Free State of DalWorth. But even that number was way too big for Cody to get his head around.

Why, in the whole West Texas Militia there were barely twenty-five hundred people, and Cody had only seen maybe two hundred of those. What did fifty thousand people look like? Or a million?—real people, not ones in Oldtimer movies. How could anybody even think about a *million* people?

Off in the distance a coyote howled sadly as though it wanted to see the moon as much as Cody did. From nearby several more coyotes joined in the lonely chorus.

Lake Paducah? Cody wondered. That's where the Nates were supposed to have some kind of camp—east of Lake Paducah along the Wichita. No, they were still too far from there—two hard days' march, anyway. But folks said coyotes always followed the Nates. No one knew why for sure, but Azle had said the Nates fed the coyotes so they would warn them if someone came near their camp at night. Maybe the Nates had come farther south than Headquarters thought. Cody shivered. Anywhere near the lake was too close to home to make him happy.

Cody didn't know much about the Nates. No one did, least ways no one he'd talked to, not for sure anyway. Cody did know that the Indian Nation had set itself up as a separate country north of the old Red River sometime after Shudderday in most of what was labeled *Oklahoma* on the old maps. Fact was that some of the old history tapes called them Okies, and the Oldtimers still did. But most folks born long after Shudderday called them Nates and said they was pretty closed-up to outsiders. Till a couple of years before now, the Nates had kept to themselves, telling Texas folks to stay south of the Red and they would stay north.

Then rumor had it two Christmases before that the eastern part of DalWorth around someplace called Paris had broken off and joined the Nates. Old Man Larkin had grinned when he shared that rumor and said that Paris and Jefferson were the only places in DalWorth good for anything anyways—like what he remembered from his childhood seventy-five years before meant something now.

No one knew for sure why the Nates had started coming south last summer around the west end of Falls Lake, first in raiding parties and then in groups of fifty or sixty claiming land for themselves. A survivor from the Falls Massacre said the Nates didn't have enough good water at home and were moving south to where there was plenty of it. The Republic had decided the Nates should stay north of the Red and that was how the water rights war between the two countries had started. Control of water rights was control of life.

Of course, it weren't really a proper war at all—not like the W-W wars Cody had read about with big armies and organized campaigns and people working hard to whip the enemy. This thing everybody called a war so far had been just a series of clashes between patrols from both countries that shot up everybody from the wrong side whenever they ran into them.

The Falls Massacre had been one of those clashes when the Nates had outnumbered the militia four to one and killed most of them—seventeen, to be exact. Cody didn't think that *massacre* was quite the right word for what had happened, but then he didn't think this was much of a war. Fact was that no one really wanted to fight it—least ways no one in the Republic—but no one wanted to open up to the Nates, either. Everybody knew that the Nates were different than real folks and didn't deserve to have no water that weren't their own.

For a fact Cody didn't want to fight the war, but there weren't nothing much else to do, what with Ann and the baby gone and all. He didn't have enough hope left in him to work his yucca farm anymore, and he felt too much guilt about her leaving to keep hanging around the old place. So he'd joined the militia. Told everyone he was going to search for Ann and the baby, them knowing and him knowing, too, that it was a lie. But it was a lie that gave him a reason for doing something—anything to keep busy and away from the farm with all its memories. He almost laughed. Even in his childhood the farm was associated with failure, like the time when he was nine and he forgot to check the fence and some wild cattle had trampled half of his grandad's vegetable—

The sound of snapping twigs almost drifted on the wind past Cody before he broke out of his dark reverie and forced himself to listen.

The wind beat gently through the grass, taunting him with

patterns of sounds, half of which could be something important, sounds he should be listening to.

There was something out there—or someone. The way the skin prickled on the back of his neck he was sure of it.

As quietly as he could, he eased his carbine's safety off, listening hard now, turning his head slowly trying to catch the sound as it moved behind the rustling screen of wind in grass.

Gimme some moonlight, he prayed, so I can see something.

Then he heard it again, another crackling of twigs off to his right.

TWO | There, Lucy thought, under the mesquite. See his rifle? See his finger already on the trigger? He is ready. He has to be. He makes the wind stink of guilt and pain.

Oh, militiaman, do not kill me now. Let me pass your camp and your rifle and your death. Then I will try to return and help you if I can.

She smiled inside. Mishla would say she was pushing her sixth sense too far trying to analyze this militiaman by the way he smelled. But Lucy knew the man hurt deep inside himself. She also knew there was no time to stop.

THREE | High above the dark plain the north wind pressed and pulled the clouds, mixing and turning them in immense swirling patterns of silver-greys and brown-grays, opening bright holes through which the moonlight splashed like elusive quicksilver sliding away over the land.

A sudden mist of light flowed across Cody and his mesquite tree. In the brief moments it took for his eyes to fully adjust to the unexpected brightness, he was sure he saw someone standing on the edge of the darkness, someone wearing a hooded cloak, dressed for traveling.

Slowly and carefully he pulled his carbine up to his shoulder and lay his cheek against its cold wooden stock. Trusting his instincts more than his vision, he aimed where he was sure the figure had stood.

"All right, hands up and move closer," he said hoarsely. He had meant to shout, but there was little power in his voice. As he peered down the carbine's short barrel he tried to steady his shaking arms against his knees. "I said, hands up and move closer." This time his voice was clearer and stronger and hung like his breath in the pale light.

The clouds overhead thickened to the texture of heavy gauze dimming the moonlight. Then the wind jerked and twisted the clouds back together, and the moonlight was gone as suddenly as it had appeared.

Cody cursed softly and reluctantly lowered the carbine from his cheek. He strained to hear something—anything that might give him more information about the silent watcher. Only the gentle sound of wind threshing the grass came back to him. It was as though the figure he had seen had dissolved into the darkness. A Scavenger, he thought, scouting our camp for tomorrow.

"Or a Nate, dummy!" he said aloud as he got quickly to his feet and moved out from under the tree. A hundred meters behind him he could see the squad's low campfire burning.

Making his way noisily around the tree he started running down the rut of a cowpath toward the fire to alert Azle and the others. He had been so caught up in his dreary mood and self-pitying thoughts that his brain hadn't fully grasped what had happened. But now his training and instincts were taking over.

He thought he saw a blur of movement off to his right, but dared not take his eyes off the dim path for fear of losing his footing. He had already endangered the squad enough without falling on his face in the dark trying to warn them.

"What is it, Cody?" a sentry asked as he neared the camp.

"Don't know," he gasped. "Maybe Nates. Saw someone out there . . . but they slipped away. Stay alert." His mind was jumping, hating these moments even as he lived them, hating the Nates and the militia and the shroud of darkness that blinded them all.

"What's goin' on?" Azle asked as she came out the last ten meters to meet him.

"Someone's out there," Cody said. "I caught the look of someone in a couple of seconds of moonlight."

"You sure?"

Suddenly he wasn't sure. Had he really seen someone when the moonlight broke through? Or had his eyes been playing tricks on him in the shifting light?

"No, I'm not sure, Azle. There wasn't enough time to be sure. But I thought I did, and I didn't want to take a chance."

"Right," she said, turning back to the rest of her extended squad. "Morgan, put the fire out. The rest of you listen up. There may be someone out there—maybe Nates even. If you even suspect anything's going on out there when you're on guard, you wake your buddy. If your buddy agrees, one of you come tell me or Cody. Now, everybody lock and load." She gave the order in the dark as Morgan doused the last embers of their campfire.

The sounds of twenty-odd bolts driving rounds into the chambers of their rifles echoed through the darkness in response. The squad had gotten her message.

"I'll take the first watch," Cody said quietly, "if that's all right with you, Azle. 'Fraid I couldn't sleep right now anyway." There was more to it than that, but Cody wasn't about to tell Azle that he felt guilty about letting his guard down. He was tired of feeling guilty every time he turned around.

"We'll both take the first watch," she said. "Then I'll take the second, and you take the third. Don't imagine anybody's gonna sleep this first watch."

"That's okay by me." For a long moment Cody stared into the night, doubting himself, but just as sure that he had seen something. "I only wish the moon would come out again," he said softly.

Azle cleared her throat. "It won't. Never does when you need it—only when you don't."

FOUR |　　Sitting very still and listening to the voices as they drifted downwind to her, Lucy knew she had been right. He was the one. Not only was the scent true, but she detected the mark in the tones of his voice, even when it was distorted in the gusting wind. Guilt left clear markers in a person's voice for the trained ear to hear just as it left its own peculiar odor—an odor different from fear or lust.

He needed healing, and Lucy would try to come back to him soon if she could. The marks were strong in him and the longer she waited, the longer his healing would take—and the more difficult it would be to help him recover.

But now there was something else she had to do, something that was far more important even than the deep healing this man would require. There were lives staked on her success.

Using the wind as a cover she moved in low, uneven strides,

blending the shuffling sounds of her feet with the rustling sounds of the grass until the two sounds were one. She tried not to hurry, tried to go no faster than the natural rhythms allowed, but her task was urgent and she had given her word.

— —
—

. . . but the way to serve God is through service to your fellow man—in the family, in the home, in the community, and in the nation, for it was one hundred years ago in the greatest Christian nation ever to exist upon the face of this earth that God's greatest will was done. In that nation, great good can be done again.

All you who sit by your radios every week listening to my broadcasts can be a part of that great service to God.

Who are these little nations that rose up when the great Christian United States was broken apart on Shudderday?

Who are these bickering little states that stand before us and dare call themselves sovereign?

Who are these groups that cry out against the reunion of a Christian nation?

We know who they are! They are the tools of the devil.

We know what they want! They want a divided people without God and church to guide them.

We know their faces, for they live among us and claim to support democracy, all the while stifling the voices of the people.

My friends, those who oppose us are the forces of evil incarnate upon our precious earth, but we can defeat them and we will defeat them because we are ". . . Christian soldiers marching as to war, with the cross of Jesus going on before. . . ."

CHAPTER 3

ONE | Cody hadn't really been asleep when Azle came to get him for the third watch. He had been lying there staring up at the closeness of the night, thinking about Ann and the baby— the baby he would probably never see, the one who would never know who his real father was.

It didn't have to be a he—it could be a daughter—but Cody always thought of the baby as a boy. Seemed natural somehow to expect a son first, and he ought to be due any time now. Might already be born for all Cody knew.

"Nothin' happenin'," Azle whispered. "Wake me as soon as it shows light. I want everybody up and ready soon as it's bright enough to see."

"Will do," Cody replied. Azle disappeared into the darkness and it was easy enough for Cody to make himself comfortable beside the dead fire and go right back to thinking about Ann.

She had been a good woman, Ann had, a better woman than he had deserved. She had given him a kind of love and affection that he had only dreamed about before, not like Deborah, not like Deborah at all. Oh, Deborah had loved him, he guessed, loved him as best as she knew how. But the thing about her had been that what Deborah wanted from him was always less than he wanted to give—less than he had to give. And what she had given him was less than he needed—or less than he thought he needed, anyway.

When Deborah had died giving premature birth to their stillborn son, Cody had felt unbearably guilty. For all the good he had been to her, he might as well have abandoned her and left her alone on the farm with her pain and suffering. He'd done everything the medwife had told him to and read and reread all the information and instructions he had copied out of Medic David's medical dictionary. But nothing he had done had seemed to make any difference, and when it was over, even though everyone had assured him that he had done all he could, he felt responsible for their deaths.

Yet after he had buried Deborah and the baby deep in the ground in the little graveyard on the rise south of the house, Cody had also felt relieved in some vague way that grew stronger in the days that followed. That unwelcomed and unexplainable sense of relief had made him feel even more guilty because he didn't understand the relief and couldn't accept it. What had Deborah ever done to him to deserve such callousness?

For a long while it had seemed to him like there'd be no getting over his guilt. But then on a trip to Dickens with his father he had met Ann, and life seemed to start over for him again right then and there in Godley's Store.

He had seen her standing there flirting with a bunch of boys off to one side of the store, and thought he hadn't seen a woman that pretty in a long time. Long thick hair the color of polished copper and eyes that seemed to burn with a blue light all their own, wearing tight faded jeans and a blue shirt tucked in at the waist, she was something special to behold, and Cody was staring at her for all he was worth, afraid maybe she'd skip out the door and he'd never see another woman that pretty again.

There were six or seven couples dancing in the aisles of the store, but it didn't look to Cody like anyone could talk her into joining them. Then for some crazy reason, she had pushed away the men standing around her and come to Cody with her hands out. When he admitted he couldn't dance, she had made him hold her in his arms and sway in time with the music. She might have been a flirt and a tease like folks said later, but somehow that night she had seen the pain in him, and without her saying anything, Cody had known that she understood him.

The boys sitting around the drink-box were playing soft music on their guitars. As Cody swayed with Ann, her body fitted to him in some kind of delicate way, he had felt more alive and more frightened than he ever had in his twenty-three years. By the time the dancing was done and the folks were leaving, he had known there was no waiting for what he felt inside.

"No telling when I'll get back this way, Miss Ann," he had said softly. "Why don't we just get married in the morning and you come home with me?" Cody was just as surprised by his impulsive proposal as he was by her immediate acceptance.

Taking her back to the farm and hearing her laughter in the fields beside him during their long days, and her soft sighs in their bed at night had given Cody joy and comfort and ease from the burden he felt about Deborah. Over time, Ann had proved to be just about everything he wanted in a wife and companion and all that he ever hoped for in a friend.

Until Kendrick Johnson.

It always came back to Kendrick Johnson. What had Ann seen in Johnson with his rough, hard hands and that smile that showed his crooked yellow teeth and looked like he'd just wrung a chicken's neck and enjoyed it? What did Kendrick Johnson have that Cody didn't? And what was the magic he used on Ann?

There were no answers for those questions and Cody knew it. Whatever Kendrick Johnson had, it had been strong enough to make Ann change, to make her slowly turn away, and to make Cody hate Kendrick Johnson and hate her too—or least ways want to hate her.

And that was the problem. He might have been able to put up with her changing, but in hating Kendrick Johnson and wanting to hate Ann and the baby she carried, too, Cody had come full circle back to what seemed to be the one constant in his life, the guilt that wouldn't give him—

A rifle barked to his left. Once. Twice. A third time.

Cody jumped and automatically pushed his carbine's safety off and rolled to his belly. Squinting into the darkness over the rifle barrel, he could see nothing. "What is it?" he called in a loud whisper.

"Something's moving out there."

"Anybody else see anything?" Azle's voice asked out of the darkness.

A chorus of quiet negatives came back from the members of the squad who were now lying alert in their circle around the cold campfire.

"Then what in hell you firin' at, boy?"

"I'm telling you, Sarge, something was moving in that draw. I saw him."

Cody shook his head. It was Morgan's voice, and he suspected that the kid was just jumpy.

"A wild cow," someone offered.

"Wasn't either. It was a person."

"Then why didn't you say that?"

Morgan didn't answer.

"All right. All right," Azle said. There was weary tension in her voice. "Everybody be on the alert. Have your flashlights ready, but for God's sake don't go flashin' them till I tell you. . . . Cody?"

"Here, Azle."

"Take Jessup and Emery and work your way out toward the mouth of that draw where Morgan was shootin'. I want to know if there's anything, or anybody, out there or not."

Cody cursed silently. The last thing they needed to do was stumble around in the dark looking for Nates. If the Nates had been there, they were probably long gone now, with all of Morgan's shooting. But he guessed Azle had to be sure about that. Nates could be laying a trap out there.

"Roland? Shelia? You ready?" he asked finally.

Two noisy shadows crawled up behind him.

"Drop all your gear except your ammo and tape that quiet if

it isn't already." As they followed his instructions, Cody hoped that if anyone was out there they had hatted-up and headed north. The only thing he wanted to find out there was natural prairie around an empty draw.

TWO | "I am Lucy, trained by Mishla," the girl chanted to herself as she marched down away from the caprock heading southeast toward Lake Paducah. "The darkened way makes the path of duty clear. I will defend the faith of my mother. All people are mine to save and heal."

The chant was one of the healing things she had learned from Mishla. Chanting kept the body in harmony and only in harmony could the body achieve its full potential. Only in harmony could the body cross the little steps of pain and break through the great wall of agony into the ecstasy of achievement. Only in harmony could she, Lucy, be all that Mishla trained her to be.

Gunfire sounded behind her, and a cold shudder went up her spine. She pulled her cloak tighter and kept walking, determined to find the braves from the Nation. It was her duty to warn them away before the Texian militia patrol found them and more blood watered the prairie.

THREE | The first show of pale grey light in the east brought a freshening breeze, as though the wind itself sought an early start on the day. Cody led Roland Jessup and Shelia Emery cautiously down a shallow draw, his ears straining to hear any message the wind might carry about Nates or other unwelcomed visitors.

Suddenly shots rang over their heads. Without thinking they all threw themselves against the side of the draw.

The sound of angry voices drifted past them, and Cody eased himself to his hands and knees in order to hear them better. It frightened him to think the Nates might be that close. Then despite the trembling tension in his body, he chuckled when he made sense of the voices. "It's the kid again," he whispered to Jessup and Emery. "Azle's chewing his ass."

"If there's anything left when we get back, I'm going to *beat* his ass," Jessup said.

"You'll have to line up behind me," Emery added as she pushed herself off the ground.

"Shhh. Keep it low." As Cody frowned at them, he realized that it still wasn't light enough for them to see his expression. "Just because Morgan's screwin' up, doesn't mean we have to. There still might be Nates out here."

Crouching low they began moving slowly down the rocky draw again. Each crunch of their steps seemed to echo into the coming day, making Cody silently curse Morgan and the Nates and Kendrick Johnson, and the draw itself which twisted and turned around chalky white outcroppings of rock that almost glowed in the predawn shadows. Every few steps Cody paused and listened, trying to decipher even the faintest sounds.

"Hear that?" Jessup asked in a low whisper.

Cody stayed as still as he could, almost holding his breath, straining his ears around the natural sounds for something— anything Jessup might have heard—wanting to hear nothing unusual. "No. What was it?"

"Gear," Jessup answered.

Then Cody heard it, faint but clear, the sounds of scuffing leather and muffled metallic thumpings, the sounds of moving men and their equipment.

The wind seemed to be shifting and he was sure the sound was not coming from their squad. But he couldn't tell if the telltale noises were approaching the draw or moving away. Moving away, he decided after a few seconds, his decision made more out of need than certainty, fearing any approaching sound that might require him to confront the enemy.

Touching Jessup on the arm he motioned up the side of the bank. Jessup signaled Emery and the three of them eased apart a double arm's length between them as they had been trained to. Slowly straightening up until they were leaning on their bellies against the bank, they peered over its edge toward the pink eastern horizon.

The ground fell rapidly away in front of them, tumbling into the darkness under the pale line of dawn. In the distance Cody thought he could detect the sheen of Lake Paducah, and for a brief moment saw something move in that elusive light.

But what? Nates? Cattle? Deer? He couldn't tell and wasn't about to commit to anything, not yet, not until he was sure. He wasn't going to be like Morgan and send shots after shadows. Anyway, by his best estimate whatever had moved was at least a mile away, maybe two. Yes, two miles, he liked that better, two miles or more—too far to have made the equipment noises they had heard.

Emery grunted loudly.

A shot cracked in the distance.

"Shelia's hit, Cody." Jessup's voice rang with panic and fear.

Cody turned in time to see Jessup sliding down the bank to Emery's side. As he ducked down to join them a second shot splattered into the draw. Tiny pieces of dirt and rock pelted his back. "Damn!" he cursed, throwing himself flat and landing on something hard that sent fire through his ribs.

For a few seconds the three of them lay still in the awful silence that seemed to mock their heavy breathing. Finally Jessup whispered, "She's hurt bad."

More shots whined over their heads chased by the barks of several rifles. Five? Ten? It was hard to tell. But Cody thought they were coming from Azle and the squad, not from whoever had shot Emery.

As he dragged himself the last few feet to where Emery lay, her body twisted like a fallen mesquite in the bottom of the draw, a terrible odor stifled his breath. His stomach turned. He wanted to vomit. Emery's bowels had emptied themselves, and Cody remembered what Azle had told him: If they smell like shit, they're dead.

Shelia Emery was dead.

Jessup was crying.

Cody pushed away from them both and heaved up the contents of his stomach in wretching spasms that tore at his ribs and made him want to scream in pain and desperation.

Emery was dead and it was his fault, just as Deborah's death had been his fault. And there was nothing he could do about it, nothing. He couldn't even stop the spasms that surged through his gut after his stomach was totally empty.

Voices shouted. Someone lay a comforting arm across his shoulders. "Easy, Cody, easy. It's okay."

But it wasn't okay and Cody knew it.

The ground trembled in shivering silence. A few loose pebbles clattered to the bottom of the draw.

"Steady, now," the voice said again. "It's only a little shake. It'll be okay."

It was Jessup's voice. Cody recognized it. Jessup was trying to reassure him, but even as his heaving stopped and he gasped for air, Cody knew it wouldn't be okay, that for him it couldn't be okay, and when the earth trembled again sending more pebbles and small rocks clattering down on his hands, some dark part of him wished this was a second Shudderday and he could die right there and then.

FOUR | Lucy sat on a flat rock soaking her right foot in the cold waters of the Pease River. The mesquite thorn had penetrated almost an inch into her sole, but after removing it and quickly treating the wound with juniper salve, she had continued her march, knowing she couldn't afford to stop until she crossed the river. The cold water would help reduce any swelling, and she could only hope she had gotten enough salve into the hole to cut off the possibility of infection.

She had done as Mishla had taught her, had put the salve on the thorn and stuck the thorn back into her foot to apply the salve, trying her best to concentrate on the litany of healing, finding new sympathy for those whom she had treated in the same manner and entreated to bear the pain before she pulled the thorn out. Now it was a deep aching hurt she would have to ignore.

In the darkened west behind her there had been gunfire and more gunfire, and Lucy feared she had missed the braves she had been sent to find. They shouldn't have been on this side of the lake at all—especially as far west as the militia camp—but she could take nothing for granted. She would first try to locate them where she had been told they were in a camp south of US-Seventy near Hackberry Hites above the Lake Paducah dam. Only if she didn't find them there, would she dare return the way she had come to search for them.

With silent resignation Lucy removed her foot from the water, dried it carefully with the inner folds of her cloak, covered the opening of the wound with more salve, then put on her sock and boot. She still had a good twelve N-miles to cover and scant time to do it in. There were three hard-roads to cross and Dunlap and Swearinginville to avoid.

Avoiding the towns was the hardest part for her, the thing she wished most wasn't necessary. But Mishla had been clear and explicit in her instructions. After the mission was finished Lucy could go to one of the chosen towns, Margaret, Crowell, or Foard

City, and send her message to Mishla, then wait for a reply and enjoy the town while she waited.

As she stood and tested her foot, Lucy smiled. Maybe it would take a long time for Mishla to reply. Maybe she would have an extra day or two—but no. The guilty man was still waiting for her, and once she warned the braves, Lucy knew she should try to find him as quickly as she could. Mishla would give her no rest, and surprisingly, Lucy no longer wanted one.

CHAPTER 4

ONE | Cody stood a grim watch as Morgan and Keene finished burying Private Shelia Emery in the rocky red soil above the draw, half his attention on the horizon, the other half keeping track of the dust cloud that marked a slow-moving string of wagons several miles to the east.

Azle had done her best to convince Cody that Emery's death had not been his fault, but Cody had only agreed with her so she would shut up. Azle's crush of concern bothered him more than his bruised ribs, but he kept all his pain silent as he grieved for the loss of Emery and the loss of another part of himself to death, grieved for shapeless reasons that pressed upon his soul like heavy storm clouds pressing down on the earth, and prayed without words to Cristodios.

With Cristodios, Cody never used words. He hated those bible-tenters who had rolled in the dirt and screamed their prayers to heaven for all the world to hear every time they got revived. He hated the Method-Baptist preacher who called himself Brother Shackleford—the one who had come from Narcisso to the little church in Chalk once a month to give them The True Word and demand public repentance—and a share of what little hard cash his faithful congregation possessed. Fact was, as a boy Cody had hated most everything that preachers and churchgoing people had tried to teach him.

But when he was eleven, Ramon—the extra-man who wore a wonderful brown felt hat he called a fedora and who sometimes worked for his father—the same Ramon who showed Cody his first-ever pictures of naked women and who had taught him how to play poker and how to cheat without getting caught—that same Ramon had sat him down on the day Cody had killed, gutted, and cleaned his first deer, and while sharpening their knives together, Ramon had told Cody about Cristodios, the loving compassionate God who knew what was in everyone's heart, and who fought with the devil to keep those hearts from going to Hell.

That was His job, Ramon had said. Cristodios didn't work miracles anymore because He was kept fulltime busy wrestling with the Devil whose strength had increased on Shudderday when some of the Evil Angels were released from that part of Hell kept in the center of the earth. However, Ramon had assured the boy, Cristodios did hear those prayers that rose straight from the soul, and if He had the time, and if the Devil gave Him a little breather, and if the prayer didn't require a miracle, then Cristodios would help as best He could.

The clang of shovels against rocks reminded Cody to scan again from the horizon back to the ground breaking away below the grave. He saw the line of oxen-drawn wagons still moving away toward the northeast ahead of their low cloud of dust. There was plenty of time for the squad to catch up with them once the burial was finished. Nothing else he saw interested him.

All that Ramon told him had made sense to Cody and he had taken it straight into his heart and held onto it ever since—least ways the part about not needing words to pray. He had never been quite sure what to make of all that stuff about Evil Angels, so he had made it a point as he was growing up of not looking for them and had always tried not to bother Cristodios any more than necessary.

And that seemed to work. Those times when he'd hurt clear down inside and ached for relief, something had most always come along to ease him over the hurt—like Ann had eased him over the hurt of losing Deborah—and Cody figured that Cristodios had found a way to take care of him, and gave thanks as silent and wordless as the prayers.

Only, after Ann left, nothing had come along to ease him over anything. Now Shelia Emery—who had been only kind to him and respectful of his rank and helpful with the cooking around the campfire—now she was dead, and the aching ground of his failure had opened to swallow another victim.

Again he forced himself to scan the land falling in shadows and gullies away through the red Permian level of the plains. He noted that the wagons hadn't made much progress, then he swept the brightening land between the wagons and where he stood until his eyes came back to the bare dirt hump of Emery's grave.

There would be no words said aloud over her now, no common prayers offered up to some common god to make the squad feel better. Cristodios knew that words wouldn't do any good for Shelia Emery now. The words, when they came, would be official and would come with tap-service back at regional headquarters in Tampico. By then it would be too late for them to mean anything to anybody. It was a rule Cody had never had to face before and he could not understand it.

"Time to go, Cody."

"Right . . . right." Cody took one last look at the grave then drew in a deep breath and followed Azle toward the head of the draw where the rest of the squad waited to begin the pursuit of the wagons. None of them knew for sure that the wagon people had shot Emery, but they all wanted some kind of revenge and the wagons looked like their best bet to start finding it.

TWO | From the cover of a thick stand of liveoak and juniper on a rise less than five hundred feet from the gravel road, Lucy carefully scrutinized each of the seven wagons.

Some were made of metal and had only two hard-rubber tires that fit up underneath them in a neat, careful way that gave away the fact they were carry-beds off of old pickups. Most of the others were made of wood and canvas with four wheels, but they too had big hard-rubber tires. All of them had symbols painted on their sides, but none of the symbols held any special meaning for her.

There were no O-U's hidden in the designs to tell her there were braves from the Nation in the wagons, no crossed red feathers to signify the presence of a healer, and no double-H to signify a herbalist. Their wagons carried only the simple marks, the Tech-T's, the circled peacebird, and symbols she recognized from Mishla's hand-colored book of clans and towns as the symbols of Vernon and Zealand.

Under different circumstances she would have offered her healing services to the wagon people just for the opportunity of meeting some of the Zealanders. She knew that their ancestors had come from across the legendary Pacific Ocean years before

Shudderday from Australia and Old New Zealand to study at the schools in Lubbock and DalWorth and even Old Austin, which was under the Mexican Sea now. For reasons lost in history, many of those ancestors were attending a meeting in Haskell on Shudderday, and sometime after that they took responsibility for the power station on Lake Stamford and made that area their clan home. It was unusual to see them this far north, and Lucy regretted losing the chance to talk to them.

As she turned away from the wagons, a distant flash of light caught the corner of her eye. It startled her for a second to have clear sunlight this early in the year, this early in the day, but she quickly recovered and pulled her hand-sized binoculars from their pocket inside her cloak and looked slowly and carefully in the bright shifting patch of sunshine for what had caused the flash.

"Militia," she whispered when she saw the uniformed figures, "following the wagons." She thought for a long moment as she put the binoculars away, then decided the risk was worth it. Without further hesitation she pulled her magnum revolver from her holster and fired two quick shots into the ground, shots whose fierce bangs echoed off the broken land and rang in her ears. Then she turned quickly down the hill, away from the wagons and away from the militia, and continued her forced-march pace. She prayed that someone in the wagons had recognized the warning signal. It was all she had time to give them.

Lucy had never been allowed much time of her own. Back as far as she could remember her days had been filled with studies and chores and endless sessions of memorization. Mishla had always been there, prodding her gently, keeping her from sitting still too long, making her think and work on her feet until sometimes she was so tired that she slept on her feet.

Their home by the crossroads outside of Childress had always been busy with people coming and going, talking in whispers or laughing loudly late into the night as they shared stories and memories with one another. Lucy had never thought of those people as anything but ordinary, and had assumed that life was full of people like that until Mishla made her spend four years in the Childress Central School. There she learned very painfully that if anyone was strange, it was she and Mishla and most of Mishla's friends.

When Lucy was younger, many of Mishla's visitors had been

braves from the Nation, many with beautiful tattoos on their foreheads and cheeks. Then there were fewer and fewer braves who stopped at their little house and those who did so always came and went at night. Lucy had understood without Mishla telling her anything that these friends were not to be talked about outside the house. In Central School she came partially to understand why. Her teachers and classmates thought the braves were dirty, ugly foreigners with no manners. Lucy had longed to tell them how wrong they were, but she couldn't.

However, Lucy had also learned to read and write English at the Childress school and as soon as she understood what was really required of her, she took to the reading of English even faster than she had to reading the healing signs and symbols Mishla drilled her on. Story books in English—*Novel* some of the brown paper ones had printed on their spines—became something special to Lucy, and although Mishla never forbade her to read them, she never encouraged her, either, seeming always to find new chores to be done whenever Lucy had settled herself with one of the books Mishla derisively called the common pap. By the time Lucy thought to look up pap in a dictionary, she didn't care what Mishla called her books, and she read every chance she got.

Even now she carried two books with her, books she had read several times each, but books she hoped she could trade for new ones. With any luck the braves might have books to trade, but if not them, then surely when she got to one of the towns she would have a wonderful choice of books to read. Just the thought of a new book made the going easier and helped keep her from thinking about what might be happening behind her.

THREE | Cody's squad got three surprises as they jogged down the uneven slope toward the wagons. First the sun came out so suddenly that it almost blinded them. Then less than a minute after the sunlight hit them, they heard the sound of two shots from way off in the distance. As the hole in the clouds closed and their eyes readjusted to the light, they were surprised to see the wagons stop on the road, seven tiny shapes fuzzed by the dust cloud of their own making.

"What d'you figure all that is?" Cody asked as he increased his pace and pulled up beside Azle.

"Nothin'. Don't know who fired the shots. They probably shot some game and stopped to pick it up. Don't care so long as they stay where they are. Makes it all that much easier to catch up with them."

Cody nodded and slowed down again to let the squad pass him. His place was at the rear, to make sure no one straggled too far behind. He didn't much like always being at the end of the line, but since the pace had never been as fast as he thought he could run, he had learned to get comfortable back there.

There were times when he wished mightily for a truck or a couple of choppers or some sturdy Mexican mules to carry them to their mission-start point. But only rich people could afford Mexican mules, and he perhaps better than anyone understood that there weren't enough trucks or choppers or the fuel to run them to be carrying routine patrols to routine places. It would take a real emergency to get them—if they had the fuel to spare.

His brother Daniel worked down in Midessa where they made gasoline and diesel oil and even airplane fuel, and had shocked them once when he came home for God Remember Day and after supper had told them that most of the gas and diesel fuel they made at his refinery that wasn't used in power plants or for the government got sold to Texico and Commanche and Wheatland—and yes, even the Indian Nation—in exchange for food credits.

Until then Cody'd never given much thought to how all the different kinds of food he took for granted got to Paducah where Mr. Burrton bought them for his store in Grow. He had only been fifteen or so then, but Daniel's revelation had come as a real surprise. After Cody married Deborah, he and his father raised yucca on adjoining farms—yucca that could be used for everything from shoe tops to cloth, to needles and thread. It was a valuable crop and they took it up to the Republic Exchange Center in Paducah once each year and were paid good money for it. If they could have raised more of it faster, they could have been rich. As it was, they raised enough to live comfortable and to hire an extra-man every now and again to help with the harder chores.

They also went out with the rest of the members of the Farm Bureau during Cotton Month and harvested as much of the wild cotton as they could. After they hauled it to Paducah and had it ginned and baled, it wasn't worth nearly as much as farm-grown cotton or their yucca, mainly because the quality was so low and it wasn't nearly so useful as the yucca, even though the Texas Independent Ginners Association always argued that it should be worth more. Of course Tiga was always arguing about something or other, mostly for the sake of doing it, his father had said. However, the cotton did bring in some extra cash that they usually spent on their annual trip to Dickens to see his Aunt Gloria. At the Trade Market there, they bought good whiskey and nails and watermelon if they had it, and lots of canned goods from the countries of Texico and Commanche in their fancy green glass jars and sealed stoneware crocks.

One really good year—the year before Deborah died—they had rented a truck from Vachel Ingram thinking they could bring back a really big load of canned goods and sell them to the folks around home. They had bought nearly fifty wooden crates full and were headed back to Chalk when the truck broke down on US-Eighty-two just shy of Willow Creek.

Cody had stayed with the truck while his father started walking back to Guthrie for help. An hour later his father returned riding in another truck with two men, but it was soon as clear as spring water that the strangers had no intention of helping. They pulled shotguns out of their truck and made Cody and his father transfer forty of the fifty cases into their smaller truck. Then they drove away laughing and that was the last time Cody and his father had ever rented a truck, and the last time they had gone anywhere unarmed. Cody still felt like he was partially to blame for what had happened to them—like maybe if *he* had gone for help, or suggested bringing their rifles, or something, it all wouldn't have happened.

As the squad topped a low rise Cody looked for the wagons again and was startled to see them still sitting on the road less than half a mile away, and coming toward the squad a group of five or six armed men evenly spread out across the road. The man in the center carried a white pennant.

"Lock and load," Azle ordered, "safeties off."

The sound of bolts driving cartridges home answered her. Cody felt the tension and an eagerness for confrontation that sent morning shivers up his spine.

FOUR | Far to the east Lucy was crossing the old Quanah, Acme, and Pacific railroad tracks and the second hard-road—Farm Road-One-oh-four, according to her hand-drawn map—at a place on the edge of Lake Paducah called Jacob's Crossing. She was pleased with the distance she had covered this morning, and pleased with the accuracy of her directioneering. But as she looked ahead she saw a dark column of smoke beginning to rise across the lake.

Her first thought was that the braves had been found. She immediately chided herself for her anxiety. There was no way of knowing what the smoke might mean, and until she knew, there was no sense wasting energy worrying about it. The one sure thing the smoke did mean to her was that she would have to be more vigilant.

CHAPTER 5

ONE | "You militia?" the man with the white pennant called.

"We are," Azle called back. "Who are you?"

The two groups had stopped forty yards apart, not quite pointing their rifles at each other, not quite trusting, but neither quite ready to make the first hostile move.

"Vernon Clan hunting party," the man answered, "with a couple of Zealander families. Been hunting down in the Pease River brakes. Got us near thirty deer and a couple of wild steers."

"Where'd you spend the night?" Azle asked cautiously.

It was obvious to Cody that she wasn't going to take anything the flag man said at face value and Cody was glad about that. He didn't like the looks of the man talking or the others with him. He didn't know why, but he sensed something wrong. Why hadn't the man recognized that they were militia?

"Camped 'bout ten miles south of Cee Vee, ma'am," the man answered. "Was that you shooting this morning?"

"We were about to ask you the same thing."

"Haven't fired a shot the last two days. Spent most of that time salting the meat for travel. You run into some trouble, ma'am? We got a healer if you need one."

The man was lying. Cody had read the symbols on their wagons and there was no sign of the crossed red feathers for a healer, nor the red cross of a medic. If they had one like they said, why wasn't it on the wagons like the law ordered it to be?

"Too late for a healer," Azle said, "but we could use a good meal. Haven't eaten proper in two days."

Cody tensed, then forced himself to let the signs of it go. Azle's lie only meant for them to be careful and not to let these wagoneers get too close to them. She was suspicious, but not enough as far as he was concerned. "I could eat a bullock," he said quickly. As her Extra it was his job to tell her that he had deeper fears.

The man laughed. "Can't afford to let you eat our oxen, but we'll feed you venison chili that'll let you taste the fire of heaven when you eat it and burn you with the fires of hell when it clears your bunghole."

Some of the squad members laughed with him, but they had all understood both Azle's warning and Cody's. Not one of the squad had clicked a safety back on or stopped paying attention—nor had the men who claimed to be Vernon Clan.

"Never met a Zealander before," Azle said, slinging her rifle under her arm and moving forward toward the flag man. "And we sure wouldn't mind sharing midday with you."

"Good, good," the man answered. "We'll set up under those trees and cook something up for you good and proper." He turned as Azle came abreast of him and his men turned with him, carrying their rifles in the crook of their arms or slung over their shoulders.

Had they been paying close attention, they would have noticed that Azle was the only member of her squad to sling her rifle. The rest of them carried theirs in various ways, but none of them more than a split second from firing position. Cody nodded to Jessup and then to Keene who lagged behind the others with him, not enough to be noticed, but enough so Cody could whisper instructions without being overheard.

"Each of you pick a buddy, and once we get even with the

wagons, do a back-to-back. Something's not right with these people. Be ready to shoot first and question later." Cody hated those words even as he spoke them, but knew it was better to be too careful than too accepting. Jessup and Keene only nodded and each moved up to pair off with another member of the squad.

Azle and the flag man were less than ten feet from the last wagon when the first shot was fired.

The squad went belly down, firing as they went. The flag man went down backwards, part of his skull missing. The men with him went down as well.

Cody fired at a rifle sticking out of the second wagon and was rewarded when a woman screamed and fell out. Then he kept firing at anyone from the wagons who moved.

Armed people were jumping out of the wagons and crawling underneath them. Rifle fire rattled and cracked around them. Cody put three quick rounds into the chest of a man with a shotgun, then reloaded.

"Cease fire! Cease fire!" Azle screamed.

Slowly the firing stopped and the sudden stillness was filled by the ringing in their ears. Cody rose cautiously to one knee. Only then did he hear the moaning and screaming.

"Cody?" Azle called.

"Here," Cody answered as he got to his feet and moved in a low crouch up to where she lay. "You hurt?"

"Yes, but not bad. Just busted my ribs. The others?"

"Don't know yet. Gonna check the wagons first." Before he could organize the squad a woman staggered around the corner of the wagon.

"Help us," she murmured before she collapsed.

After checking all the wagons the squad found eleven women and two young boys bound, but uninjured. Three of the Vernon men were still alive. Five men and a woman were dead. Cody put Keene to treating their own wounded and placed a guard on the men. Then he began to piece together what had happened as Mary MacEarnest, the woman who had collapsed, told him how fourteen men and the dead woman had ambushed the Vernon and Zealand men in their camp on the Pease near Copper Breaks five days earlier and killed them all.

"Called themselves the Caddos," she said. "Raped us all at least once since then—her watching most every time." She twitched her head toward the woman's body. "Took their turns and did it real gentle like . . . like we were supposed to feel grateful for it." She kept her head down when she spoke, but there was fiery anger in her voice. "Said they were taking us back to Copper Breaks after they sold off our meat. Then last night six of the men left. We heard shooting early this morning, and right after that they got us rolling. Left me untied to help guide them . . ."

" 'Scuse me, ma'am. Jessup! How many of them buzzards we got? Dead and alive."

"Nine. Six dead, three alive. Shall I kill them?"

"Not yet." Cody turned back to Mary MacEarnest. "Sorry about that, ma'am, but those six didn't come back, did they?"

"No, uh, Mr. . . ."

"Cody, ma'am. Just call me Cody. Did they say anything else, ma'am, anything about Nates?" When she looked up into his eyes, he guessed her to be no older than he was.

"No, Mr. Cody. They didn't say anything else." Without warning she burst into tears.

"Riders coming," Singleton announced, "on muleback— from the west and coming fast."

TWO | Lucy sat in the pale shade of a clump of ashe juniper eating dried fruit and sipping occasionally from the small cup of water she had allotted herself for her midday meal. It didn't matter to her that she was close enough to Lake Paducah to easily fill her canteen. Water discipline was water discipline, regardless of the quantity available. That was how Mishla had taught her, and that was what Lucy felt most comfortable with.

On the hill opposite where she sat half a mile away the remains of the fuel tanker blazed steadily under the center of a black column of smoke in the middle of US-Seventy. Well back from the fire off the side of the road were several wagons, a truck, and five people who sat around a small fire of their own, obviously cooking their midday.

They weren't braves—Lucy had made certain of that—and they weren't paying much attention to the burning truck. Maybe they had accepted it as beyond their control. Or maybe they had set it on fire. Whatever their reasons, they didn't seem overly concerned about anything. They had no guards out, nor lookouts, and their only weapons seemed to be their holstered pistols. Lucy took heart from that and hoped that if one of them saw her when she moved on around her hill that they would leave her alone. Even if they didn't she felt sure she could outrun them.

What worried her was the thought that the braves she had been sent to find might have set this fire. If they had, they had probably also left the encampment. And if they—

"Stand up, missy," a gruff male voice said from behind her.

"I mean you no harm," she answered as she placed her cup carefully on the ground and gracefully rose to her feet, turning to face him at the same time.

"Perhaps not, missy," the red-bearded man said, holding a long-barreled pistol casually pointed at her, "but a body cannot be too sure in these times. Where be you heading?"

"To visit Aunt Mishla in Foard City," she answered quickly, trying to read the expression on his hairy face.

He squinted with laughter at her. "Mishla doesn't live there anymore," he said.

Lucy felt a huge wave of relief sweep through her. "You're the man they call Johnson?"

"One in the same," he answered as he holstered his pistol. "And who would you be?"

"Mishla calls me Lucy."

"Ah," he said, as though that meant something to him. "Well gather your gear, Miss Lucy, and come join us for midday."

"I've come with a warning," she said as she picked up her cup and carefully emptied it back into her canteen.

"Time enough for that while we eat."

Lucy followed him down the gentle slope and was surprised that he said no more until they reached the group around the fire, three men and two women—one of whom had long copper-colored hair and was very pregnant. Lucy couldn't imagine why a pregnant woman had been sent—

"Mishla's Lucy," Johnson said, interrupting her thoughts, "I would like you to meet the Quentin brothers, Hector, Max, and Wendel. Then this here's Suzanne Quentin, Hector's wife, and"—he indicated the pregnant woman—"Ann Johnson, my wife."

They each nodded in turn, but none of them spoke or even smiled. Lucy felt very uncomfortable, more so because none of them were braves. "My honor to serve you," she said with a bow.

"You'll meet the others later."

"Others?"

"Surely you don't think we'd be sitting here so casually if there weren't others watching for us?"

"But I didn't see anyone when——"

"You weren't supposed to," Johnson said. "Even Mishla would not have seen them."

Lucy felt foolish and a little stupid. How could she have missed all the guards and any sign that these were braves from the Nation—except they weren't. She knew they weren't. "I am impressed. But are you not worried about someone finding you close to this mess I assume you caused?"

"On the contrary, Mishla's Lucy. We are hoping for someone to find us. One of our trucks is out of gas and the driver of this tanker was most uncooperative. Now we are hoping someone more generous will turn up. In the meantime you can share our food and pass on Mishla's warning."

Suddenly Lucy wasn't hungry and for the first time in her life seriously wanted to disobey Mishla's instructions. There was something hard and cold about these people—something ruthless—that gave her the willies.

THREE | The riders never stood a chance. By the time they realized that the militia squad had control of the wagons, fifteen rifles were pointed at them.

One man was stupid enough to try to pull his pistol, like maybe he'd been watching too many Oldtimer movies. He was dead before he even got a good grip on the pistol and fell heavily out of the saddle. His mule bucked.

A second man reached for his pistol. One bullet blew out the side of his head. The second exploded out his back in a shower of blood, flesh, bone, and cloth.

The other four held their hands high and begged for mercy.

"Dismount," Cody ordered. Then he turned to Mary MacEarnest. "Are these the others?"

"Yes," she answered softly.

"Tie them up good. Morgan, you stand guard over them. Now's the right chance to use that trigger-ready finger of yours. They move any way that makes you jumpy, shoot 'em."

Cody was glad the prisoners were Azle's problem. The way he felt at that moment he would just as soon as killed them as tied them up. Maybe more so. One of them had killed Emery.

Their partners had killed Frederico Santos and wounded Azle, Lloyd, Hermosa, and Pollard.

He went back to where Azle lay in the shade of the fourth wagon, a five-inch-wide strip of green bandage wrapped around her ribs under her combat bra. There was also a bandage on her left leg just above the knee. "Four new prisoners, Azle. Total of seven. What do you want to do with them?"

"Let me think on it a minute, Cody. What would you do with them?"

"Shoot them now," he said half-seriously, "and be done with them. We can't go dragging prisoners all over the Republic while we're hunting for Nates."

"Cody," Melindo called from the other side of the wagon, "you'd better come look at this."

"Don't shoot them yet," Azle said as Cody stepped away to see what was bothering Melindo.

Melindo pointed silently toward the southeast. A black cloud was in full rise from somewhere beyond the horizon. "What burns like that?" she asked.

"Oil," Cody answered, his eyes riveted on the smoke. "Lots of oil. . . . Damn!" He spun on his toes and headed back around the wagon. "Something's burning hard off in the southeast," he said as he squatted beside Azle. "Can't tell how far away it is, but it's making smoke like oil or gasoline."

"Don't worry about it. Sounds like a problem for the road patrols. Help me sit up," she said, holding out her hand.

Cody pulled her gently into a sitting position. "That feel better?"

"Some." Azle grimaced. "But not much. How far do you reckon we are from Dunlap?"

"Three miles. Maybe four. Why? Is that where you want us to go? Seems to me we'd be better off dropping down US-Eighty-three to Paducah and letting Sheriff Pietro help us. I know him. He's a good man and a friend of my father's. He can get these folks back to where they belong, and Paducah's got a real medic to check you all out."

The light shifted and Cody looked up to see Mary Mac-Earnest.

"Mr. Cody, we hate to be bothering you, but we feel the need to go straight aways back to Copper Breaks and get our men. They weren't proper buried, and, and—well, it just seems like we have to do it."

"That settles it," Azle said, shifting her position to ease the pressure on her bandaged ribs. "Help me get my shirt on. We're going to Paducah. It's a whole lot faster to get to Copper Breaks from there than it is from Dunlap."

FOUR | "This is the warning," Lucy said, "just as Mishla gave it to me. Beware the militia and stay off the roads. Go carefully north and cross at Groesbeck Creek. Your tribe awaits."

"Where's Groesbeck Creek?" Johnson asked.

"North of Copper Breaks," Max Quentin answered. "Easy country once you get past Quanah."

"So, we go to Copper Breaks first, pick up the rest of the tonkaweya, then head for Groesbeck Creek." Johnson paused. "You're welcome to come with us, too, Miss Lucy."

She shook her head, and Johnson laughed.

CHAPTER 6

ONE | The seven wagons bearing their load of women, militia, and prisoners barely made it to the outskirts of Paducah before a tremendous line of thunderstorms rolling out of the northwest caught up with them. Cody led them through to the west side of town to the old school gymnasium that had a big gap in one of its end walls, and they pulled the seven wagons under its sheltering roof. Within minutes the squad had begun unhitching the oxen and Mrs. MacEarnest had the grim-faced women preparing a meal. The gym smelled of mildew and use, but Cody barely noticed any smell but that of the meat curing in the Vernon wagons. He had the prisoners hauled out of the wagons and roped together with slipknots around their necks, then told Iola if they made any fuss, she could just shoot them.

By the time he came back around the last wagon, Azle was beginning another of her arguments with Morgan, even as Morgan helped lift her out of the wagon and set her on a pad of tarps on the concrete floor.

"Dammit, boy, it's not the same. Can't really call somebody friend 'less you've shared hard biscuits with them while you were fightin' for your lives." Azle paused, as though she were trying to find exactly the right words. "See, kid, it's 'cause that after you've fought together and survived together, you can grin at each other's bloody mess, throw arms around each other's shoulders, and laugh and cry together." Azle paused again and squirmed gingerly under her bandages. "We all got a little taste of it today—but just a taste. It's goin' through lots of things like that gets you real friends, the stickin' kind of friends."

"Other ways, too," Cody said, surprising himself as much as Azle and Morgan. He sat cross-legged on the floor, not knowing that he'd ever really thought about friendship like Azle was talking about it, knowing only that their argument had triggered something in him, something that was pushing to get out, so he just followed the thoughts off the top of his head.

"Seems to me that sometimes friendships are built on lots of other little things, with maybe nothing really dangerous hard like you're talking about. Maybe all it takes is a row of little things over lots of years, like brush and dirt slowly filling a runout, until instead of erosion you've got a piece of land you didn't have before, and that's what friends have—something they made together that they didn't have before."

"You got friends like that?" Azle asked.

Cody hesitated, thinking of Ann, and then, because he couldn't help it, thinking of Kendrick Johnson. Once Cody had thought he had that special kind of friendship with Ann, but he guessed that maybe you couldn't have that kind of friendship with a woman, 'cause there was always something else there cutting away the fill between a woman and a man. If you both stuck with it, you might stop the erosion, but with a woman you probably never would fill the runout, like somehow it just wasn't natural to fill in the spaces.

"No," he said finally, "I never did, but my daddy does. Him and Bono Davis been neighbors and friends like that long as either of them can remember. They never did nothing like you're talking about—least ways not that I ever heard of. Year after year they just kept working on that runout that divided their property until they got solid fill and grass to take hold and it wasn't a runout no more."

Morgan looked puzzled. "How can they tell where their property ends and begins?"

"Damn, boy, don't you know anything? That's not the point," Azle said before Cody had a chance to speak. "Point is that maybe Cody's right. Maybe there are some folks who can build friendships that way. I just never had or knew one like that."

"That's 'cause you've been in this damned militia since your momma pushed you off her tit," Melindo said, giving Azle her lopsided grin. "Told me yourself you joined before you—"

"You just swallow what I told you, Private," Azle said. There was a hard edge to her voice, but a twinkle in her eyes that seemed to brighten the grey light in the old gym.

"Go ahead, Melindo," Cody laughed, adding his grin to hers. "Azle's more tractor than plow, anyway. What'd she tell you?"

"Who the hell are you people?" a voice boomed from the opening in the wall.

Cody immediately stood up. "Sheriff? Sheriff Pietro? It's me, J. F. Cody." He walked to greet his father's old friend as the sheriff waited by the gap just far enough in to be out of the rain, one hand stroking his beard within easy reach of his shoulder-holstered gun.

"Well, I'll be cussed and left for the devil hisself," the sheriff said as Cody walked out of the shadows. "Who you got with you, boy?" He held out his hand and Cody took it gladly.

"Some folks from Vernon that got ambushed up in Copper Breaks but we found them south of Cee Vee, and some of the crud that did it—the mules belong to them—and my militia squad. We're going to need Doc David if he's around."

"So you're a leader so soon?" Pietro asked and they walked back to the pile of tarps where Azle lay. Most of the squad members and the Vernon women moved to join around them.

"Just the Extra. Squad leader, here, Sergeant Azle, caught a bullet in the ribs. Broke 'em good, but didn't get through to her lungs. Thirty-two caliber black powder pistol that—"

"Don't get up," Pietro said to Azle as he approached. "I can see you don't need the moving around. We'll get the doc over here pretty quick, and somebody to lock up the mules . . . and their shit," he added, nodding toward the prisoners, "but I sure am surprised you all got here this fast." Giving Azle a smile, he squatted down in front of her, his stainless steel, Albany-Ruger .44 magnum riding easily under his arm.

"You were expecting us?" Cody asked, sitting down on the tarps beside Azle. He was suddenly too tired to squat.

"Sure. I sent a message to Tampico last night asking them—"

"We were just out on routine patrol followin' rumors of Nates. Headquarters didn't send us here."

"Don't matter," Pietro said. "You're here and that's what counts. We got some sure enough Nates over on the east side of the lake—near Hackberry Hites north of the dam, Jeremiah—and I was fixin' to go after them just as soon as I got some militia help, so it looks like you're it."

"Maybe you better check these prisoners first," Azle said. "They might be the people you're looking for."

"Might be some of them at that, Sergeant, but not the main party. Near sixty of them were seen 'bout last sundown, and old Patricia Brighton open-throttled all the way across the lake in the dark to tell me. Used up damn near a month's worth of gas doing it, too. They'd of had to fly to get from where she seen 'em to anywheres near Cee Vee."

Cody cringed at the news. It was twelve N-miles—fifteen as the road twisted—from his daddy's place to Hackberry Hites, and that was too damn close for comfort. "When you want to leave?" he asked.

"Hold on there," Azle said. "If I recollect correctly, I'm still the leader of this squad—wounded or not."

"We're talking home ground here, Azle. We're talking people I grew up with, spitting distance away from where my daddy is right now. We're talking about something—"

"I didn't say we weren't goin'," Azle said. "I just thought you might let me make the decision." She grinned quickly. "So, Sheriff, what's the fastest way to get us there and how much local help can we expect?"

"The Bureau's got twenty-two people with a radio on call at Chalk Landing and Tiga's got thirty-three or -four on call here, with boats to carry fifty."

"What's Tiga?" Morgan asked.

"The Texas Independent Ginners Association," Cody answered. "All your reading and you never heard of them?"

"I guess I did, but never called Tiga."

"Well, you should of. If it hadn't been for Tiga, and the Bureau, and the Co-ops and Aqha, and groups like 'em, this Republic would—"

"Aqha?"

"This Republic would have been in big trouble after

Shudderday. Aqha, boy, is the American Quarter Horse Association. All that school-learnin' clogged your brain, didn't it."

"Come on, Sarge. How am I supposed to know everything you know? You're older than the caprock."

The brief wave of laughter that followed was interrupted by Mary MacEarnest. "What about our men, Sheriff?"

"Pardon?" Pietro said as he stood and took off his sweat-stained grey felt hat.

"Our men. Our husbands. These murderers buried them up in Copper Breaks and we've got to go get them and take them back to Vernon for proper burying."

TWO | For three hours Lucy had sat with Kendrick Johnson as the fuel burned steadily from the truck, but no other vehicles came to investigate the column of smoke. She had eaten with then, shared their water and some sweet cookies they called nillas, but at no time could she engage any of them in real conversation. The longer she spent with them, the more uncomfortable she became. Yet for reasons she couldn't cipher, she felt compelled to stay with them a while longer.

Her sense that something was wrong about these people increased when several braves drove in from the south in a small Crosby truck. It was easy to tell they were braves by the tattoos on their foreheads, and it was always easy to tell trucks pieced together in Crosbytown because they always had two headlights on the right side, and only one on the left. Some people even called them Crosby-eyes, and then anything that was lopsided or in any way abnormal was a Crosby by default.

The braves who drove the truck were just as Crosby as their truck was, wild-eyed and crazy-sounding, shouting words Lucy couldn't understand as they squealed their truck to a halt. They were either drunk, or drugged, or both, but when Johnson ran over and gave them instructions, she did catch something about "many boats" before they roared off to the north, weaving from side to side over the hill and out of sight. What concerned Lucy was that Mishla had taught her that hangers—alcohol and most drugs—were banned from the Nation. The only commonly used drug was maryjanis, and its use was reserved for ceremonies and special occasions like birthdays and wedding orgies. No true brave would shame his or her tonkaweya by letting themselves be ruled by hangers—especially in front of non-braves like Johnson and the Quentins.

"What was that all about?" she asked Johnson casually when he returned to where they were all seated around the little campfire.

"Looks like we're going to have to leave here before we get that gas we wanted," Johnson said without looking at her.

Suddenly the ground trembled and they all paused and unconsciously adjusted their bodies to more stable positions. Johnson sat down.

"You go north and I go east," Lucy said when the quake subsided.

Johnson turned to her with a strange grin on his face. "Not quite, Mishla's Lucy. You'd better be coming with us for a while. Maybe to Copper Breaks where the tonkaweyas moved. Maybe all the way to the border. Who knows?"

She was startled by what he said. Perhaps he just didn't understand her role in all of this. "I cannot. I must go to Foard City and seek my instructions from Mishla."

"Mishla be damned," Max Quentin said. "She's not paying us. The Nates are." He paused, spat into the fire, then stared openly at Lucy with a leer all too easy to read as it spread across his face. "Besides, me and Wendel been ready for some soft-stuff for too long. Why I'll bet you can cure what ails us, you being a healer and all."

It took Lucy a long moment to realize what he meant, and when she understood, she was so outraged she didn't know what to say. Almost instinctively her right hand reached reassuringly inside her cloak for the handle of her pistol.

"Go easy, girl," Johnson said, flicking his eyes from hers to where her hand rested. "Max was just teasing. You got to give him some room for that. He don't mean you any danger."

Max smiled. "Course I don't."

Lucy smelled his lust, and her earlier discomfort now settled into a thin layer of fear that threatened to cloud her judgment. She mentally brushed the fear aside and looked without expression from Max Quentin to Johnson and back again. To the west great black thunderstorms rumbled, making the sky tremble as the earth had. "Course you don't," she said, mimicking Max's tone as her fingers closed around the handle. "And I don't mean you any. So you just go north like your message said, and I'll just go east like Mishla instructed, and both of us will be where we belong."

"I told you, you have to go north with us," Johnson said.

"And I told you that I have other duties to—"

"Shut up, bitch."

Lucy was startled by Ann Johnson's command, but more startled when she looked at the pregnant woman and saw her pointing a large pistol at Max Quentin.

"Now, Ann . . ." Max said very slowly.

"Mrs. Johnson," Lucy said, "I appreciate what—"

"Shut up, I said. Fill your canteen and get out of here. Go southeast and stick to the high ground." Ann Johnson was talking calmly and steadily as though she gave these kinds of instructions every day. Her aim never wavered from the center of Max Quentin's chest, and everyone else around the fire seemed frozen by her performance.

"When you hit the creek," she continued, "follow it till you come to a small rock dam. Foard City's a fast hour's walk due east of there if you take the hard-road when you hit it."

"Thank you," Lucy said, rising slowly, her right hand still inside her cloak, her fingers still resting on the checkered wooden grips of her revolver. "My canteen is full, so I will be on my way." She backed slowly away from the group, then turned quickly, and without hesitation shifted into the healer's hurry down the slight slope, her strides too fast to be called walking, but too slow to be running.

Several times she checked to see that no one was following her, then checked once more before heading up a rocky draw that would take her to the ridge top. Only as she climbed the draw, did she wonder why Ann Johnson, who had barely spoken the whole time Lucy had spent with her, had chosen to help her leave.

She didn't know the answer, but she did know that she could not follow Ann Johnson's directions and advice. No tribe leader, no tonkaweya leader, no party leader would have permitted what Lucy had seen with Johnson and the others. *When in doubt, do what you sense is right*, Mishla had always said.

This was one of those times when Lucy would have to follow what her instincts told her was right. She would go to Copper Breaks to find the tonkaweya, to meet its leaders, to cipher out what was wrong, and what this republican and his nasty partners were really doing, and how they had control over the braves.

After ten minutes she stopped and opened the leather tube that held her maps and compass. The map wasn't detailed enough to be a great deal of help to her except for figuring that a heading of sixty-five degrees from her approximate location would bring her to Copper Breaks or the road that bordered it on the east. That and the cover of the approaching thunderstorms were all the help she needed.

For luck she would trust to Cristodios and whatever fortune He chose to bring her—having little faith in that kind of luck, but never failing to give appropriate thanks for it when it came her way. As a child she had prayed and wished for all kinds of things, but never got them—at least not in any way she could associate with her prayers—so that she finally quit expecting things and merely accepted them as they came in the course of living.

At the moment Lucy wished for a mule. Might as well have wished for a horse for all the good it would have done. A year or so after Shudderday, after the Refugee Riots, after hundreds of millions of people had died mostly from starvation or fighting to get food or from the smallpox virus that had climbed up from the quake-opened graves and swept through the survivors, folks managed to restore some sense of order.

Only after all that did ranch people begin to realize that there were damn few foals dropping from the surviving mares. Something had sterilized most of the studs, and no one really knew what, but they called it stud fever even though it affected about eighty percent of the mares as well.

Didn't take long for horses to become scarce and fertile ones to become damned valuable—valuable enough for the governments to control them and their breeding. Every few years a rumor would circulate that someone in Texico or Commanche had produced a small herd of studs, but no one ever saw any horses produced by these miracle herds, and all a practical person could do was learn to walk efficiently and hope someday to be able to afford a good mule. Now as Lucy walked she harbored exactly that hope.

However, despite any hardships, she was glad for this world. She had read the old books warning of nuclear war, and was glad that Mother Nature had intervened before mankind blew itself to radioactive dust. She was glad that humankind had been given a chance to rebuild the world, and glad she was a part of that rebuilding. Perhaps most of all, she was glad to be Lucy, Mishla's messenger doing whatever she could to serve. Step by step she let that gladness carry her toward the future and Copper Breaks, until her dark curiosity about Kendrick Johnson's group pulled her down to an awareness of questions she had no reasonable answers for.

CHAPTER 7

ONE | Cody pulled his collar higher and his hat lower to try to keep the rain off his neck and out of his face. He didn't know how Patricia Brighton could tell where she was going in this storm, but as the boat bounced steadily over the waves he caught an occasional glimpse of Hackberry Hites hovering like a white shadow behind the grey sheets of water and knew the boat didn't have far to go.

He had known Patricia Brighton all his life—or more accurately, she had known him all his, for she had been the attending medic at his birth. Older than his father, but telling no one her true age and ageless in her own way, she was a woman who said little, did a lot, and generally found ways to make almost everyone who came into contact with her love her for one reason or another, usually personal. Mostly it was the way she treated people, like they weren't only family, but good family, close family. She expected family things of them because that's what she gave. To everyone's surprise but her own, people treated her like family, too, and did for her the way they would do for their own, helping her add on to and take care of her place, sharing God Remember Day dinner with her, and making Republic Day one they always celebrated as her birthday as well.

Well after Shudderday, but before the Republic broke away from what was left of the United States and Old Texas, Patricia Brighton—Abbot then before she married the unlucky Neal Brighton who got himself killed digging for gold and silver in the Van Horn Mountains—had gone to Fort Worth and studied medicine and come home a Doctor of Osteopathy while still only in her early twenties. But she always called herself a medic, not a doctor, because she had a real prejudice against M.D.s.

She was heard to say afterward, whenever anyone asked her

why she'd gone there instead of Dallas, that the medical school in Dallas could hardly keep going, which was only what they deserved after the bad reputation their M.D.s earned in the years right after Shudderday, and that was why anyone who wanted a good medical education went to Fort Worth. It was a point people didn't argue with her too often after they'd riled her once on the subject.

Then, when the Republic was formed, she had gone immediately to Lubbock and told the folks at Texas Tech that they had to start a medical school whose graduates would be called medics. They did, and that's what they were called, medics—even though most people and the Oldtimers always called 'em "Doc." She taught there at Tech, and even lured some of her old professors out of Fort Worth to become citizens of the Republic and teach beside her. There wasn't a medic or a medwife or a nurse Cody had ever met who hadn't gotten some of their training from Patricia Brighton.

It had surprised almost everybody when she retired and took up an abandoned farm on the North Wichita slough, saying she had given enough to the Republic and it was time she got some back. But she kept on giving, of course, and pretty soon she was never alone out there because friends, or students, or foreigners from DalWorth and Commanche and even Texico, if they could get visas, would always be visiting her. People around there like Cody's father got to calling the place Brighton Bayou and put up signs showing folks how to get there.

"We're almost there, Jeremy," she shouted at him over the slackening rain.

He watched as she expertly maneuvered her boat through the waves to the lee side of her dock between two larger boats. Jessup jumped out and secured the bow to a post, then tied off the stern so that there was a two-foot gap between the rocking boat and the yucca-padded dock. Cody led the way, and one by one the seven armed people in the boat followed him. The last to come off was Patricia Brighton who first secured a fitted tarp over the steering wheel and instrument panel.

"Take them up to the barn," she said pointing to the surge of militiamen and civilians filling the dock. "Plenty of room in there for all of you, and the oxen won't mind."

Cody nodded. "Thanks. Will do." He turned and waved to the crowd. "This way," he shouted as he began trudging up the hill. The rain had slackened to a drizzling mist that was almost worse than the downpour on the lake, and as Cody led the Tigas and militia into Patricia Brighton's barn, he thought longingly of the captured mules they had left in Paducah and how useful they would have been, and suddenly he was very pessimistic about catching the Nates.

TWO | The more it rained, the slicker the ground became. Lucy had to slow up time and again to make way across a muddy runout or go around a draw suddenly filling with water. She crossed two barbed wire fences protected by owners' seals on the posts, but eight more she cut, finding no seals and wanting whatever animals were contained by them to have the freedom Cristodios intended for all living things. She would have cut the sealed fences as well, but Mishla had made Lucy swear years before that she would leave them intact no matter how much she hated them. Sealed fences meant the land was in use, and people had a right to protect their property, she guessed.

She crossed US-Seventy for the second time that day without seeing anyone and wished that she dared follow it to Texas-Six, and Texas-Six north to Copper Breaks. That route would probably double the distance she had to travel, but if the rain continued, it probably wouldn't be any slower. Either way she wasn't going to get there until late that night. Again she followed her instincts and stayed off the roads.

Rain and bad terrain had been her companions five years earlier when Mishla had sent her on her first independent mission following the Red River west from Estelline to the Little Red, and the Little Red to Caprock Canyons. There she had met Cynthia Ironeyes, a healer from the Nation, and they had exchanged pouches and herbs and spent three sodden days together waiting for the Red to subside some, so Cynthia could travel the safer north side of the river back to Altus where, she told Lucy, the leaders of the western tonkaweyas were in council.

It was from Cynthia that she had first learned about the Nation's water problems, and from Cynthia that she first came to a fuller understanding of the world outside the Republic. Cynthia had done some serious traveling in her fifty-two years, from New Cleveland in the Old United States that called itself the True United States, to the Arkansas coast, north to New Nebraska, to as far west as the Free State of Utah where she said men gathered wives like she gathered herbs. She had told Lucy about having met a woman in Utah who was the eleventh wife to her husband, and her barely pregnant with their first child—his eighteenth—when he married his twelfth wife.

The woman had even taken Cynthia to see the ruins of the Salt City and said that on Shudderday, which they called The Day of the First Rapture or sometimes just Holy Day, the Wasatch Fault had swallowed the great temple and most of the Salt City as a sign from God that her people should return to their original ways. From what she saw, Cynthia figured that meant having big families with one husband, lots of wives, dozens of children, and lots of boys and young men called the Deseret Demons who stole as many girl-children and women as they could and carried them down to Las Vegas where they could be sold for horses or silver bars—a sixteen-year-old girl of reasonable looks bringing sometimes three hundred ounces or more from the rich California Quakers who dared to live where the mountains shuddered every day.

Of course, Cynthia said she didn't believe most of that and said Lucy shouldn't either, but wasn't it awful if it was true, and Lucy had said that it couldn't be true, that no one would sell another human being—at least she couldn't let herself believe that they would. So both of them had agreed not to believe it and laughed together, Lucy knowing all the while that Cynthia thought it probably was true, but because it happened somewheres else to somebody else and they couldn't do anything about it, it was just easier to live with the lie.

Like the so-called True United States, Cynthia had told her, where the Joiners and New Federalists and a hundred smaller groups were arguing about how the Indian Nation and the Missouri Coalition and every nation west of the Mississippi should be forced back under their government, as though they had any say in who did anything west of the Mississippi. Those folks were living a lie, that was for sure.

Before those precious three days in the rain with Cynthia in Caprock Canyons, and another two days with her six months later on the Nation's side of Doan's Crossing, Lucy had associated rain with being cooped up in the house doing the most tedious of mending and learning chores. After those times she had come to associate the rain with times of learning and understanding. She knew she was only using that association to comfort herself, but now as she marched steadily down toward the Pease River and Copper Breaks, she didn't mind the rain at all. It was the fear of what she would find when she got there that nagged at the back of her mind.

THREE | Azle hobbled through the groups of men in the huge old barn calling for him. "Cody? Cody? Where the hell are you?"

"I'm right here, Azle. What the dickens are you doing walking around? I promised Doc David you'd stay off that leg so you could come this far."

"Don't sass me, Extra. Doc Brighton wants you up at the house. Said it's important and that you should come straight away."

"All right, I'll go up there, but you sit yourself down. We can't do anything until the Bureau men get here and the rain stops anyway, so there's no sense you wasting your strength."

"Hell. You sound like Morgan. Just get up to the house."

Cody did as he was told, buttoning his collar against the wind and driving rain, bending over low with the barrel of his carbine as far up his sleeve as it would go, walking up to the house, forcing himself not to run so he wouldn't fall down, but wanting to run the whole time to get out of the cold. March hadn't promised any good weather yet.

He let the spring-hinged door to the mudroom slam behind him as he shook off the water and took off his wet coat and hat. The carbine he hung upside down on the deerhorn rack under his coat, then put his hat on top of that, remembering the first time he had been in this house as a small boy and how he had stared in wonder at all the antlers nailed in a row along the wall, thinking Patricia Brighton must be a famous hunter to have killed all those deer. It was years later before he learned that people gave her sets of antlers every year and she had so many that she started giving them away, but there was one set of antlers on that wall, the one with fourteen points, that had belonged to a deer she had shot right there on her place.

"Get in here, Jeremy," Patricia Brighton called. "There's chicory on the stove, and some soup in the pot if you're hungry."

Cody settled for a cup of hot chicory, glad for the bitter taste that cut through the sugar she'd sweetened it with and braced him against the chill of his damp clothes. When he walked into the large room off the kitchen he was surprised to see not only his father, but also three strangers—foreign strangers by the look of them—sitting in a circle around the stone firepit, with the funnel chimney that hung upside down from the ceiling.

Two of the strangers, a dark one and a red-nosed one, were trying to talk at once. The third, a skinny old woman in a healer's dress covered with symbols, sat staring into the fire, but Cody could tell that she was paying close attention, so he just nodded to his father and took a seat close to the fire. Rain pelted the metal chimney cap, and water hissed occasionally inside its hot pipe—background for what the strangers were arguing about.

"And I tell you that it's a common problem we're facing," the largest and darkest of the men said evenly as he looked from face to face with the eyes of a man who knew he was right. "It doesn't matter where they came from. They're a threat to the Indian Nation and to your Republic. They have to be stopped, and they have to be stopped soon, or they're going to hook up with Goodfox or his New Federalists and get too strong for any of us to stop. Then we'll all get to pay for them in bloodshed."

It took several moments for Cody to realize that the man was a Nate—a Nate right here in Patricia Brighton's house. But why? What was he talking about?

"Dammit, Hadley, our government won't listen to this," the red-nosed man said. "Lubbock's not going to believe anyone's behind these groups except your government itself. They already think Goodfox is your agent, and they'll see these new raiding parties as renewed attempts to force the water issue."

"They'd better believe it," Patricia Brighton said. "There's evidence enough. Jeremiah, tell these men what your militia squad found."

For a moment Cody didn't say a thing, then when he found his words, he directed them at the red-nosed man. "A bunch of raiders calling themselves Caddos killed a Vernon and Zealander hunting party up at Copper Breaks—killed the men and boys, that is. They raped the women." The healer was peering at him with her head cocked to one side. The look on her face bothered him for a second, but he shifted his eyes to his father whose smile helped him plunge on.

"Tried to ambush us, too. Weren't any of them clearly marked as braves—no tattoos or anything—but their gear was

Nate—uh, what I mean is, it was Nation-made equipment they were carrying including Wooley-and-Wolfe pistols. We got some of them in Sheriff Pietro's jail over in Paducah."

"You say they weren't marked?" Hadley said.

"That's right, sir, least not where we could see it. One of their wounded did have a snake tattooed . . . well, on his private parts, if you know what I mean."

"The Nimenim."

Every face turned to the healer expecting her to say more. Her eyes held the fire. "The Nimenim. The people of people. Started as a religious cult forty years ago. Only their genitals are marked. Most of them lived along the Red keeping pretty much to themselves."

"I had thought them only rumors," Hadley said.

Cody thought briefly about Ann's tattoo, but knew that wasn't what hers meant.

"You mean you knew about them?"

"Yes, Mr. Terry, I had heard about them. But one hears many rumors which turn out to be nothing more than that."

Terry? Winslow Terry? Cody wondered. The Attorney General of the Republic? Here?

"What else can you share with us, Mishla?" Patricia Brighton asked.

The woman looked up. "There is little else I know, except that if the Nimenim are indeed involved, and are part of the raiding party this young militiaman has told us about, then I am afraid I have been of unwitting assistance to them."

Cody heard years of sorrow and fatigue in Mishla's voice and saw from the look on his father's face that he heard it, too.

"In what way?" Terry asked.

"I sent one to warn them . . . because I was told they meant no harm to anyone and their tribe needed them back."

"You warned a Nate raiding party?" Terry bucked his stubby body forward in his chair, his face flooded with a rage that almost matched his nose.

Mishla nodded.

Rain beat harder against the roof and filled the momentary silence. "I would have done the same," Patricia Brighton said, "if I had thought they meant no harm. But the ones I saw yesterday sure meant harm to someone."

Terry was sputtering, obviously searching for words to express his outrage, when for the first time Cody's father spoke.

"None of that matters now. What matters is what we are to do immediately, and what our two countries can do together to fully investigate this matter and bring the raiding to a halt."

"Jeremiah," Patricia Brighton said in a tone that demanded his attention, "who's your best mud tracker?"

Cody thought for a second. "Me, I guess."

Terry found his voice. "Then take your squad and go after those killers."

"A squad's too big and too slow," Cody said, suddenly realizing that he was being volunteered for a dangerous job. "I'll take four of my best and send for help when we find them."

"There's something else that may be important," Mishla said, her voice breaking in the words, "something I should have realized before now. Their leader is a man who used to work at Pantex."

Terry sucked in air. The rest of them looked at her blankly.

"Pantex is where the old U. S. of A. assembled its nuclear bombs before Shudderday—where they still store radioactive materials. He was a guard there until eight or nine months ago. I don't know why it might be important to know that, but down in my bones I'm sure that it is."

"Plutonium," Terry said. "They store plutonium at Pantex."

FOUR | Lucy wasn't sure if she was camped above Canal Creek or Cedar Creek. The little cave she found was dry and she had managed to get a fire started and made some stew out of her dried rations. Outside darkness was almost upon her and she knew she would have to put the fire out soon, but she allowed herself a few minutes of luxury to continue reading one of her books, *Goodbye to a River*. It had been written long ago about a Texas she could scarcely believe existed, but she liked the writing and the stories because she knew the man who had written it loved the land like it was his own.

The rain had stopped and the damp earth smelled round and full as she settled down to read, content in knowing that if she got up with the sun she could be at Copper Breaks in an hour or two. She was immediately caught up in a story about a settler on the Brazos and the Indians closing in on him, so that it took her a few seconds to realize that the shots she heard in the distance were real and not from her imagination.

— —
— —

. . . nor be those foolish people who tremble not at the presence of the Lord, and do not understand—those foolish people who have eyes but do not see, who have ears but do not hear.

The leaders of the Republic of West Texas claim to be wise, but they are foolish people.

The leaders of the Indian Nation claim to be wise, but they are foolish people.

The leaders of the Free State of DalWorth claim to be wise, but they are foolish people.

For those foolish leaders do not see the hand of God at work, nor hear His voice calling them together.

But we hear. You and I hear. We know what the will of God means and that only the foolish oppose it. We know what God wants from us. We have polished our weapons and girded our loins for the upcoming struggle of reunion.

Pray, dear friends, with all your hearts. Pray that those leaders will see the light of truth. Pray that your neighbors will listen to the word of God. Pray for yourselves, for God's strength and He will join you when the battle comes and . . .

CHAPTER 8

ONE | Cody and his team of four volunteers sat up with Azle and Attorney General Terry until well past midnight, plotting the course they would take, the radio channels they would use, and the overall objectives of their mission. After much debate it was decided that they would follow the old Hackberry Road to US-Seventy, then strike north from there for Canal Creek and follow it in to the Pease where the southern range of Copper Breaks climbed north from the river.

Terry made it clear that the team was to make no contact with these Nates—or Nimenim fanatics if that's who they were—but were to track them and keep the county militia headquarters in

Quanah informed if they had something significant to report, or if the Nates made a run for the border. Their backup contact if they needed one—which they shouldn't if they did their job properly, Terry had emphasized—would be the sheriff's office in Crowell. Azle would take the remainder of the squad plus the Bureau men and Tigas and search from the dam west around the lake back to Paducah.

"I also want to bring in two planes for air reconnaissance," Terry said.

"Negative, sir. Absolutely not."

"Cody's right, Mr. Terry," Azle said. "If the Nates hear or see planes it is only going to make them more cautious."

"Might even make them change their minds about a rendezvous at Groesbeck Creek with their tribe," Cody said.

"No sense warning them that they're being watched," said Azle.

"I don't think we can take that chance, sir—least ways not and answer the questions you and Commissioner Hadley want answered."

Senior States Commissioner Oytant Hadley from the Indian Nation had left shortly after dark, taking Mishla, the old healer, with him. A small single-prop airplane equipped with pontoons had arrived at dusk, and taken off in the darkness and rain as easy as if the pilot had done it from there before. Patricia Brighton had given Hadley a full hug and a grim smile when she said goodbye to him on the dock, and Cody had heard him promise to take care of himself.

It had all been so strange, so much like a story rather than real life. Even after Cody curled up on a pallet of hay in the barn to try and get a few hours' sleep, it all seemed like a dream gone off the tracks, too much like the train that had derailed near Russellville and wrecked its engine. Azle's squad had been part of the cleanup after that and Cody knew he would never forget the sight of that engine lying on its side, the boxcars folded around it, their boxes and crates strewn whichever way, jars of rotting vegetables stinking up the air, and buzzards circling overhead.

Before he gave in to the fatigue that was pulling him toward sleep, he tried to push that train image away, not wanting to think that such a thing could happen to a plan as happened to a train.

But the image persisted into his dreams, the sound of the

rain on the corrogated roof becoming the sound of a phantom train, the wind of it rushing past him dark and cold toward the accident, dragging him with it and through it and over it and under it, forcing him to look at the bodies in the wreckage, the bodies of Deborah and the baby and Ann and Emery, that melted into the bone-camps where Shudderday refugees had piled their dead and the piles of bones still loomed over him until he awoke sweating and cold and guilty and angry and decided without much consideration not to go back to sleep.

Fumbling in the dark through the bottom of his buttpack, he found the little plastic cigarette case he hadn't touched for almost three weeks. Taking one of the slightly damp readyrolls from the case, he lit a match and inhaled slowly, drawing the cigarette smoke deep into his lungs, appreciating the catch in his throat, the fresh taste of the tobacco, fighting the urge to cough, wondering what it was about a cigarette that was so satisfying, especially when times were rough and a man needed some private calming.

"Got an extra butt?" Jessup asked from the darkness.

Cody held out the case and matches. "You can't sleep either?" Jessup's hand found his by the glow of the cigarette and eased the case and matches from his fingers.

"Nope. Well, maybe a little." The match flared. "But between the rain and your moaning, I decided to give it up as a bad habit. You want to talk about what's bothering you?"

"Remember the Russellville train wreck? Well, I dreamed I was in it in some way, only I wasn't, I was watching it happen, but all the time it was dragging me along. I was moaning, huh?" He took another long drag on the cigarette, his mouth already tired of the taste, but his lungs clamping onto the smoke.

"It's five-thirty," Jessup said. "Should I wake the others?"

"Might as well. We should be ready to go after breakfast as soon as it gets light out there."

One by one Jessup woke them—Ed Kolmer, the squad's best brush-country tracker, Juanita Brisas who would operate the vintage PRC-25 radio that Patricia Brighton had produced for them out of her cellar, and Donna Melindo who could kill a jack at five hundred yards with the scoped, long-barrelled, .308 Winchester she carried. As quietly as they could they gathered their gear and followed Cody up to the house by the light of a kerosene lantern hanging beside the back door.

After they stacked their equipment in the mudroom, Patricia Brighton greeted them in the kitchen with a large platter of scrambled eggs, biscuits, little strips of venison fried crisp, and a huge pot of chicory. Attorney General Terry was already sitting at the table drinking his chicory and looking them over with an expression that seemed too self-satisfied to Cody.

"You got everything you need, Sergeant?"

"I'm no sergeant, sir," Cody said. "Just an Extra."

"You're a sergeant now," Terry replied. "You'll need the rank if you have to cope with Sheriff York in Crowell. Bertha's got a high opinion of herself and who she should deal with, so from now on you're Sergeant Cody. I'll make it permanently official as soon as I get back to Lubbock." He scribbled something in a small notebook.

"Thank you, sir," Cody said as evenly as he could, not that he wasn't pleased by the promotion, but that he would sooner have gotten it a different way and from someone else besides Terry. He didn't see any reason to tell the Attorney General that Bertha York was his mother's first cousin and his brother Daniel's godmother and that he had always called her Aunt Bertha. "I'd like to make Roland Jessup my Extra, then."

"Done," Terry said quickly, adding another notation to the notebook before closing it.

"Now eat hearty," Patricia Brighton added. "You have a long rough way to go today."

TWO | Lucy awoke to a dismal dawn, but the rain had stopped and there was a hint of warmth in the breeze that blew in from the south. There would be time enough to wake up to joyous dawns alive with pink and orange promises of sunshine and heat when summer came. For now the dawn matched the task at hand.

Slowly she stretched the cramps out of her body, taking the time to warm every muscle group, knowing the fastest way to injure herself would be to start out cold. It took her fifteen minutes to do the job thoroughly, but she felt better for it. She took a compass heading, checked her map, decided that the creek below her had to be Canal Creek, and set out again toward the east-northeast.

Part of Copper Breaks had been a state park before Shudderday, a big stretch of mesa broken by lots of runouts, gullies, and draws—the breaks of its name. Lucy had heard an

Oldtimer from Thalia tell Mishla once that Copper Breaks had been open land dotted with tamarisk and juniper—saltcedar and post cedar most folks had called them—the breaks being a place where a man could hunt jackrabbits for a full day without seeing a decent shade tree or a park ranger. He swore that Shudderday had ruined the Breaks because now they were covered with mesquite and liveoaks as well as the cedar, most of it too thick for a man to walk through.

"There are even cane brakes in the Breaks," he had said with astonishment, and added wistfully "probably deer, too," except he was too old to hunt deer any more and his sons wouldn't do it for him—saying that venison was too dry, and besides, it was easier to hunt wild cattle that just stood there and let you shoot them whenever you were hungry, than it was to hide and wait for deer or try and stalk one all day for a decent shot and then only get fifty or sixty pounds of dry meat for your trouble.

Lucy wasn't much for hunting, but she did like venison, especially venison chili made with chunks of bacon in it, and she'd done her share of hunting for deer and cattle both to keep meat in Mishla's freezer. Lucy liked rabbit, too, but cottontails were hard to find anymore near Childress, and jacks were so disease-ridden that even ignorant people had learned not to eat them. Fact was most people wouldn't even feed jacks to their dogs. They'd just shoot them and leave them for the buzzards.

Sometime or other she had eaten most anything to be found on a good republican's table, or a brave's, for that matter— squirrel, armadillo, snake, possum, dog once, when she didn't know what it was, dove, quail, duck, chicken, and turkey. Turkey and venison were her favorites. Just thinking about them made her hungry and she unconsciously reached into her food bag and put a handful of dried fruit to her mouth.

As she chewed in rhythm with her walking, she wondered if the shots she had heard the night before were from hunters or if they had been fired by someone doing something else, something she wouldn't like if she found out about it. Lucy had only heard three shots, but one would have been enough to worry her. This was her twenty-second mission for Mishla, yet in all that time she had never gotten used to hearing shots in the distance when she was in the country alone. Something about it always, always made her uncomfortable.

THREE | Tomball Abbot, Patricia Brighton's fifteen-year-old grandnephew, took Cody's team from Brighton Bayou to the old Hackberry Road in the same boat Cody had crossed the lake in the day before. As soon as they landed and adjusted their packs and ammo belts, the team headed down the side of the road doing the soldier's shuffle, an easy jogging pace that they could keep up for two or three hours without a break. They had fourteen N-miles to travel, half by road and half across country, and Cody wanted them to make as good a time as possible before they hit the rough country and had to pick their way along and watch for Nates at the same time.

Terry had arranged roadblocks at Crowell on US-Seventy, on FR-Six, and on the Kirkland Road at the Summer Bridge—one of the few bridges Cody'd ever seen that hadn't suffered Shudderday damage—but neither he nor anyone else thought the Nates would be foolish enough to travel the hard-roads. Cody had only agreed that it wouldn't hurt to be on the watch for the Nates wherever they might be.

During the boat ride it had occurred to Cody that for all Terry's participation in the planning for this mission, he had offered very little in the way of support—some roadblocks, radio contacts in Quanah and Crowell, and the radio, of course, which had been Patricia Brighton's idea, not Terry's. That was it.

Don't make contact and you won't need support. That's what they had taught him at the Jayton Militia School back when he'd done his mandatory year of service before he married Deborah.

Watch without being watched. Move without being seen. Return with accurate information.

They made it sound easy at the school, and made people feel stupid if they didn't succeed when they practiced up the Double Mountain Fork of the Brazos Valley. Of course, the instructors had been going out there for a long time and knew all the places a good observer would choose, so they'd go straight to those places and catch a student trying to hide and watch, and chew ass from there back to camp.

Three times they had caught Cody before he finally understood what he had to do to keep from getting caught again. The fourth time he went out he had given up the best observation points and had chosen places that weren't quite so good, but gave him better chances of not being found—and he had moved from place to place, never staying too long in any one. When he returned to camp he had reported what he had seen as accurately as possible, and although he had gathered less information than some of his captured classmates, he was one of three who hadn't gotten caught. He had learned his lesson.

Thinking about that experience made Cody feel better about the mission and with a smile he called back over his shoulder, "Anyone want to pick up the pace?"

He heard several grunts of disgust before Juanita Brisas trotted past him, radio and all, and began to pull away. Half a mile later Cody's smile was gone, but his body had settled into the new pace as they moved down the road.

Then a sharp pain stabbed Cody on the right side, just above the waist. He recognized it as a running pain and tried to think himself past it, but the ache of it cut through his concentration, and he remembered Deborah clutching her swollen stomach while tears rolled down her contorted face. With the thoughts of Deborah came the guilt, and with the guilt came thoughts of Ann and his son. At least he hoped it was a son. April, Doc David had said.

This was March, and the pain in Cody's side was easing, and surely the baby hadn't been born yet, and why had Ann run off with Kendrick Johnson, and how had he been so stupid as to let Shelia Emery get shot? *And why and why and why and why and why?* asked that nasty little voice of guilt in his head, and he had no answers except the tears that bounced off his cheeks as he doggedly kept up with Juanita's pace.

FOUR | Lucy was working her way across a deep runout when she smelled the smoke and knew at once it was mesquite burning. It was with some relief that she located the thin column of smoke just south of where Canal Creek joined the Pease. The saltcedar was thick in the bottoms, so she worked her way slowly back up the steep hill until she found a secluded place from which to observe the river and its banks.

What she saw made her frown with uncertainty.

She counted nine men sitting around a small fire eating and talking quietly—too quietly for her to make out what they were saying. Near them was a loaded pickup wagon covered with a tarp. Occasional laughter punctuated their conversations. But the striking thing about them was that five of the men wore the tan uniforms of the Indian Nation. The other three wore the grey-green uniforms of the West Texas Militia.

Lucy had never seen braves and militiamen sharing a meal, nor heard of it, nor talked to anyone else who had ever mentioned such a thing. Her healer training made her want to stand up and shout out her presence, to walk down to the camp and congratulate these men on their courage and humanity. The naturally wary part of herself forced her to stay low as she began working her way closer to where they sat, pausing every few steps, hoping to hear what they were saying.

Without seeing or hearing anything, Lucy sensed someone above her and sank down in the center of a small saltcedar thicket, daring neither to move nor look about.

"Hello the camp," a male voice called from somewhere up the hill. "The password is 'meat.'"

Lucy recognized the voice as Kendrick Johnson's and wondered how he had managed to get there so quickly. She prayed swifty to Cristodios that he couldn't see her while she waited as still and silent as the mockingbird that landed on a branch close to her face and stared at her.

CHAPTER 9

ONE | Cody recognized the sound and cursed.

The airplane flew low over their heads then made a high arching turn and flew straight back toward them. Cody cursed again when the twin-engined Beechcraft waggled its wings before turning northeast and climbing toward the high clouds.

Apparently Terry had ignored his argument and Azle's and had decided to use reconnaissance planes anyway. Might as well send the Nates a written announcement to warn them that everyone knew they were there. What the hell was wrong with Terry, anyway? Didn't he know that he was risking the whole mission doing this? Or was there something else going on here, something Cody had missed?

"Take ten," he said, jogging to a halt by a stand of young liveoak. "And gather round. I need some advice." It suddenly occurred to him that Terry's attitude had changed from when he had first told them to go after those killers to when he had told Cody not to make contact. But what had been the turning point?

By the time the team settled into a rough circle, Jessup was already half-finished rolling a cigarette. Kolmer and Melindo were opening their canteens, and Juanita Brisas was slipping out of the radio harness. Jessup handed the cigarette to Cody.

"Thanks," Cody said. He automatically lit the cigarette and took a long draw, holding the smoke in his lungs for a second before expelling it slowly. He'd quit smoking. At least that's what he'd told himself—and he really had. This was only his second cigarette in three weeks—well, third, if he counted the one he had shared with Jessup the night before they left Wolf Flat, but he'd only had two or three hits off that one. No, he'd quit the habit, and now he'd just smoke one every now and again because he wanted to, not because he had to.

"Looks like Terry sent his planes anyway," Brisas said, breaking the silence that had settled around them. "You want to do a radio check and find out why?"

"Can't. Told Terry we would only call in information reports and that's all we're going to do. Just because he broke his word doesn't mean we—"

"Dammit, Cody. Don't use that everyone-else-jumping-off-the-bridge argument with us."

Cody took another long draw on his cigarette. He resented Jessup's interruption, but quickly decided to let him say his piece. It was obvious that they were all upset by the plane.

"Once Terry broke the deal, it's broken and all promises are off. He's the one who should—"

"He's taking chances with our lives, not his," Kolmer said in his low, gruff way that always hinted at disapproval. His eyes were fixed on the wrinkled map spread on his thighs.

"But he's not in command here. Cody is." Melindo gave him her lopsided smile. "So what are we going to do, Sarge? Track Terry down and shoot him?"

Grasping the cigarette between his thumb and forefinger, Cody carefully brushed the fire off its end so he could save the rest of it for later. It was always a bad sign when he did that, a sign that he was falling back into old habits, but for the moment he had other things to worry about and Melindo's joking suggestion didn't change that.

"That's why I wanted your advice," he said slowly. "Maybe Azle'd have a quick answer for you, but I doubt it."

"Damn straight," Jessup said.

"Does seem like the Attorney General has made it a lot tougher for us to sneak up on those Nates—if that's really what we're supposed to do. How far we have to go, Ed?"

"We ought to hit Canal Creek anytime now. Four miles from there to the Breaks," Kolmer answered.

"And what does that do to our time? An hour and a half? Two hours?"

"Sounds right—if we don't have any trouble," Jessup said.

"Suppose we cut the angle and head straight for where Six crosses the Pease?" He had already guessed most of the answers, but he was buying himself time to think and giving the team time to come to the same conclusion he had. There didn't seem to him but one thing left to do and still follow their orders.

Kolmer measured with a small plastic ruler. "Six miles plus some, probably—all across the drainage slope."

"Then we continue as planned," Cody said. "We head for Canal Creek and follow it to the Pease. Then we do like we said we would do. We watch, listen if we can, take notes, and report to headquarters—and do our damnedest not to get caught at it."

"And if we see that plane again?" Jessup asked.

"If we see that plane or any plane—or if anything else happens to put us in danger, we stop to reconsider. That's all we can do for now. If we have to split, our escape and evasion point is the Raggedy Creek Bridge on Six. Doesn't that sound pathetic from your leader?"

"Sure as hell does," Melindo said with a brief laugh, "but I ain't got nothing better to offer."

"Jessup?"

"Sounds reasonable to me, Cody."

"Then let's get moving."

TWO | Cramps tightened Lucy's legs and back and she longed to stretch her body to relieve them, but she knew she dared not move until Johnson and the tonkaweya withdrew their guards and moved away. She couldn't see them, but she could clearly hear the voices of many people down in the Pease bottoms, sometimes arguing, sometimes laughing, but always seeming to grow in number and volume.

For some reason they weren't doing much to conceal their presence. Maybe they knew there was no one around who could be a threat to them. Or maybe they were just too arrogant to worry about being discovered. Or maybe they were just being careless. Whatever their reasons, their actions worried Lucy, making her increasingly unsure of what she should do.

Several times during the two hours she had sat in her clump of saltcedar people had walked by close enough for her to hear their breathing. When they stopped, she had frozen her position, her whole body hidden under her dark brown cloak, and prayed that they would come no closer. Miraculously, two of them had paused to urinate behind the saltcedar as though they were marking their territory before climbing up to stand guard at the top of the bank, but neither of them had seen her.

If she could have slipped away undetected, she didn't know where she would have gone. There was something more happening here than a peaceful tonkaweya scouting for land for their tribe. The tonkaweya had something in its possession that most of them were not very happy about. Even now another loud argument was taking place below her.

"And I say it's stupid," a baritone voice said. "Even if we do get it back, what are we going to do with it? Explode it somewhere? Use it against the Texians? It's too dangerous to—"

"It's none of your business," Johnson's voice responded. "Chief Townsend sent you to follow my orders. Until we return to the Nation, I am the tonkaweya leader."

The other voice said something Lucy couldn't make out, but she heard disgust in his voice.

"How dare you dispute my leadership!" Johnson roared.

A smacking sound was followed by shouts from several voices. Lucy longed to peer through the saltcedar to see what was happening, but caution kept her still even as a new sound buzzed the valley.

A plane! By the time she realized what it was, it was overhead, the steady growl of its twin engines filling the air. Then it was gone, a fading sound lost in the grey morning.

Hectic shouting echoed below her with Johnson's voice rising above the others. "Hide everything! Everything! And uncover that machine gun!"

THREE | "There it is," Melindo said, pointing almost due north of them. "And it looks like it's spotted us again. It's coming straight this way."

Melindo was right. The plane had circled twice and was now headed straight toward their position at the head of a short draw leading down into Canal Creek. Cody stood there feeling helpless as the plane flew lower and lower, wondering what it could mean.

Suddenly a package fell from the plane. A small parachute opened, breaking its fall, and the package drifted toward large cedar thicket several hundred feet away.

Cody turned to watch the plane which waggled its wings before heading west. Whatever Terry is up to with this damned plane must be really stupid—or really important, Cody thought. "Okay, let's find out what it is," he said, heading out of the draw toward the thicket.

By the time Cody reached the thicket, Ed Kolmer had unfastened the parachute and was folding it up. "Might come in useful," he said.

"Might." Cody stooped down and inspected the package as though expecting it to bite him. It was a standard militia box two feet to a side with yucca straps holding it closed, and its only markings were the letters R.W.T.M. stenciled on each side. With great reluctance he undid the straps and carefully lifted the lid as the rest of the team crowded around him.

Sudden silence held the team still as Cody took an official envelope off a plastic bag marked with radiation symbols. Inside the envelope there was a single sheet on which was printed a message that Cody read to his team.

RADIATION PROTECTION UNIFORMS.
TO BE USED FOR SHORT-TERM EXPOSURE TO RADIOACTIVE MATERIALS ONLY.
NOT CLEANABLE. NOT REUSABLE.

Beneath that was a typed note that he also read aloud.

*Use of these uniforms may become necessary if you come into
contact with cargo carried by the Indian Nation party currently under
your observations. Take all conceivable caution, but bury that cargo
at least six feet deep and mark the location clearly. Proper disposal
will follow.*

*Avoid all contact if possible, but if unavoidable, follow instructions
on the inclosed uniforms.*

> *Good luck,*
> */s/Winslow Terry*
> *Attorney General, Republic of West Texas*

"What the hell does that mean?" Jessup asked.

"I'll be damned if I know," Cody answered as he passed the
note to Melindo, "and I'm not real sure I want to find out. It's
reconsideration time, team."

Slowly he sat down and wondered what in the name of salt
and water was going on? He didn't know anything about
radioactive materials except that they were damned dangerous,
but he clearly remembered what Terry had said in Patricia
Brighton's living room.

Had some Nate stolen a nuclear bomb? Were there still
nuclear bombs around? Why in the world would anyone want or
need one? It didn't make any sense—none at all.

FOUR | The plane did not return, and after a few
minutes Lucy heard the tonkaweya hitching oxen, loading
wagons, and preparing to move out.

An engine coughed to life. Orders were shouted back and
forth. The guards trotted down the hill past her hiding place.
Wagons rattled as they bumped over the rough ground. Little by
little the sounds retreated around the bend and out of hearing
distance.

Lucy still refused to move. Even though she couldn't hear
them and dared not look for them, she felt sure the tonkaweya
had put out a rear guard. The Texian Johnson obviously
understood things like that. Hadn't he caught her hiding once
before?

To calm her thoughts and ease the burning sensations that
had replaced the cramps in her legs and back, she repeated the
litany of healing to herself, over and over until she was sure she

had done it at least ten or twelve times, wondering, as she had more than once before, how such a simple thing could block the body's messages of pain.

Only when she stopped did she feel the pain again, and when she finally decided to move, the pain burned back through her nerves like a fire out of control. First she straightened her back, slowly, carefully, deliberately, letting the blood return to angry muscles. Then with her hands she pulled her left leg out in front of her, clenching her jaw against the deadweight tingling that jabbed her like a thousand pins. Rhythmically she massaged that leg until she felt the sensations returning to normal in a sudden rash of itching over her skin. She repeated the process with her right leg, then massaged them both until she felt confident that they would bear her weight.

Raising herself first to her knees, and then putting her left foot under her, she stood very slowly, steadying herself against the cedars. Her knees felt weak, as though they weren't ready to do much work, but she knew that would pass. The next thing she wanted to do was empty her bladder and have a good, healthy bowel movement. Then and only then would she be ready to follow the tonkaweya. As slowly as they would have to travel, she was sure she could easily catch up with them.

Lucy made her way cautiously down the hill, waded across Canal Creek, and walked to the center of what had been the tonkaweya camp site. From the tracks she guessed they must have had seven or eight wagons—far more than a raiding party would have, but not nearly enough for a settling party—just another fact that refused to fit into a clear picture.

Her nose led her to their trench latrine and she gratefully used it and the small roll of paper they left behind before kicking dirt into the latrine and filling it up. The paper she slipped into one of the many pockets in her cloak. Any good tonkaweya would have filled the latrine before leaving camp—but then, this tonkaweya had been in a hurry, and there was ample evidence that it was not a good one.

Perhaps they had left some other clues around the camp that might help her understand who they were and what their intentions were in the Republic. She covered the ground systematically, following the various sets of tracks that led into the camp, looking slowly around where each wagon had sat, prodding the ashes of their fire and the loose piles of dirt where they had obviously sat, searching for anything, anything at all.

After twenty minutes she had found two US-coins—a quarter and a nickel—a piece of paper obviously torn off a tobacco pouch, a copper button the size of her thumbnail which she put into a pocket, and a shiny, folding fork-and-spoon combination that she also put into her pocket after reminding herself to boil it before using it.

She had covered the campsite twice and was ready to leave when a spot of yellow under a small log caught her eye. She almost dismissed it, but instead, turned back and pushed the log back with her foot. What she found was a torn yellow and black decal no larger than the palm of her hand that looked like it had been very carefully peeled off something. Even without the words she would have known what it stood for. "RADIOACTIVE MATERIALS," it said around its three-petalled flower symbol.

But what in the world was a tonkaweya doing with radioactive materials?

"Find something interesting?" a voice asked.

Lucy spun around and saw two men, one of them holding a shotgun leveled at her.

"Looks like Kendrick was right," the other one said.

Only then did she recognize him as Max Quentin.

CHAPTER 10

ONE | "And I still think we ought to cut down to Crowell and find out what in the tale-of-holy-horses is going on," Jessup said with a wave at the box of radiation suits.

Cody nodded slightly to indicate he understood. He didn't agree, but he wanted to hear how each of them felt before he made his final decision. "What about you?" he asked Melindo.

"*Cabeza de vaca*, Cody! You're the head of the cow. You lead and we'll follow," she said with a straight face.

"I think Donna's right," Brisas added. "You're the head of the cow." She paused, a tight grin tugging at the corners of her mouth. "Better the head of the cow than the rear of one."

For a long moment Cody contented himself with staring north over the Pease brakes, glad that they could inject humor into this situation, and understanding exactly what they were saying.

They were right—it was his decision. That was all there was to it. He could call Crowell for information. He could take the team there. Or they could add these radiation suits to their packs and continue searching for the Nates.

"At least let's call in," Jessup said, as though reading Cody's thoughts.

"And let the Nates know we're here?" Melindo said in disgust. "Wasn't Terry's air force bad enough for you?"

"Sure it was. But we don't know that the Nates have a radio, and we certainly don't know that even if they do, that they're monitoring all hundred channels on that thing."

"Fifty-two," Brisas said. "Only fifty-two of them work."

"Dammit, Juanita, I don't care how many—"

"You made your point," Cody said quietly. "Now I'm afraid it's time for me to make mine." He looked from face to face before he continued, trying to read beyond their words to their emotions. "We'll each take one of these suits and keep looking for the Nates. We'll stay off the radio like we agreed until we have something to report, and we'll follow—"

"Crap. If you weren't going to listen to us, why'd you bother asking?"

Cody was startled by Jessup's attitude, but knew better than to make an issue of it. "I listened, Roland, but I think we have to do it this way, that's all. . . . Some Nate kills me, you can make the decisions. Until then, you're stuck with mine."

Jessup shook his head and glanced at Melindo and Brisas before he spoke. "I'm sorry, Cody. I know you're doing what you think you ought to, and I didn't mean nothing—oh, hell. It's just that I'd feel a clear sight better taking a shot at this thing if I knew you were as worried as I am."

"Take my word for it. I'm worried. I've got no more idea about what's going on than you do, and what little I know about radiation scares the hell out of me. But I figure at least Terry's watching out for us, so we might as well get on with the job we were sent here for." Cody took the bag containing the top suit out of the box, surprised by how heavy it was. "One size fits all, it says here—though I'll tell you right now I don't want to see how that works. Anyway, grab one and let's get packed up and on our way."

As they followed his lead, Cody felt a sudden wave of apprehension. Was he really doing the right thing? Was this the smart decision? Or was it only right because it was what the

Attorney General Terry wanted? What if one of them got hurt or killed because he chose the wrong thing?

With a frustrated shake of his head he pulled his pack on and stood up. He couldn't afford to second-guess himself. If something went wrong, he would take responsibility for it like he took responsibility for everything else.

Responsibility. He'd been taking responsibility since he was a kid, taking it even when it wasn't his, because if he took it, people patted him on the shoulder and praised him and he needed that kind of reassurance. But if something went wrong—even if it wasn't his fault—he'd take the guilt, too. Why not? What was a little more guilt compared to the great load of it he already carried?

TWO | Lucy squirmed in the well-worn saddle as she readjusted her body trying to find a more comfortable way to ride the white-faced ox. They'd been riding for almost an hour and she had already determined that she couldn't get her hands untied. The yucca rope was small, but tough and tight, and pinpricks of numbness were beginning to tingle in her fingers. She turned to face Max Quentin who rode beside her on a Mexican mule. "Can't you untie my hands now? Please? I can hardly run away from you riding this."

He stared at her for several seconds from under the brim of his dirty brown hat before he spoke. "Sure, missy . . . for the time being you can ride with your hands free. Bayhylle, hold up," he called to the man in front of them who was riding a brown ox much larger than Lucy's.

Quentin pulled her ox to a halt then urged his mule in close beside them. "Hold your hands out nice and steady, missy, and don't do nothin' stupid. I'd hate to have to shoot you—most of all 'cause Wendel would be vexed to beat-the-witch if he found out I'd caught you then wasted your body." His strange, hazel eyes looked hooded and deadly.

"I promise to do whatever you tell me," Lucy said. She held out hands as steady as her voice, neither betraying the emotions churning inside her. "We're supposed to be working for the same purpose, aren't we?"

"Yeah . . . well, we'll see about that. For now you just ride like I tell you." His long, dirty fingernails had little trouble loosening the knots. After he untied them he coiled the rope neatly around his hand, secured the little bundle, and shoved it into a leather bag that hung from his saddle horn, all the while watching her intently.

Lucy looked down as she rubbed circulation back into her wrists. She hated the hungry look in his eyes and remembered again his insulting comment the day before about what he and Wendel wanted from her. As she looked up she caught Bayhylle staring at her with a look that matched Quentin's, and could smell his lust.

"You ready to go?" Bayhylle asked. "Or you got something else in mind? Like a soft-stop, maybe?"

Quentin laughed. "Not yet. And not here. Be time and roll enough for that later."

Bayhylle spurred his ox. "You just make sure I get some when the bedroll's out."

"Yeah, I'll do that, Bayhylle, 'cept you'll have to take thirds behind me and Wendel and as small as you are, no one's gonna know if you get any."

"Speak for yourself, breed," Bayhylle called over his shoulder. "I heard you calling snake in the morning just so you could find yours."

Again Quentin laughed. "Only when it's cold." He reached out and slapped Lucy's ox with a quirt. "And this one sure don't look cold to me."

Lucy pulled her cloak tighter around her as her ox jerked into motion behind Bayhylle. No matter how much she had tried to ignore what they were saying, Lucy trembled with anger and fear. How dare they . . . How could they . . . The questions were easily answered. She had been used before.

His name had been Ioni—Paul Ioni, a brave in good standing with his tonkaweya and his tribe. But on her first visit to the Nation, Paul Ioni had displayed his true feathers.

A walk to pick herbs. Then grabbing her under the trees. Pinning her down. Tearing her clothes. Stabbing between her legs over and over. Missing. Cursing. Dying before either of them heard the bark of the rifle.

Lucy had left him there—tears burning down her face, black maws threating to swallow her mind—running blindly through the spring morning—fleeing a voice she dared not listen to—lost and seeking in the unfamiliar breaks until she stumbled upon a group of women behind an old barn.

Two of them had taken her to Mishla's mother's house where sisters and neighbors and gentle friends comforted her, where no one spoke directly of what had happened, where there were gifts presented in shame by relatives who crawled in the door, where the name of Paul Ioni was never mentioned again, where she was soothed and loved and sedated until the whole memory was pushed into the fuzzy distance, and sometimes years later she wondered if the memory was real.

It was. Though Paul Ioni had failed, though her hymen had remained intact, though the bruises on her arms and legs had faded within weeks, the bruises on her heart and mind had taken much longer to heal.

At twelve she had gone innocently with Paul Ioni, and he had sprung the beast of his lust at her with no warning she had recognized. Now, ten years later, she was going with these men against her will, the warning of what they intended seen and heard and understood clearly enough to make her want to scream in rage and terror.

THREE | "There's the old bridge," Melindo said, pointing east.

Cody had to squint before he could see it. When he finally picked out the partially collapsed span that ran like a dotted white line from the green trees on the south to the naked pink dirt and white rock on the north, he understood again how Melindo's eyes made her such an excellent marksman.

The first time he had seen the Copper Breaks bridge he had been seven or eight years old and his Grandad Cody had taken him to the Breaks on a hunting and fishing trip. Except they hadn't done much hunting and very little fishing. Instead they had wandered the old park, talked to a bunch of the Oldtimers who lived there, and then come home. Yet Cody had sensed even then that the trip had been more important than it seemed— important in some basic way that puzzled and pleased him at the same time. That was the trip he always thought of as the story trip, because Grandad Cody had told him lots of stories then— only they didn't mean as much to Cody until years after Grandad had died.

He'd taken Cody to a place called Peace City south of the bridge, past the old Foard and Hardeman marker stuck in the riverbank, and told him about how after Shudderday thousands of people had gathered there in a great fundamentalist revival where stirring preachers had convinced people that the end of the world was upon them and they should come to Peace City to hear the One-True-Word and receive the spiritual manna of God.

Between Cody and his grandfather that day they had counted close up to a thousand marked graves laid out in ragged rows among the mesquite near shallow depressions that made them both feel there were more graves that weren't marked, and thinking about walking on top of all those bones had made Cody shiver.

His grandfather had tried to explain to him that it didn't matter that those people had died there because people were starving to death all around the old country then anyway, and maybe these had died feeling some peace and consolation, and at least the world had missed the devil's radiation they would have got if there'd have been a nuclear war before Shudderday. Not that there weren't some nuclear fallout, his grandfather had said, from the melted reactors that weren't shut down properly— especially the ones in Russia that the scientists said had already started falling apart anyway—but all in all, the world had gotten off pretty clean.

Near the road they also found a historical marker on its side, half-buried in the mud, that told about another town called Pease City that had been near the same spot, that made them wonder what the connection was between Peace and Pease. But come late afternoon Grandad had sworn that whatever that place was called it was bad ground for people, and took Cody away from there. They never talked about it again, but Cody never forgot, and every God Remember Day when he went to the cemetery, he would think about that trip.

The bridge disappeared from sight as Cody led his team deeper into the Pease bottoms. Something told him that they were alone there for the moment, but he remembered his grandfather telling him the Breaks were never empty, and remembered how, almost to prove him true, minutes after his grandfather's telling, a Scavenger had rattled around the bend and up to their camp, his wagon filled with nameless pieces of metal and plastic that instantly fascinated the young Cody. While he had walked around the wagon, staring at the Scavenger's collection of junk, Grandad and the Scavenger held a low conversation with Cody only hearing mention of the

Nates—which they both called Okies—and a curse about the Joiners who wanted to put the US-States back together again.

Years later when he was fourteen, sitting by Grandad's death-bed, he had asked about that Scavenger and his grandfather had wrinkled his pale skin into a frown that made the blue veins on his head look like they were going to pop right through.

Then in his faint, raspy voice he had said, "Don't you never become a Joiner, boy, or one of them damn New Federalists. The rest of the old states only want Texas oil and gas. And that US-government damned near ruined us before Shudderday."

Cody remembered the words ever so clearly. "Can't trust them yankee states," his grandfather had said. "You just swear you'll always fight for West Texas independence, and don't never give in to anything the Okies want, 'cause everyone knows that Okies can't be counted on for nothing but lies and—"

The scent of smoke brought Cody out of his revery. He signaled a stop and sniffed the air.

"I smell it, too," Brisas said. "Smoke."

"Not much of it, though." Slowly and carefully Cody scanned as much of the bottom land as he could see through the saltcedar, juniper, and mesquite brakes, looking for any sign that might help. Again it was Melindo's eyes that found the answer.

"There." She pointed down toward the river. "Just on the other side of that creek. From here it looks like a ford. Lots of wagon tracks."

With great skill and patience the team moved quietly through the brakes as they closed the half-mile between them and the ford.

There was indeed a fire on the other side, and Cody could see five or six unusual wagons with what looked like glass tops, but no matter how hard he squinted, he couldn't make out what was in the wagons. All he could see were the plants and bushes on the other side of them. Were the wagons empty? Or were they carrying some hidden cargo?

"What do you make of that?" he asked Jessup who had moved up beside him to peer across the river from the shelter of the saltcedars.

"Damned if I know," Jessup whispered. "Juanita, Donna, take a look at this."

The two women moved up to take Jessup's place while Kolmer guarded their rear, but from the expressions on their faces Cody could tell that neither of them recognized anything about the glass-topped wagons, either. All of a sudden a chill ran down Cody's spine as he wondered if these were the kinds of wagons radioactive materials were carried in.

FOUR | Lucy wasn't surprised that they weren't headed north, nor that they were following fresh wagon tracks. She assumed that Quentin and Bayhylle were taking her to join the rest of the tonkaweya, and she hoped her assumption was correct. Once with the tonkaweya she was sure they wouldn't do what they were suggesting.

Max Quentin had taken her gun, her sheath knife, and even her steel and flint. He hadn't found the narrow emergency pouch that hung under one arm inside her shirt. It held extra flint and her antique Jack Crain knife—its three-inch stainless steel blade sharp enough to use as a scalpel, and strong enough to skin an ox. Or stab a man.

Nowhere in the Healer's Code was there any prohibition against using it to defend herself, but this knife was doubly special. It was a MUST-Kit—a Medical Utility Survival Tool Kit—complete with antiseptic, sutures, and sterile tape stored in its hollow handle, and it was a gift from her father. There was something repugnant about the thought of using it as a weapon, something in the very idea of it that rasped against the core of her being.

I consecrate my life to the service of humanity. I consecrate my practice to the healing of my patients. I promise them dignity, diligence, and compassion. I swear to respect all human life, and to do all within my power to teach others the same respect. So long as life fills me, I will . . .

All that is in my power . . . But how can I teach others to respect me? And how can I respect them if . . .

If . . . if . . . If it gets dark before we reach the tonk-aweya, what will happen then? If they try to force me, what will I do? What can I do?

The ox stumbled and Lucy snapped back to the present and looked quickly around. The wagon trail was climbing away from the river now, past the pink and white bands of soil, past small clumps of juniper, and past the shelter of the trees. She knew that once they were out of the breaks they would be much more exposed, much more easily seen, and she tried to remember what towns were marked on her map anywhere near here.

Medicine Mound was the only town—and suddenly she wondered if the tonkaweya was heading for the medicine mounds themselves. It made sense. The mounds were grounds sacred to many tribes of the Nation. Mishla had told her that after Shudderday, tribes would gather there in the spring for council and ceremonies, but that was before the buildup of hostility between the Nation and the Republic.

If that's where they were going, she felt a little better. Even Max Quentin and Bayhylle wouldn't dare try to violate her on holy ground—not in the presence of the tonkaweya. Would they?

CHAPTER 11

ONE | As Cody stepped from behind the trees with his carbine cradled easily in his hands, he knew that three other carbines and Melindo's .308 were sighted in on the group across the river, but that didn't make him feel any less vulnerable.

"Hello the camp!" he shouted.

"Hello yourself," an old woman shouted back at him. "You want to shout, or come across?"

The woman was dressed all in brown—a simple dress that looked like wool, a heavy sweater, and a low-crowned hat with a floppy brim. She certainly didn't look dangerous, but Cody wasn't about to take any chances. "Identify yourselves!"

Stepping closer to the water, she cupped her hands around her mouth. "We're of the Megargel Producers, free growers from the Seymour region. And you, by the looks of you, are militia. Come share some midday with us."

Cody had no idea what a Megargel Producer was, nor a free grower, and though he knew where the town of Seymour was, he'd never been that far east. "A little late for midday," he shouted back. "Where be you headed?"

"Right here . . . or close enough by. No settlement law against that up here, is there?"

"No, ma'am, there isn't. Just don't cross any sealed fences." Cody waded into the river, the shock of the cold water up his legs rattling his teeth, his hands holding the carbine high and ready. "How many of you are there?" he asked as he sloshed closer to her.

"Seventeen, counting me. That outnumbers you about three to one, young man, but we mean no one harm—though I suspect them others with you won't quit pointing their rifles at us until you're sure we're who we say."

Cody was surprised that she'd spotted his team, and equally as surprised to see that despite her wrinkled brown skin, she looked much younger than she sounded—probably wasn't a month past forty-five. He was relieved to notice that she was not tattooed like a Nate. "You're right about that, ma'am, though we certainly don't mean you no harm, either. Just trying to find some Nates that are supposed to be along this part of the river."

"Wouldn't be a group with six wagons and a truck, would it?"

"Could be. I take it you seen them?" He was standing on the low bank now, facing her, seeing nothing but openness in her face, and thinking that if she was a Nate, she was a damned slick one. Her eyes kept flicking from his face to his rifle, so he cradled it in the crook of his left arm and let his right hand drop to his side. He was taking a chance, but somehow he felt like it wasn't a bad chance—at least not yet.

"We did peer for a while at a group like that, but don't know for sure they were Nates. Just saw them heading north, three, maybe four hours ago. We was on the bridge—didn't know it wasn't no good—and they was turning up a draw a mile or so east of there. Fact is, we back-followed their tracks to get here. Seemed to know—"

"Harriet! Tell that boy to come eat or leave us alone," a man called from behind her. "Yours is getting cold."

Harriet waved dismissively. "That's Guido. He's always wanting me to do something I ain't doing at the moment." She paused and looked straight into Cody's eyes. "You gonna eat or not? Guido's right, you know."

Cody decided to trust her and was immediately surprised by how much better that made him feel. When he signaled Jessup and the others, he had no reservations about Harriet and her group. Might as well meet these people and see who and what they were.

As soon as the rest of the team emerged from the trees across the river, Harriet turned and started walking to the half-circle of wagons. Only then did Cody realize he had totally forgotten to ask her about the wagons. "Hold it, Harriet!"

She turned, startled.

"What's in those wagons?" he asked, holding his rifle in both hands again.

"Seedling flats, mostly, though we got a few early peas good and up."

Cody shook his head, his finger resting on the trigger guard, ready now, and suspicious. Behind him he heard the team wading across the river and hoped they saw the change in his attitude. "You'd better explain that."

Harriet put her hands on her hips, a look of amused disgust on her face. "Seedlings, boy. Vegetables. Tomatoes. Beans. Dwarf corn. Weren't you listening? We're free growers looking for a place to summer that's—"

"What's a free grower?"

She dropped her hands and slapped her legs in frustration. "You come see for yourself, 'cause sure enough I'm not going to stand here and try to explain it to you."

Again Cody read only honesty in her words and expression and let himself relax. "All right, Miss Harriet, you show me what you're talking about because you might as well be talking Mexican for all the sense you're making to me."

She turned once more and he followed her, Jessup and the team now close behind.

"Everything okay, Cody?"

"I think so. Said they were free growers and she's about to show me what that means."

When they came up on the wagons Harriet pointed under the clear top. "Seedlings," she said. "Flats of them. Soon as it warms up a bit more and we find a good place, we'll transplant them and garden till the crops come in."

Cody stared through the top and saw a bottom crammed with racks and trays all containing tiny pots full of little plants. "Are these . . .?"

"Tomatoes mostly in there," Harriet said, moving on to the next wagon. "This is the bean wagon, though Guido's got some fancy stuff like mint and oregano in there, too. Then the next one is dwarf corn—gonna have to get that in the ground pretty soon—and there's squash and cabbage and lettuce."

"You mean you tote all these things around and grow them in wagons?" Cody asked. "Why? I mean, what's the point?"

"So's we can plant them wherever we please, when we please. That's what free growers do. And ain't it about time you told me your name? I'm Harriet Shaw." She held out her hand.

Cody accepted it. "J.F. Cody," he said. "This here's Roland Jessup, then Juanita Brisas, Donna Melindo, and Ed Kolmer." As he was making the introductions, the other members of Harriet Shaw's group came up and soon everyone was introducing themselves to everyone else.

It was only after all of that was over and they had settled around the fire eating some fine stew of Guido's making that Cody asked, "Where did you say you were from again?"

"Megargel," Harriet said. "We belong to the Megargel Producers Co-op, but we're free growers and decided to try our hand at growing somewheres else."

"Summered and wintered in Grayback," Guido added, "but Leon and Harriet heard about some fine land up near Middleburg, so we thought we might try a summer there—until we got here. We liked this bottom land as soon as we saw it. Looks good to us, and close enough to reach the towns without them being down on us. Course, we might move on later. Depends on the sun and such, like when we have a really good summer with lots of sunshine, we sometimes keep the tomatoes blooming from June to September. But when we have a bad summer—"

"They ain't interested in all that, Guido. They want to know about that group of wagons we saw from the bridge."

"We'd appreciate it," Cody said, "anything you can tell us."

Guido wiped his mouth. "Watched them through my binoculars for close on to ten minutes, I did. Seemed like a strange-looking party to me, and I couldn't figure out why they were traveling cross-country instead of by the roads, but then I guessed they must be pretty rich and it wasn't none of my business."

"How many of them were there? And why do you think they were rich?"

"Six wagons—all in pretty good shape it looked like—and a battered old pickup that was leading them. Plus some folks on oxen and mules—more mules than I've seen together anywhere except at auction once. Anybody owns that many mules has to be rich." He paused as though considering that point. "I didn't exactly count them, you understand," he said, looking evenly at Cody, "but if I were guessing, I'd say close to thirty of them in the main group."

Cody swallowed a half-chewed mouthful. "There were two groups?"

"Three, actually—least ways three that I saw. There was a

little mounted group out front—five men all on mules—then the main group with the wagons, and then as we was coming over the bank into the bottoms, I saw a man and a woman on oxen, and a man on a mule following the tracks. That'd make close to forty all told, I guess. . . . That woman had a funny way of sitting her ox, like her hands were tied or something, but maybe she just wasn't used to riding. Or maybe she was sick. Why, I've seen people spend five minutes in the saddle and be sick for the next fifteen, puking their guts out and—"

"Did you notice anything else unusual about any of them?"

Guido shook his head. "No. Nothing I recall. But I'll tell you what, young sergeant, I think that woman on the ox wasn't going with them 'cause she wanted to."

Cody's heart jumped. "She wasn't full pregnant, was she?"

"Not hardly. Skinny, almost."

Since it wasn't Ann, for the moment he didn't care who it was. He wanted to know something more important. "Did you notice anything unusual about their wagons? Anything at all?"

"Not unless you call the pickup pulling a wagon unusual. All looked pretty normal to me."

Cody had another flash. "That woman wasn't carrying a baby, was she?"

"No again, Sergeant."

"Damn. I was hoping . . ." He let the sentence die when he saw the expression on Jessup's face, then yawned unexpectedly, the fullness of his stomach making him suddenly sleepy.

For a few seconds Guido stared into the fire and Cody was about to tell the team it was time to pack up and hike off their midday when Guido spoke again.

"I wasn't always from Megargel, you know. Was born and grew up in Jermyn—that's over in Big Jack territory. Problem was that everybody in creation claims that land. DalWorth wants it 'cause it controls the Trinity River. Commanche wants it for the growing land. I don't know why West Texas wants it—maybe just to aggravate the other two." He paused a second and sneezed.

"Blessings," Cody said. He didn't want to be rude, but he had no idea why Guido was telling him all this.

"Anyway, like I was saying, when I was a boy—ten years old, I remember, 'cause my mother gave a party for my friends before we left—my folks and me went down from Jermyn to visit my cousins near Bryson and had to stop for a train. I remember that, too, 'cause it was the first train I ever saw. It wasn't very long, but my daddy said there must be something dangerous on it, 'cause after the caboose came an empty flatcar, and after that a boxcar with red and yellow diamonds all over it."

He looked up at Cody and grinned self-consciously. "Don't know why I'm telling you this, Sergeant, except that the folks I saw kind of treated their last wagon the same way. Only one of them ever came close to it was the one driving the team, and he was riding the lead oxen of two-pair-and-one. Nothing unusual about that, is there?"

TWO | The only sure indication Lucy had that they were catching up with the tonkaweya was the fresh smell of oxen droppings on the trail—too fresh to be more than thirty minutes, maybe an hour old. Without reason she took heart from that, and even more encouragement when Bayhylle spurred his ox into a trot. She kicked her ox to follow, but Max Quentin jerked the rope to the ox's nose ring. With a bellow it stopped.

"Don't you go hurrying, Miss Lucy. No need to rush yourself like that. Why, I'll bet that if we wait here, old Wendel will drop back with something that'll help us relax."

His leer told her he wasn't talking about hangers—although he might be talking about them as well. No matter what happened, she knew she couldn't lose control of herself. If she did, well, it would just be better not to. There was no accounting for what might happen otherwise.

"I remember a time or two when Wendel and I was young that we went regular with a couple of girls from Sowells Bluff. Used to row across the river to see them, we did—took us an hour or more each way. But they always made it worth it for us once we all got shuck of our clothes. Whew! Some times we had with them girls. But maybe you don't want to hear about that, huh?"

Lucy stared at him, biting back the words she wanted to say, trying to find some way to reduce the threat of his presence. Through the stink of his body she could smell his hate and his lust, but maybe if she could keep him talking . . . "Not so, Mr. Quentin. Where is Sowells Bluff? And whatever happened to those girls?"

"Sowells Bluff is in the Nation, now, on the Red. Used to be part of DalWorth, but it was the fight for it that lost us the Benge girls." He smiled and scratched his chin under his beard.

"Stormy and Charlotte they were called, and Stormy was mine and Charlotte was Wendel's, but when the argument about who owned what land got hot, their old man moved them down near Greenville, and even though Wendel went down there looking for them once, we never did see either of them again. Course their old man never knew about us—would have killed us if he did 'cause they was pretty uppity people, anyway, being related to the King-Hills and the Van Zandts and all them—so in the end it weren't no big nevermind to . . ." His words trailed off as he looked at her suspiciously. "Why you asking about all this?"

Lucy forced herself to smile. "You asked me if I wanted to hear about it, and I was curious. It sounded like an interesting story to me and gave me a chance to get to know you a little better. Were you and Wendel in on the fighting for—" She stopped suddenly at the sight of Wendel Quentin riding up to them—alone.

"So," Wendel called, "Bayhylle wasn't fooling me. You did find her."

"Doing exactly what Kendrick guessed, snooping around our camp. Found something she shouldn't have, too."

Despite the early afternoon warmth, Lucy shivered.

"Well, he wants to see her," Wendel said with a frown, "so you'd better bring her on."

"Aw, what's the hurry?" Max asked. "We ain't going to get a chance this good again. You know?"

Wendel shook his head. "Later. We'll figure that out later. Looks like Johnson's going to have a baby born on us pretty soon, so this one's got work ahead of her. You understand that, missy?" For the first time Wendel looked directly at her.

"Yes. Of course. You have no medics or medwives. I will be more than happy to assist Mrs. Johnson with the birthing—"

"She ain't Mrs. Johnson. Just claims to be. She's actually married to a man from over—"

"Shut up, Max! And be careful," Wendel added more quietly. "Kendrick hears you saying stuff like that he'll fill your face full of knuckles and your ass full of lead."

"I don't give a good god—"

"Just shut up. And learn some patience. We can deal with Kendrick after we meet Goodfox." He took the nose-ring rope from Max and turned to Lucy. "Come on, Missy, there's need of you."

As her ox plodded steadily up the hill behind his mule, Lucy puzzled over what all this meant. She was convinced that this was no ordinary tonkaweya, and that they were dealing with something bigger than a raiding party in West Texas territory. But so far the pieces refused to fit into a pattern she could decipher. The burning fuel truck. The threat to take her with them. Ann Johnson setting her free. The Texian militiamen and braves sharing a campfire. The argument about leadership. The Quentins, who would have been ejected from any decent tonkaweya. Kendrick Johnson and his pregnant wife. And not the least, the radiation warning label. What did it all mean?

A noise brought her back to the moment. An easy mile ahead of them on the trail she saw first one, then two of the wagons. The noise she had heard was the sound of a pickup. Even when at Wendel Quentin's urging she kicked her ox into a trot, it seemed to take forever before they caught up with the wagons. He led her wide around the last one, then up to the third from the end where Kendrick Johnson greeted her from the back of his mule.

"I said you would be coming north with us, Mishla's Lucy," he said with an unreadable twinkle in his eyes. "Tried to tell Ann she was going to need you when she let you go, but she's a stubborn one, that's for sure. She's in the wagon ahead. You go up there and tend to her. And make sure she and the baby are all right."

"My duty," Lucy said, "but there are no guarantees, Mr. Johnson. I'll do my best to see that there are no major—"

"That they're both all right," he repeated.

The scowl that darkened his face warned her to guard her tongue. "If she's in labor, we'll have to stop soon and prepare her properly—boil water and all those things."

"We'll stop when I say, Mishla's Lucy, not when you say. Be close to dark by the time we get to Medicine Mounds. You get Ann to hang on till then and I'll get you whatever you need."

"Don't be so stupid," she said without thinking. "Babies come when they're ready to, not when some ignorant man tells them he's ready to receive—"

"You heard me," he said before turning his mule away. "You hold that baby till sunset."

He spurred the mule and rode toward the last wagon, but Lucy knew she had made her point with him. Wendel Quentin guided her ox up to the wagon Johnson had indicated and told the driver to stop. Lucy dismounted and climbed into the back of the wagon. Ann Johnson was lying on a thick mattress on top of the load. "It's Lucy the healer, Mrs. Johnson. I've come to help with—"

"Damn! I thought I got you away from us. What's the matter with you, healer? You stupid or something? You think you're involved in some game as you run your little errands? Damn, damn, damn. Get out of here."

Lucy shook her head. "I can't. I think I'm a prisoner."

"Not for long you're not. We'll find—" Ann broke off in a low moan. "God! It hurts. It really hurts."

CHAPTER 12

ONE | Guido had been wrong. It was nearly two miles east of the bridge where the wagon tracks turned north away from the river. Now the afternoon light was fading fast under dark clouds that loomed in from the south as Cody and his team followed the tracks up out of the Pease brakes toward the red, rolling prairie above. Thunder rumbled in the distance.

"We're gonna catch it," Kolmer said.

"Think we'll lose their tracks if we do?" Jessup asked.

Kolmer shook his head. "Have to rain for years. These ain't just new tracks, and even if they were, one of those wagons they got is loaded heavy and cutting deep. We could probably follow that one across anything 'cept granite."

Cody nodded in agreement. The only time Kolmer said much in one lump was when he knew exactly what he was talking about. "Ed's right. Let's get our rain gear on and keep our eyes open for some shelter. No sense in getting caught out in the rain if we don't have to—not if it's not going to gain us anything on the Nates."

"You want to set up tents up there?"

"Not if we can find something better."

As they paused to unroll their ponchos and put them on, thunder grumbled in the sky, louder and closer this time. When it subsided Melindo called to them from the top of the trail. "Easy going from here on."

"You see any sign of those wagons?" Cody called back.

She shook her head. "Just the tracks heading north. There's

some kind of building about half a mile northeast of here. Could be a barn, but the tracks don't lead there."

"Hold what you've got and keep your eyes open. We'll look at it together."

The thunder settled into a regular pattern, drumming in the dark clouds that grew high out of their black roots below the southern horizon.

Suddenly Cody's knees buckled and he fell to the ground. Only as he fought to regain his balance on his hands and knees did he fully realize that the ground itself was shaking.

It was an earthquake—the worst one he had ever felt. And the longest. He counted by one-thousands for a full thirteen seconds before the ground stopped trembling.

Kolmer whistled through his teeth as he climbed slowly to his feet. "Damn bugger, that one."

"I've never felt one that strong," Brisas said. She was still sitting on the ground leaning back against her radio pack, her face pale, her body trembling.

"Bet none of us have." Cody crawled over beside her and offered her his hand. "Together?"

She took his hand and they helped each other to their feet. Large raindrops spattered them and splotted on the damp soil. "Let's get to the top before we get caught in the runoff," Cody shouted as a fierce wind ripped at them from above. What would they do if this was another Shudderday, if the tectonic plates were shifting again?

A shiver ran through their feet.

Instinctively Cody and Brisas reached for each other. By the time they held each other by the arms the shiver had stopped.

"Aftershocks," she shouted, as she let go of his wet poncho. "Folks are in bad trouble wherever that thing's centered."

Again the ground shook for a second, then stilled, then trembled again. And again. And again. Each little shock made Cody and the others wary of moving even as they fought the wind in order to stand still. Rain poured down on them, hard blowing rain that turned the dirt under their feet into slick mud.

"Up! Up!" Cody shouted. "Get to the top!"

It took almost fifteen minutes for the four of them to struggle up to where Melindo waited—each step they took a sliding, mud-sucking search for traction on ground that refused to hold beneath them.

Once they all reached the top of the trail, Cody spread them out, then Melindo led them without words through the blowing rain toward the building she had seen. When they reached it, they circled it very carefully and discovered it was a shed, a three-sided shed made of rusted sheet metal and weathered boards. But except for some junk piled against its back wall, it was empty and they gladly took shelter under its noisy roof.

"Look," Melindo shouted in Cody's ear. She pointed to one end of the long shed that was closed in. The door to that closed-in part had a latch fastened on the outside.

After placing Melindo to cover him, Cody cautiously opened the door. In the dim light he could see nothing, but the overpowering stench of rotting flesh sent the remains of Guido's stew lurching from his stomach in spasms of nausea.

TWO | "I don't know," Lucy said. "I have no way of knowing. I know what to do—how to deliver your baby when it's time. I've done that. But I don't know how to tell if this is false labor. Could, like as not, be the real thing. So far you haven't dilated any, and your water hasn't broken, so there's just no way I know of anyone could tell." The other thing she'd seen when she checked Ann, she kept to herself, but she knew now that the woman belonged with the tonkaweya.

Ann sighed. "The cramps seem to be easing. Does that mean anything?"

"Only that your body's not ready yet. This could go on for a couple of days or even a week before serious labor starts. Or your baby could be born in a couple of hours. With your first it's just too damned hard to guess what will—"

"All right," she said with a limp wave of her hand. "All right. I get the point. Leave me alone, now. I can't seem to keep my eyes open."

Lucy felt ill-trained and inadequate as she listened to the gusting pattern of wind and rain on the wagon's vinyl top, grateful that Johnson had decided to stop, but worried about how he was going to provide her with enough hot water when the time came. Hot water was one of those essentials for sterilizing her knife, cleansing the mother, and then the baby—and for sterilizing the thread that would tie off the umbilical cord. When she looked at Ann she wished that true labor would start so they could both get this over with. "I'll be right here if you need me," she said.

"Fine. Just fine." Ann whispered sleepily.

Leaning back against one of the side supports, Lucy gave brief consideration to the idea of climbing out of the wagon and stretching her legs, rain or no rain. However, she really didn't want to get wet, and she certainly didn't want Johnson raging at her again. He was in a foul mood that she was sure could not be blamed on the weather or his wife's condition.

If Ann was his wife.

What had Max Quentin said? That she was married to some other man? How long had she been with Johnson? And if what Max Quentin said was true, whose child was about to be born? Kendrick Johnson's? Or someone else's?

And what was Wendel's comment? Something about taking care of Johnson when they reached Goodfox? Who was Goodfox? Why did that name ring such a— Then she remembered. Father Murray Goodfox was one of those radio preachers—a Joiner or worse—who wanted to reunite the old U.S. of A. as some kind of holy . . .

Lucy's head jerked and she realized she had been nodding off. Someone was untying the front flap.

"How is she?" Kendrick Johnson asked gruffly as he stuck the upper half of his body into the wagon, dripping rain from his wetsuit onto the pillows under Ann's head.

"She's sleeping," Lucy whispered. "She needs the rest."

"What about the baby? Why isn't it here?"

His tone seemed to imply that Lucy was somehow responsible for the fact that the baby hadn't been born yet, and that angered Lucy. "I told you I'm not a medwife. It's too soon for me to tell anything yet. Could be false labor. Have you figured a way to make hot water for her?"

"Don't worry about it. You just worry—"

"I have to worry about the whole damn thing," she hissed, "especially if we're going to be stuck—"

"Go away," Ann mumbled. "Leave me alone."

Johnson jerked his thumb toward the flap. "We'll talk outside."

Lucy only nodded, angrier than she thought she had reason to be. Yet as she pulled on her cloak and carefully eased herself up on her knees without disturbing Ann, all the reasons for her anger seemed to pour through her thoughts. Johnson, and the Quentin brothers, and Ann, and being held against her will—

only now she couldn't leave because Ann needed her, so she wasn't staying against her will, but that just increased her anger.

She unzipped the rear flap, saw a face, and shrieked.

Ann moaned.

The face disappeared into the rainy darkness.

Johnson came sloshing up from the front of the wagon. "What in the blazing hell is wrong with you, woman?"

"Qu-Quentin," Lucy managed to say with a stutter as she fought for control of her pounding heart. "Max Quentin. He was right here, staring at me as—"

"Of course he was," Johnson said. "I told him to watch this end of the wagon so's you didn't make a run for it."

Lucy slapped him so hard his hat flew off and landed in a puddle. "How dare you!" she screamed. "How dare you question my ethics as a healer. I would never abandon a patient."

She climbed down from the wagon and hovered over him as he bent over to pick up his hat, surprised by the force of her anger. "You may be used to people who do things like that— scum like the Quentins," she shouted, "who have no morality that's noticeable—but I'm not one of them. You get that through your head right away. You understand me?"

As he stood up, he hit her so hard, her ears rang. Then everything faded into cold, wet darkness.

THREE | "Dogs," Jessup said, setting his tiny camp lantern on the ground. "Must have dug under that back wall. Looks like they ate most of that bag labeled poison. No wonder they died the way—"

"Enough," Cody said above the din of the rain on the roof. "I'll believe anything you say. Just don't bother me with the details. My stomach won't take them. You find anything interesting in there?"

"Yes and no. Found some tools—rusted to no good, most of them—four cans of Lamesa oil that look pretty new, and a big metal storage box that looks like a safe 'cause the key has to fit up inside a little hidey-hole."

"Anything in it?"

"Locked tight and nobody gave me the key."

"They won't, neither," a deep voice said.

Cody and Jessup looked up to find themselves confronted by

two people in rain slickers standing just under the roof with shotguns leveled straight at them. "Easy, now," Cody said. "You wouldn't want to be doing something wrong here."

"And neither would you," the closest man said. "Samuel, shine the light on these boys."

From the other side of the shed a hissing light appeared out of the darkness and revealed that none of Cody's team members had their hands on their weapons. It also revealed that the shotgunners were a man and a woman. "We're members of the West Texas Militia," Cody said as evenly as possible, "and we're out tracking some Nates that went through here."

"Saw 'em," the man said, the barrel of his shotgun never wavering, "an ugly looking bunch, and too damn many of them to boot. How do we know you're not with them?"

"Our uniforms should be enough—"

"Don't mean nothing, boy. Some of them Nates was wearing our militia uniforms. What else you got?"

"Are you sure? About the uniforms, I mean?"

"Sure as I'm standing here with my finger on the trigger," the man answered. "Been a lot of folks around here lately. Now, what else you got to show you are who you say you are?"

"Our I.D. cards," Cody said.

"Show me yours . . . real slow like, so's I don't get nervous and accidentally pull this trigger."

"Now, Kenneth, don't be threatening—"

"Hush!" he said, cutting the woman off. "They move, you shoot them. I want to know who it is that's trompin' over my roof and rootin' in my shed."

"I'm going real slow," Cody said as he pulled his right arm under the poncho. He knew he could reach his pistol, but he also knew that could get someone killed, and these people were only protecting what was theirs. Yet having to look down the wrong end of a shotgun angered him deeply.

"I'm putting my hand on my sleeve pocket and unbuttoning it. Now I'm reaching for my I.D. card. Now, I am pushing my hand back out here where you can see it." Cody held the card out to the man, aware again of the smell of rotting flesh, but also of the gasoline smell of the lantern.

"Samuel," the man barked, "get that."

The light moved closer and behind it Cody saw a boy about eight years old. His face was badly pocked—probably from smallpox—and he looked frightened but determined. The hand that reached out to take the card was missing two fingers.

Cody dropped the card and grabbed the boy's wrist, jerking him off his feet and into Cody's lap. Somehow the lantern landed right side up beside them.

"Let me go! Let me go!"

"Samuel!" the woman gasped.

The boy struggled, but Cody held him fast. Everyone else seemed frozen in the glaring light.

"Now," Cody said to the man, "you look at that card as long as you want to, but until you put those shotguns down, I'm hanging onto the boy."

"I'll blast one of these others!" the man growled as he shifted his aim toward Brisas.

"No, Kenneth! No!" Suddenly the woman dropped her shotgun and stepped in front of the man. "These people haven't done anything to us. And if they're who they say they are, they're here to help us."

"She's right, sir," Brisas said. Her carbine was pointed directly at the man's head. "You can put that shotgun down now."

Cody knew the situation had gotten out of hand, but didn't know how to bring it to an end. If he hadn't grabbed the boy, none of this would have happened. And if he didn't do something quickly, someone was going to get hurt—and it would be his fault. "Please, mister, put the gun down."

The man pushed the woman aside and backed up a step, keeping the shotgun aimed at Melindo and Kolmer. Rain spattered on his slicker. "Let the boy go first," he said slowly.

The woman stood by a post looking from the man to the boy and back again.

"Juanita, point somewhere else," Cody said.

Brisas hesitated for a moment, then raised the muzzle of her carbine until it pointed at the roof. Her finger still rested on the trigger.

"Now, Kenneth"—Cody hoped his use of the man's name would ease some of the tension—"if you will point your gun away from us, I'll let Samuel go."

The ground trembled.

The woman lurched forward and grabbed the barrel of the shotgun. It fired with a deafening roar.

FOUR | Lucy heard the patter of the rain on the vinyl top and awoke to see Suzanne Quentin's dim profile. "What . . . where . . .?"

"He really hit you," she said, "but you certainly deserved it, talking to him like that! It's women like you that make it hard for all of us—not knowing your place and not having sense enough to hold your tongue." She paused with a faint smile. "But you'll learn. If Kendrick don't teach you, Max and Wendel will."

Pushing herself up on her elbows, Lucy felt a little dizzy as she looked around the neatly crowded interior of the wagon. The side of her head throbbed and there was a faint ringing in her ears. "Who's watching Ann?" she asked.

"Kendrick. Said he'd call for me if you wasn't back up when she come around. You better go over there."

Lucy stared long and hard at Suzanne Quentin before forcing herself to sit up. She paused, lightheaded for a moment, then reached for her cloak which was rolled up neatly at her feet. "I didn't mean to cause you trouble," she said as she straightened out the cloak and began to pull it on. "I didn't realize that Mr. Johnson was from the old school."

"Ain't got nothing to do with schools. It's got to do with knowing your place and acting proper. Didn't your momma teach you anything?"

"Didn't have one—least not after she gave me birth. Died of the tetanus."

"Mine died of scarlet fever," Suzanne said, the critical tone gone from her voice, "but I was ten by then and it scared me something awful. I'm sorry about yours."

"Me, too. And I'm sorry about yours. But I'm glad you got to know yours." Despite the circumstances and Suzanne Quentin's attitude, Lucy felt an odd kinship with this woman.

"Your daddy die, too?"

"Yes, when I was sixteen," Lucy said, "but I never knew him too good." She thought about the few times he had visited her at Mishla's and how every time he left too soon, and how between times she had missed him, and hated him for being gone, and loved him all at the same time. She pulled up the hood of her cloak with a shake of her head. "Which way's their wagon?"

"Straight behind," Suzanne said. "Be careful with Kendrick. He's got a mighty short temper."

Lucy smiled. "Thanks, I will." She unzipped the front flap and crawled out onto the wagon seat and into the rain. As quickly as she could she zipped the flap closed, not wanting Suzanne Quentin to have to clear up any more of a mess than Lucy had already left her. She climbed carefully down from the seat, holding on all the time, then felt her way back along the wagon.

The night was cave-black in the blowing rain, and beyond the wagon she could see nothing. Then she heard a woman cry out, and she knew that Ann Johnson's pains had started again. With steady determination she pushed herself into the blackness in the direction of the laboring woman.

CHAPTER 13

ONE | The blast from the shotgun tore a hole out of the edge of the shed's roof.

Before the report died, Jessup tackled the man and ended up in a heap with him and the woman—the three of them struggling in the rain and the mud.

Samuel screamed and jerked himself sideways out of Cody's arms.

Kolmer and Brisas jumped to their feet and Melindo grabbed the boy's slicker and pulled him back to her.

It took several minutes to get everyone untangled and under control, but finally the eight of them were sitting peaceably around the lantern, sharing its warmth as well as its light, grinning uncomfortably at their muddy condition. The shotguns rested beside the team's rifles and the radio, all in an orderly row against the back wall of the shed. The front of the shed now had a nasty leak.

The woman reached into the damp earth and picked up Cody's I.D. card. After wiping the mud off of it and reading it carefully, she handed it back to him. "I'm sorry, Mr. Cody, and I'm sure Kenneth is, too, but times have been strange and hard around here these last weeks."

Only then did he notice that her face was as pocked as the boy's. "It's all right, ma'am. We understand that you got to be careful living out here by yourselves. I'm just glad no one was hurt in the middle of all that."

"So am I, Mr. Cody," the man said. "Praise the Lord."

"Amen," the woman and boy said at the same time.

"Please, just call me Cody."

The man stuck out his hand. "I'm Kenneth Lockett, and this here's my wife, Maria, and our son, Samuel."

As though meeting for the first time they all introduced themselves around the circle, sharing handshakes and nods until all names had been spoken and acknowledged.

"Have you been born again, Mr. Cody?" Mrs. Lockett asked.

Oh, goodness, he thought, what can I say to that? The last thing he wanted to do at the moment was get snared in a born-again-or-not discussion. Seemed every fundamentalist sect had its own definition for that and its own interpretation of the true meaning of the Bible. Cody only understood the Method-Baptist way because he'd grown up hearing it. But that wasn't his way. Maybe he should just explain that somehow. "If you mean in the sense of believing in Cristodios, I, uh . . ."

"How many Nates passed here today?" Jessup asked.

Cody could have blessed him for changing the subject.

"'Bout forty or fifty, I'd guess," Mr. Lockett answered, "assuming them last three were Nates."

"How long before we got here?"

"Four hours, maybe. Not much more than that." Mr. Lockett paused, staring out at the blackness and blowing rain. "Listen, Mr. Cody, I truly am sorry about what happened. I mean, it's just been kind of bad on us this last month or so. Someone stole half our cows in the middle of the night a week or so back—fifteen of them to be exact—and I suspect it was Nates what done it, though I can't be sure. But whoever done it pretty well trampled down our garden when they come through here. A couple rode across the roof—that's how we heard 'em—but by the time I got up here they was gone in the dark. Even took our riding oxen."

"Did you say they rode across your roof?" Brisas asked.

Lockett smiled. "That's right, missy. We're full dug in about forty yards from here, complete with a chimney we can pull down inside if need be—which is what we done today when Samuel spotted them Nates."

"You live underground? What about the quake today?"

"Didn't bother us much."

"It was fun," Samuel said suddenly. "We got a periscope and everything. Papaw made it out of some stuff he traded with a Scavenger, and I can see real good with it, too, like I did today when them Nates was coming, only I was outside when I saw them first, but I watched 'em with Papaw while Daddy and Momma stood guard, and Nana and Mamaw watched the babies, because we got pigs, too, see, but only little ones is down in the house. The hogs and sows without piglets stay in the pen." The boy beamed as though he had just given a prize recitation.

"Talks a mite, don't he?" Lockett said to no one in particular. "But he's a good boy and a help to us."

"Isn't your Papaw going to be worried about all of you?" Cody asked the boy.

"Naw. He can see inside the shed with the periscope."

"Just what is this periscope thing, anyway?" Jessup asked.

"Well, it's kind of like looking out a little window, only you're underground and the window's above ground. Papaw—"

"You can explain to him later," Mrs. Lockett said. "Right now I think we ought to invite these men into the house where we can all get cleaned up and I can see to supper for all of us."

"Really, ma'am, that won't be necessary. We'll stay dry and warm here, and with a little fire we can cook up our rations—"

"Nonsense, Mr. Cody. Tell him, Kenneth." The determined look on her face as she stood up warned against disagreement.

"Maria's right. Usually is. You all come on down and dry yourselves out while it's cooking. It'll be a mite cramped in there, for sleeping, but better than this old shed. It's the least we owe you after . . ." He stood up and glanced at the still open door of the end room. "I see you found the dogs."

"You mean you left them there?" Jessup said.

"Yep. Only way to warn the others. Packs of them run wild around here, but they've learned not to eat poisoned meat, so I thought I'd remind them that this is poison country. Might help keep them away from my pigs. But I guess I'm going to have to get them out of there pretty soon. Smell's getting awful."

Mrs. Lockett cleared her throat and the rest of them stood.

Cody smiled. "We'd certainly be pleased to accept your hospitality, ma'am."

"Follow me," Samuel said, picking up the lantern. "I'll show you how we go."

Two | Lucy dipped the rag in clean water, twisted it tightly and gave it to Ann Johnson to replace the one she had clenched in her teeth.

"Check me again," Ann said before putting the fresh rag in her mouth.

Knowing there was no sense in arguing, Lucy took the lantern off its hook, moved to the foot of Ann's mattress, and lifted up her dress. Ann spread her legs automatically. Lucy held the lantern as close as she dared without burning Ann or setting her dress on fire and checked her. "Still no dilation," she said, lowering the dress. "I'm pretty sure it's false labor."

"But how? Why?"

"I don't know how or why," Lucy said as she moved back beside Ann and hung the lantern on its hook under the vent hole. "All I know is that sometimes the body does that, like it's practicing or something, and there's nothing we can do to change it. Do you have any calendar idea of when you're due?"

Ann clenched her teeth with a frown and twisted the rag around her hand. "April first," she said after the pain passed. "That'll be nine months to the day from when I think I got pregnant."

With a tilt of her head Lucy did a fast mental calculation. "Thirty-seven, thirty-eight weeks, now. If you got pregnant when you think you did, this is right at the beginning of the normal range for birthing, so it could happen any time in the next three or four weeks. And I think your body's going to wait at least part of that time."

When Ann didn't respond, Lucy was content to make herself comfortable and sit quietly beside her patient listening to the quiet brrring hum of the lantern and the sounds of their breathing—Ann's labored, hers light. She was beginning to feel uncomfortably warm, so she leaned back and pulled the front zipper down another couple of inches and folded the flap out.

A cool damp breeze greeted her effort and she remembered another time like this when it had been her father whose sickbed she sat beside in a similar breeze. He was having a recurrent bout of malaria—common malaria Mishla had called it, but Lucy had found nothing common about it. For two long days she had tended to him, watched him shake with the chills, burn with the fever, and sweat to the point of dehydration. Following Mishla's instructions she treated him with the very expensive quinine salts from Colorado mixed with water—as much water as she could force him to drink.

On the morning of the third day he had gotten out of bed, declared himself better, and given Lucy a kiss on the forehead and a cloth-wrapped package which he made her swear not to open until after he left. Then he did just that. He left.

The package had contained the antique MUST-Kit knife with its finely-honed stainless steel blade and an excellent Arkansas stone to keep it sharp. Its four-inch-long hollow handle was packed with emergency medical supplies and wrapped with braided nylon cord. A note stuck in its sheath told her the knife had been made by Jack Crain, a famous pre-Shudderday knifemaker from Weatherford, down in Commanche, and that her father had bought it from an old medic in Missouri. The knife's history made her appreciate it all the more.

In the package under the knife her father had left a rambling letter telling her that he loved her, but that he never knew how to be a proper father, and that he hoped she understood that no matter where he went or what he did, he never forgot about her, and that someday he would find a way to make it all up to her. That day had never come. She had seen him one more time after that, before word came that he had died in the Ozarks.

Ann snored softly and Lucy was brought momentarily back to the present, glad that her patient was getting some sleep, and more sure than ever that they were not faced with the beginnings of true labor.

Several months after receiving the news of her father's death, another package had arrived—one with four books in it and another rambling letter that he had written in a town called Willard when he knew he was close to death. The most important and exciting of the books was a copy of *Taber's Cyclopedic Medical Dictionary* in excellent condition. But there was also a small regular dictionary, and a two-volume set of wildflower identification books that someone had added notes to about the medicinal properties of many of the plants.

The letter described how he had come by the books, and the places he had been, and the things he had done and seen, half of which Lucy didn't understand or care anything about at the time. She was looking for something more important and found it in the last three pages.

There her father in his tiny, cramped handwriting told Lucy about her mother—who her mother's people had been, what kind of schooling she had received, and where she had lived near Gilliand before he met her in Lubbock—but most important of all, what kind of person she had been and how much he had loved her.

Those final pages, which she read and reread over the years, had persuaded Lucy to forgive her father for many of the things he had failed to do for her. Yet they had also made her feel like her roots had been stripped away—first by her mother's death, then by her father's—and that she only belonged where someone chose to take her in, not where she had a natural right to go. If only she had known—

The sound of the zipper startled her, and she turned to see Kendrick Johnson crawling in through the front flap.

"Well, Miss Lucy, I take it there's no baby yet?"

"I believe it's false labor," Lucy said quietly.

"Then she won't be needing you for the rest of the night?"

"No, I don't think she will."

"Good. You can go now and I can get some sleep."

Suddenly it occurred to Lucy that she had no place to go. "Where can I sleep?"

Johnson laughed. "With the Quentins for all I care. Now, get out of here."

THREE | Cody sopped up the last of the gravy on his plate with the loaf-end of Mrs. Lockett's bread, and as he stuck it in his mouth, he marveled at the nature of their underground home and the size of their family. In addition to the three Locketts they'd met in the shed, there were Kenneth Lockett's parents, Maria Lockett's mother, who was introduced as Nana Fernandez, and year-old twin baby girls. As soon as dinner had been served Nana Fernandez had taken her plate and the babies into another room, claiming the babies would be too much trouble at table.

"You want more, Mr. Cody?"

"No thanks, Samuel. I believe I'm quite full." Truth was he would have liked more, but he had seen Mrs. Lockett dealing out smaller portions to her family than to his team, and he couldn't eat any more without feeling like he was cheating them.

"You're welcome to it," the senior Lockett said, "'cause spite of the way Maria doled it out, we got pigs enough to make more and lots of it." He looked directly at his wife when he spoke, and there was an amused look in his eyes.

"Now, Father, there's no need in fussing at our guests—"

"Or at me either," Maria said as she began gathering the plates and dishes. "The Good Lord knows I do my best to keep your meals ready when you want them and water in the cistern and hams cured and smoked. I certainly don't need any unsaved man telling me how to—"

The old man laughed and patted his wife on the arm. "You listening to her, Mother? She sounds just like you, and still doesn't know teasing when she hears it."

His wife smiled quietly and covered his hand with her own as she rose to help her daughter-in-law. Samuel joined them.

"Never did cotton too much to religion—even when the pox came through again six years ago and everyone was converting," the old man said, "but me and the babies are the only heathens left in the family—not that anybody but me thinks they're with me, but when I rock them we talk about it and I know they're on my side."

His family ignored his comments, but Cody was taken with his manner and his speech. "How long you been on this land, sir?"

"No need to call me sir, boy. Only Samuel does that anymore and it's just as well." He pushed back from the table and rocked his chair back on its rear legs. As if in response to an automatic invitation, Samuel started climbing into his lap and the chair came down on the plank floor with a bang. They both laughed at some private joke.

"That was certainly a delicious supper," Jessup said. The rest of the team murmured in agreement. "Made me sleepy."

Cody acknowledged the hint with a slight nod. "Maybe it's time we went back to the shed and settled in for the night."

"Nonsense," Lockett, Senior, said. "You'll sleep down here where it's safe, dry, and warm. You'll have to use the floor, but it's better than that wet ground."

"There's a problem with that," Cody said after hesitating for a second. "None of us is going to sleep very well without a guard out. We're too used to having somebody on watch all the time. Not that I mean to say that we feel unsafe here, but—"

The old man laughed and pointed at Kenneth. "See. I told you they'd want that."

Kenneth shook his head with an amused grin.

"Good for you, boys—and girls," Lockett added with smiles for Brisas and Melindo. "I was four years captain of the Vernon Locals, back when things was really bad, and I know how you feel. But that don't change nothing. Just 'cause we mount a guard don't mean that you can't sleep here between times, does it?"

"I guess not, Captain. We gonna use your periscope?"

"Nope. It's great in the daytime, but it don't hear worth a damn at night, so—"

"Father, please! Your language!"

"Yes, dear. Anyway, like I was saying, Cody, it's not much good at night, but there's a snug place on an outcrop a hundred steps from our door where you can see most of the surrounding countryside, hear good, and stay fairly dry if it's still raining up there."

"Sounds good to me."

"I'll take first watch," Jessup said. "Unless you want it, Cody?"

"No. Go ahead. Juanita, you take second. Ed can take third, Donna, fourth, and me, last. Anybody want to swap?"

None of them did, so that was how they started. An hour later everyone in the house was either in bed or bedded down on the floor except for Cody and the captain, who seemed to be in charge of checking everything before he went to bed.

"I'll tell you what, Cody," he said as he fussed with the coals in the stove so the bank was to his liking, "I wouldn't have no complaint if you all stayed around here."

"Why's that, Captain?"

"Because I got a nasty feelin' in my gut that tells me things are going to be poppin' in these parts any time now—like they were fifty years ago—and I figure five extra guns just might keep us safe and sound."

FOUR | After crawling out of the wagon bed angry and frustrated, then sitting on the seat for thirty minutes or so, Lucy had come up with a solution.

By pulling the weather flaps all the way down to the footbox, and by sitting sideways on the wagon seat, she had managed to create a relatively dry spot to sleep. She wasn't going to be any too comfortable, she knew, and she was probably going to be stiff and sore in the morning, but it was easier to accept those conditions than to search for a place in one of the other wagons, all of which—except Suzanne Quentin's—had only men in them so far as she knew.

Two hours later she was beginning to wonder if she would ever fall asleep. No matter how she arranged her cloak and her pack as padding, cover, and pillow, she managed to find some bone that pressed hard against the unyielding wooden seat, or one of several riding bruises from her trip on oxback. Then by pure chance her body found a comfortable position, and she knew that if she counted her breaths, slowly and steadily, and kept her mind focused on the sound of the rain, that she could relax her body enough to go to sleep. Just as she was slipping over the edge, the rain stopped and hushed voices demanded her attention.

"It's gonna kill us if . . . get rid of it," someone was arguing, "and I say . . . it or him."

"Him in charge . . . until we contact Father Goodfox . . . there has . . . or don't need to know."

"You'll find out when we get to the train."

Lucy was alert now. The last voice had been Max Quentin's, but he, too, was speaking in hushed tones. Then as if they realized they were too close to Johnson's wagon, the voices moved away, and Lucy lay on the hard wooden seat in the damp darkness frustrated and afraid.

Who were these people? What did they have to do with that Joiner priest, Goodfox? She tried hard to remember anything else she could about him, but fatigue kept sidetracking her thoughts. The only other thing that jabbed through her memory was a phrase, *the holy instrument of God*, but she shrugged it off. Nothing about Johnson's group could be confused with anything holy.

— —
—

. . . *concludes another in our series of pre-recorded patriotic broadcasts from Father Murray Goodfox. Please send your donations to Unification Fund, St. Joseph Church, Rhineland, Knox County, Republic of West Texas.*

This is Sister Paula Kathryn. May the Lord bless you and keep you. May the Lord make His face shine upon you and be

*gracious unto you. May the Lord lift up His countenance upon you
and give you peace. . . . And remember, Father Goodfox will be
broadcasting the mass live every day from Holy Thursday through
Easter Sunday.*

CHAPTER 14

ONE | Cody awoke trembling, afraid, unsure of where
he was in the warm darkness.

Then he remembered the Locketts and the underground
house and knew it was the earth trembling, not him. That
worsened his anxiety about where he was. He was used to
trembles and little shakes every now and again, but not like what
had been happening over the last three days. And he certainly
wasn't used to being underground when the earth shook like
that.

The old man entered the room carrying an oil lamp turned
way down. He walked stiff-legged first to the Franklin stove,
then to the cabinets beside it, checking to see that all the doors
were closed.

Cody yawned on purpose before he spoke. "Little shake
there liked to of scared me, Captain, especially being down
here."

"Been a long time since we had this many shakes close
together. Hard to remember one as strong as we had yesterday,
either." Captain Lockett spoke very softly and pointed up at the
planked ceiling. "But don't worry about being here. It's a good
house, a strong one. That wood up there's just to make it pretty.
Above that is steel reinforced concrete and all around us, too.
My brother Allen and I built this house back when the ground
really did shake regular. Built it to last. Hasn't even cracked
much in all these years."

"I believe it." Cody stood up, carefully stepped over Ed
Kolmer's snoring form, and edged himself around the kitchen
table to the open side where he pulled out a chair and sat down.
The old man's words made him feel a little better, but he was still
uneasy. "Could you leave me that light when you go back to bed?
I don't believe I'm going to sleep any more."

Captain Lockett put the lamp in the middle of the table. "I'm gonna fix some chicory blend for me. You want some?"

"Well, I'm not sure I'm ready for anything yet."

"Give it a try, son. I make it myself. There's a little kola in it along with the chicory, and some milk thistle, some soy and mesquite beans, a touch of mint, and a dash of real coffee. May not sound like much to you, but I think it'll surprise you. Perk you right up."

"Why not. Sure, Captain, fix me some, too." Cody yawned naturally this time as he watched the old man fill an old percolator with water, then open a tin of ingredients and measure them into the percolator's basket. After he put that on the stove and added a few small sticks to the fire, he opened one of the cupboards and took out two large mugs.

"Time was," the captain said unexpectedly as he leaned back against the counter next to the stove, "when there weren't no law out here at all. Oh, there was in the towns, and if something got big enough out in the country—like feuds or something like that—then the law would come out from Vernon or Quanah or Crowell or wherever they was and bring some kind of rules and their version of justice to folks in the country. But them lawless times was almost past by the time I joined up with the local militia."

The first shot of water tapped the glass knob on the percolator, and a hint of aroma escaped the spout.

"Odd thing was and still is that Oldtimers never seemed to understand what was needed in the way of law and order. You ever notice that? Like they always expected it just to be there? And when it wasn't, they couldn't understand why."

Cody nodded. "Yep. Either that or they thought there shouldn't be any law at all except their vigilante committees and them committees ought to be allowed to do what they damn well pleased, when and where they wanted to."

"Exactly." He paused and sniffed. "Smell that?"

"Smells fine, Captain." It struck Cody as odd to be in pursuit of Nates, but sitting at this old man's table watching for something hot to drink and listening to him talk about things. Cody guessed that was part of being a militiaman, too—letting folks talk to strangers when they hadn't seen any in a while—and maybe picking up some useful information in the listening.

"Be ready soon. . . . Anyway, like I was saying, Oldtimers out here are pretty damned stubborn and independent. Friend of my daddy's tried to explain the why-of-it to me once. Said that before Shudderday folks in Texas—especially west Texas— thought of themselves as Texans first. Then, maybe, they thought about being part of the United States and the world. But for them, this was the center of all that was important in the universe. If you ever read any of the old history books on Texas, you'll see that in them, like Texas was something bigger and better than anywheres else."

"I know," Cody said, "and it really shows in the old museums. You ever been to those museums in Crowell, the ones in the old depot and firehouse?"

The old man smiled. "More 'n once."

"Then I don't have to tell you. They even got a book there that talks about Texas royalty—peerage they call it. Seems to me it's that kind of thinking that maybe helped save us after Shudderday, and how we ended up with the Republic. Folks wanted to hold on to as much of the old state and the old ways as they could—"

"Because tradition means something around here—not like those candy-assed folks in DalWorth. Place's full of con men, whores, and Joiners."

Cody shook his head. "Never been there, and don't know that I'd go if I had the chance. Been to Lubbock, though. Fact is, when I was there last, I heard talk about Joiners and the New Federalists meeting in Nashville, Tennessee, and that they were hard at it trying to pull all the old US-States back together again." He hesitated a moment, held still by memories. "My Grandad hated those folks—especially the ones on the radio. Said they'd be the death of Texas, and if we couldn't shoot them on sight, we ought to steer clear of them."

Captain Lockett moved the chicory pot off the burner, but it kept percolating. "All preachers are about worthless, and those ones on the radio like Goodfox and Jarvis are plumb out of their minds. Your grandad sounds like a smart man to me."

"Was. Taught me lots of things I didn't appreciate when I was growing up, and some I did—most all of them useful and sensible, so's hard not to think about him near every day."

For the next two hours they drank up the captain's pot of chicory blend and talked about the attitudes of people they had known, and conclusions about what made the people in the Republic special and better than other folks, and why everyone hated Nates—until it was time for Cody's turn on guard. Even then the Captain walked out with him in the damp morning, not talking, but acting like their talk wasn't quite finished. Then he said goodnight and headed back to the house with Melindo.

By the time Cody climbed up on the outcropping of rock the first show of grey was cutting under the dark eastern sky and he was glad he had chosen the last watch. But no sooner had he gotten himself comfortable than it started to rain again, not heavily, just a blowing mist that kept soaking his face and beard so that he felt chilled almost immediately. He thought about the captain's hot chicory blend, and how it really had been good, and how he would liked to have brought some up with him.

"Getting soft," he said aloud as he scanned the eastern horizon through squinting eyes. From his vantage point he could see north, east, and south—about two-hundred-seventy degrees that contained all the natural approaches to the area. To see west he would have to climb to the top of the outcrop, but then he'd only be looking at country too rough to travel through.

It was from here in this partially sheltered spot that Samuel had spotted the Nates the day before and where Cody hoped to see anything worth seeing. There wasn't much. As the sky lightened he saw some cattle moving against the southeastern horizon, saw and heard a turkey flap its ugly way down toward the river—remembering the taste of smoked wild turkey, and having to still the itch in his trigger finger—and saw the flicker of a fire to the north-northeast.

The fire made him wipe the mist from his face and take out his binoculars. There still wasn't much light, but in this case that was good. It made the fire easier to find—not that finding it did him any good. Five to six miles away, it was too far to make out any details, and as dawn forced its light under the overcast sky, the fire got harder and harder to see until Cody couldn't find it any more.

No sense in worrying about it. Could be anybody's fire. But something made him figure otherwise—something that had been growing in aggravation since the first day of this mission. It was like an itch he couldn't reach or scratch. Whatever it was forced him toward a decision he'd been avoiding.

Before they left Lockett's place this morning, he was going to have Brisas raise Quanah on the radio and see what kind of help they could get from the north. If the Nates were anywhere near the medicine mounds, his team was going to need some assistance, because between there and the Red River was easy ground and a fast shot at Groesbeck Creek. He had to assume they still had at least a four-hour lead on him, and that was more than the team could make up.

And if the Nates really were carrying some kind of dangerous radioactive material, Cody was less and less willing to have his team do this job alone.

TWO | Lucy awoke with a start as she had six or seven times during the night. Her neck hurt. Her legs ached. Her back was stiff. Her knees popped and her back complained when she slowly forced herself into a sitting position.

Inside the wagon she heard both the Johnsons snoring. The rain had stopped and outside she heard conversation and quiet laughter. When she opened the weather flaps she smelled cooking bacon and mesquite smoke. With practiced patience she began stretching her muscles, limbering up, preparing for whatever the day was about to bring her.

By the time she finished stretching she heard the Johnsons stirring in the wagon and decided she'd rather be off their seat when Kendrick Johnson got up. She slipped on her pack and cloak and rolled back the weather flaps just in time to be greeted by Suzanne Quentin.

"How is she?"

"Fine," Lucy said as she climbed down to the soggy ground still feeling stiffer than she wanted to. "Looks like false labor to me. She slept most of the night without interruption, so I suspect that her pains were just aggravated by all the traveling she's done lately."

"Best not tell Kendrick that," Suzanne said. "He ain't been in none too good a mood lately anyway. You ready to eat some breakfast?"

"Just as soon as I relieve myself."

"Over there." She pointed to a clump of juniper about fifty yards away with a grey piece of cloth hanging on one of them. "When you're finished you can wash out of the barrel on our wagon, then get yourself something to eat."

"Thank you, Suzanne. I appreciate your help."

"Ain't nothing more than manners."

She turned away before Lucy could say anything else. Lucy took the hint and headed for the junipers.

"And just where do you think you're going, Missy?" Max Quentin asked from behind her.

"There," she said, pointing to her destination.

"Maybe I'd better go with you so's to be sure you don't try to run away."

Lucy pushed her anger aside and tried to keep her voice neutral and steady. "I hardly think that's necessary, Mr. Quentin." A tall man with a facial tattoos of a brave was approaching him and Quentin looked uncertain. Lucy decided to raise her voice so the brave could hear her. "You keep forgetting that I'm not trying to run away."

He glanced at the brave, then back at her and snorted. "Go on. Go pee. But if you stay in there too long, I'll have to send someone over to drag you out."

Her back was already to him and as she walked to the latrine she refused to respond to his warning. In her heart she really did want to escape these people, but she felt triply bound to them—by her duty as a healer to assist Ann Johnson, by the mystery of the radioactive sticker, and because of that, by some sense of duty she felt as a citizen of the Republic.

She knew there was more to it than that, knew there was something more important than those things involved, a deeper fascination that she couldn't explain or defend, but which made her reluctant to leave. However, if she didn't get away from them, she was at constant risk from the Quentins.

Then as she was readjusting her britches, she understood. It was the implicit danger, the feeling of being close to the edge of trouble that fascinated her. But the Quentins brought the danger to life with threats she had to acknowledge, and that was going too far for her. They pulled her fears to the surface when she wanted and needed to keep them hidden and under control. And it was her own fear that she couldn't cope with. Understanding that let her realize what she had to do.

She went straight from the latrine to Hector Quentin's wagon where she saw Suzanne wiping dishes clean. After looking around to make sure no one was in earshot, Lucy said, "Suzanne, I may need your help with something."

Suzanne looked suspicious. "Like what?"

"Like helping me get away from here as soon as the baby's born so I can go home," Lucy whispered as she washed her hands, adding the lie about going home to appeal to Suzanne's sense of what was fitting and proper.

"I can't," Suzanne whispered back. "If I did, Hector would beat me till I bled—and if he didn't, his brothers or Kendrick would. I don't want to know anything about it," she said with an angry shake of her head. "Now leave me alone and go eat your breakfast."

Drying her hands, Lucy said, "I'm sorry. I should have realized the danger it would put you in. Forgive me." But even as she turned away, anger boiled in Lucy's heart. Her only ally in this false tonkaweya was Ann Johnson, and there was no way Ann was going to be of much help now. She'd done her best for Lucy and Lucy hadn't been sharp enough to understand that her release was also a warning.

Lucy rounded the wagon and walked without hesitation past several braves to the cook fire where a huge cast-iron skillet with chunks of bacon popping quietly in it rested beside the coals. Beside the skillet was a pot of something white and mushy which Lucy assumed was grits. Using her canteen cup as a plate, she scooped in some of the grits and with the fork in the skillet put a large piece of bacon on top of that. Then she moved to a dry-looking flat rock not far away and sat down. From one of her pockets she took her spoon and tasted the grits. To her surprise it wasn't grits at all, but some kind of sweet corn mush.

During all of this, none of the ten or twelve braves within polite distance had spoken to her, nor had she spoken to them. In fact, they were going about their business as if she didn't exist, which was just fine with Lucy for the moment. After everything else that had happened, she could hardly expect anyone from this tonkaweya to act with honor toward her.

Forcing herself to eat slowly, Lucy tried to concentrate on the best possible way to escape. It would have to be someplace drier than this, or anyone who wanted to would be able to track her down. If she could get her hands on a mule, that might help, but better to sneak away somehow and her absence not be noticed for a while. Only then would she stand a fair chance of not being found. The question then was when would be—

A scream interrupted her thought. Ann!

Then she heard Kendrick Johnson yell, "Shut up, bitch!" followed by a loud slap.

And Ann Johnson screamed again. Without thinking about anything else, Lucy dropped her cup and spoon and rushed to help her patient.

CHAPTER 15

ONE | "Hardeman Station, Hardeman Station, this is Bearcub. Come in, Hardeman Station. . . . Hardeman Station, this is Bearcub. Come in, please. . . . Come in, please. . . . Still nothing," Brisas said, twisting and adjusting the knobs on her radio. "I'm not getting anything. Maybe Quanah's not monitoring."

Cody shook his head in frustration. "Dammit. Terry told us he would have them monitoring this frequency around the clock. Suppose we had an emergency for them?" He had expected an immediate response—expected, perhaps, that there was a deeper urgency and importance in their mission that would have the Attorney General himself ready to receive their every report. Now he was angry because Quanah wasn't even listening. Maybe it was time to call Aunt Bertha. "Try Crowell."

Brisas changed frequencies and began calling, "Foard Station, Foard Station, this is Bearcub. Come in, please. . . ." She smiled. "Acknowledged, Foard Station. Stand by for Bearcub Leader." Brisas handed the headset to Cody.

"Foard Station, this is Bearcub Leader. Request conference with Sierra Bravo Yankee as soon as possible. Repeat. Request conference with Sierra Bravo Yankee, as soon as possible."

"Acknowledged, Bearcub Leader," a faint voice said in his ear. "Sierra Yankee is currently unavailable. Can you monitor this freq? She should be available shortly."

That figures, Cody thought, but there was nothing to be done about it. "We understand that Sierra Bravo Yankee is not there, and we affirm that we can monitor," he said. "This is Bearcub standing by."

"Now what?" Jessup asked as Cody handed the headset back to Brisas.

"Simple. We follow these tracks while we wait for Sheriff York to call us back."

A look of concern crossed Jessup's face. "You're not even going to try to contact Vernon?"

"Not yet, Roland. We'll give York thirty minutes or so to get back to us before we do that."

"Wouldn't hurt to go ahead and try them, would it?"

"No," Cody said, the irritation he felt slipping into his tone, "but if Vernon answers and then Sheriff York calls back, we're liable to have two stations trying to tell us what to do—both at the same time. Doesn't seem like a good idea to me."

"Better two than none."

Cody spat into the mud and shook his head. "Boy, Roland, sleeping on that nice floor last night sure didn't do *you* any good, did it?"

Jessup's brows wrinkled in scowl, then his face broke into a sudden smile and he laughed softly. "So who got to sleep? I was awake half the night listening to you and the old man one-upping each other with tales that would shame a huckster at the district fair." He paused, his expression half-serious. "You lost, by the way. The old man beat you solid."

"Never happened," Cody said, returning his smile, relieved that Jessup had decided to abandon his protests. "Captain Lockett's just older, not better. Now, we might as well hat up. We can do three or four miles while we're waiting for Crowell to call back. Will that give you any trouble with the radio, Juanita?"

"*Nada pro-blemm, señor.*"

"Phew!" Melindo shook her head as she shrugged on her pack. "Your Mexican is worse than mine. You'd have thought our parents would have taught us better."

Brisas laughed. "My parents didn't even speak Spanish or Mexican at all—only my grandmaw. The little I know I picked up from her, or the kids at school, and then later I learned some more from a couple of the guys in my basic training company."

"I'll bet they taught you all the famous dirty words," Jessup said. "*Casa del crapo. Punta bella. Chica tu madre.*"

"Yeah, and lots worse than that—words that would make you blush, Roland." She shrugged her shoulders roughly to settle the radio on her back.

"You'll have to blush while you walk, Roland, but you can take the drag so no one will see you." Cody stepped out with Melindo, Brisas, Kolmer, and Jessup falling in behind him. He had already discussed their order with Jessup, so he knew Roland's feelings weren't going to be hurt, and the humor was a good way to start the day. Even Kolmer had allowed himself an expression that looked like a smile.

"Bye!" Samuel Lockett called from the lookout rock as they headed north away from the shed.

Cody waved and the others did as well. Kenneth and Maria had already gone down to the bottom land along the river to check their cattle traps, and Cody guessed that Captain Lockett was using his periscope to watch them leave.

In a way, Cody wished they didn't have to leave. He'd taken a strong liking to the captain and Samuel and thought the Locketts about as kind and decent as folks got in these parts. Fact was, he liked Kenneth and Maria Lockett in spite of their fundamentalism because they had the good manners not to press it on someone who believed otherwise. Their caution the day before had been totally understandable, and even if their methods had been a little extreme, he held nothing against them for it. Probably would have done the same thing if he'd been through what they had.

Now as he trudged through the red mud beside the wagon tracks, he thought about the little bag of chicory blend the captain had given him along with a complete list of ingredients printed carefully on a small slip of tough paper—yucca paper made by Nana Fernandez, he said.

Yes, they were good people, and Cody hoped he might get to see them—

The ground shivered and made him pause. The whole team stopped, each standing with feet spread, arms out, ready to go to ground if the shiver turned into shaking. Two or three seconds later it was gone, but they waited just in case.

"Somethin' bad's happening somewheres to somebody," Kolmer said gruffly, surprising them with his sudden words. "That big one yesterday must have been a fierce mothershake of a plate-shift to be sendin' out all these aftershocks."

"Let's just hope it's nobody we know," Cody added as he began walking again. "Probably one of those Missouri shakers just giving the yankees something to think about."

"Why do you say that?" Melindo asked as she fell in behind him.

"Oh, I don't know. When I was down at Jayton they had one of those earthquake people down there—Opal Schwartz her name was. Anyway, she claimed you could feel the difference between at least three different kinds of shakes by the aftershocks. Said the ones from the Pacific felt like humming in the ground, kind of, and the ones from the Rockies were jerkier, and the ones from the New Madrid in old Missouri had more bounce to them."

Brisas laughed. "Never noticed stuff like that. You believe it?"

"Didn't believe it at first," Cody said with a shake of his head, "but we felt a couple fair size shakes while I was down there, and she swore that the first one was a Pacific quake and the second was a Missouri quake. I couldn't tell if I really did feel the difference, or if I just wanted to, but I did write the dates down like she suggested and next time I got to Paducah I took those dates to the seis-station, and sure enough, according to their calculations anyways, that Miss Schwartz had guessed 'em right on."

"So now you're an earthquake expert?"

The sarcasm in Jessup's voice was sharp in a friendly kind of way, but that didn't bother Cody as much as the fact that Jessup had moved up almost beside them. "Not hardly—least ways, not about earthquakes. But I know that I've felt differences often enough and was able to test my guesses right two or three times after that, and if I pay close attention to the feel of a shake, I think I can guess fair enough where it's coming from. But that sure don't make me an expert."

He looked over his shoulder at Jessup. "According to the militia, though, I am an expert in team maneuvers and discipline." This time the sarcasm was heavy in his voice.

"I think I hear the drag calling me," Jessup said with an exaggerated grin as he slowed down to let the others pass him.

"And Crowell's calling us," Brisas added. They all stopped as she acknowledged the call and gave Cody the headset.

"This is Bearcub Leader," he said as he put the headset on.

"That's a cute name," Sheriff York's voice said in his ear. "Who gave you that one, Nephew? Terry?"

"He's the one. How you doing, Aunt Bertha?"

"Pretty fair, boy. What's goin' on with you?"

"We're hot on the trail of some Nates and are going to need some help," he said. As quickly as he could he filled her in on the details and concluded with, "If Terry doesn't want them to make it back to the Nation, somebody's going to have to cover Two-eighty-seven between Quanah and Chillicothe, 'cause if they get north of there, well, I think they'll be home free."

"And you tried to reach Quanah?"

"Did, but couldn't raise an answer. Oh, and there's one other thing," he said quickly. "Terry had some radiation protection suits dropped to us and said the Nates—"

"Damn that snake! I told him—" She stopped suddenly, then restarted just as quickly. "I'll get through to Quanah and Chillicothe and Vernon if we have to. But you listen careful, boy. If you have to tangle with them Nates, don't you mess with nothing in their wagons. You got that? Nothing."

"I understand," he said evenly. "No matter what happens, we don't go near their wagons."

"Right. Now get your ass off the air and on the road—but monitor this channel and I'll keep you posted on what Terry wants to do and what's happening."

"Will do," Cody said. "Take care."

"You're the one who needs to take care. Foard Station, out."

"Bearcub, out." With a feeling of resignation he handed the headset back to Brisas. Somehow, talking to Aunt Bertha hadn't made him feel any better. "Listen up," he said quietly. "Just in case you didn't catch all that. Aunt—uh, Sheriff York said that under no circumstances are we to approach the Nate wagons. Whatever this radioactive business is, we don't want to get involved with it. You understand?"

They nodded in acknowledgement just as another tiny ground-tremor swept under their feet.

TWO | Much to Lucy's surprise, one of the braves beat her to Johnson's wagon and jumped in through the weather flaps.

Kendrick Johnson shouted in surprise. Someone grunted. Ann screamed. The wagon rocked.

A second brave climbed up to the seat. Max Quentin tried to pull him down. A third brave joined the struggle. Then a fourth. Then Hector Quentin.

Lucy reached inside her shirt and pulled her MUST-Kit knife, then moved around them and headed for the back of the wagon.

"Help me! Oh, God! Help me!" Ann shouted.

The brave and Johnson grunted and growled as the wagon shook with their fight under the vinyl top.

A shot rang out.

Lucy swiveled in time to see Wendel Quentin tackled by a brave and fall to the ground, his pistol flying from his hand. She barely hesitated before running to snatch up the pistol. As she turned back to the wagon, Johnson fell out and landed on his back. Three braves pinned him to the ground. Six others held the Quentins, each with an arm twisted high behind his back.

For a moment everything was silent except for a soft whimper from the wagon.

Without thinking, Lucy shoved the pistol into her belt, pushed two braves out of the way, and climbed up past them, her knife still in her other hand.

Then one of the braves spoke. "You shame us, Kendrick Johnson," he said angrily. "You and the Quentins are a stink upon our tonkaweya."

"I'm your leader," Johnson shouted.

"Where did he hit you?" Lucy asked as she sheathed her knife and crawled down next to Ann.

She whimpered again. "In the face, mostly. I covered— I tried—" Her voice broke into sobs.

Lucy wrapped her arms around Ann and held her firmly while she cried. What startled her was how controlled Ann's crying was and how clearly she could hear the argument going on outside the wagon.

"Chief Townsend made him our leader. We cannot—"

"No man can be forced to follow a bad leader. The rules of the tribes allow for change."

"And the rules of the tonkaweya—"

"Enough!" a deeper voice shouted. "Are we going to play and talk about rules, or are we going to decide on the basis of actions—his actions—their actions—what is to be done?"

"I'm for Johnson."

"Me, too."

"Go to hell, all of you. That's where he's going."

Ann's sobbing had subsided to whimpers, and Lucy blocked out the sounds of the argument. Her first priority had to be Ann's health. Only after caring for Ann could she worry about herself and the tonkaweya.

"Shhh," she said, stroking Ann's matted hair, its copper color now darker for want of washing. "Shhh, it'll be all right. We're not going to let him hurt you again."

"He will," Ann insisted. "He hates the baby."

"But why? Why would he—"

"Because!" She looked away, then closed her eyes. "Because he thinks maybe it's not his," she added softly, "and no one can tell him for sure that it is."

"That's not mine to deal with," Lucy said, still stroking Ann's hair, feeling her heart go out to this woman she didn't really understand at all. "I don't care who its father is. All I care about is that it gets born safe and healthy, and when it is, that you're the same, so's you can love and care for it for a long time."

"Wouldn't that be fun?" Ann said bitterly. "What makes you think I'd have a chance of that with him?"

Despite everything that had happened, Lucy was shocked by Ann's tone and attitude, but she wasn't going to give over to it and let it change her thinking. "So you raise it on your own—or with some other man. There's better than Kendrick Johnson in this world that would be glad—"

Ann burst into violent tears again, and suddenly Lucy put the pieces together—what the Quentins had said, and Ann, and herself—until she saw the pattern. There was another man, someone better than Johnson, and Ann had left him, walked away while she was pregnant and didn't know whose child she was carrying. If that didn't beat all.

"Miss Lucy," a voice called from the wagon seat, "if Miss Ann is all right, we've got need of you out here."

"In a few minutes," she called.

The other end of the wagon opened suddenly and Suzanne Quentin started climbing through. "Is she . . .?"

"I think she'll be all right."

"They got some nasty cuts and a shot brave out there. I'll stay with her if you want to tend to them."

"Thanks again, Suzanne." The young woman looked long into Lucy's eyes before she answered.

"You're welcome."

"Miss Lucy," the voice from outside called again.

"Coming," she answered. "Coming."

CHAPTER 16

ONE | Cody had strained against the morning breeze, listening for another shot, but heard nothing. Now as he watched Brisas fixing the broken radio strap, he wondered who it was.

"You still worried about that shot? It was a long way off," Melindo said. "Could have been anyone."

"Or could have been the Nates," Kolmer said.

Jessup dug a pack of ready-rolls out of his pocket and offered one to Cody. "Donna's right about one thing. Whoever it was, was a long ways off."

Taking the cigarette and the offered light, Cody inhaled deeply, sending his lungs into an instant craving for more. "How much longer?" he asked.

Brisas cocked an eyebrow. "You want to go on without me?"

"No, dammit. I just want to know when you're going to have that thing fixed."

"Easy, Cody," Jessup said. "Easy. Juanita will have it finished when it's finished. Just relax and enjoy your cigarette. If that won't do you, Donna and I can scout ahead while you—"

"I won't be much longer, Cody."

"Sorry," he said. "Didn't mean to snap at you. It's not knowing what's up ahead that bothers me. But Roland's right. I'm going to give myself permission to take this break and enjoy my cigarette for the day." He sat down on the damp rocks, grateful for the waterproof seat of his uniform pants, leaned back against his pack, closed his eyes, and wished it was true, that he really could give himself a break.

Problem was, there weren't no breaks for a leader. No matter what he told himself, or what the others said, in the end he was responsible for what happened. Twenty-four hours a day, good or bad, he had to lay claim to the results and take what came with them.

One of the nice things about being Azle's Extra had been that he didn't have to shoulder that much responsibility. When things got too heavy for him, he could just turn to Azle and say, "This one's yours," knowing she'd take it because she had no choice. Now he didn't have no choice. Nothing unusual about that. If he thought about it long enough, he knew he'd been taking responsibility since he was a boy—being the one his parents had bragged on, getting patted on the head, or sometimes getting a US-dime to spend on the next trip to Grow at Mr. Burrton's store.

He enjoyed the taste of the cigarette as he remembered the boy he had been. When he'd done his chores, most times without having to be told, and volunteered for a little extra he didn't have to do, parents and grandparents took notice. They'd tell him he sure was grown up, and he'd stand there, looking at the floor, not knowing exactly what they meant—except that whenever they said it, they were happy with him, and he liked having them happy almost as much as he liked the little presents and treats they slipped him out of sight of his brothers and sisters. Ramon had said it was like always knowing he could draw to an inside straight. Took Cody years to understand that, too.

It had been a simple step from there to come to believing that being responsible meant pleasing people—and even though he knew now at twenty-eight that it didn't mean anything of the sort, he couldn't shake free of the notion. It was like part of him always wanted to—always had to—please people, or feel guilty if he didn't.

He blinked, not wanting to think about guilt, and took another long drag from the cigarette, noticing that it was almost gone, wishing he had another, then reminding himself with a mental curse that he had sworn to quit them.

Pleasing people had been basically easy when he was only Azle's Extra. Now as the team leader, it wasn't—and worse, he knew it wouldn't be. His job was to carry out this mission, not to worry about pleasing anyone but Attorney General Terry—and any commander Terry put between them. Smiling, Cody took the last drag, holding the cigarette between fingernails, trying to get as much of the smoke as he could without burning himself. Make Terry happy, and Cody knew he would get a reward. Like being a kid again. Then the smile faded. Problem was, the reward would probably only mean more responsibility, and that wasn't what Cody wanted.

"Tie this knot and I'll be done," Brisas said. "Just cross your fingers that my stitchin' will hold the weight."

Kolmer held the radio as she put her arms through the straps. She shrugged carefully, settling it onto her back, then fastened the quick-release band that connected the shoulder-straps under her breasts. After adjusting the band's tension, she held out her hand and Jessup passed her carbine to her.

"Ready?" Cody asked.

"One more thing." She slipped the headset over her cap and immediately tilted her head. "Uh-oh. Cody, you better take this. It's Vernon."

"This is Bearcub Leader," he said as he took the headset.

"Stand by for the Attorney General," a woman's voice said through a distant rush of static.

"That you, Sergeant Cody?"

"This is Bearcub Leader," he repeated. He wasn't going to break standard procedure, even for Terry.

"Okay, Bearcub, you listen up real carefully. We're sending out road patrols from Vernon, Chillicothe, Quanah, and Kirkland. Tampico's trying to get a chopper up. Whatever you do, don't let those Nates slip south of you. We're going to try to pin them against Lake Pauline. You hold the line from Medicine Mounds to Texas-Six. Sheriff Pietro has a couple of deputies, six Bureau men, and those women from Vernon heading for Copper Breaks, but you'll have to hold Six until they get there."

Cody couldn't believe his ears. "Uh, sir, would you say that again? I mean,"—he fumbled to get his map out of his shoulder pocket—"it must be six, seven miles from Medicine—"

"Seven-point-two N-miles," Terry said.

"But sir, how am I supposed to cover that with five people? Even if I could space my team out, the Nates could drive right between us and we'd never know the difference."

"Then you'd better find the Nates and keep them in sight, young sergeant, because you're all I've got at the moment to keep them from retreating south. Now get your butts moving and monitor Hardeman Station. Terry, out."

"Yes, sir," Cody said to the static in the earpiece.

"What's the matter?"

"Not a damn thing, Roland. Give me another cigarette." As Jessup was digging the cigarettes out of his pocket, Cody let Brisas take the headset. Only after he'd lit the cigarette, taken a long drag, and blown the smoke out did he tell them. "The Attorney General, Mr. Rednose Winslow Terry himself, just ordered the five of us to block seven-point-two N-miles between Medicine Mound and Texas Six while he brings in the reinforcements from the north. Nothing wrong with that, is there?"

"Shee-it. How are we supposed to do that?"

Cody laughed bitterly. "His alternate suggestion was that we find the Nates, keep them in sight, and prevent them from heading south. Course, if we miss them and they do decide to head south, then our asses are cotton and Terry's gonna be driving the picker—or a chopper, 'cause that's what he's trying to get from Tampico."

"But they can't be hard to find," Melindo said, "not as long as they stay with these wagons."

"True. As long as they stay with the wagons and don't have a rear guard out and don't circle on us, they won't be hard to find." Kolmer spat in disgust. "What's your plan, Cody?"

He sighed, exhaling great lungfuls of smoke. "We follow the

tracks. Whenever they cross wide-open ground, we circle through cover if at all possible. We go slowly and carefully and don't take any risks we don't have to."

"I don't understand," Jessup said. "How's this different from what we've been doing? I mean, okay, so now we're supposed to prevent them from turning south, but all along we've been trying to catch up to them and tell headquarters what they're up to. What's changed?"

"Everything. If they spotted us before, we could split and hide, and meet up somewheres later. Now we're supposed to stand and fight regardless of the odds."

"Sorry, Cody, but I still don't see the problem. Terry wants us to block them? Fine. We track them like before. When we find them, we shoot their oxen and mules, then run like hell. Let Terry and his chopper finish them off. Can't no brave from the Indian Nation run faster than I can if I'm being chased."

Cody shook his head. Jessup's idea didn't seem right, but he wasn't exactly sure what was wrong with it. "And if they spot us first? What then?" He heard the anger in his voice, but didn't know why it was there or how to stop it.

"Easy, now, both of you," Kolmer said, stepping toward them with an intense look of concentration. "First of all, Roland, Cody's the leader of this team whether you like it or not. You been riding his decisions since we started out, and I figure it's about time you quit."

Jessup cleared his throat and looked away.

"And you, Cody, you're so busy being mad at Terry, you're not listening to what Roland said. There's sense in it—even if you don't want to say so."

Cody looked up at Kolmer, then over at Jessup. Only then did he notice that Melindo and Brisas had moved to either side of Kolmer. "You two siding with Ed?"

They nodded. "He's right on both counts," Brisas said.

"But you're the leader," Melindo added, "no matter what."

"Right," Jessup said unexpectedly. "I guess I've been riled in one way or another about this thing since the beginning—thinking that we should be looking for revenge, not spying—and I've been taking it out on you." He held out his hand. "Sorry."

"No apology necessary," Cody said, accepting the hand-shake. "I've been doing part of the same thing." He suddenly felt very uncomfortable. "Okay, so Roland's right. We keep on with what we were doing, only we're a lot more cautious about it. Juanita monitors Foard Station for new information, and we all stay ready to shoot up the Nates' animals and beat it—for where?"

"Medicine Mound?"

"The town?"

"Yes."

"Easy enough," Cody said, checking his map. "If we have to split up, you head east. If you hit a hard-road, follow it east and south. That should be the road into Medicine Mound. If you hit railroad tracks first, follow them north. Anything else?"

Kolmer grunted. "Yeah. I think we ought to lock and load."

"With safeties on." Cody led the way by feeding a round into the chamber of his Albany-Ruger carbine and clicking the safety into place. "Melindo, you're the best eyes we got. You lead the way. Then me, Brisas—"

"I'll take the drag," Jessup said.

"Right. Let's go then." As they stepped out behind Melindo, each ten paces behind the person in front of them, Cody had a low shuddering premonition in his gut that they were in for more trouble than anyone could guess.

The clouds opened for a second or two and let through a milky shaft of sunlight. Then darker, heavier clouds slid under the hole as a grey, gloomy pall covered the land with dull light and a soft, misty drizzle.

TWO | Most of the tonkaweya was gathered around the cookfire and the sounds of the argument rose and fell behind Lucy and her last patient where they sat under the extended weather flap at the back of Johnson's wagon. She tightened the bandage around his arm until the brave winced slightly.

"I do not meant to hurt you further," she said, "but we must make sure it is tight enough to stop the flow of blood." She admired the finely drawn hat with red and blue feathers tattooed on his right cheek, and was struck by the clean, sharp smell of him and let herself enjoy it with a smile. He couldn't have been more than sixteen or seventeen and he had not spoken the whole time she dressed his wound. "May I ask your name?"

"My personal name is Tinker Oberly," he said, "but

everyone just calls me Tink—except my mother who is half Osage and calls me Chief Tinker—but that's a joke between us, you see, because there was once a famous Osage chief by that name—Oberly, too, even though my father only claims to be part Choctaw and none of his people know where or when the Oberly name entered his side of the family. Before Shudderday, though."

She almost laughed at this sudden outburst of information, but she did not want him to misunderstand. "Well, Tinker Oberly, I think that should take care of you for the moment. However, you should know that arm is going to be very sore for a long time. Quentin's bullet took a fair chunk of muscle with it, and you're going to have to exercise regularly after the surface heals to keep it from getting permanently stiff on you."

"How long, Miss Lucy?"

"How long for what?"

"How long until the muscle grows back?"

"It won't," Lucy said simply. "What you'll get is a little scar tissue that will help fill the hole, and you can build up the muscle that's left underneath it, but what got shot away will never grow back. Muscle just doesn't do that."

"Then ask her!" someone shouted.

"Miss Lucy," another voice called, "please come here when you are finished with Tink."

She stood up and hitched up her pants against the weight of the revolver heavy in her belt. "All right," she said with a wave before turning back to Tinker. "Think you could find me a holster and a belt?" she asked.

A sheepish look crossed his face as he rose to his feet. "Actually, I know where yours are—and your pistol, too. Johnson put them in our wagon for safekeeping. I'll get them." He turned quickly and headed toward one of the other wagons.

Lucy smiled after him then walked over to the cookfire.

"We've got a question or two for you, Miss Lucy."

"Not until you answer some of mine," she said firmly.

"As you wish," the same man said. "What would you ask?"

She looked at him carefully, trying to take the measure of this tall brave, but the common leather pants and jacket told her little. His pupils, though, seemed too small for his blue eyes. "First of all I want to know what tonkaweya this is and who besides Johnson has claim to leadership."

"We are from the Ardmore Council of Five Tribes. We are from two tonkaweyas, Wyandot and Seneca, and I am Elroy Sashahunder," he said.

"And you claim leadership?" she asked, relieved to know who she was speaking to, but wanting confirmation.

"I am the leader," Sashahunder said.

"Damned if you are," Hector Quentin said from where he was tied to a folding chair. Beside him was Kendrick Johnson, who was gagged, as were the other two Quentins beside Johnson. They were all tied to wooden folding chairs.

"You're only the leader of the Wyandot," a shorter brave said. "Mike Young speaks for the Seneca."

"Then let him speak," Lucy said, adopting the formal style she had learned at home, "and I will listen to him and to Elroy Sashahunder." Tinker came up beside her and held out her pistol and her holster belt with her sheath knife on it. As she took them and started to put them on, she saw Kendrick Johnson's head jerk and anger burn in his eyes.

A shorter, stockier brave wearing faded bib overalls over a heavy denim shirt stepped forward on the other side of the fire. "I am Mike Young. Our questions go to you because we know you were sent with the message," Young said. "What were you told, and what leader were you commissioned to tell it to?"

"I was told to deliver a message from Chief Townsend that you were to return to your tribe across the Red from Groesbeck Creek, and I was told that Kendrick Johnson was the leader I should deliver it to, but if—"

"See! We told you that she would—"

"Hold!" Lucy commanded. "You did not let me finish." She looked around the circle of faces, some paying close attention, others looking totally unconcerned. Looking directly at Mike Young she noticed a slight tic under one of his eyes before she continued. "I was also told that if Johnson was not with the tonkaweya I was to deliver my message to Elroy Sashahunder."

"I do not believe it," Young said flatly.

"I have no proof except my word," Lucy said, "but there was a second message—a poem message—I was told to use if my word was doubted. Do you need to hear that now?"

"Yes," several men said at the same time.

Lucy closed her eyes and concentrated for a second before reciting the message Mishla had taught her.

> *January comes*
> *Tenderly holding the year.*
> *Look! The way is clear.*

"What the hell's that supposed to—" A brave clamped his hand over Hector Quentin's mouth.

"She tells the truth," Sashahunder said.

"Just because she knows the opening of *True Beginnings*, doesn't mean anything," Young insisted. "We must use the radio to verify what she says."

Lucy was startled. "You have a radio? Why was I sent to you if you have a radio?"

Sashahunder answered her. "Because your government radio-monitors could locate us if we use it, and they would bring the militia down on our necks."

"Shit," Young said. "The Quentins burn a fuel truck. Garringer and his Caddos break off on their own looking for God-knows-what. We drag a trouble-wagon around and leave tracks all over creation, and you worry about anti-radio-monitors? Cut us some slack, Elroy. The Texian militia knows we're here and are probably—"

"Chief Townsend said to use it only for emergencies, and that's what we are going to do. This is not an emergency."

"Yet," Young added in disgust.

"Perhaps Mr. Young is correct," Lucy said. "Perhaps it is time to consult with your chief." She looked from Sashahunder to Young and then to their four prisoners tied to the folding chairs, all gagged now. "Someone has to decide what should be done here, and since you seem at odds for settling it by yourselves . . ." She let the implication hang.

Sashahunder looked hurt, but Young didn't exactly look pleased by what she had said, and Lucy had the sudden feeling that she was only privy to the surface of their dispute, and that something deeper and far more important was at stake here than which brave should represent the combined tonkaweyas.

"Very well, set up the radio," Sashahunder said. "Let us see what Chief Townsend has to say about his Texian leader who beats a pregnant woman—and the non-braves scum who follow him and put a stink on our lives. You call him, Michael Deerfoot Young of the noble Seneca, and tell him about this man you wish to continue following."

The anger and sarcasm that dripped from his voice were infectious, and Lucy heard herself talking before she realized she was going to say anything. "And ask him what the tribe would do to men who plan a rape in front of their victim." Her voice trembled, but she stared defiantly at the Quentins. "Ask him that," she said, "and tell him I await his answer with my patient." With that she turned quickly and walked to Johnson's wagon.

Suzanne and Ann were both alseep when Lucy climbed into the wagon, and she was glad. She needed time to calm her emotions. What had happened out there? Why had she said what she did? There were no obvious answers, but as she tried to explore what had motivated her to speak up so clearly, she realized that in speaking she gave herself some relief. However, before she followed that thought, Suzanne woke up, and immediately started talking about Ann and the baby and how she hoped she had children one day, and on and on, until Lucy realized that Suzanne had crossed some barrier within herself in order to share this much. That made it easy for Lucy to relax and play the part of a good listener.

An hour later Tinker came for her. "They have the radio working," he said, "but no one answers. Now we will have a meeting to decide what should be done, and they wish for you to participate." He tried to smile, but failed. "Your vote will be counted as a true member of the tonkaweya."

"Go on," Suzanne said. "Ann's been no trouble to me so far, and if something happens I can't handle, you're in hollering distance."

"Very well." Lucy left the wagon and walked with Tinker to the fire. Twice he started to say something, then stopped with a shake of his head. "Something bothers you, Tinker?"

"You will see soon enough."

Much to her surprise, one of the braves greeted her with her spoon scoured shiny-clean and her canteen cup brimming with hot tea. "Thank you," she said, "I am very—" She cut herself off when she saw the Quentins opposite her. They were no longer tied and gagged, and they were armed.

Max leered at her. "That's right, Missy. Everyone gets to vote on this, and your side's going to lose."

The shiver that ran down Lucy's spine was more anger than fear, but the fear was there all the same.

CHAPTER 17

FATHER MURRAY GOODFOX | The sun hid behind a thin layer of clouds, casting pale shadows over the rocky land on the edge of the Ozarks. Thick, early stands of blue chicory dotted the sides of the broken road, huddling against fallen limestone blocks and collapsed bridges like flowers against headstones. Confederate violets peeked underneath the grass in the medians flanked by ragged yellow louseworts and the white blossoms of spring beauty.

Soon the dwarf larkspur would release its lavender blossoms, followed closely by the pink and yellow goat's rue along the broken road-cuts in the hills. In a month or so if the warm southern breezes continued, there would be the competing purples of day flowers and beggarweed and heal-all and spiderworts shading the hillsides.

But always first to blossom were the erigina followed quickly by trembleweed with its slender stalks and tiny white flowers dancing to the subtle rhythms of the earth. For the past week the trembleweed had danced almost continuously.

Even with the show of wildflowers, this land always looked rougher than he was accustomed to, but Father Murray Goodfox had come to like the craggy limestone hills and dark green trees of the Missouri Ozarks. He didn't even mind the snow when he came here in the winter—mostly because there were almost always closed trucks to ride in and warm company to keep. Yet it never failed to surprise him that the snow did not soften the texture of this land he had come to appreciate on his regular visits.

But now, being pursued by the Ash Grove Boys, he wished for the familiar hills of the Nation or the rolling farm country around home—and better roads. Holy Father, how he wished for better roads and less shaking earth. They were only two hundred miles from the New Madrid fault, and it was obviously acting up.

Goodfox leaned on the door and asked, "How much time do you think we have?"

"Two hours at the least," Nyllan answered from under the

hood as she concentrated on the repairs she was making to their truck. "Enough to get to the airfield, load the controller, and get out of here." She held up a frayed wire and shook her head before tossing it away over her shoulder. "I don't know how I ever let you talk me into this," she said as she stuck her head back under the hood, "but it's been kind of fun up till now."

"That is a unique way of putting it. I can see the lurid type in one of those Tulsa tabloids. 'Rhondasue Nyllan Captured With Renegade Priest: Says It Was Fun.' Might even carry your picture and old man Truman could put you in one of his public enemy scrapbooks." He glanced at the canvas-wrapped controller in the bed of the truck, thought about the operating codes for it hidden in his church back in Rhineland, and allowed himself a brief smile.

"You make fun of H.S. all you want," she said, scooting her body deeper into the engine well, "but that old man's still a damn sight smarter than anyone I ever met but you. And I'll tell you what, my hot-bodied priest, if we're not careful H.S. will find a way not only to stop us, but to get rid of us at the same time."

Her words angered him, but he quickly pushed the anger aside. She was right, of course, but she didn't have to keep reminding him. "Any progress under there?"

"It's almost finished. Get in and get ready to start it when I tell you."

Goodfox slid onto the bench seat behind the steering wheel and after depressing the clutch, put his hand on the ignition switch, and pumped the accelerator.

"Not yet, dammit! Wait till I tell you!"

With a long sigh he forced himself to lean back against the yucca-cloth seat. Even Rhondasue cursed him. Was there no one in this world who didn't curse him? Or who wouldn't soon enough?

Probably not—at least not right away. Later they would come to understand and appreciate him. But until then, one way or the other he had angered or would soon come to anger almost everybody in these old divided states. Even the Joiners—his natural allies—didn't understand, and they wouldn't until he put his plan into action and accomplished his holy mission. Then they would see the advantages of his plan and fall in behind him so that together they could rebuild the ideal country that Shudderday had destroyed.

"Now," Nyllan called.

Again he depressed the clutch pedal and pumped the squeaky accelerator. Then he flipped the ignition switch. The engine roared to life before he eased off the accelerator and let it drop to an idle.

"Good," Nyllan said, standing beside the open hood with a smile on her face. "Very good, even if I do say so myself."

"Good enough to get rolling?" Goodfox asked.

"Yes, Murray, good enough to carry us all the way to the airfield. After that, who gives a damn?"

"I wish you'd quit cursing," he said with a shake of his head as he handed her a fairly clean rag.

"Comes with the package. You like my mind and my skills— and my body? Put up with my tongue." She slammed the hood down.

"Point to Rhondasue," he said.

"Move over."

He put the truck in neutral, released the clutch, and maneuvered himself awkwardly past the floorshift lever to the passenger side. The tension between them was like a taut strand of barbed wire. "You mad?"

"Yes—no—yes. Hell, I don't know," she said as she slid in behind the wheel and closed the door. Putting the truck in gear she guided it into the center of the road. "It's just that sometimes your attitude really bugs me, you know that? Like no matter what you do, sometimes you're such a prude you won't admit even to yourself that you do it"—she paused and threw him a brief smile—"or that you've got as many faults as the rest of us in this world."

"Not true. I know my faults better than you think. But I also know that I have an obligation to overcome them."

"And make others do the same thing, right?"

"It's my job."

"It *was* your job. Not any more, Murray."

"It's still my job—regardless of what the bishop says. Just because he thinks he's taking my church away from me doesn't mean I'm no longer a priest. He can't take my vows away. He can't defrock me because he hates my politics. Consequently, if I sometimes insist on behavior—"

"Consequently bullshit. All that crap you tell yourself is just to ease your conscience. The rest of it doesn't mean pig piss. You do what you damn well please, and you know it."

The silence between them was filled by the rattling of the truck and the sounds of the engine. Staring out the window as they bounced along the broken pavement helped him calm himself. No matter how much affection he felt for Rhondasue Nyllan, sometimes he just wanted to lash out at her, to slap her face until she stopped goading him every chance she got. He automatically asked God's forgiveness after that thought and assumed it was given.

It was a difficult task God had chosen for him, one which he didn't totally understand, but one which he knew he had to accomplish regardless of the hardships he might encounter. God had led him to Rhondasue so that she could help him, just as He had led Sister Paula Kathryn to him years before. Rhondasue had the skills he desperately needed—and a body whose delights he had come to crave.

Oh, Lord. For that, too, he had asked forgiveness—every night, but only after they had exhausted their passion. When she was in his arms with her body wrapped around his, he could not think of sin, could not believe that this wonderful, joyous experience was not part of God's plan as well. Only when they were sated and she slept softly beside him did his conscience emerge and nag him, making him question over and over his defense of their actions until he admitted his sin once again and begged in whispered prayers for forgiveness for every venal and mortal sin he might have committed.

"Now you're the one who's mad," Nyllan said, keeping her attention on the fractured I-road that was their fastest route to the airfield.

"No, just thinking . . . about God." For the time being he wasn't in the mood to talk.

"Talking to yourself again?"

She was teasing, but he didn't like it. What troubled him was that she was the cause of his nightly torment. Yet each morning, in the rational mind of daylight, he had absolved himself with that pure certainty that God had indeed brought her to him. And if he had to physically hold her in God's service, who was Murray Goodfox, lowly priest of the New Dominican order, to question God's will?

In the mornings, his rationale was clear and simple and seemed to come straight from heaven. In the afternoons, he held on to that understanding as a blessing from God. In the evenings, he cushioned himself with faith in his perceptions of

God's will. And later, in the dark, in the midst of their passion, he did not care.

Thus his doubts were limited to a few sleepless hours when he was tired and weak—vulnerable to dark, evil forces much stronger than he. Yet, perhaps there was some proof that he was under God's hand, because even in the grip of those forces that tried to divert him from the duties he must perform, he always found his relief in prayer. For Murray Goodfox that was proof enough.

"You *are* mad at me."

Goodfox refocused his eyes and turned with a smile to look at her freckled face. "No, Rhondasue, I am not mad at you. Quite the contrary. With a sure and holy purpose I need not examine, I am coming to a better understanding of God's direction for our lives."

She snorted. "God does what God does, and we do what we do, and if the two of them meet, it's God's luck or ours—but that's all it is, luck. And if you're coming to some understanding, you're coming to an understanding with yourself." She paused and squinted. "And we're coming up on the cutoff to the airfield. Get the map out."

He wanted to refute what she said, but that could wait until they were safely away from the threat of capture. Pulling the map out of his canvas shoulder bag, he asked. "What exactly are we looking for?"

"Alternate Seventy-one to Carthage."

"Okay," he said after studying the map, "what was that exit we just passed?"

"Missouri Thirty-seven."

"Then it's the exit after next."

"Good. Guess you better get the weapons out."

From the same canvas bag Goodfox took out two Albany-Ruger revolvers and laid them on the seat within easy reach. Then he pulled out an old Stevens shotgun whose double barrels had been sawed down to twelve inches, and whose rear stock was nothing more than a pistol grip. He opened it, dropped two buckshot shells into its chambers, and snapped it closed, letting it rest across his thighs with his left hand on the grip. Once he had loathed these weapons, but now they felt natural in his hands, extensions of his will and God's.

For seemingly endless minutes they rode along in silence

until the crude exit sign came into view. "We shouldn't have any trouble," she said as she drove the truck down the exit off the old I-road, "but if we do, remember that Bell is on our side."

"Of course," he said, watching as Nyllan carefully turned north on Seventy-one. Goodfox knew that Bell was on his own side—the side of profit—but at least in this case Bell would also be serving the good of the country. "There's the sign."

"I see it." She turned right onto a dirt road at an old rusted sign that said TRUE OZARK ANTIQUES. A mile and a half farther she turned right on another dirt road and came to a stop in front of a low wooden building. "This should be it."

"Doesn't look like much," Goodfox said as he opened the door and climbed out of the truck with his shotgun at the ready.

"Well I'll be damned! Rhondasue, Father Goodfox, didn't expect you two this early—or this well armed, either."

Goodfox returned Bell's smile with one of his own, wondering again how one man could be so black. Father Irving would look pale beside him. "Made good time, Bell, plus we're kind of in a hurry. Your plane ready?"

"I was just topping off the fuel, Father," he said as he reached out and shook hands. Then he looked in the back of the truck at the canvas covered box. "This your cargo?"

"That's it," Nyllan said. "Not too big for you, is it?"

Bell laughed. "Not half too big."

"Move it gently, though," Goodfox said. "It's full of electrical equipment."

"I know. Satellite controller, Rhondasue said."

"What!" Goodfox couldn't believe it. Anger locked his tongue and he stared at Nyllan.

"Relax, Murray. Bell's on our side."

"I sure am, Father," Bell said as he began maneuvering the controller toward the tailgate, "but even if I wasn't, I got no idea in the world what the hell you'd want this thing for."

Goodfox turned away from both of them and busied himself reloading his canvas shoulder bag, trying to still his trembling fingers, wondering how he was going to force the states back together if his every move became common knowledge. The controller and its operating code were his locks on the power he had to have to reunite the states and then to begin building the earthly kingdom of God.

CHAPTER 18

ONE | "I think I'll go back and let Nana Fernandez and Mrs. Lockett fix me lunch," Jessup said, staring at his dry rations with disdain as the team squatted in a circle eating their midday meal.

Cody grinned. "As long as you bring some back for all of us, I have no objection." He paused and looked up at the sky. Even though the rain had stopped, the clouds still hung dark and low over them. "From here on we're going to have to be extra careful. The Nates could be anywheres around the mounds and you can bet they'll have lookouts watching for us."

"Don't you think they've probably gone on?" Melindo asked.

"Let's hope they have." He looked north to the medicine mounds and silently prayed that they had indeed moved north. "But we can't bet on that. From here on we have to stick to the cover of the trees. We'll stay as close to the wagon tracks as we can, but we can't risk being spotted."

"Wouldn't it be a bitch if they had gone on and were hitting Two-eighty-seven about now," Jessup said, "while we were sneaking through the brush like a herd of three-legged armadillos."

"Yeah, it would, Roland, but it would be a worse bitch if they were sitting up there somewheres waiting for us."

Kolmer spat loudly. "But, but, but. But everything. Are we going to get on with this, or aren't we?"

Cody was startled by Kolmer's question. "You objecting to this break?"

"I'm objecting to all this talking. Dammit, Cody, we know we got to be careful. We understand what we're up against. We ain't new at this either, you know, and ain't nothing made easier by talking it into the ground." He shook his head and water dripped off his cap. "God, I hate this."

Only then did Cody realize how deeply his team was affected by this crazy mission they were on. "Me, too, Ed. Everybody. Nothing we can do about it right now, though, except follow through doing our best." He stood up. "All right, maybe I've talked about it too much. Maybe Ed's right. But I'm done talking. Donna, you ready to take the point again?"

As she stood, so did the others. "Ready as I'm gonna get."

"Roland, you want me to take drag for a while?"

"I'm fine, Cody."

"Ed? Juanita? Anything either of you want to add before we get moving again?"

Kolmer shook his head. So did Brisas, and Cody felt no better about this than he had when he talked to Terry. He also knew that his team was ready for something to happen, eager and anxious at the same time, and he hoped that would give them an edge, not a handicap, when something did happen.

"Lead us out," he said to Melindo.

Most of the mesquite trees were just close enough together to give them decent cover, and not so close that they had to fight their way through the thorny branches. Melindo picked and chose her path with one eye watching ahead for trouble from the mesquite and the other, for signs of the Nates. It was Cody's job to make sure they didn't wander too far away from the road with its fresh wagon tracks.

The going was steady, but noisier than Cody wanted it to be. Fact was, he had never found a way to keep a patrol on the march quiet—and neither had his instructors at Jayton. Cloth rubbed cloth. People breathed. Ground debris snapped and crunched. Pebbles rattled down hills. Put more than two people on the trail together and you had noisy business. It was that simple.

He remembered seeing a movie at Old Man Larkin's house one time where some soldiers were moving through the woods and didn't make a sound. He'd asked Mr. Larkin how they did that, and Mr. Larkin had laughed and said that when they made the movie they just turned the microphones down so they didn't pick up the sound. Cody'd been too young to understand exactly how they could do that, thinking that microphones would pick up every sound, but he did understand that it was a trick. Now he wished he could pull that trick here and hush the noise his team was making.

The wind gusted steadily from the south, helping to mask their noise as it scurried through the trees. Overhead the clouds seemed to be thinning, and for the first time since he could remember Cody prayed they wouldn't get sunshine. Not now. Not today. Not when they needed all the help they could get to remain hidden from Nate eyes that might be watching for them.

As if to spite him, a huge hole opened in the clouds and a pool of hazy sunlight bathed the ground between them and the closest medicine mound.

Immediately Melindo signaled for them to get down. She stared ahead for long moments, then turned back toward Cody with a grim look of determination and held up two fingers beside her head.

Nates. She had seen Nates.

TWO | The vote on what the combined tonkaweyas should do had not been as simple as Max Quentin had predicted.

Eighteen braves, most of them from the Wyandot tonkaweya, had sided with Elroy Sashahunder. Fifteen braves from the Seneca tonkaweya plus the Quentin brothers had sided with Mike Young and Kendrick Johnson.

However, twenty braves—including Wyandot and Seneca, and Tinker Oberly—had so far refused to choose either side, arguing that a more fundamental question of allegiance had to be recognized, and that under no circumstances could anyone divide this group until they had been released by Chief Townsend.

Their stance caused an eruption of arguments that might have been humorous had Lucy not been caught in a serious problem. Elroy Sashahunder had told her she must choose, but Lucy had refused. Her duty lay with Ann Johnson. Her safety lay with Sashahunder—at least that's what it looked like to her. There was no choice in that. Ann Johnson and her unborn child had to take first priority.

But she waited, wanting the tonkaweyas to settle their dispute before she announced her intentions. If Tinker's group won, she wouldn't have to announce her duty and choose. Then the Quentins couldn't be sure she was going to stay with them because of Ann.

As she sat by the fire sipping her tea it occurred to her that if the Quentins thought she was committed to Ann, they might not watch her so closely, and she might have a better chance to escape. No. She refused to give them that satisfaction. Let them wonder.

Listening now to the groups arguing, she slowly saw something about them that struck her as rather odd. Except for Tinker Oberly and a few others, most of the braves in the uncommitted group had no facial tattoos. In Sashahunder's group, tattooed faces far outnumbered untattooed faces. The reverse was true for Mike Young and his Seneca group. She couldn't think of why that might be the case until a little chunk of forgotten information clattered noisily to the floor of her awareness.

Several years earlier after one of their visitors from the Nation had left in the middle of the night, Mishla had told Lucy about a religious cult in the Nation that was growing in influence and power—especially along the Red River where Lucy would have to travel.

They called themselves the Nimenim—the true people. Members of this cult were noted for their fundamentalist religious fervor, for their secret societies totally closed to all outsiders, for their blind allegiance to their leaders, and for a questionable code of honor. They were also known for rejecting certain fashions, including tattooed faces, but were reported to tattoo their genitals—men and women both.

Lucy might never have thought much about them after that except that the information had so upset Mishla that for three nights she restlessly prowled the house, or read her books, but she didn't sleep. That in itself was highly unusual. Mishla was a firm believer in six hours of sleep every night. So when she had insisted that Lucy always keep a suspicion open for the Nimenim, Lucy knew they were more than another fundamentalist religious sect looking to convert the world to their way of thinking.

Over time, Mishla's warning had been tucked away by her mind because in all her travels across the Red and into the Nation after that, she had never been given cause to think the warning was important.

Swallowing the last of her tea, she realized there was no way of knowing if Mishla's warning was important now. If these braves were Nimenim, she had no idea what they were trying to accomplish here, but she did know she would have to pay closer attention to them. And how Ann Johnson fit into—

"You look unhappy, Miss Lucy."

Lucy blinked in the sudden brightness of soft sunlight and

realized Tinker Oberly was standing almost directly in front of her drinking from a large dipper.

"Don't let all this argument worry you. It is our way and we must follow it. In the end we will win."

"Who, Tinker? Who will win?"

"Our side," he said with a smile. "Even the sun shines with favor on us."

Before she could ask him again, he turned and walked back to the loudest group, dropping the dipper in the water bucket on the way. There was a certain bounce in his step that told her he was enjoying all this, and that puzzled her even more.

She poured herself another cup of tea from the large pot and was just sitting down to enjoy it when a sudden quiet snapped her attention back to the braves. They were all listening intently to a man who was trying to talk between gasps. What he was saying gave Lucy an indefinable kind of hope.

"Only three . . . don't think they saw me . . . hard to tell. Could be the point . . . of a larger group. Less than a mile," he said, pointing south.

"Prepare to move out," Kendrick Johnson said. "I want to be rolling out of here in ten minutes. Nathan, you and Paul get your militia uniforms on. Mike, Elroy, give me two pickets each to the south."

Young and Sashahunder exchanged looks, then nodded almost simultaneously. For the time being the argument was suspended. Lucy understood that with mixed emotions. By choosing to remain united and to run rather than fight, the tonkaweyas had increased her opportunities to escape in the confusion, but they had also increased the dangers to Ann Johnson.

Lucy stood and knew without question that she dared not try to escape under those conditions. The baby's welfare and Ann's had to come first. As she walked toward Johnson's wagon, Lucy wished the baby had been born last night and freed her from this duty. Shaking her head to dismiss those thoughts she began thinking about how she could best help make Ann comfortable.

A mule brayed in fear.

A shot rang out.

Lucy twisted around in time to see one mule fall to the earth. Its legs jerked and kicked. Another mule reared to the echo of the second shot and collapsed in a spasmodic heap beside the first.

Someone screamed orders. A third shot felled one of the oxen hitched to Johnson's wagon.

With a startled cry Lucy ran toward the wagon, her only thought to protect Ann.

THREE | Murray Goodfox paced impatiently as Bell supervised the refueling of his airplane. It had taken more than three hours for them to fly from the little airfield near Joplin to this even more primitive field outside Okmulgee in the heart of the Nation.

"Calm down," Nyllan said from where she sat under the shade of a small tree. "You'll wear me out just watching you. Besides, Bell told you there was no way we could get there today, anyway, so there's no sense in worrying yourself like this."

"What am I supposed to do? Pray for patience? If the boys can't handle Johnson, we're going to be back to an ugly zero."

"So, it'll slow you down. Won't stop you, will it?"

He paused and stared at her for a few seconds before answering. "Maybe it won't stop me, but it will certainly slow down God's work. And where that is concerned, I cannot abide delay. One doesn't hesitate where God is concerned, or—"

"When the work of the merciful Lord is at hand," she said, finishing the sentence for him. "I know. I've heard it before. But dammit, Murray, what about mysterious ways and all that? So we were a day later than you planned getting away from H.S. and the Ash Grove Boys? So we're going to be a day later getting back to Rhineland? So what? Maybe God has a—"

"Stop! Stop! I've told you time and again I will not put up with your constant readiness to put everything off on God just to humor me. God doesn't work like that. He works by helping His servants, not by doing the work for them. He works—"

" 'Bout ready," Bell called. "Better drain your bladders now, 'cause the next leg is the longest."

"He works in mysterious ways," Nyllan said. "I'm gonna go pee. You?"

"I already did."

"Don't say Bell didn't warn you when you're up at two thousand feet and have to go."

Goodfox turned away without answering and walked quickly to the little outhouse marked GUYS. As he stood over the smelly hole and relieved himself, he realized he was reciting the rosary silently in his head. Rhondasue did that to him—frustrated him with her mocking ways and her lack of faith. Yet he knew the frustration was his problem, not hers. She could not choose to frustrate him. He could only choose to be irritated and angered by her actions.

The choice was his alone. If he chose to be irritated by an instrument God had led him to, he couldn't blame the instrument or God, he could only blame himself. At the very least he should have learned that much with Paula Kathryn.

That old familiar realization made him smile. How many times had Father Dibole cautioned him about that failing? How many nights had he prayed in the Blessed Mother's grotto to overcome it? How many miles had he walked on his knees at the seminary in Windthorst in penance for his uncontrolled emotions?

And before then? Before he found his faith? Before he had broken with the old life? Even then he had suffered because he did not, could not, would not come to terms with himself. That had cost him a wife and child, but after he found God, and God led him to Windthorst, he had learned what had to be done. Now his life was a penance for previous sins, and he must not confuse his private emotions with signals from God.

No, he thought as he left the outhouse. He had to choose internal peace, the peace that came from trusting in God alone. He had to choose not to be irritated and angered by Rhondasue. And in the choosing he knew he would be granted patience in bearing his crosses, and come one step closer to God's pure intent.

When the time came to issue the holy warnings, to announce the holy purpose God willed for his people, Murray Goodfox would be pure of heart and mind, ready to bring the truth and justice of the Lord to the United States, and then to the world. But to be so prepared, he must be ever vigilant to purge himself of all failings so that God could use the vessel of his body to pour the oil of holy peace upon the troubled waters of the world.

As he climbed aboard Bell's plane, Goodfox felt much better than he had in weeks.

"Nice to see you smiling like that," Nyllan said.

"All praise goes to God, Rhondasue. All praise to Him."

CHAPTER 19

ONE | "I think it's time we circled west," Cody said.
So far Melindo had done all the shooting, downing two mules
and two oxen with five well-placed shots. Now the Nates were
returning fire, shooting wildly in the team's general direction,
and Cody decided it was time to shift positions so the Nates
would have less chance of locating them.

Not that the team was in any real danger. Unless the Nates
had themselves a good sniper with a big piece of glass on a long
rifle, they weren't going to hit nothing this far away. Melindo had
estimated her range at nine hundred yards and set her scope for
that distance. Four hits in five shots sure seemed to confirm her
estimate.

There weren't nothing much Cody and the others could do to
help her except to keep their eyes out for approaching Nates and
keep her moving after every three or four shots. Truth was, the
Nate camp was way past the accurate range of the team's short-
barreled Albany-Ruger carbines, even if they used the cali-
brated peep sights that gave the A-R's acceptable accuracy out to
four or five hundred yards—for a good shooter, of course.

Once, when Cody was nineteen and a trainee at Jayton
Militia School, he had shot six bull's-eyes out of ten at four
hundred measured yards with no wind, and he and his instructor
had both considered that damned good. But he knew he could
never shoot as good as Melindo, because to do that took more
than skill and hard practice. It took a certain breed of intuition,
so that the rifle and the scope kind of became extensions of
Melindo herself. Least ways, that was how Melindo described it.
Said that on her good days, she got this special feeling—like the
rifle was a part of her arms and her eyes at the same time—and
when she felt that, she knew she could hit damn near anything
she wanted to.

This was obviously one of her good days.

Cody halted the team a hundred yards or so west of where
Melindo had fired her first shots, wishing again that the clouds
would cover the sun. It had been ducking in and out of big holes

making it easier for the Nates to spot them. That was the last thing he wanted. As long as Melindo could pick off the Nate stock one by one without being seen and drawing return fire, he and the rest of the team were going to be a lot happier.

Melindo crept forward through the mesquite until she had a relatively clear view of the Nates and again took aim. Her next shot staggered a large ox that stumbled forward and pitched its rider into the mud. After the following shot, the ox fell beside him.

Suddenly the Nates unleashed a machine gun that sprayed the trees well in front of the team with a rash of bullets.

"Back away," Cody ordered.

"But Cody, they're not coming anywheres close to us."

"No sense in taking a chance. Back away. We'll swing northwest and hit them again."

With a reluctant nod Melindo backed out of her firing position and followed Cody to the northwest. The machine gun fire stopped. The team went farther this time, searching for a spot with good cover and a clear view of the Nates. Much to their surprise, when they found that spot, they saw the Nates had already gotten their wagons moving—but they were off the worn track, heading east into the brush through the heart of a huge patch of sunlight.

"I have to get closer," Melindo said immediately.

Cody scanned the area. "There." He pointed to one of the low, hat-shaped mounds to their north. "There's good brush cover up there."

She nodded. "We'd better hurry. Even that may not be close enough."

Just as they started to move again, a rifle shot whined past close over their heads. They instinctively crouched lower as a second shot followed the first. Some Nate was working out the range and apparently had the accuracy to threaten them.

"Now what?" Jessup asked with a deep frown.

"We circle back the way we came," Cody said as he turned and started moving in a low crouch. "No way we can get to that mound without exposing ourselves." None of them argued with his decision as they turned with him.

A third shot splintered a mesquite tree about twenty feet in front of them.

"Bracketed," Melindo said.

Cody immediately turned south just as the clouds finally

blotted out the sunlight. He ran in a low crouch in and out between trees for fifty or sixty yards with the team close behind him. No shots followed them, so he stopped under a larger-than-average mesquite. They were all breathing heavily.

"Juanita, crank up the radio. It's time we find out what kind of help we've got out there."

TWO | Lucy braced herself again, using her body to cushion Ann's as the wagon jolted over the rough road.

The sounds of firing were farther away, now, and for many reasons Lucy prayed that they would stop altogether. There was no doubt in her mind that whoever was doing the shooting was part of the West Texas Militia. No one else could have been senseless enough to shoot mules. What a shameful waste!

Only as she recalled the terrible sense of loss she had felt when the first mule went down did she realize that something else very important had happened. The shots had been—

The wagon dipped sideways then bounced out of a hole. Lucy clutched Ann's shoulders and tried to hold her steady.

Ann cursed with a moan. "It's starting," she said. "It's starting again."

"Shhh. Shhh. You're going to be all right." Please, she prayed silently, please don't let this be labor.

"Oh, God, it hurts!"

"The medicine I gave you will help soon. But you have to help, too, by relaxing as much as you can. Don't tense your body. You're not going to roll anywhere and I'll see that you don't bounce too hard. Just try to go with the motion and—"

"But I'm going to be sick!" Ann screamed. She jerked away from Lucy, gagging and gasping, turning her body sideways across the rolled bedding that protected her.

The wagon lurched again. Lucy twisted toward Ann and wrapped her arm around her shoulder. "Gently, gently," she whispered. "Breathe deeply. Use your mouth. Deep breaths, Ann, take deep breaths."

Ann shuddered, sucking in air through her mouth in short, wet, panting gasps, but she stopped gagging, and after another lurching minute or so, pushed back against Lucy. "Okay. Okay. I'll be okay," she said between breaths.

Lucy pulled her gently to the center of the mattress and

pulled the bedroll with her as tight against Ann as she could get it. Her main concern was to protect Ann from as much jostling as possible. Ann's breathing was becoming more even and her eyes were closed, letting Lucy hope that the concentrated Mormon tea she had forced Ann to drink from her little flask was taking effect.

What else could she do? She had been trained as a healer, not a medwife, and she had been afraid even to give Ann the Mormon tea. The question about whether or not it could be given to a pregnant woman had never occurred to her—nor, apparently, to Cynthia Ironeyes who had taught her about its effects in calming a patient. All Lucy knew was that it worked and that if anyone needed calming, it was Ann.

As she worried about the tea and Ann and the baby, Lucy absently stroked Ann's brow, letting her warm hands gently massage the furrows until Ann's breathing slowed into long, even measures interrupted only by the bouncing of the wagon and an occasional murmured moan. Maybe the tea was working by now. Maybe she could relax a moment and begin thinking about the future of—

A sudden thought stilled her as though some greater hand had pushed aside her worries and revealed an idea that seemed as strange to her as it was appropriate. Whoever had been firing at them back at the campsite had been deliberately shooting animals instead of people. That was a strange thing. Who would do that? And why? Why wouldn't they be aiming for people as well as animals? Could it have been someone other than the militia? But who? Who?

She paused and listened as though the occasional distant shot might tell her something, give her some answer to this living puzzle. Instead she heard curses and moans that could mean only one thing. There were men hurt out there, and as soon as possible she was going to have to treat them. So much for her questions about who would shoot only animals.

The wagon came to an abrupt halt. Voices were shouting, arguing. Others were telling them to be quiet. Lucy decided she had better find out what was going on and eased herself from under Ann whose eyes flickered when she moved.

"It's all right," Lucy said. "I'll be back in a minute." As quickly as she could she climbed out the end of the wagon, surprised by how dark it was becoming, and turned in the direction of the voices. What she saw started her. The Quentins and Mike Young and some of his braves were holding Kendrick Johnson and Elroy Sashahunder at gunpoint.

"You!" Max Quentin yelled at Lucy when he saw her, "get yourself over here."

Tucking her hands inside her cloak, she walked slowly toward the group, resting her right hand on the butt of her pistol, trying not to let her anger and fear show, wondering what was happening now and why the Quentins were doing this. She stopped an easy ten feet from both groups.

"We've had a change of plans, Miss Lucy," Mike Young said. "You'll have to come with us."

"Where?" she asked.

"Don't worry yourself about that."

"They're going to leave me and Ann here," Johnson said.

Only then when she looked at him did Lucy realize that he had been wounded. His left arm hung by his side and blood had soaked the shoulder of his jacket. He was still armed, but his pistol was holstered. She immediately shifted her eyes back to Young. "If that's true, I cannot go with you, because I cannot leave Mrs. Johnson here," she said. As she shrugged her shoulders and readjusted her cloak, she eased her pistol from its holster and held it flat against her stomach, ready to use it if necessary. No one was going to force her to leave Ann.

"You don't get a choice, Missy," Max Quentin said.

"Try to make me," she said with a sudden defiance in her voice, revealing and cocking her pistol at the same time. "I stay with Ann Johnson. You go where you damn well please."

As Wendel Quentin swung his pistol in Ann's direction, Young slapped his arm away. Almost simultaneously a brave shoved a shotgun barrel in Wendel's ribs.

Hammers clicked. Guns came up. Fingers tensed over triggers. Now there were three groups armed and waiting for something to happen.

THREE | As the plane broke through the low clouds and began its descent toward Marysville, Father Murray Goodfox stared out the window at Falls Lake which stretched sixty miles into the western horizon. That huge body of brackish water had been like a perpetual taunt from the devil after Shudderday. It beckoned with promise to everyone who came near it, only to turn them away when they got close enough to smell or taste it or see the long swirling oil slicks spreading from the wells beneath its surface.

Falls Lake was one of the stranger mysteries of Shudderday, one of those things that shouldn't have happened, but did. Like the uplift that held back the Mexican Sea and the new springs that kept appearing in West Texas while wells suddenly went dry in the Nation, Falls Lake had appeared unpredictably, and now its foul waters covered over fifteen hundred square miles on two sides of the old Red River bed from the Dennison Dam to what was left of Falls City that had been called Wichita Falls, once.

As a child in DalWorth, he had taken clean drinking water for granted until his parents—especially his mother—had begun teaching him how very valuable water was to the survival of every political entity. DalWorth was lucky. It had an even dozen major reservoirs fed by the Trinity River watershed, plus a large number of wells that had suddenly turned artesian after Shudderday. In fact, DalWorth had such a surplus, it had sold water to the Nation until the Red River uprising when two hundred tonkaweyas had swept south across the Red and claimed some of the water for themselves.

Pat Mayse Lake, Lake Bonham, Lake Lavon, Roberts Reservoir, Moss Lake—each an important water source, each name etched into Goodfox's memory as the site of a battle for the rights to that water. Now, thank God, there was a truce, and even in the disputed Grayson County area, the Nation drew water from the northeast part of Roberts Reservoir, and DalWorth drew water from the rest of the lake. But it was a fragile truce at best, and Goodfox knew that only his plan for reunion could cleanse the map of lines that divided people and provide water and resources for everyone.

The plane bounced as it turned into the wind for the final approach to Marysville, and he lost sight of Falls Lake.

"A bullet for your thoughts," Nyllan said.

"Mother," he answered. "I was thinking about Mother and what a remarkable woman she was. Did I ever tell you that she was one of the founders of the New Federalist Party?"

"No, but I knew she was a Joiner."

"That came later." Goodfox shook his head. "After the New Feds got too big for their principles, as she used to say, she resigned as DalWorth Coordinator for the New Feds and became a fire-spouting Joiner."

"Is that when you joined?"

He laughed and patted her knee. "No, that was well before I joined that group. Back when Mother joined, I was married and living up in Atoka. I was spouting my own kind of fire."

"You weren't a tribalist, were you?"

" 'Bout to land," Bell said.

As the plane thumped down on the grassy runway, Goodfox laughed again. "Oh, yes I was—through and through. Why not? My father was more than half Osage. My mother was of mixed tribes, like you, and proud of every ounce of her Indian blood." His voice had grown louder to compete with the sound of the engine, so he paused and watched as Bell brought the plane almost to a halt, then turned it and headed toward a little cluster of buildings.

Nyllan tugged at his sleeve. "So when did you become a Joiner?"

He tapped his ear and waited until the plane stopped and Bell shut off the engine. "Years later," he said finally as he released his seat belt, "after I became a priest, actually. Took me that long to understand what was so important about reunion."

As he started to climb out of his seat, Nyllan put a hand on his arm. "Will you tell me more about it later?"

Her question startled him. "Of course, if you want to know, I'll be glad to tell you about it."

"And about what you think the reunion ought to be like?"

There was an open kind of need in her voice that touched him. "Everything I can, Rhondasue. Everything I can." He turned to Bell who was checking things off on a clipboard attached to his thigh. "How long will we be here?" he asked.

"Until tomorrow."

"What?"

"Until tomorrow, Father. We've fought winds all the way from Joplin, and there's no way I'm going to fly this plane any further before it gets a thorough mechanical checkup. Wouldn't want something falling off, would we? Besides—"

"But you said—"

"Father," Bell said gently, "I said we would try. Besides, even if we could fill up and take off, where the hell would we find to land in the dark? 'Cause that's what it will be in an hour or so, pitch dark. Relax, Father. We're in Nimenim country. They'll take care of us."

CHAPTER 20

ONE | At least we got some of them, Cody thought as he looked east. The Nates had moved totally out of range and he had stopped the team while Brisas called Foard Station again on the radio. Already the horizon faded into a dark, thick grey lined with blue-black clouds. An hour of light left, he thought, maybe less. I sure as hell don't want to track the Nates by sound.

"Got 'em," Brisas said, holding out the headset for Cody.

"This is Bearcub Leader," Cody said into the mike.

"The answer to your question is—nothing until tomorrow."

"Dammit, Aunt Bertha, we could lose them in the dark."

"I know that, Jeremiah," her voice said calmly in his ear, "but that's a chance we'll have to take. Terry's got patrols all up and down Two-eighty-seven, so the Nates will have a hard time breaking through to the north."

"But I told you, the last time we saw them, they were heading east." What in the hell was the matter with Terry, anyway, he wondered. Couldn't Terry see that—

"I told him that. He said for you not to worry about it. Said you should track them as far as light would allow, then rest easy for a long day tomorrow."

Cody cursed. "With some help, I hope."

There was a long pause before Sheriff York answered. "He didn't say, Jeremiah. . . . There's something else big going on that's got his attention, but I don't know what it is."

"Leaving us shorthanded and out of luck," Cody said with a disgusted sigh. "Okay, Aunt Bertha. We'll do what we can. Bearcub Leader—"

"Jeremiah, there's one other thing . . ."

"What?"

"The Quanah-Vernon-Crowell triangle has been declared off-limits." There was a quaver in her voice. "Terry's already evacuated Medicine Mound and Farmers Valley. The folks from Margaret are just coming in here, and the Raylanders are going to Lockett."

"Why? What about the Locketts?"

"I just told you that the Raylanders—"

"No-no. I mean the Lockett *family*," he said. "They live a couple miles east of Copper Breaks."

"That's Quanah's jurisdiction, but I'll let them know."

"Good. Now, why is it off limits?" Cody asked.

Again there was a long pause before she answered. "Terry's got some almost positive evidence that this group is carrying eighty grams of plutonium missing from Pantex. There was a man named Kendrick Johnson who worked there and—"

"Kendrick Johnson? Are you sure?" His heart jumped and he could hardly think. "*Kendrick* Johnson?"

"Terry's sure. Seems this Johnson fellow disappeared shortly after the plutonium did, but their records up there are apparently such a real mess, and they didn't catch any of it missing for a while."

"So what's this plutonium good for?" As he asked the question his mind was really on Kendrick Johnson, and Ann, and the baby, and wondering what in the name of Cristodios was going on.

"Well, it's very radioactive, very poisonous they say, and lasts a long time. The old United States used to make bombs with it—nuclear bombs."

Cody's jaw dropped with a tiny groan. "Unh . . . bombs? Is that—? Who would—? . . . I don't understand," he said slowly. Only then did he realize that the team had crowded closer and was listening carefully. "Maybe you'd better explain."

"I don't know any more, Jeremiah. I'm sorry. I don't even think Terry knows any more. All Lubbock knows for sure is that there's some radioactive materials missing—part of which is the plutonium—and that Kendrick Johnson worked there about the time some of it disappeared, and that they think he's leading this group you're following. And that's it. I'm sorry."

An angry chill ran up his spine. "And that's it? That's it? Terry wants us to follow these Nates who are carrying God-only-knows what kind of dangerous stuff, and that's it?" His voice rose with every question. "That's all the information he can give us? Well, that's not enough, Sheriff York—not damn near enough."

"Jeremiah, I don't want to hear you talking like a—"

"I don't give a sheep-shitting damn what you want to hear!" he screamed. "You tell Terry that if he doesn't get us help and a lot more information, he can find some other suckers to do his scut work for him."

His sudden rage startled him and made the rest of the team flinch away from him. Brisas almost jerked his headset off, and as he readjusted it, he listened for some kind of rebuttal from Aunt Bertha.

"You still there?" he asked angrily.

"I'm still here. Are you calming down?"

"Negative. You pass on my message. Bearcub Leader, out." He yanked the headset off and tossed it to Brisas. "Turn that damn thing off."

Brisas switched off the radio without looking directly at him. Fact was, none of them was looking directly at him.

"You want to hear it all?"

They nodded. "Damn straight," Jessup said.

As quickly as he could, Cody repeated what Aunt Bertha had told him and explained that she didn't know anything more than that. Then he said, "I lied to her. I'm going to follow those Nates. But none of you have to come with me. They can't order me to do it, and I won't order you to."

"Then why the hell are you going?" Jessup asked.

Cody looked at the blackness that had swallowed the eastern horizon—praying, hoping, knowing that Ann and his baby were out there somewhere. He hesitated for a long moment, considered not telling the team, but finally accepted the fact that he owed them the truth. "I have to. The man they say's leading them Nates is the man who stole my wife and baby."

TWO | "Easy, boys. Easy," Hector Quentin said. "There ain't no sense in shooting each other up."

"Then you will leave the healer alone," Young said. "We will take Mrs. Johnson and the healer with us."

"Now dammit, Mike, there's no sense—"

Young glared at Max. "Either you and your brothers accept my decision, or you go alone, with no braves, no wagons, and no mules."

"All right. All right. We do it your way. But we better hurry. God knows what the militia is up to now."

"Explain," Lucy demanded, bringing all eyes back to her. Most of their guns were lowered, but hers was still pointed at Wendel Quentin. She didn't understand any of this—including why Johnson was now siding with Sashahunder against the Quentins—and she was not going on without explanation.

"Miss Lucy," Young began, "we will need your services as a healer, and because we are under great pressure, we must deviate from our previous plans. Please accept our—"

"Talk straight," she said quickly. "Either you tell me what's going on here, or you can just go on without us. I'm getting a little tired of being jerked around by a bunch of shameful braves and their wretched friends." She was surprised by her vehemence, surprised that she had dared speak her mind so openly, and pleased all at once by the looks on their faces.

"We have been ordered south by Chief Townsend, and we need you to go—"

"Lies," Johnson said. "He's lying through his teeth. No one ordered us to go anywhere."

"That's right," Sashahunder added. "No Wyandot heard this order from Chief Townsend."

"The radio message said, 'Meet your father at Rhineland before Easter Sunday.' Who else would have sent that message?"

"But you're the only one who heard it," Sashahunder said.

"You question my honesty?"

"Hell, yes."

"None of this has anything to do with me," Lucy said angrily. "And since you refuse to tell me, Mrs. Johnson and I will stay here with her husband until the baby—"

"Her husband's not here," Max Quentin said. "Her husband lives down in Chalk. Name of Cody."

"More lies." Johnson spat. "Go on, traitors. Leave us here. But the load-wagon stays."

"It belongs to Father Goodfox."

"No, it doesn't, Young. It belongs to me. I stole it and I say where it goes."

A pistol barked. Johnson spun to the ground with a brief growl of pain.

Sashahunder knelt beside him. "Damn you, Quentin."

"Next?" Max Quentin asked, his pistol waving back and forth at Sashahunder and his Wyandot braves.

Lucy had to force herself to relax the grip on her own trigger. All she really wanted to do was blast a stump-sized hole in Quentin. That realization stunned her. How had she built up so much hatred for this man that he made her want to violate all her training? The answer that came back to her was simple. How could she not hate him?

"Enough!" Young shouted. "It is decided. We will take the load-wagon, the Johnson wagon, and the Number Two supply wagon south to meet Father Goodfox at Rhineland. All are free to join us or return to the Nation with the Wyandot. Choose now."

Both the division of loyalty and the speed with which they chose surprised Lucy. In less than a minute there were two distinct groups—the smaller, mostly with facial tattoos, standing behind Sashahunder, and the larger, mostly without tattoos, behind the Quentins and Mike Young. Only then did she realize that she had not seen Tinker Oberly since they had run from the gunfire. But there were at least ten or twelve braves missing. She suspected they were out on guard and hoped Tinker was among them.

"It is settled," Young announced. "Miss Lucy, you may tend to Johnson and the rest of the wounded, then prepare to leave with us within the hour." He looked down at her pistol still pointed at Wendel Quentin. "And don't worry, no one's going to hurt you."

Slowly, almost reluctantly, she lowered the barrel then tucked the pistol back into its holster. Tending the wounded would give her time to think—and time to decide what risks she was willing to take, because she didn't believe Mike Young's assurance. Not for a minute.

THREE | "You're the one who told me we had to be flexible," Nyllan said. "Practice what you preach."

"I don't need your clichés or your reminders." Goodfox stared at her for a second, then shoved another spoonful of the thick beef soup into his mouth.

"If you don't need reminding, why are you so damned upset?"

He swallowed quickly. "Because," he said, wiping his chin, "we don't know what's going on with the Quentins. Suppose they couldn't get the materials away from Johnson? What then? What if they didn't get the message to meet us in Rhineland?"

"So try the radio again. Try calling them instead of Townsend. But for God's sake, calm down."

"That's the point, Rhondasue. For God's sake, I can't calm down. If I don't get control of this situation soon, we—"

She slammed her hand flat on the table. "You beat everything I've ever seen, Murray Goodfox. You know sure as clouds cover the sky that there's no way to get control until everyone gets to Rhineland. You keep trying to get me to meditate and learn to accept the natural rhythms of life, but you're worse than Bishop Malone—strung out on your own nervous frustration."

When she paused, he started to speak, then closed his mouth. She was right. Again.

"I can't make everything right for you. You can't make everything right. No one can. . . . God, listen to me. I sound like you." Pushing away from the table as she stood up, Nyllan shook her head. "Go pray for yourself. Or go run laps around the airfield. If you can't accept the *is* of this situation, take your frustration out on yourself. Just leave me out of it. I'm too tired to cope with you." With that she turned and walked out the front door of the tiny cabin that had been provided for them.

Pray for yourself, Goodfox thought. Pray for yourself. Didn't he wish he could. Father Dibole had been only too correct when he had told Goodfox that his most difficult parishioner would live in his heart. It was true. Always it was true.

He sighed and pushed the bowl away, no longer hungry for that kind of food. What he needed was something more sustaining, something that would continue to give him energy as he worked through the difficult days ahead. What he needed was a renewal of faith. Slowly he folded his hands and rested his forehead on them.

Dear God, he prayed, *help me in my struggle to do Your will. Teach me again the meaning of patience. Make me steadfast of purpose and diligent of heart as I follow Your direction. Help me again to accept Your plan for my life, and to fulfill it Your way with Your guidance. I am a weak vessel, Lord, unworthy and unfit. Strengthen me, I pray, in the name of the Father and the Son and the Holy Ghost. Amen.*

His eyes were moist as he realized he felt no better for the praying, no more patient, no more content, no more accepting of the unacceptable situation. Was this God's will, too, that he struggle internally even as he joined the struggle against God's enemies? Was this how God was preparing him?

He didn't know. He just didn't know, and the not knowing

added to his misery. If only he could come to the understanding of it all as he once had, maybe he could then—

The sound of a plane's engine revving interrupted his thoughts. "Bell," he said aloud, "testing his plane."

Only when the revving changed pitch did his gut turn with a terrible suspicion. He jumped up and pushed the table aside as he hurried to the door. Throwing it open, he ran outside just in time to see the dim shape of Bell's plane taxiing toward the end of the runway.

"No!" he screamed. "No! Get back here!"

Already he was running, trying to put himself between the plane and the runway. "Stop!" he shouted. "Stop! Damn you, Bell! Stop!"

The plane turned. The engines roared. Goodfox hurled his body forward, trying to grab the wing.

Then it was gone, rolling down the runway, leaving Murray Goodfox sitting on the ground, cursing the pain in his wrist and the treachery of men.

Nyllan reached him as the plane left the ground and disappeared into the darkness. "What happened?"

"He left us! The traitor left us. Help me up."

"But why? I don't understand," she said as she put a hand under his arm and helped him to his feet.

"And you think I do?"

"Father? Father Goodfox?" a voice called from the darkness.

"That's Bell!" Nyllan exclaimed. "We're over here!"

"Then who . . ." His voice trailed off as he stared into the darkness.

"They stole my plane," Bell shouted as he ran over to them carrying a small lantern.

"The controller!" Goodfox said suddenly. "They got the controller."

"Maybe not," Bell said. "I unloaded it while I was doing maintenance. It could still be in the shed."

Goodfox started running for the maintenance shed with Nyllan. Bell ran close behind him shouting, "The bastards stole my plane!"

CHAPTER 21

CODY | Night wind—a steady breeze from the south-west, cool but not cold—shuttled through the trees in noisy little spurts of energy. Black silhouettes of clouds outlined in pearlescent grey slid up the sky in silent denials of warmth.

The team had huddled under a large mesquite that was rooted in a slight rise two or three feet above the surrounding plain. Because of its location, the ground underneath its branches wasn't quite as muddy, but it trembled ever so gently, once, twice, three times, like it, too, was shivering in the dampness. Then all was still.

"It's too damn dark," Kolmer whispered when the trembling stopped. "Can't see more than fifty feet out there. Too risky to keep going."

"For you, maybe," Cody said, "but not for me." He was pleased that they had all chosen to come with him, but he didn't want them slowing him down. Still . . .

Jessup put his hand on Cody's arm. "Use your head, man. We know we're close. What more do we need? We dry-camp, get up before it's light, and close in on them then."

Cody nodded slowly. Roland was right. "All right. That makes sense. But I want us on the track as soon as it's light enough to see. I've got to know if she's with them or not."

"We'll find her," Brisas said. "I can feel it."

With practiced restraint they quietly spread out under the tree and after a few minutes Cody could hear some of them chewing their dry rations. He still sat on his rolled-up poncho, his heart aching, his head full of questions without answers.

This whole operation had gotten totally out of hand as far as he was concerned. From the night he had seen that cloaked stranger in the moonlight until now, the path they were taking kept twisting away from him like a copperhead into the brush. But maybe he was going to get a chance to pin its head down now. Maybe he was going to get some answers after all.

He shifted off his butt and unrolled the poncho, faced with the decision of sleeping under it or on it. Kolmer and Jessup had doubled up and so had Melindo and Brisas, each pair sleeping on one poncho and using the other tied to the tree limbs for shelter from the mist and rain. He decided to sleep on the poncho and depend on his hooded jacket with its bottom-rolled flaps to keep him dry.

It didn't take long to arrange himself, and he was just punching his pack into a comfortable pillow position when Jessup said. "You want first watch, Cody?"

"Yes. And last, too. You all draw among yourselves for the rest of them."

"Will do. I'll take last with you. Think we could smoke a cigarette?"

"Probably, so long as we smoke 'em facing west. You got one for me?" Cody knew they probably shouldn't—just in case the Nates might see the glow, but right now the thought of a cigarette was more seductive than the worry over whether the Nates might see them.

"Here," Jessup said. "Juanita's got the second watch."

A hand reached out of the darkness cupping the telltale ember of a smoke. Cody sat up, took the cigarette carefully from Jessup's fingers and eagerly brought it straight to his mouth.

God, it tasted good.

He remembered once when he'd been sick and Ann had followed Medic David's instructions to the letter and refused to let him smoke. Then one morning after he'd gotten out of bed for breakfast and after that sat with her and a cup of chicory on the narrow porch watching the color-show of an early summer sunrise, she'd surprised him by giving him a fancy-wrapped pack of Knoxville ready-rolls. She'd even struck the match for him, and to this day that sulphur smell of a match and the special taste of tobacco smoke just flat made him feel better.

Even now. He resisted the temptation to take exaggerated drags and forced himself to smoke it slowly and cleanly so that the fire never burned more than a quarter of an inch or so from the end. The smoke stayed cooler that way and the cigarette lasted longer, and he was determined, absolutely determined to enjoy every positive feeling it gave him. But as he drew near the end of it, regretting its loss even before it was gone, his mind turned to his real loss.

What was he going to do if Ann really was with this group of Nates? Or if Kendrick Johnson was and she wasn't? Or if she was and he wasn't?

He put the cigarette out in the damp earth and readjusted his position so that he could lean against the tree while staring off into the eastern darkness.

What was he going to say to her? *Ann, I'm sorry I made you unhappy, please come home?* What would he feel when he saw her again?

And what about the baby? What if the baby had already been born and Kendrick Johnson had given it a name and Ann had agreed, how could he change his baby's name?

That question almost made him laugh, and suddenly Cody actually did feel better. It was silly to worry about all of that. Whatever happened would happen, and his worrying wasn't going to change one bit of it.

An abrupt trembling caught him as off guard as the abrupt shift of emotions that accompanied it, and for a brief instant guilt threatened to overwhelm him. He almost laughed a second time—or cried—he wasn't sure which as he steadied himself against the dangers of both. To laugh would be to lose control of his emotions. To cry would be to lose control of his mind. He might not be able to control anything else in this world, but he should certainly be able to control himself.

Tears rolled from the corners of his eyes.

So much for mind over anything, he thought, letting the tears flow without making any attempt to stop them. Better to cry now, than tomorrow, if and when he came face to face with Ann and Kendrick Johnson. Better now, than some time when he had to make quick decisions. Better now, when no one could see him.

After the tears stopped, he checked his watch and was surprised to see that it was almost time to wake Brisas. How strangely time moved when emotions were loose—sometimes like a pregnant cow carrying twin calves, and other times like a jack on the run. He was in no hurry to go to sleep, so he didn't wake her until thirty minutes after her scheduled time.

Much to his surprise, he got his body comfortable, pulled his carbine in close behind him, nested his head in his pack, and moments later felt Jessup gently shaking his arm.

"Getting pink in the east, Cody."

"Right," he answered, pushing himself up on one elbow. His left shoulder and arm ached and his neck was stiff as though he hadn't changed positions all night. Pushing himself all the way into a sitting position he rubbed his eyes, then looked at his watch. 6:05. Time to empty his bladder.

Mist, he thought as he stood up, slung his carbine over his shoulder, and walked downwind. Better mist than drizzle. After he relieved himself he felt much better. Then as he walked back to the camp tree he heard a distinct sound in the distance. "Roland, you hear that?" he asked when he saw his Extra dark against the greying sky.

"Somebody starting their breakfast?"

"That's what I thought. Pots and pans. They must think they really got away from us. Wake the others."

"Right."

For the next fifteen minutes Cody listened carefully to the sounds from the Nate camp, trying to figure out the exact direction they were coming from. By the time the team was up and ready to go, he had the direction down to about ten degrees. What he couldn't decide on was the range.

"Here's your pack, Cody," Melindo said.

"Oh, thanks. I was listening so hard I didn't—"

"I knew you wasn't sleeping. 'Sides, it didn't take long for me and Juanita to pull your stuff together. Eat this."

He accepted the dried food bar from her without comment and took a big bite, forcing himself to chew slowly and steadily. "Okay," he said after he swallowed that bite, "first we call Foard Station, then we locate the Nates, and depending on what Crowell's told us, we either try to take them ourselves, or we play the sniping game again. Any questions?"

There were none and Brisas was already cranking up the radio. She handed the headset to Cody almost immediately.

"This is Bearcub Leader," he said quietly. "We are close to the Nate encampment. When can we expect reinforcements and how many will we get?"

"No reinforcements until some time this afternoon," a strange voice said in his ear.

"Are you positive?"

"Affirmative, Bearcub Leader. Information verified by Sierra Bravo Yankee."

"Understood, Foard Station. Bearcub Leader out." He handed the headset back to Brisas. "No help on the way," he said simply as he looked from face to face, "so I guess that means the sniping game again."

"Don't look so worried, Cody. That's what I'm here for," Melindo said. "You just pick out the folks I'm not supposed to shoot and leave the rest to me."

"You all ready?"

They nodded.

"Good. Then here we go."

Two hundred yards down the trail a shot rang out. Jessup gasped, gurgled, and collapsed. The team hit the mud.

A second shot spatted in the mud near Cody's head. He couldn't see anything ahead of him, just trees. Then a fourth, and a fifth, and a sixth.

"Help," Brisas cried after the sixth shot.

"There!" Kolmer shouted as his carbine started barking round after round into the trees.

Cody followed his aim and saw what Kolmer was shooting at. He wasn't sure it was a Nate, but it was the only target he saw, so he, too, began sending shot after shot toward the motion in the trees.

Behind him Melindo was crying. Suddenly Brisas crawled up beside him without her radio. "Jessup's dead. The radio's shot to hell. Where are those sons of bitches?"

Kolmer had stopped shooting and Cody did too. "See that little cluster of cedar? There was something moving just to the right of that. You support Ed. I'll check Donna."

He crawled back to where Donna Melindo had collapsed over Jessup. She was crying gently. Much to his surprise, when he pulled her off, he realized she was hit, too. There was an ugly red splotch centered on her left breast around a dark, wet hole. He could hear her lung bubbling.

A sucking chest wound. God, he'd read about them, but he never thought he'd actually have to cope with one. How had this happened? What had he done wrong?

Kolmer and Brisas were firing again, on their feet and moving forward. Should he join them? A glance at Melindo said no. Without thinking he opened her jacket, then took out his pocket knife and cut open her blouse and her combat bra. The amount of blood startled him.

"Help me, Cody. Please help me."

"Easy, Donna. Take it easy. You're going to be okay." He pulled the adhesive-backed plastic patch out of her first aid kit and stripped its backing off. But as he looked at her wound, he couldn't decide how to apply the patch. Should he try to wipe the blood off her breast, first? No. This adhesive was supposed to stick even under water. He centered it as best he could over the bullet hole and pressed it into place, squeezing blood out from under the edges. In order to make it lay flat, he had to pinch it over her nipple, but much to his relief it held. He pulled her jacket closed and snapped it to help keep her warm.

"Cody!" Brisas called. "Hurry!"

He took out one of the morphine tubes with its built-in needle and stabbed it through her jacket into her arm like he'd been taught. "Donna," he said as he emptied it slowly into her muscle, "I have to go." After taking the needle out, he picked up his carbine. "I'll be back. You understand? I'll be back."

Her eyes were closed, but she nodded slightly, and that was all he needed. Without waiting for more he stood up and ran toward where he could see Kolmer's huge form through the trees. He was panting hard by the time he got there and knelt beside the tree Kolmer was using for cover.

"They got a white flag out," he said.

Cody peered around the tree, and sure enough saw a Nate in bib overalls standing away from a group of wagons holding a white shirt tied to a stick. Behind him there were eight or ten Nates with their empty hands up in the air, and two more Nates lying on pallets on the ground. It was immediately obvious that this was only part of the group they had been following.

"Where are the rest of you?" he called.

"Left us," the lead Nate answered.

"Cover me," Cody said. He stood up and stepped from behind the tree, holding his carbine leveled at the Nate with the shirt. Certainly wasn't the whole group they'd fired on yesterday. "When'd they leave you?" he asked as he got closer.

"Last night. Patched up our wounded and left. All we want to do is go back to the Nation, mister."

"Is that why you fired on us?"

"That was a mistake."

One of the men on the pallets was trying to sit up and Cody automatically swung his rifle in that direction and froze. The man on the pallet was Kendrick Johnson.

CHAPTER 22

LUCY | For hours the wagon had rocked and pitched, shifted and twisted through the night, their drivers using walking guides with lanterns to keep them on the rutted gravel roads. Pausing only once—giving the women time to relieve themselves—the braves had abandoned the pickup truck which had finally run out of gas, and transferred its meager contents to the supply wagon before jolting off again into the darkness. Then when they reached their first hard-road, Mike Young had ordered the wagons stopped and he and the Quentins had left on muleback.

Lucy didn't know why they had stopped or where they had gone and didn't care. All she wanted was the opportunity for herself and Ann to get some much needed sleep. As soon as she realized what was going on, she had made Ann and herself as comfortable as possible atop the old mattress, so that by the time she heard the mules leaving, she had lost touch with the reality of the moment and thought she was hearing braves leaving Mishla's house in the middle of the night.

She was startled awake by the trembling of the wagon and the bawling of the oxen. Dogs howled in the distance. Never in all her life could she remember so many quakes so close together. Never. For a long moment she wondered why they were like this and where they were centered, but her drowsiness soon dulled her idle curiosity. Earthquakes came when they came, shook who they would, and slipped back underground until the next time. All a person could do was accept them and go on living. Let the seisers worry about the whys and hows.

Morning light colored the translucent windows in the wagon's vinyl sides a dull greenish-grey, and the rattling of chains told her the oxen were being hitched to the wagons.

"Are we leaving again?" Ann asked in dismay.

"It sounds that way. How are you feeling?"

Ann shut her eyes, shook her head, and frowned. "I don't know any more. I'm tired. I hurt. The pains come and go, but nothing seems to lead to anything."

Lucy raised herself on one elbow and looked intently at Ann. "If you're not cramping, that's good. How do you feel otherwise?"

"Relieved."

"But why?"

"Because we got away from Kendrick."

"From Kendrick? Why didn't you want to stay with him? He's your husband, isn't he?"

Ann's eyes popped open. "No, he's not, and I couldn't stay with him. I had to get away. You don't understand about us, and I can't explain it to you—not now. I'm sorry he got hurt, but I'm glad he's not here any more. Can you understand that?"

"Miss Lucy, Ann, if you have to use the latrine, you better do it now," Suzanne's voice called from the rear of the wagon. "They said we're going to be leaving soon."

"Thanks," Lucy called back. Turning to Ann she asked, "You want to use the jar?"

"Ugh. I hate that smelly thing. Just help me out and I'll be okay."

It took several minutes for both of them to climb out of the wagon, and by the time they did, Lucy was surprised to realize that it was well past dawn. Suzanne showed them the latrine, and they used it as quickly as they could, pausing when they returned to the wagon to wash their hands and faces. Lucy wished most of all that she could bathe all over and put on clean underwear.

Mike Young was waiting for them. "How you two doing?"

"Better, now," Ann said as she sat on the tailgate drying her face.

"Well, it'll be easier from here out. Paved road the whole way to Medicine Mound. And even better after that, but I'll save that for your imagination. Now, get yourselves loaded. It's time we rolled this caravan."

"Mike! Mike!" a brave called from the last wagon. "You better come see this."

Young turned his mule and headed back to the brave. Lucy helped Ann into the wagon and was about to climb after her when she heard Young call her name. As quickly as she could she ran to join them.

Propped up against the wheel of the last wagon was a bloody brave. It took Lucy several seconds as she kneeled down beside him to recognize that it was Tinker Oberly.

"Found him in the wagon," the brave was saying. "Must

have crawled in there after he got shot. Wonder that stuff in there didn't already kill him."

"Get me some hot water and bandages," Lucy said.

"We don't have time for that," Young said. "Put him in the supply wagon and do the best you can. Once we get to Medicine Mound, you can treat him right."

"But," Lucy protested, "he needs attention—"

"'Scuse me," the brave said, pushing her gently out of the way and stooping to pick Tinker up.

Lucy followed him to the supply wagon. "Make sure he's as flat as you can get him," she said. "I'll get my pack and be right back." By the time she explained to Ann what was going on, and got her pack and canteen, Suzanne had climbed in the wagon.

"Mike said you'd need me."

"Good. You ride here, and I'll see what I can do for Tinker." She hurried back to the supply wagon and a brave helped her climb in.

Tinker was lying on a folded tarp, his face wiped clean of blood, his eyes half open, his lips dry and split. "Hi, Miss Lucy," he said as she pulled herself up beside him. "Looks like I caught it, don't it?"

"You'll be all right, Tinker. What happened?" she asked as she pulled clean bandages out of her pack and opened her canteen.

"Got hit—twice, I think. Crawled into the wagon. Passed out, I think. . . . Woke up once last night . . . tried to call for help. Voice wouldn't work right."

"Looks like you caught another right where I patched you up the last time," she said as she wiped dried blood from the edges of the bandage on his left arm. The wagon was rolling, now. "Guess you thought one hole was better than two." She surveyed him for a minute then asked, "Where else were you hit?"

He raised his right hand to reveal a dirty cloth bandage caked with mud. "Wrapped it last night. Pretty dumb, huh? Right hand, left arm . . ."

Taking his hand, she reached into her pack and pulled out her blunt scissors. "This may hurt, but we have to cut you free." As carefully as she could she cut away the bandage and peeled it partially away from his hand. Only by patting water on it could she loosen it enough to get it off. Without hesitation she bathed his hand as soon as it was free, then heaved a little sigh of relief when she saw where the flesh was torn away between the third and fourth metacarpal joints. "Can you move your fingers at all?" she asked.

"Yes, but it hurts like hell. See?"

"Good, Tinker. It doesn't look like it did any serious damage, but it's going to take a while to heal." As she cleaned his wounds and bandaged them, she tried to draw him out again about his background and family, but he was too busy fighting his pain to say much. The process was complicated by the movement of the wagon, and only when she finished did he speak.

"You know what's in that other wagon, Miss Lucy?"

"No, Tinker, I don't."

"Radioactive stuff," he said. "I'm worried, too, because I read once about how that can kill you real slow and awful like. Is that true?"

"I don't know, Tinker, but I can find out." Remembering the decal she had found back at Copper Breaks, she fought to control a shudder as she opened one of the outside pockets of her pack and pulled out her *Taber's*. Flipping to "Radiation" she began reading, then saw the length of the entries and immediately knew that she didn't have enough information. "What exactly is in the other wagon, Tinker? What did you see in there?"

"There are four buckets—each about the size of an ice cream freezer, you know what I mean? Shiny like that, too." When she nodded, he continued. "Anyway, they're sitting in this rack kind of thing that's tied in the center of the wagon. I was layin' next to them most of the night. Had to hook my legs on the rack to keep from bouncin' all over the wagon."

"Were any of the containers open?"

"No."

She smiled and closed her book. "Then I don't think you're in any danger. Now, if you're comfortable, I'm going to leave you for a little while and go see about Mrs. Johnson."

"I'm okay," he said with a weak smile.

"Good. You just rest, and I'll come back and check on you."

He closed his eyes and nodded.

The wagon wasn't going very fast, so after she gathered things into her pack and slung it over one arm, she climbed over the tailgate and jumped to the ground. By walking quickly she could pass that wagon and catch up with the Johnson wagon. One of the things she noticed immediately was that there weren't many braves with the wagons, not nearly as many as the night before. She would have worried about that if she was not far more worried about Tinker.

Taber's didn't spend two and a half pages on something that wasn't important. If Tinker had been exposed to radiation, was he radioactive now? Was she in danger? Could he have contaminated her? If he had, what about Ann? Would she now be a danger to Ann? The only answers she had access to were in her *Taber's*, and she had to know those answers before she came near Ann again.

She pulled herself up on the step at the rear of Ann's wagon and stuck her head in. "How's she doing?" she asked Suzanne quietly when she saw Ann's eyes closed.

"Been resting the whole time—sleeping now."

"Fine. I'm going to walk for a ways and get the kinks out of my legs. You need me I'll be right out here." She stepped off the wagon and pulled *Taber's* out of her pack, then slung the pack into the wagon, letting it rest against the tailgate before she let go of it.

Walking and reading wasn't the easiest thing in the world for her to do, especially when she had to walk fast enough to keep up with the wagons, but this problem was far too important to let that bother her. She read every entry from "Radiation" through "Radiation Accidents" to "Radiation Syndrome" with growing anger and frustration.

If Tinker was right, if the containers had been closed, then the only person who might be affected was himself. Lucy had to assume that was true for the moment, had to assume that she was in no danger and didn't represent a threat to Ann. But why would anyone want radioactive materials? And why would they endanger themselves carrying it across country?

"Watch it, miss," a voice said from over her shoulder.

Looking up she saw the wagons pulling to a halt beside a low metal building with an odd roof. For a long second she didn't realize that the odd roof was actually the top of a train engine on the other side of the building. A quick look around confirmed that they were in Medicine Mound—a town with fifteen little buildings, two silos, and a railroad station.

The station swarmed with braves, some of them loading small crates into a boxcar, others beginning to load the first oxen and wagon on a flatcar under the direction of Max Quentin who stood leering at her. Lucy closed her book and turned to Ann's wagon just as Mike Young directed Max Quentin to the station then walked up to her himself.

"Studying?" he asked with a smile.

"Yes—studying how people die from radiation sickness. What in the name of tribal honor is going on here?"

"Shhh!" he said, putting his hand roughly on her shoulder. "You just see that Miss Ann and her goods get loaded into the second car behind the tender. Soon as we get rolling I'll explain it all to you."

"Rolling? Rolling where?"

"Don't you worry about it." He paused and released her arm. "Look, Miss Lucy, I mean you no harm, and I won't let anyone else harm you, but I don't have time to explain the how-comes and what-fors now. You do what I tell you and you'll be all right. Just get Miss Ann and yourself loaded, and like I promised, we'll talk about it."

"What about Tinker?"

"I'll get him to you—and some hot water, too. We can drain it from the boiler. Anything else?"

Hesitating only for a second she looked straight into his dark brown eyes. "What about the . . . canisters?"

"Don't you worry about them, either. They'll be in the last car with a good guard and a quick release. Now, please, get going. The longer we stay here, the greater the danger."

"I'm going to count on that explanation," she said as she stepped reluctantly toward Ann's wagon, her thoughts more cluttered with worry than ever. Mike Young was lying to her. She was sure of it.

CHAPTER 23

GOODFOX | "It's the best team-of-four and wagon I've got, Father," Louis Eagil said softly, "and I know you probably don't have DalWorth dollars, so I'll sell you the lot for a hundred Nation dollars."

"Pay him," Goodfox said to Nyllan, "and get a receipt—with a good description of oxen, yokes, and wagon. I don't want to be stopped for stealing and not be able to prove we didn't." He turned away from them and walked back toward the little building where they'd spent the night. Rhondasue would take care of the details, and soon enough they could be on their way.

What a joke. On their way in an oxen wagon when they should have been flying into Rhineland. Now they had one hundred fifty miles or more to travel by road through DalWorth, Big Jack, and almost all the way across the fifth militia district of West Texas, carrying an illegal radio, forged safe-conducts, and a satellite controller.

Nothing to it. All it would take was God's direct intervention for the next five or six days.

As he closed the cabin door, he admitted to himself that things weren't quite that bad. At least the woman who had stolen the plane hadn't taken the controller. Apparently she hadn't wanted it, because when they got to the hanger after she had taken off, the controller was still sitting exactly where Bell had left it. Strangely enough, the radio was sitting on top of the controller, and Bell swore it had been in the plane when he went to the outhouse. Goodfox sat down at the table and began putting his pistol back together. Maybe she had just wanted the plane. God knew they were few enough and valuable enough.

Bell, of course, had raged with anger for the rest of the night—raged at Barton Haggerlotten, the field boss whose common-law wife, Dolores del Noches, had stolen the plane, and at Jimmy Jack Haggerlotten, the hanger-boy who hadn't stayed with the plane when he was supposed to, and at Goodfox and Nyllan for letting them talk him into this trip. Only when he started blaming the theft on God had Goodfox intervened.

Didn't do much good, he thought as he screwed the pistol grips into place. Bell had walked off into the night still swearing under his breath, not understanding as Goodfox finally did, that God had left them with the radio and the controller. That was a positive sign Murray Goodfox could neither ignore nor deny, so he accepted it as a gift from God's wisdom.

But there were things he hadn't accepted, things he was still fighting to accept, like the long journey that faced them now and the destruction of his timetable for reunification. God would have to be patient waiting for that acceptance.

After putting the pistol back in his shoulder bag, he pulled out his new map—copied from Louis Eagil's original map, a geodetic topo-map, Eagil had called it, full of details the likes of which Goodfox had rarely seen before except on some of those old originals belonging to the church. It showed the northeast corner of Old Texas from Williams to Texarkana to Wiergate to Eden. The Mexican Sea and Falls Lake along with the expansion of the Red River had been colored in pale blue by hand, and the borders between DalWorth, West Texas, and Commanche were marked with faded pink lines and broken stripes designating the disputed territories.

Goodfox would have loved to have owned such a map, but he had been quite content to be allowed to copy it, tracing as carefully as he could the printed red lines and hand-drawn green lines that marked the roads. The only route worth considering from Marysville to Rhineland was the most direct one—over to Saint Jo on the border, then from Montague going north of Bowie through Gault on one of the green roads to Vashti, and from there to Windthorst. From Windthorst it was a straight shot to the Rhineland Road off of old US-Eighty-two.

Seymour would be the big problem. There was no clean way around it. But maybe they could just pass through like they knew what they were doing and no one would question them. Don't act suspicious, Father Dibole had taught him, and people won't suspect you—always easier taught than practiced, Goodfox had come to learn, but a lesson well worth learning. If he could get Rhondasue to stay calm, they just might make it to Rhineland after all.

The door swung open and Nyllan walked in with an unusual smile on her face. "You got it all figured out?" she asked as soon as she saw what he was doing.

"I have determined our route, if that's what you mean."

"Hot damn," she said as she sat down across from him. "Murray's figured out the road. But what the hell makes you think I'm going with you?"

Her question startled him. "I, uh, well, I had no reason to think otherwise."

"Took me for granted again, didn't you." It wasn't a question, it was a statement.

"Yes . . . I suppose I did. Can you forgive me that?"

"I'll forgive you damn near anything but that," she said, pushing her chair back and standing up again. "It's your worst goddamn trait, you know it?"

"Please, Rhondasue, I didn't mean to—that is, when you agreed to come and help me, I assumed that meant for as long as it took to get the job done."

"You assumed. You assumed. You always assume. Yesterday you assumed I would fix the truck, so there was no reason for you to thank me for it, was there?" Leaning forward with her hands on the back of the chair she answered her own question. "Hell, no. You always assume things about me. Do you remember where all this started with us? 'Come up to the Ozarks with me to see your Uncle H.S.,' you said, 'and help bring peace to the world.' Then it was, 'Help me escape from here, Rhondasue.' Then it was, 'Find us a plane, Rhondasue.' Now it's, 'Find us a wagon and load your gear,' without even being asked."

"Point to Rhondasue," he said with a little smile that felt out of place on his lips. There was a hint of falsity in her voice that bothered him.

"I don't want your goddam points, Murray," she shouted. "I want your sexy body and your brains and your respect. And I want to be asked before you just take off and expect me to follow you into God-knows-what-or-how so that you can become pope of the world."

"That's not what I want, and you know it." Anger vibrated his words. "I only want the establishment of God's kingdom on earth as He directed me to establish it. You, of all people—"

"All right. Can it." She threw up her arms and crossed them in front of her face. "I've heard that hymn before. So you're doing God's work. Well, He didn't ask me to go any further," she said as she lowered her arms and put her hands on her hips, "so I guess I'll just be hanging around here till something interesting comes along."

Goodfox felt suddenly lost. Was she serious? Did she mean it? He couldn't tell. "But why?" he finally managed to ask. "You know I need you, and you certainly know that I want you, so—"

"How? How do I know those things?"

"All the time . . . I show you those things all the time."

She snorted and straightened her body, folding her arms over her breasts. "Your body does, but your mouth doesn't."

His face flushed and he wished he could hide his reaction. "Please, Rhondasue, don't do this to me. I need you. I really do. And I want you to come with me . . . not just for your body, and not just for your brains . . . for all of you. I need your laughter, too, and your—"

"You don't need my cynicism, you said."

"That's different. What I meant was that I—"

"No, it's not. I been telling you and telling you, but you just don't listen, Murray. I come as a package. You can't just take the parts you like and then complain about the rest of me. That stinks, and I won't put up with it." Suddenly she swung a leg over the chair and sat down, pulling it up close to the table and leaning forward.

"You got to take all of me, Murray—all of me or none of me. That's the way it works. Or it doesn't work. But there's no way I'm going to put up with halvesies. Not any more. You want me, you take me as I come. You quit bitching about me all the time. And you stop naming me as the one who dragged you into sin."

"What?"

"I'm not always asleep when you pray, you know. Shouldn't do it aloud like that—'specially when you're blaming me right after screwing me. I didn't pull you across any line you weren't already rushing across on your own, so I ain't going to play the devil in your prayers. You want to blame somebody, blame the guy who started it all. Blame yourself."

Goodfox took in a long, ragged breath and slowly let it out in a trembling sigh. Panic edged into a corner of his consciousness. His whole body trembled and as he clutched the table, it, too, trembled as the earth itself shook in sympathy. Then it stopped, but he didn't. His breaths became deeper and more frantic. Silent prayers filled his head in cadences as ragged as his breathing.

"Goddammit, Murray," Nyllan said, pushing away from him. "You hyperventilate on me again, and I swear you'll never see my ass again, much less kiss it."

He locked his elbows and clenched his teeth, fighting for control, his prayers never stopping, his mind frantically searching for something to hang onto.

Nyllan stood up. "I mean it, Murray. Even reunion isn't—"

"Wait," he managed to say. "Wait. . . . Please?" She was the key. She was the answer. He couldn't let her go. He had to take control. "Please? Please?"

Slowly she sat back down and put her hands over his, a puzzled look filling her face. "You really do need me, don't you?" she asked.

"Yes," he hissed, the trembling in his muscles slowly coming under control, but not the trembling in his heart. "I do."

She laughed too quickly and unexpectedly. "I now pronounce us wretch and wench. Let the devil and the U.S. beware."

Goodfox didn't understand the joke, but he laughed too, a laugh full of strain on the edge of tears.

"Come on," she said, slapping his arm. "We've got to get going while we can make some distance today."

"Right. You're right." He shook his head quickly trying to clear his thoughts and the tears from his eyes. "We do have to get going." He stood as she did, then stepped around the chair into her waiting arms.

Suddenly they were both crying softly and holding each other, Goodfox not sure why, or what it meant, but understanding that something very important had happened to them here, knowing that God had given him another sign that he couldn't ignore. If he was going to accomplish God's ends, he would have to do it with Rhondasue by his side as his helpmeet and his comfort, for God had said, *It is not good that man should be alone. I will provide a helpmeet for him that together they may serve.*

Those words came so automatically to his thoughts that it took a full second or two before he acknowledged that they were from the marriage ceremony. Was that God's message? That he should marry Rhondasue?

He hugged her more fully, holding her head against his shoulder as he stroked her hair, feeling joy and confusion and full of questions, praying for patience and answers, fearing an understanding that would deny her to him.

"We really do have to get going," she said.

"I know. I know." Easing her away from him he kissed her forehead, then her nose and cheeks, then her mouth—softly, carefully, joyously, to a lingering conclusion.

"God, I hate you, Murray Goodfox," she said as she snuggled her head into his shoulder.

"Why?"

"Because I can't have all of you."

"Only God has all of—"

"Shhh." She laid a finger over his lips. "Talk to me about God when we're on the road. Not now."

"For everything there is a season."

She laughed softly. "Couldn't resist, could you?"

"Bad habit."

"That's what you are, all right, a bad habit," she said with a smile as she pushed herself out of his arms. "Now get your junk together, then come help me load everything. Old Man Eagil and the Haggerlotten boy put the controller in the wagon, but they left the rest of it to us."

"Thanks."

"For what?" she asked as she picked up her leather duffel bag and the yucca-cloth ammunition pouch.

"Just thanks," he answered. "I'll be ready in a couple of minutes. Did Eagil think he could find us a rifle?"

"A thirty-thirty with a three-by scope. Threw it in with ninety rounds for another seventy-five bucks. Claimed he killed a deer with it once at three hundred yards."

"Yeah," Murray said with a chuckle as he carefully refolded the map, "and his mother killed a bear with her kitchen knife."

She laughed and then walked out the door. Goodfox paused to watch her go with a prayer of thanks to God for bringing her to him and another beseeching His protection on the trip they were about to take in His name.

CHAPTER 24

ONE | "You," Kendrick Johnson said wearily as he opened his eyes.

Cody stared down at him, seeing how pale he looked under his beard, seeing the bloodstained bandages on his arms and one leg, and hating him all the same. "Where's Ann?"

Johnson started to laugh, then coughed violently. "Gone," he said as the coughing eased off. "Gone."

"Gone where? With the rest of your group?" He felt the rage trembling inside him and fought to keep it under control.

"May I answer that?" a voice behind him asked.

"Gone where?" Cody repeated, his eyes never leaving Johnson.

"With the Seneca tonkaweya," the voice said.

Cody turned around very slowly and glared at the blue-eyed man sitting with the rest of the Nates under the watchful barrel of Kolmer's carbine. Beyond them Brisas was sitting beside Melindo, who looked just awful in her torn and bloody uniform. "What the hell's that mean?"

"With their people. I am Elroy Sashahunder, leader of this

group, the Wyandot tonkaweya. The other tonkaweya is led
by—"

"Dammit! What the hell's a tonkaweya?" Cody tried to hold
his voice steady, but it was all he could do to keep from shooting
this man. Jessup lay dead out in the brush. Melindo had a
sucking chest wound and wouldn't live long if a medic didn't get
to her, and this son-of-a-bitch was talking nonsense.

"It's a group," Sashahunder said quickly, "like a clan or
something to you people. Tonkaweya just means people who stay
together."

"And your clan is called what?"

"Wyandot. We are from the Ardmore Council of Five—"

"I don't give a slow shit if you're from the gates of hell,"
Cody said, his voice shaking even as he fought to keep it steady.
"I want to know what happened to Ann Cody."

An indecipherable look crossed Sashahunder's face, and he
glanced at Johnson before he spoke. "The Ann we had with us
called herself Ann Johnson."

Cody spun back around and brought the barrel of his carbine
to within an inch of Johnson's face. "You miserable, goddamn—"

"It's not what you think," Johnson said, his voice strangely
unafraid. "but you kill me if you have to."

"Back off, Cody. Killing him won't do no one no good."

"Stay out of this, Ed. It's got nothing to do with—"

"He's right," Brisas added. "Killing him isn't going to bring
your wife back, or Jessup back, or save Donna."

"I'm not going to kill him. I'm just going to blow little pieces
away until he tells me where Ann is." Cody pushed the muzzle of
his carbine against the side of Johnson's nose. All the hatred he
felt for this man seemed centered in his trigger finger. All he had
to do was squeeze just a little more, put a bit more pressure on
the trigger, just enough to release part of that hate and—

"Kendrick told you all we know," Sashahunder said. "They
took all the mules, the best of the oxen, and left—headed east—
to Medicine Mound, we think."

The Nate's words touched something in Cody and slowly he
stepped back from Kendrick Johnson and let the muzzle of his
carbine drop slightly. Then he pulled the trigger.

Mud spattered all over Johnson's face and chest. His eyes
filled with fear.

Cody laughed, pleased with the ugly joke. But something

inside him cut the laugh off abruptly, like it hadn't even been his and somebody had snatched it from him. Let Kendrick sweat it for a while, he thought. "Juanita, where's the radio?"

"Out there, Cody, but it's busted."

"Get it anyway. Maybe you can fix it."

"Cody, I don't think . . ."

He turned to look at her as she stood up and saw the disapproval in her expression, but his head was filled with thoughts of Ann and the baby—and Melindo lying there wounded because— "Look, Juanita, either we make the radio work and call for help, or you get to run all the way to Quanah to get help for us. Which will it be?" He tried to smile at her, but his face wouldn't cooperate.

"Okay, Cody, I'll get it. Let me take a couple of these Nates and bring Jessup in, too."

Cody didn't want to see Roland's body, but he couldn't say no. Already the buzzards were circling under the low, grey clouds. Roland deserved better than that. "Do it," he said, "but either of your helpers does anything stupid, you shoot them first and worry 'bout it later."

"Gotcha. You and you," she said, pointing her carbine to pick them out, "on your feet."

He watched as she made the Nates tie their right legs to the ends of a four-foot piece of yucca rope off one of the wagons, then herded them lockstep out of the camp. Deep in his gut he knew she would be all right, but he was worried about her anyway. Maybe he should have sent Ed with her and stood guard over these Nates himself. Or maybe he—

Stop! a voice in his head shouted. No more blaming. No more guilt. Not today. Not now. No. No more.

"All right, Sashahunder," he said, walking over beside Kolmer, "you say you're the leader of this group. Suppose you tell me what you all are doing in the Republic."

"I cannot do that."

"You damn well can—or you can die. Might die anyways, seeing as how we shoot murderers in this country. But if you tell me where my wife is and what you were after and what the rest of your group is up to, headquarters just might get a little soft and let you live."

"I cannot tell you or anyone. It's a matter of honor." His face was set firmly around his narrow blue eyes.

"Then you'll die a dishonorable death in front of a firing squad." Cody shook his head. "God, I hate you bastards."

The long silence between them was filled with the chirping of birds and the rustle of the wind through the trees. The damp earth smelled like rotting flesh, and Cody cringed inside, wishing he was somewhere else—anywhere else.

"There is something I can tell you," Sashahunder said, "only because they have . . . Mike Young, the leader of the Seneca—the other group—has broken faith with our . . . with what we're supposed to do."

"So spit it out."

"It is very hard."

"Harder than dying?"

TWO | The train was traveling slowly southward as Lucy finished redressing Tinker's wounds in a small room at the end of the car Young had assigned him to. At least Mike Young had kept his word about the hot water. Two braves had brought her three gallons of it in a stoneware crock with a spigot. Young had also come up with a yucca box of bandages, a bottle of antiseptic solution with a spray top, and some antifungal cream, neither of which she had ever seen or used, but she recognized the markings of the Wewoka Medical Company stamped on all of them, and felt no hesitancy about using them.

"Am I going to be okay, Miss Lucy?"

"I don't know," she answered honestly. "Your wounds won't kill you, but I've got no guess about the other." Forcing herself to keep looking at his troubled face, she continued, "I just don't have any way to tell, Tinker. If those containers you lay next to were sealed properly, and if they're the right kind of containers, then you've got nothing to worry about. But I don't know how to answer those questions."

"You like rockin' country?" he asked unexpectedly.

It took her a moment to understand what he was saying. "Yes, I do, but I don't get to hear much of it. The closest station that plays it is in DalWorth, and we can't pick it up very well where I live."

"Who do you like best?"

"The Bridgeport Ramblers, Paradise Island, and the Dixie Shakers. There're some songs by Alan Parker that I like, too, like 'Blue Creek Revival' and 'Woman of the Plains.'"

He smiled. "If you like Alan Parker, you'd really like Doyle

Stout and Amy Rogers. They do, like, real hard ballads and real fast country-joes—the kind you can polka to."

"Do you polka?" For some reason she was surprised and at the same time felt closer to him.

"You bet. My momma taught me when I was a kid. Why, given the chance, I could polka your legs off, lady."

Lucy laughed as she stood up. "That I'd like to see you do, Tinker Oberly, so you work on resting right now, and some day maybe you'll get a chance to live up to your words."

"Live up to what words?" Mike Young asked from the open doorway.

"A promise to dance," she said, turning to face him. "And speaking of promises . . ."

"I promised you some answers, didn't I? Well, Miss Lucy, you follow me. Tinker, you take care of yourself."

She followed him out of the little room and down a narrow corridor toward the front of the car, matching her steps to the gentle rocking of the train. Lucy paused long enough by the door of Ann's room to see that she was sleeping, or at least resting, and Suzanne was crocheting something that looked like a baby's cap.

"In here," Mike Young said, indicating a room barely large enough for a small, folding desk and three chairs.

Instinctively she took the chair with its back to the front of the train. "I want the truth," she said quietly as he sat down across from her.

"The truth is relative. I thought every healer knew that."

Her back straightened. "In other words, you're not going—"

"I'm going to tell you what I can," he said barely loud enough to be heard over the clack of the wheels, "then I'll let you decide what the truth is. You know the Nimenim?"

"Yes," she said, leaning forward in spite of herself.

"I am Nimenim. We are true believers who wish to prepare the world for the Second Coming. *But the way of the cross is hard and crowded by the unbelievers*, as Father Goodfox has told us. Do you understand what that means?"

She understood more than she realized, understood that she was in the hands of fanatics—and suddenly knew she had overestimated the goodness necessary for people to see themselves as instruments of God. "It means," she said carefully, "that you are on some kind of holy mission. Is that correct?"

His face was radiant with enthusiasm and his dark eyes narrowed in a pleased squint. "It is. We are part of the great plan

that will reunite the states. That is the first step toward building
an earthly home worthy of the Rapture."

"What does that have to do with the here and now?"

"Ah, that I cannot tell you, Miss Lucy, except to say that the
plan is beginning and soon there will be a sign from Heaven to
acknowledge His blesssing."

"And that radioactive stuff you have back there?"

"That will be part of God's punishment for the unbelievers,
for He said that when the time came, many men would die of the
water because it was made bitter."

She didn't know exactly what he meant, but she knew she
was frightened when one of Mishla's favorite verses from the
Bible flashed into her mind. "*And the foundations of the earth
will tremble and the earth be utterly broken and rent asunder.
Isaiah,*" she said in reply to his startled expression. "Is that what
you're going to do? Blow up the world?"

"No," he answered quickly. "We have no such intentions."

"Then what in God's name are you going to do with that
nuclear abomination you're dragging around the countryside?"

He looked at her for a long moment, and when he finally
spoke, the horror of his words belied the look of serenity on his
face. "Poison the waters of the unbelievers."

THREE | "That must be the Saint Jo Road," Nyllan
said as she studied the map.

Goodfox pulled firmly on the reins that ran to rings in the
lead oxens' noses, and they responded with a slow turn to the
right onto the packed gravel road. "How far from here?"

"Twelve stat-miles. If you keep the oxen moving, and the
road stays good, we can probably make it right before nightfall."

"No. We'll camp this side of Saint Jo and cross the border in
the morning. If the DalWorth Border Police are like the ones out
of Bowie, they're mean, ugly, and trigger-ready. I don't want to
risk coming up on them at night. Besides, in all this planning,
we never did decide what we were going to say to them."

She laughed. "You just put your cassock on and the words
will come to you. Tell them you're on a pilgrimage to take me to a
nunnery and to visit your old seminary."

"One look at you and they'd know better."

"You'd be surprised, Murray. I can look real plain and

frumpy if I have to. You've got a bigger problem with the controller and the radio. Which reminds me, aren't you scheduled to make a broadcast tonight?"

He snorted. "Yes. From Rhineland, where I've got a real antenna and fifty thousand watts of AM power. Hard to reach out with our little shortwave."

"You haven't even tried," she said disapprovingly.

"Yes, I did," he said. "Somebody took the batteries."

"Why didn't you tell me? We could have asked Eagil if he could get us—"

"I did. While you were in the outhouse. He said they'd been asking for six-volters like that for the past three months. Probably why Dolores stole them and not the radio. Or maybe Bell stole them in a fit of childish spite. Who knows? God's will be done."

"You're the most hot-and-cold man I've ever known. First you scream and rage, and then? God's will be done. If it's God's will be done, why bother with the screaming?"

He frowned. "Because it's God's way of reminding me how weak a vessel I am."

"Bullshit. It's because you're human just like the rest of us and you don't need God to remind you of that. You've got me."

"That's the holy truth,' he said bitterly. "I can depend on you to keep track of my failings for me."

"So stop the wagon and let me off if I'm too hard on you. They got jobs for people like me in DalWorth."

"Oh, you'd like that, working regular hours for some company that didn't care about anything but how much work you put out for them. Boy, you'd feel right at home there."

"Don't be so damn sarcastic. I could do that kind of work."

He shook his head. "You could no more work for one of those communications companies or somebody like Temco-Texas than I could go back to being a simple parish priest."

Nyllan laughed suddenly and encircled his right arm with hers. "That'll be the day, when you're a simple anything."

"So you think you'll stay for the ride?"

"Hell, yes. Where else could I find comfort like this with a man as crazy as . . . Murray, what's that up ahead?"

He stared, using the wide brim of his hat to shield his eyes from the glare, and saw something coming toward them. "I don't know," he said as he pulled the oxen to a halt. "Better get the guns out."

CHAPTER 25

ONE | "What do you mean, you don't know? You were lugging radioactive plutonium around in the back of a wagon and you don't know what your people were going to do with it? That's the stupidest thing I've ever heard."

"It's true," Sashahunder said from his seat beside Johnson. "Kendrick stole it and told our chief. We were just supposed to help Kendrick take it back to the Nation. Only our chiefs know what was to be done with it."

"So what happened?"

Sashahunder tried to explain the rift, but the politics of it all made no sense to Cody and he finally told the Nate just to shut up. He didn't understand and he didn't want to hear any more. All he understood was that Johnson was weaving in and out of consciousness and was of no use to him, and that Ann was with the other group of Nates, and he was powerless for the moment to chase after them. And the anger. He understood how very angry he was.

When Brisas came back with the radio and the Nates carrying Jessup's body, Cody set her to work trying to salvage the radio, and the Nates to digging four new graves—three for the Nates, one for Jessup—beside five graves the Nates had filled the day before. He would just as soon have shot the Nates and gone on, but even if they were dead, he still couldn't leave Melindo behind, so there was nothing to do but put up with all of it and try, try to control the anger that churned inside of him.

The wet ground made each shovelful doubly heavy, and five hours later when the Nates finished burying their own and Jessup, the eastern sky had darkened under the clouds. "Juanita," Cody called, "you want to leave that for a minute? I'm going to say a few things about Roland."

Brisas left the radio, picked up her carbine, and walked over to stand beside Kolmer so that the Nates were between them and the grave.

Suddenly Cody realized that he had no idea what to say, but he was determined to do better by Roland than they had by

Shelia Emery. "You Nates all kneel down and bow your heads," he said, "'cause I'm about to pray and I don't want a one of you looking anywheres but down."

After they were all on their knees with their heads bowed, he nodded to Kolmer and Brisas who kept their heads up, then continued. "We're gathered here like this because Roland Jessup was a good man, deserving of our respect. He was a good tracker, a good friend, and a fair hand at poker. I'm going to miss him, and I 'spect others are, too. You know I don't ask for much," he said, turning his face toward heaven, "but I do ask that You take Roland into Your care. . . . And these Nates, too, I guess. Amen."

"Amen," the Nates and Kolmer and Brisas all said at once.

"Okay, that's it. You Nates stay right where you are. Juanita, how you coming with the radio?"

"I think we're going to be able to broadcast, Cody, but we ain't going to receive *nada*."

"Broadcast, then. Tell whoever you can what our problem is." She turned back toward the wagons and he looked at the Nates. "Sashahunder? I need something from you."

"What?"

"Food—and a promise that you— Oh, hell, never mind that. Here's the deal. You'll tie yourselves on short ropes. If any of you try to escape, we'll kill all of you. Understand?"

Sashahunder hesitated. "Sergeant Cody, you can hardly expect us to agree—"

"Do you understand or not? Yes or no?"

"Yes, but that doesn't mean that—"

"Shut up. It means that if any one of you tries to escape, we'll kill the rest of you. You don't have to like it or agree to it, you just have to understand how it works. Got it?"

Again Sashahunder hesitated.

"Ed, kill one of these bastards so's they'll understand."

Kolmer got an ugly smile on his face, brought his carbine to his shoulder, and sighted down on the closest man.

"Dammit, don't," Sashahunder said. "We understand."

Cody kept his face expressionless. "Good. Now which two of you are going to cook us some supper?"

TWO | The train was still rolling slowly southward as Lucy and Ann ate the thick soup one of the braves had brought for them. Lucy couldn't get her mind off of what Mike Young had said. They were going to poison the water with their radioactive material.

Poison the water!

The idea was so horribly inhuman she had no way to cope with it. *Taber's* might not tell her exactly how that would work, but from what *Taber's* did say, she knew the effects could only be devastating. She'd read a yellowed copy of *Hiroshima* in the Childress School and it had given her nightmares so bad that she'd blocked that memory until she read *Taber's* entries. But now she had no idea of what she could do or how she was going to cope with this awfulness.

The only thing she was sure of was that she had to escape as soon after the birth of Ann's baby as possible. "How are you feeling? Any cramping?"

"You sound almost hopeful."

"Sorry," Lucy said with a shake of her head. "I didn't mean for it to sound that way, but I've got to get out of here, Ann. I've got to warn people what this tonkaweya is going to do, and I can't leave you until after the baby's born."

"You can leave any time you please. Lots of babies have been born without help before now, and lots more will be born the same way after."

"That's not the point. Once I accept a duty, I cannot just walk away from it because its timing doesn't suit my plans."

"Crock. Go if you need to. I sure won't hold it against you. Suzanne can help when the time—"

"No. Suzanne isn't qualified." Lucy paused. "Do you know what this tonkaweya is carrying?"

Ann looked puzzled. "What do you mean?"

"I *mean* did you know that one of the wagons had a load of radioactive material, and now that stuff's on the train, and, oh, never mind. It's not your problem." Why am I telling her this? she asked herself.

"Radioactive? But why? That is . . . my baby?"

Lucy saw the distressed look on Ann's face and knew that her

patient didn't know anything about the radioactive cargo. "I
don't think you or the baby are in any danger, yet," she said,
coaxing all the reassurance she could into her voice, "but maybe
you should plan to come with me as soon after the baby's—no,
that won't work. We don't have that much time." She pulled her
pack up from the floor and took out her map. "Ann, I need your
help."

"With what?"

"This map only shows one set of tracks, from Medicine
Mound south almost to Crowell where it branches, the Sante Fe
south toward Knox City, and the Crowell-and-Weatherford
southeast to Seymour. The train's going to have to slow down,
maybe even stop sometime before Crowell or in Crowell. When it
does, you and I are getting off. Please?"

Ann's face was a mask of unreadable emotions. "All right,"
she said finally, "but you have to do something for me, too."

"What?"

"You have to promise to take care of my baby if . . . if
something happens to me."

"Nothing's going to happen to—"

"Promise! And I don't mean give it to someone else. I mean
you, you take care of it."

For a moment Lucy hesitated, suddenly realizing what she
was agreeing to. "What about Kendrick? What if he comes to
claim—"

"Kendrick's got no right to my baby."

"But as the father . . ."

"He's not the father. If its father comes and wants the baby,
that's okay."

Lucy waited, surprised to hear Ann say for sure that Johnson
wasn't the father of her baby . . . except Ann had . . .
"Who is the father, so I'll know if he comes?"

"His name's Jeremiah Cody, and he's a good man, and God
knows why I let Kendrick take me away from him"—tears
streamed down her face—"or how I could have hurt him the way
I did when he wasn't nothing but good to me, or why . . ." Her
words trailed off into a shuddering sob.

Moving across the small compartment to sit beside her, Lucy
was more confused about Ann's relationships than ever. Had
Johnson swept her off her feet with some wild romantic notion, or
had he forced her in some way to join him? Ann cried steadily, as
though she had been storing these tears, holding back these

emotions until she could hold them no longer. Lucy could do no more to help her than offer the comforting shelter of her arms and body as a refuge for Ann's naked release of pain, rocking her gently in time with the rocking of the train.

When Ann's crying began to slow down, Lucy gave her a bandana and Ann gratefully wiped her face and blew her nose in it several times before she regained control of herself. "Forgive me for that," she said softly.

"There is nothing to forgive. There is nothing about crying that requires forgiveness. If anything, I should apologize for causing you pain."

After blowing her nose again, Ann looked up at Lucy. "There's something you ought to know, but I'm not sure that it makes any difference, now. You see, Kendrick is my brother, and I owed him a lot—more than I could ever repay—so when he told me I had to leave Jeremy and come with him, I—I—I just didn't see where I had a choice."

"I don't understand. How could you owe your brother more than you owed your husband?"

Ann turned her face away and looked out the window at the fading light in the west. "When we were barely teenagers," she said in a small, steady voice, "my stepfather raped me and tried to choke me to death because I wouldn't promise not to tell anyone. Kendrick heard me screaming, and broke in and beat him up and he died, my stepfather. He died."

She paused again, chewing on her lower lip, staring without focus. "You see, Kendrick's not my real brother, even though I've always thought of him like he was. He's actually my stepbrother." With a slow, almost mechanical blink, she turned from the window and looked straight at Lucy. "He killed his own father to save my life. How could I owe anyone more than that?"

Lucy didn't know what to say, but deep in her gut she understood a little more about Ann and Kendrick Johnson. Yet, she was sure there was still more to it than Ann had told her, and it all made her more determined to get Ann out of this mess.

"Ann, listen to me," she said softly. "Mike Young told me that he and the rest of this tonkaweya are hooked up some way with that renegade priest, Murray Goodfox. Young told me point-blank that they were planning to poison the water somewhere with that radioactive stuff they're carrying. You and I have to get off this train, then I have to find the local military commander or the sheriff, or someone, and warn him. God knows how many people will die if this tonkaweya isn't stopped."

"And God knows you won't stop us," Young's voice said from the doorway.

THREE | The approaching vehicle was a pickup truck that slowed and almost seemed to stop when it got within a mile of them.

"Guns ready," Nyllan said.

Goodfox stuck his pistol in his belt and pulled his coat over it, hating the thought of having to use it, but recognizing in himself the excited tension of anticipation that told him he would use it if he had to. As he watched the truck approach, he wondered again if there was some deeper significance in the events of the past two days than he had so far recognized. Surely God had reason for allowing those events, and even though Goodfox knew he would never understand even a fraction of God's reason, he also knew there was holy merit in searching for that meaning.

From the time Nyllan had spotted the vehicle until the truck came to a slow stop beside them, almost ten minutes had passed. The driver, a red-bearded man with long shaggy hair, looked up at Goodfox. "You two taking that wagon to Saint Jo?"

"Might be," Goodfox said, knowing that Nyllan had her pistol under the blanket in her lap pointed at the man.

"That's the only town this road goes to," the man said with a grin. "Couldn't interest you in a six-volt radio battery or two, could I?"

Goodfox fought to control his face. "You have some for sale?"

The man laughed. "That I do, Father. Old man Eagil swore it really was you, but I had to hear your voice for myself to believe it."

"You talked to Mr. Eagil?" Nyllan said.

"Indeed I did. I got a place 'bout three miles this side of Saint Jo and he called me on the radio. Said you would be heading this way but wasn't sure you'd take this road like he told you to, so I thought I'd better come take a look while there was still some good light left, 'cause to tell you the truth, Eagil's been known to exaggerate the truth every once and again and I really didn't expect to find the famous Father Goodfox coming down my road."

Once the man got started, Goodfox wasn't sure he would ever stop his run-on explanation, but when he did, Goodfox asked, "Do you really have batteries for sale?"

"For you, Father, they're free. Come on to my place. There's stew on the stove, a warm fire burning, and a boosted antenna you can hook your radio up to."

"You are one of the faithful?"

"The wife and me listen to you every week. We ain't Nimenim you understand," the man said with a laugh, "but we sure are believers in what you say. Name's Varginik A. Shearina—and don't ask where I got a name like that. Folks gave it to me and then died, and I was stuck with it, but it ain't so bad, because it gets conversations going with people, and pretty soon when we get to know each other they all call me Vargin, which I'd be pleased if you would, Father—and you, too, of course, Miss . . ."

"Nyllan, but my friends call me Rhondasue."

"Fair enough, Miss Rhondasue," Vargin said with a quick glance from her to Goodfox. "How about it, Father? Will you honor us by staying at our place and making your broadcast from there?"

"We would be pleased," Goodfox said, automatically adding a prayer of thanks. God had again provided.

"Then tell you what, Father. You just follow this road about four miles—you ought to make it inside an hour—until you get to an open gate chained to post oak on your right. Turn in and after you pull through the trees you'll be able to see the house. Wife and I will be waiting for you there."

"God's blessings on you." Goodfox leaned out and signed the cross above Vargin's face. "We look forward to sharing your meal and meeting your family."

"See you later," Vargin called as he backed the truck in a half-circle. Then he sped off down the road.

"Something's wrong about this," Nyllan said.

"What? What do you mean?"

"I mean I've this feeling," she said, "and my feeling is that there's something wrong about this man and his invitation."

"So what do you suggest?" Goodfox asked, only aware of the sarcasm in his voice as he spoke. "Should we turn around and go back because you have this *feeling*?"

"Shit, I don't care, Murray. Forward, or back, what does it matter? But for the sake of reunion, let's keep our eyes and ears open from here on down the road. Maybe I'm just jumpy . . . and maybe not."

Goodfox slapped the oxen with the reins and they started up again, but whatever good feeling he had about Vargin had been swept aside by Nyllan's feeling. Even if she was wrong, she was right. They couldn't be too careful.

———

———

. . . will come when God will offer us the great opportunity of rebuilding a nation in His name as the new United States of America. And when that day comes, do not let Him catch you asleep, or fearful, or claiming excuses why you cannot serve His cause.

For when that day comes you must choose either to serve God, or to serve Satan.

When that day comes you must either take up the banner of righteousness, or deliver yourself into the hands of Satan.

For on "that day shall this song be sung in the land; Open ye the gates, that the righteous nation which keepeth the truth may enter in," and America shall once again be a righteous nation that does not forsake the ordinance of God.

Have faith, my friends, and prepare yourselves now for the day of glory to come. Listen to these radio messages—not to hear me, Father Goodfox. No. Listen for the power of God using my voice to enter each and every heart that listens for Him and welcomes Him into . . .

CHAPTER 26

ONE | The long evening and most of Cody's night passed in misery. Once each hour as he sat by Donna Melindo, he broadcast his distress call for five seemingly endless minutes, hoping against the darkness that Foard or Hardeman or Wilbarger Stations would receive his signal and send out a chopper to pick Melindo up and tell him what to do with the Nate prisoners.

During each intervening hour, he hovered beside her and reviewed again and again his actions leading up to the skirmish that had so severely wounded her and cost Roland his life. He was sure there were a hundred things he could and should have done differently that would have spared them. Yet no matter what alternatives occupied his thoughts, he couldn't quite convince himself that they would have made any difference.

Brisas and Kolmer both offered to make the radio calls during their watches, both of them assuring him that he had done all he could and the Nates couldn't escape, neither of them able to persuade him to give up the radio or get some rest.

Cody knew what he was doing was stupid. There was no sense and no purpose in putting himself through this torture of second-guessing, but no matter how many times he tried to think about something else, his mind snapped back to the solid history of his failures and clung there like a hound on a coon's neck, refusing to free him from his guilt.

At three, when Brisas was taking the last watch, fatigue finally made the decision Cody had been unable to make on his own, and he turned the radio and Melindo and the Nates over to Brisas, then stretched out on his poncho under the wagon.

Persistent waves of tiny quakes jerked him around the edges of sleep, nagging his thoughts in and out of consciousness. A series of shapeless monsters pursued and punished distorted images of himself for sins he knew he had committed but could not remember. In his lucid moments he tried counting by thousands—one thousand, two thousand, three thousand—hoping to fall back into sleep before he reached ten thousand, but instead, being dragged off by a new image somewhere between three and seven, until at last Kolmer shook him gently and said, "Light's coming, Cody."

Slowly he climbed out from under the wagon and stretched. Had he slept? He didn't know, nor did he really care. His body ached from his ankles to his head. His nose was clogged, and his throat was raw, but suddenly none of that mattered. From the south he heard the sound of an approaching helicopter.

"Flashlights!" Cody shouted as he spun around and started digging through his pack.

In a minute he and Brisas and Kolmer were shining their flashlights up into the grey morning sky. They could see the searchlight of the helicopter as it turned east too soon to see them.

"Damn!" Kolmer said.

Cody frantically blinked his light at the chopper, forgetting about codes, wanting only to attract the chopper's attention. Slowly it circled back to the north, then seemed to head straight for them before it turned toward the west.

"We're here!" Cody shouted even as a familiar sound clicked behind him. Instinct made him turn in time to see Kendrick Johnson rising on one elbow from his pallet, a pistol in his shaking hand.

Time hung motionless between them. Then a blur fell in front of Johnson as the gun fired harmlessly into the mud. It was Sashahunder—hands still bound behind him—now lying atop Kendrick Johnson.

Kolmer had his carbine to his shoulder.

"No," Cody commanded. "He saved us." He charged to the pallet and ripped the revolver from Johnson's hand, throwing it back toward Kolmer and Brisas. Then he helped Sashahunder to his feet "Why? Why'd you do that?" he asked as he wiped the mud off Sashahunder's face.

"Honor. There is none in shooting someone in the back."

"Even an enemy?"

"Even an enemy, Sergeant Cody."

"Well, thanks. I'm still not sure I understand, but we're all certainly grateful, and I'm sure headquarters will—"

"It's coming, Cody!" Brisas shouted.

He turned and saw that the chopper was now on a straight bearing to where they all stood. The clearing in the center of the camp might be big enough for the chopper to land if— "Get back! Everyone get back!"

The pilot never attempted to land. He brought the chopper into a hover fifty feet above them and moments later two troopers rappelled down to the ground. One of them started toward Johnson as soon as he was down.

"No! There!" Cody pointed to Melindo under the poncho-curtained wagon. He didn't care if Johnson died before the medic could tend his wounds. Just save Melindo, he thought.

The second trooper, a sergeant, came up and gave him a quick salute as the chopper moved up and away. "Lieutenant Cody?"

Without thinking he returned the salute and corrected him. "It's *Sergeant* Cody."

"Not according to these, sir. I'm Sergeant Goldstein and these are orders from Lubbock for Lieutenant Cody."

Cody accepted the yucca-cloth packet the trooper handed

him and opened it quickly. It contained four pieces of paper. The first was an order promoting him to First Lieutenant. The second directed him to proceed by chopper to Crowell, there to meet a train in pursuit of the Nates. The third charged him for a small Geiger counter and a new radio, one of the new PRC-100's with half the weight and four times the range as their old PRC-25. The fourth piece of paper was folded, sealed, and stamped, *TOP SECRET: For Your Eyes Only. Destroy after reading.*

TWO | Mike Young had heard what they were talking about and had laughed at them. Then he had immediately locked them in their compartment.

The train rolled all night without stopping. Lucy quickly jimmied the crude lock, then she and Ann took turns staying awake, listening for telltale signs that the train was slowing down. It stopped three times, but there were always people in the corridor outside their compartment. It was rolling again by the time the sky began to brighten and actually seemed to be going faster than it had all night.

"It has to slow down when it gets to Crowell," Lucy said. "When it does, I'll jump first, then I can run beside the train and you can swing down to me." It sounded good, but Lucy had never done anything like that before and wasn't at all sure how it would work.

Even as Ann agreed, the train increased its speed and was soon rolling into the northern outskirts of Crowell through the grey light of dawn far too fast for even Lucy to jump, much less for the pregnant Ann to follow her. They both cried when they realized what was happening, but once through Crowell, it was Ann who first sensed that the train was quickly slowing.

"Get ready to jump," Ann said, forcing Lucy to her feet, "as soon as you have the chance. You may not get another."

"But Ann!"

"Do it, Lucy, please? for me and my baby? If they've got that radioactive stuff like you said, somebody has to do something to stop them."

Lucy knew Ann was right. Someone did have to stop Young and his renegades, and she couldn't do it herself. She didn't even know what to do. But she did know that something very basic had changed in her these past few days—something she couldn't quite put in words, but that she felt down inside just as surely as Ann felt her baby.

In the midst of all this turmoil Lucy was discovering a new strength within herself. How long had it been since she'd thought about Mishla? Longer than at any other time in her life. Whatever this thing was, it encouraged her to act on her own in a way that she had never considered before.

"All right, Ann. I'll do it. My prayers stay with you."

"And mine go with you."

They hugged briefly, then Lucy closed her pack tightly and held it under her cloak as she peered into the aisle. "Bye," she whispered as she stepped out of the compartment. Ten short steps took her to the door at the end of the car. The platform between cars was empty. The last of Crowell's buildings was already slipping away by the time the train slowed enough for Lucy to jump.

With only the slightest hesitation she stepped onto the platform and launched herself into the tall grass beside the tracks. Instinct made her roll when she landed. Fear made her lay still when she stopped rolling—fear that she might have been seen, and fear that she had broken every bone in her body.

The rest of the train passed her and kept rolling south, and she prayed quietly that she wouldn't be missed, or if she was, that Young wouldn't send someone back for her. The odds were pretty good, she thought, but she wasn't willing to risk being seen until the sounds of the train faded into the distance. Only then did she try to move, first her arms, then her legs until she was sitting up.

She couldn't see more than fifteen feet through the grass, so Lucy forced herself to her hands and knees, and then, shakily, to her feet.

Looking down the track, it took her a moment to realize what she was seeing—two braves, less than a mile away, pumping a handcar north toward her. One of them waved.

Instinctively she felt for her gun, then pulled it out and assured herself that it was ready. She picked up her pack and put it on under her cloak. There was little chance she could outrun the braves, but Lucy intended to be as close to Crowell as possible before they got within range, and then she was going to make a lot of noise to rouse local curiosity.

With great determination she climbed up to the roadbed and began hurrying north as quickly as she could on the uneven surface. She tried running on the ties, but there were spaced wrong for the length of her stride and after stumbling several times, she moved back to the heavy gravel beside the tracks.

A quick glance over her shoulder showed her that the braves on the handcar were gaining, and the closest buildings in Crowell still seemed to be a mile or more away. Pausing for a moment to catch her breath, she heard a faint voice calling her.

"Miss Lucy . . . Miss Lucy . . . wait . . . wait for us."

Did they really expect her to wait? Did they think she was that stupid? Lucy couldn't believe it. They were close enough now for her to see that both of them were carrying rifles, and they might not be in range of her pistol, but she was in range of their rifles.

She turned and started running faster, her eyes searching for a path near the tracks that would let her make better time.

"Miss Lucy . . . please, wait . . ."

Were they afraid to shoot her? Was that it? Something jostled her questions, something she'd noticed about them . . . the way one of them . . . It was Quentin—Max Quentin behind her!

Fear spurred Lucy even faster.

THREE | Despite Nyllan's worry, Goodfox found Vargin and his wife, Shirlito, open and honest people, bright with curiosity, but restrained by good manners. The meal Shirlito had prepared had been simple—steak, beans, cornbread, and pickled watermelon, all in much larger quantities than the four of them could eat—but very pleasant and satisfying.

Goodfox could not say the same about the broadcast. It had been easy enough for Nyllan to make the necessary connections to feed his signal through Vargin's signal booster and antenna, but when they raised Rhineland on the alternating security frequencies of the modified shortwave, Sister Paula Kathryn had difficulty patching her shortwave receiver to the AM transmitter. Nyllan had monitored the AM broadcast on a radio in the other end of the house, and after he finished, she had reported several static-filled interruptions, one lasting almost two minutes.

But at least he had made contact with Rhineland, and Sister Paula could begin the preparations there for the big broadcast to be made as soon as he arrived. That was the most important thing—for all to be ready when he arrived. Despite the security system that alternated frequencies every two seconds, he had not dared ask if the Quentins had arrived, and Sister Paula had said nothing that could have been interpreted that way. Consequently, he had told her to be gracious to any guests who arrived in his name at St. Joseph's and left it at that, having faith that his followers would understand what had to be done.

It was his fault, of course. He had made no provisions for this possibility, assuming that he would be in Rhineland when the Quentins arrived, and thus having no contingency plan for his church to fall back on. However, Easter was still four days away, so there was ample time to bring all the elements together in time to make the first broadcast.

Out of deference to their hosts, and perhaps as a rebuke to Rhondasue as well, Goodfox had decided they should sleep separately. But he hadn't slept very well, and now as the pale pink light of dawn colored the shadows of the small room where he lay, he wished again that it didn't matter to him what people thought. It shouldn't, he knew that. But it did. He wanted to be properly regarded as the priest and leader of the people, and if that meant being what Rhondasue called hypocritical, then he guessed he was.

Except he couldn't be. God had brought Rhondasue Nyllan to him to be his helpmeet, and in the rosy dawn he decided that never again would he force the two of them to sleep alone just because of what someone else thought. If God meant for them to be together, what mortal priest was entitled to question that?

"Murray, get up," Nyllan's voice commanded through the closed door. Before he could respond she was in the room with him, fully dressed and armed with her pistol and the shotgun. "Something's going on. I told you I didn't like this setup."

"What are you talking about?"

She tossed him his shirt and pants. "I'm talking about the fact that Vargin was up in the middle of the night talking to somebody on his shortwave, and now, as far as I can tell, there's no one in the house except you and me."

"Maybe they have early chores," he said as he pulled his shirt on over his head.

"Maybe they do, and maybe they don't. But it's time you got dressed anyway. If chores took them out, we'll know soon enough. No reason we can't load the wagon while we're waiting to find out, is there?"

He shivered as he stepped onto the cold floor and pulled on his pants. "No reason at all." Did Nyllan have reason to be so suspicious, or was she just overreacting? "However, I would like to know why you're so concerned."

"Dammit, Murray. Vargin and his wife are gone. We're less than three miles from the DalWorth border carrying at least one thing they'd be interested in—two if you count yourself—and you want me to be calm and relaxed?"

"I just don't want you to panic."

"Panic, hell." She was standing by the door, the shotgun casually ready in her hands. "I'm just being sensible. Horny toads got spikes so they can hide from trouble. You and I don't. Hurry up, will you."

"I'm almost ready." He supposed she was right about all this caution, but for the life of him he would never understand how she came by her suspicions so naturally.

Outside an ox moaned in distress.

CHAPTER 27

CODY | The meaning of the secret orders Sergeant Goldstein had handed him was all too clear to Cody. He and the reinforced platoon that would meet him in Crowell were totally expendable.

> . . . Pursue, engage, contain, and defeat the enemy force at any necessary cost . . .
> Secure all radioactive materials and hold for the proper authorities . . . maintaining regular contact with the nearest military headquarters until relief and reinforcements arrive and you are relieved of command.
> /s/ Winslow Terry
> Attorney General, Republic of West Texas

And a personal note on the end to Cody from Terry.

> The welfare and security of The Republic and perhaps the North American continent may be at risk from the irresponsible actions of

your target group. We are counting on you to do everything necessary to stop them. Our prayers are with you, Lt. Cody.

With a great sense of weary frustration, Cody read the orders one more time, then put a match to them and held them at arms length as they burned. If this mission was so damned important, why was Terry trying to get it done with only a reinforced platoon? There was something basically very wrong about that unless . . . unless Terry was dealing with even bigger militia problems somewhere else.

Was that it? Was all this trouble between the Republic and the Nates finally turning into a real war? Cody shuddered at the thought, and as though echoing his concern, the earth shuddered under his feet in a set of slow, tiny tremors.

"Lieutenant? Can I talk to you a minute?"

Cody dropped the burning orders and walked quickly to where the medic was kneeling beside Melindo. There was an IV in each of Melindo's arms, one of plasma, the other of saline solution, and their bags were still swaying in response to the quakes. "How is she?"

"I think she'll make it just fine, sir, if we can get her to Chillicothe as quickly as possible, but we only have one chopper. How do you want to handle this, sir?"

"Brisas," he called without hesitation, "crank up that Prick-100 and get me Foard Station. It'll take all day to get this job done with just one chopper." The medic looked at him questioningly, and with a brief flash of amusement Cody realized how natural it felt to be giving orders. "You take her and the wounded Nates with him," he said with a flick of his head toward Sergeant Goldstein, "as your guard. Then I want that chopper and Goldstein back here as fast as that pilot can push it."

"I got 'em, Cody," Brisas called.

"Tell them I want to talk to Sierra Bravo Yankee in person, immediately if not sooner, and if they give you any shit, tell them you're operating under direct orders from the Attorney General."

She grinned. "Can do, Lieuuu-tenant Cody, sir."

"What about us?" Sashahunder asked.

"You'll stay put. I don't have enough transportation to haul you around the countryside right now." He looked at the Nate's dirty face and a strange feeling of concern swept through him. "Don't sweat it, chief. I'll get the word to headquarters that you aren't the ones they need to worry—"

"Sheriff York's on the horn, Cody."

He walked quickly over to her and took the handset. "This is Bearcub Leader," he said quickly. "That you, Aunt Bertha?"

"Sure is, boy. What the hell's goin' on out there?"

"More than I can tell you now. You heard from Terry?"

"Damn sure did—right after the border train ran through here without stopping not twenty minutes ago. I figure it was some more Nates, but we didn't follow them because of Terry's orders. He said I should give you everything I could."

"They were probably my Nates. They could have captured the train at Medicine Mound." But why would they be heading south? he wondered. "Aunt Bertha, you got a chopper and five or six troops you can get out here to me? I got some Nate prisoners I need to get shed of."

"No chopper here. I thought Terry said he was sending one to you?"

Cody frowned and shook his head. "Okay, Aunt Bertha, you call Chillicothe for me and tell them the chopper's coming in with one of our wounded and a couple of wounded Nates. Hold on a second." He put one hand over the mouthpiece and shouted to Goldstein, "How many people can that chopper carry?"

"Seven including us."

"Okay. Aunt Bertha, make that five Nates, all of them wounded more or less. And tell them I want a guard squad sent back with the chopper to take care of the rest of these prisoners I got. Then as soon as they get back here, me and what's left of my team will fly down there to meet you."

"Gotcha, Jeremy. Anything else?"

He thought for a second before answering. "That old train engine the Hysterical Society's got in the museum still run?" He remembered riding on it as a child for some holiday celebration or other, but—

"It does. You want me to get it ready?"

"Yes. And a couple of those cotton cars Tiga keeps on the siding—get them ready for the troops Terry's sending."

"Got a boxcar belongs to Aqha you can have, too. That it?"

"For now. . . . Oh, one thing more, Aunt Bertha. Do you have a track repair supervisor there?"

"Yes. Mrs. Millsap. You want to talk to her?"

"Yeah, that, too, but what I want most is a track map with any information about track and bridge conditions that she can give us, okay?"

"I see what you're thinking, Jeremy. I'll get to work on all of this and we'll see you later."

"Roger." He gave Brisas the handset and turned to Goldstein who was sharing a cigarette with Kolmer. It was the first time Cody could remember seeing Kolmer smoke. "Sergeant, get your chopper back here, and tell him to land if he thinks there's enough room."

Five minutes later the pilot set the chopper down in the center of the clearing, blowing everything that was loose out of the way in the process. While the medic supervised the loading and Kolmer kept watch over the Nates, Cody conferred with the pilot. He was surprised for a second to find that he knew who she was, and that she remembered him from his training down at Jayton, and he was pleased when she understood right away what he wanted done.

"Be back in thirty minutes!" she shouted.

"Thanks! See you then!" Cody backed away, she shut her door, and moments later the chopper rose, nose slightly down. With a surge of power it lifted out of the clearing and over the low mesquite, turning quickly and heading northeast toward Chillicothe, its distinct sound so foreign yet so familiar.

Cody caught himself saying a silent prayer to Cristodios for Melindo's sake. Please, please don't let her die.

As he turned back to where Kolmer and Brisas were waiting, it suddenly occurred to him that he had meant to say something to Kendrick Johnson before the chopper hauled him off, had meant to tell him that if the Republic didn't shoot him or put him in prison for life, that he was as good as dead if Cody ever saw him again.

He had meant to say that, wanted to say that, but he hadn't said it, because deep down inside he knew that the moment for killing Kendrick Johnson had passed, and there was no way to get it back . . . not for what had already happened. If he was going to kill Kendrick, he should have done it when his anger was overflowing.

Not sure of what his unwillingness to kill Johnson said about him as a man, Cody tried to shake off all those thoughts, but there was one thing that refused to let go. He *had* killed something in that overflow of anger, and only now did he understand what it was. He had killed what little remained of his love for Ann. That was why he hadn't been able to shoot Kendrick Johnson. How could he shoot a man who had stolen something he no longer cared about?

Cody's heart denied that lie as soon as he thought it. He did care—whether he wanted to or not. He might not be able to love Ann any more, but he could not stop caring about what happened to her—and to their baby. Yet in giving in to whatever magic Johnson had used on her, Ann had given up any claim to Cody's love, and now he understood that he had given up his love for her as well. With a shake of his head he dismissed Johnson and tried to dismiss his thoughts about Ann.

"You all right, Cody?" Brisas asked.

"What? Oh, sure. I was just thinking about Donna."

"The medic said she'd live."

"I know. I know." He looked distractedly over at the Nates. "Sashahunder, I want you and the rest of your group to sit over there in front of that wagon where we can watch you easy. And I don't want you moving around or talking."

After the seven remaining Nates had straightened the tarp blown by the chopper and sat where he told them, Cody said, "Juanita, you and Ed might as well hear this now. The orders I got from Terry make it pretty clear that he doesn't expect most of us to survive the rest of this mission. You two already been through hell, so if you want out, when we get to Crowell you can skip the rest of this."

"Don't be stupid," Brisas said with a deep frown. "We owe those Nates something."

"Damn straight," Kolmer added. "You're not telling us we can't go, are you?"

It was more of a relief than Cody expected to hear that they both wanted to stay with him. Somehow he would have felt very alone if they had chosen otherwise. "No, Ed. If you both want in for the whole show, you're in, and I'm glad."

They exchanged quick glances, then Brisas said, "We figured something like this was happening after you read those orders, and, well, I really want to go with you, but I want somebody else to carry the radio."

Cody was surprised. "Why?"

"'Cause I want to be free of it to fight when there's fighting, instead of being tied to this thing."

"She deserves it, Cody."

If they hadn't both looked so serious, Cody might have laughed. "All right. If one of these reinforcements we're going to pick up is qualified to handle the radio, you got it. But if none of them are, you can get somebody else to carry it, but you're still the operator. Fair enough?"

Brisas smiled. "Okay by me."

"Good." They settled in to wait for the chopper's return, and while they were waiting Cody thought about his father and remembered that scene back at Patricia Brighton's house as though it had been months before instead of only four days ago. God, the things that had happened since this patrol started.

Once, after Deborah had died, his father had sat him down very seriously and told him about the early troubles between what were now the Republic and the Indian Nation. He'd talked about the New Federalists and the Joiners, and how the Republic was the only hope for the people of West Texas, and that there was no way and no reason to pull the old United States back together again.

In his grief and guilt over Deborah, much of what his father had said hadn't registered with Cody. But now it was beginning to seem like it was more and more important to remember what was said and try to understand it. He had the overwhelming feeling that he was going to be faced with choices he couldn't have made even a week ago and still wasn't ready to make. There was no way he could shake Terry's order and warning, yet Cody hated the feeling of being caught up in something so important that his decisions could make a difference for the whole Republic.

Nothing he'd done in his whole life had prepared him for that kind of responsibility—least ways nothing clear enough for him to draw out of. It was like asking someone who had never seen a bridge to build one. No, that wasn't quite right. He had seen others doing what had to be done—making the choices that had to be made. If that was all he had, then he'd just have to make the best of it when the time came. Maybe Terry had exaggerated. Maybe this wasn't all as big as—

"Chopper coming," Kolmer announced.

Cody got to his feet when the sound got louder and stood watching as the chopper circled, hesitated, then moved in a slow hovering turn and landed in the clearing. Sergeant Goldstein got off followed by five militiamen.

"She's all yours, sir!" he shouted over the noise of the chopper. "Good luck!"

"Thanks." Cody motioned to Brisas and Kolmer and the three of them climbed aboard the chopper. When it lifted off, a shiver of excitement doubled by nervousness raced through him and made him wonder where all this was going to end.

CHAPTER 28

LUCY | Lucy fired once, twice, a third time, shooting too quickly, wasting precious ammunition in her panic to escape Quentin and the brave who chased her.

Their handcar never paused.

She turned and ran off the roadbed toward the weathered silo less than two hundred yards away. The young, shoulder-high mesquite trees tore at her cloak, slowing her down, stopping the desperate driving of her legs.

A quick glance over her shoulder showed Quentin off the track now followed by the brave. Calling her, "Miss Lucy, Miss Lucy . . . damn bitch!"

The pistol was heavy in her hand. Tears ran down her face. Her heart overflowed with panic. Again her cloak caught. She turned to free it and fired again at Quentin, hitting him finally, watching him spin and fall in a time slower than reality.

Her cloak pulled loose. The brave helped Quentin to his feet as she turned yet again and zig-zagged through the trees.

Where was the silo? She couldn't see it. Had she turned the wrong way? Lucy kept running, dodging trees, afraid to pause and get her bearings, seeking only escape.

Her ragged breath tore at her throat. Her side ached. Her heart fought to escape her ribs. She paused, bent over, desperate for oxygen, sides heaving like a winded horse, the roaring of her blood in her ears blocking her hearing.

She heard the growl as something hit her from behind and she was thrown down to the cold, wet grass. Her pistol! Twisting viciously around, she brought the gun up. As she squeezed the trigger, her hand went numb.

The sound deafened her. The pain tore at her chest. A long, white moment of calm filled her mind, then faded into darkness where she spun slowly, calmly, deliberately down toward the warmth of gentle arms that reached up and cushioned her fall.

Mishla was tearing yucca-cloth into strips. Lucy was helping her, holding the bolt of tough fabric as Mishla had taught her, using the weight of her small body to work with the weakest parts of the cloth, shifting her weight, feeling the heavy press of the bolt against her.

"Well, damn. Stupid bitch wasted herself. Wendel's gonna hate this. Come on, Tuck. Let's get some soft-stuff."

Mishla was tearing yucca-cloth into strips . . . tearing strips for streamers . . . strips for red streamers on God Remember Day. Lucy was doing her best to help her, trying to hold the bolt the way Mishla had taught her, trying to make the weight of the bolt and her own weight, one weight, making the fabric yield along its weakest lines, letting herself fall under the heaviness of the bolt pressing insistently against her body.

Her legs squeezed around it, the yucca-cloth was tearing, tearing, tearing . . .

Lucy saw light. She felt the cold damp air between her legs. She smelled the odor of him. She smelled his anger and his hatred. She heard something rip and felt it, too.

It was Paul Ioni again, bruising her breasts, stabbing, hurting, forcing her thighs farther and farther apart, splitting her up the middle—wet with tears of shame, crying for the darkness she could not find, the frightened animal in her body twisting in panic, turning in flight, fighting the weight, the pain, the raw force of him tearing deeper and deeper, cursing, screaming, crying . . .

Mishla holding Lucy in her arms, stroking her hair, rocking her gently, saying,

"I killed the snake, I killed the snake, I killed the snake. It's gone now, child, gone now, child, gone now, killed it . . . gone now . . ." Trying to breathe, knowing for certain she was going to die on the cold, wet ground.

"—going to die. If you want yours warm instead of cold, you'd better get it now while she's still got enough fight left in her to make it fun."

"I can't do it. It's rape. I can't."

I can't. The voice. I can't. Remember the voice. I can't, I can't, I can't.

CLICK-CLICK.

Where's the pistol? Who has the pistol?

"You can. You'll do it anyway. When we get to Rhineland I don't want the likes of you saying I did it just because you didn't have the balls for it. You just drop them pants and hump her good and fast—"

. . . and fast, and fast, dear God . . .

" 'Cause if you don't I'll blow you away with her and say she killed you. Now, get on her, you Nimenim bastard, or you'll find this gun up your asshole and you'll be sporting a new one."

A new one, a different one, slower, crying, grunting, hurting . . . fighting again, twisting away, arching back, rolling up . . . always the pain, the pain, high and low. Curling, curling, tighter and tighter into a ball, chest on fire. No air, no breath, to die at last . . . the cold, cold wind stinging between her legs, waking her up, bringing her back from the comfort of death.

More heat. God, no! Stabbing behind, filling her. Not again! Not this!

Forcing its hot way, pinning her under the weight—the weight, the shifting, pushing, pumping weight—again, and again, and again, with growling rhythms of grunts and moans until the light flared and faded, lost in the dark well of pain and horror.

Where is the yucca-cloth?
All torn to shreds.
Where is the weaver?
Gone to bed.
Who will remember, who will cry?
No one will care in the sweet bye and bye . . . bye and fly . . . higher and lower, swooping wind, taking the breath away, climbing toward the heat of the sun, leaving the earth behind.

"Leave it behind, I said. Nothing else we need. The buzzards will take care of the evidence, and this way it looks like she killed herself. Come on. If we're going to catch up with them at Foard City, we have to get going."

Going . . . going . . . listening to footsteps walking into the windsounds, gonesounds, sobbingsounds, roaringsounds-and-sounds-and-sounds-and-sounds . . . and sounds floating alone through time and space . . .

"Oh, my God, Jason. Quick, get my bag. Call Sheriff York and Medic Leigh. Hurry, Jason, hurry."

Hurry? Hurry? Why hurry, hurry, hurry?

"Be still, child, still. Help is coming. How did this happen? Who did this? No, don't talk. Just be still."

Be still? Hurry? Lucy smiled, giggled into the blinding white

*beacon, laughing through the light into the sweet warm comfort
of darkness. Letting go of the darkness, letting go of the light,
letting go . . . go . . . go . . .*

Shock.

The word rested in the center of her dim consciousness like
it ought to mean something.

Shock.

She knew the word. She knew what it meant. She just
couldn't put the two together.

Shock.

Wait. Running. Shooting. Pain. She remembered the pain,
but she didn't know why. How had she hurt herself? What had
she done wrong?

The pain. It hurt all over—inside, outside, all over—
scraping away at her with all those strange sounds and
disconnected voices—new voices, soothing voices, urgent,
tender, concerned, all over and all around her. . . . What did
they mean? What were they talking about? Numb tingling
spreading through her chest and into her arms. What were they
doing? Who were they?

Who are you? Who are you?"

Why didn't they answer? Why wouldn't they tell her?

Another pain, sharper, grating her bones. A cry of triumph.
"Got it!"

The ache deep in the side of her chest and all she wanted to
do was sleep, sleep, sleep.

"Miss Ilseng? Miss Ilseng?"

The woman's voice nagged at her.

"Miss Ilseng? Can you hear me? I'm Medic Leigh. I know
you're a healer, and I have to know if you're allergic to penicillin
or sulfa? Are you? Can you hear me? Are you allergic to either of
those antibiotics?"

"Me?" Lucy heard the word part her lips like a thick grunt.

"Yes. Miss Ilseng, you've been shot, and raped," the
woman's voice said. "I need to know if you're allergic to either
penicillin or sulfonamides."

Raped? Shot? Allergic? The answers pushed their way up
through the protective shock that congealed the thoughts in her
brain. "No. Not allergic. Not me. No. Not shot. Not me. Not
raped. Not Paul. Not me. Not me."

Tiny pains, pricks on the edges, then floating away, drifting in the darkness . . .

I am Lucy, trained by Mishla. The darkened way makes the path of duty clear, clears the path of duty, to the faith of my mother I will defend when all the people are mine to heal and save. Mishla's Lucy, trained and ready, always obedient, born of faith of fathers lost beyond the grey, empty sky, cupping the friends of my travels beyond the second moment of time.

Lucy suddenly heard muffled voices somewhere close by, but when she tried to open her eyes, her body refused to cooperate. It was as if she was separate from her body, as if her mind had pulled away. She couldn't feel the bed under her, but she knew it was a bed. She also knew the room was warm and so was she, but she didn't know why. When she heard herself sigh like a stranger, she was suddenly afraid.

What had happened? Something—something important—but where and what and when she didn't know. *When we get to Rhineland . . .* There was a dark veil behind an opaque curtain between her and the past. The train, and Ann, and being locked in by Mike Young. What after that? Ann had escaped.

No, not Ann. Lucy. She had escaped, gotten off the train. How? It hurt to think so much.

Again she tried to feel her eyes, or move her body, or feel something, but there was no response beyond a vague sense of heaviness, like something was holding her down.

The memory of panic flashed like a sudden light from behind the edges of the veil, and then it was gone.

Someone had held her down. When? Where? The memory stayed dark, but she smelled new yucca-cloth and remembered Mishla and how they had torn strips from the bolts of yucca-cloth to dye red for the grave streamers of God Remember Day. Then, for no reason at all, she remembered Paul Ioni, and how nice he had been to her, and how she must have done something terribly wrong because after that he was gone and no one would talk about him.

The veil tore a little and she saw him. It wasn't Paul.

Lucy counted slowly, ten, nine, eight, seven, six, trying to relax her mind and free her memories. Five, four, three, two. Again. Ten, nine, eight . . . but nothing happened.

She heard her body struggling with a long breath and gave

up. Something was very wrong with her, but she would have to wait to find out what the sickness was. Patience was the answer.

Letting go of everything, Lucy let the simple rhythms of a quiet stream making its way through rounded rocks distract her from thinking. It was such a simple sound, yet such a complicated sound, too, full of hidden harmonies and counter-pointed melodies all quietly blending into a peaceful, soothing—

Quentin. Max Quentin. She remembered.

Suddenly she could feel her body again, feel the deep, aching pain in her chest, and the raw, burning itch between her legs, and she cried. In an instant she felt it all and remembered it all and heavy sobs wracked her body. The pain was like tearing flesh.

She coughed, and groaned with the central hurt of it, then coughed again. Screams tore through her body. Rage jerked her muscles in terrible spasms. Tears choked her.

Then the voice was there again, the soothing, calming voice, and soft arms holding her firmly, rocking her gently. She remembered that comforting after Paul Ioni, and now, again, after Max Quentin, and suddenly she wondered where this comfort came from and why it was always a woman who brought it to her.

Lucy could feel now, could feel herself crying, could feel the wounds from the dark memories, could feel the tender concern of whoever held her, could feel the changes which had caught her up and swept her into unknown seas, and she could feel the loss of something that had no name.

CHAPTER 29

GOODFOX | Vargin and his wife were nowhere to be seen in the barn, nor did they answer when Nyllan called their names. But the oxen were yoked to the wagon which was standing just inside the door to the widest of the two aisles that ran the length of the barn.

"See, there's nothing sinister going on here," Goodfox said.

"Then where are they?" Nyllan asked as she walked cautiously around the wagon and peered at its contents.

"What business is that of ours? They have been gracious hosts. If something called them away this morning, why can't you accept this final gesture of their hospitality for what it is? For the love of God, Rhondasue, I don't understand—"

"Shut up."

She held up her hand when he started to protest, and the look on her face told him to pay attention rather than argue with her. At first he could hear nothing more than the gentle moaning of the wind under the eaves of the barn. Then he realized it wasn't the wind. It was somebody. He held his pistol up and nodded to her.

Nyllan motioned toward a walled-off area at the other end of the barn and started creeping slowly in that direction with the shotgun level in her hands. Goodfox followed down the other side of the center stalls, his palms sweating in the cold morning dampness of the barn, his hands trembling ever so slightly wrapped around the revolver, his eyes darting left and right, afraid that at any second someone or something was going to attack him from the shadows.

Each step they took seemed to echo in the barn. The straw snapped like twigs beneath their feet. The mud squished up through the straw releasing the stench of urine and manure.

Something metal clattered to a wooden floor.

Goodfox crouched, knees flexed, arms straight out in front of him aiming the pistol at the sound.

"Damn," a man's voice said.

"Vargin? Is that you?" Goodfox called. He saw Nyllan shaking her head, but he ignored him. "Vargin?"

"In here, Father," Vargin answered loudly, "you're just in time to help."

Again Nyllan shook her head, and again he ignored her. Lowering his pistol, he stepped up to the doorway and peered cautiously in.

"Shirlito and me took this damned pump apart—pardon my language, Father—but it looks like it's going to take more than the two of us to get it back together." He glanced down at Goodfox's hand. "You looking for trouble, Father?"

Goodfox blushed. "No, not exactly. But when we couldn't find you and you didn't answer our call, we got a little scared. After all, I'm not the most welcomed—"

"I understand, Father." Vargin grinned. "You could stay here on this place with us for a year and be safe, 'cause we got respect around here. But a mile down the road? You're in no-man's-land with Joiners and Nimenim and DalWorth Rangers—and more than a few little gangs looking for easy food and money. It's all right, Father. You had no way of knowing."

"There, Rhondasue," he said as she moved up beside him, "I guess your caution wasn't totally out of place."

With a shake of her head she set the shotgun down by the door. "Let's get this pump back together so we can get on down the road."

"Sorry about the scare," Shirlito said.

"No problem."

With the four of them working together they had the pump reassembled in fifteen minutes, then went back into the house where Shirlito insisted on cooking them breakfast before they left. Only when they were finished and she had packed biscuits and roast beef sandwiches for them in a yucca-cloth bag was she willing to let them go.

Nyllan and Vargin loaded the shortwave and tied it down while Goodfox changed into his cassock, brought the rest of their gear out of the house, and put it in the wagon.

"How'd you plan to cross the border with this?" Vargin asked.

"You think they'll want to know what's under the canvas?"

"Maybe. Maybe not. Actually, Father, you being a priest and all, they might not even bother you in Saint Jo. It's going through Bowie that you're going to have trouble."

"We're not going through Bowie," Goodfox said. He would have told Vargin they were going through Gault, but the look on Nyllan's face stopped him short.

Vargin scratched his head, then bent down and started drawing in the mud. "Well, from Saint Jo you can either go through Montague on Fifty-nine to the Gault cutoff, then head west from Gault on Eighteen-oh-six to One-seventy-four and that will take you straight through Big Jack into Windthorst. Or you can go through Hardy, Forestburg, and Smyrna down to Sunset, which is a whole lot longer, but hardly patrolled by the rangers. Then there's county roads from Sunset to Newport and on up to One-seventy-four at Buffalo Springs, but it's a hard route to follow if you don't already know it."

"Are those the only choices?" Nyllan asked.

"No. You could go from Saint Jo through Dye and Mallard

over to Salona and Fruitland that way, but it's all back roads and rough country—slow going with the oxen."

"Which way would you—"

"You saying there are lots of patrols the Gault way?" Nyllan cut him off with a look that hardened her words.

"That I am, Miss Nyllan, but if I wanted through DalWorth fast and didn't mind the chances, I'd sure go that way."

"Thank you," she said before Goodfox had a chance to speak. "We'll certainly take your advice into consideration, but you understand that we can't tell you which way we're going, don't you? No sense in implicating you in any way."

Vargin looked from her to Goodfox and shook his head. "I'm not sure I do, lady, but if that's how the father sees it, I'd be the last one to argue with you."

For the first time since they had met this man, Goodfox understood Rhondasue's distrust of him. There was a flash of something hidden in Vargin's eyes that spoke of deception. Then it was gone, and Goodfox wasn't sure he'd seen anything at all. "Thank you both for everything," he said, signing the cross over each of them, "and God's blessings upon you." When he turned, Rhondasue was already on the wagon seat, reins in hand.

"You are most welcome here any time, Father," Shirlito said. "We are honored to serve you."

"We all serve together," Vargin added.

After he climbed on the wagon and they had pulled out of the barnyard, Nyllan whispered, "Turn back and wave, and tell me what they're doing."

Goodfox did as he was told. "Shirlito's waving back. Vargin's walking into the house."

"Damn! That's what I was afraid of."

"What are you talking about?" he asked as he turned back to face the front.

"Why didn't I plan for this? Murray, he's gone to use his radio, to warn somebody that we're coming, probably the New Federalists in Saint Jo."

Goodfox was startled. "That's the most ridiculous thing I ever heard of."

Nyllan slapped the oxen hard with the whip and they responded with a slight increase in speed. "Dammit, Murray, the man's a New Federalist as sure as you're a New Dominican. So was Eagil if we'd just been smart enough to see it. Shit!"

"Can you explain all this sudden revelation—without cursing?" He had no idea why she was so sure about—

"You're damn right I can. Dolores del Noches stole Bell's plane, but not our radio or the controller. There's no other plane available, but we get this team and wagon—guaranteed to slow down our arrival anywhere. Vargin's not really worried about how we'll get through Saint Jo—am I going too fast for you?"

"I'm listening, but I still don't follow."

"Then listen harder. Last night Vargin was on the radio to somebody. Today he's trying to find out which route we're going to use to cross DalWorth. And then he said, 'We all serve together,' and whose motto is that?"

"The New Feds', but that doesn't mean anything." He was getting a little tired of this and it showed in his voice.

"We've got to steal a truck," she said as they pulled out the gate and onto the Saint Jo road.

"Rhondasue Nyllan, until you give me better evidence than you have so far, we will steal nothing."

They rode for a few minutes in silence, then with a hard jerk on the reins accompanied by protests from the oxen she brought the wagon to a halt. "Fine, Father Murray Goodfox, sir." She handed him the reins and dug the weapons bag out from under the seat. "You just go ahead and do what you think is best. I'll wait for the announcement of your death on the radio."

The sarcasm in her voice didn't match the look in her eyes, but Goodfox knew that she was quite capable of walking away from him and never looking back. Yet he refused to give in to her irrational behavior. Maybe it was time he drew the line and let her make the hard choices.

"If that's the way you feel," he said slowly. "Just leave me the shotgun and my pistol. You can take the rifle."

"You keep the rifle," she said bitterly as she climbed off the wagon. "You're going to need all the firepower you can muster."

"Rhondasue . . . don't do this to me."

"You're doing it to yourself, Murray, and I'm sick and tired of your discounting everything I tell you." For a long moment she stood looking up at him, then dug her pack out of the wagon. "You said once that I had good instincts, but you hate like hell to depend on my instincts." She took her pistol from the weapons bag and some of their dried rations and stuffed it all into her pack.

"So you go on," she said with a new tone in her voice. "You go on trusting people and taking them at face value, and when they've got you pinned to a wall, or nailed to a cross, and you know you're going to die, you remember that I tried to warn you."

Her tears touched him, but her words only set his determination not to give in. "You're being irrational. Climb back up here and let's move on."

With a sad chuckle she snuffled and spat, then looked back up at him. "Well, Murray, like I said before, it's been fun. See you at the funeral." Turning away she shrugged on the pack and began walking back toward Vargin's house and Marysville.

Goodfox slapped the oxen repeatedly with the whip until they started moving again. With every little bounce of the wagon he fought the urge to turn around and call to her. If this was the way she wanted it, this was the way it would be. If this was the way God wanted it, this was the way it would be. The glory and praise to Him. Amen. Amen. Amen.

Much to his surprise, there were tears running down his face. Then it was even harder not to turn around. But he wouldn't do it. He couldn't. She had made her choice and he had made his, and God would watch over them both.

With that conviction firmly set in his mind, he rode steadily westward, rare patches of sunlight peeking through the overcast to spread brief moments of warmth on his back before disappearing again. Before long he stopped crying, but a storm of emotions raged against the shores of his heart. He prayed for relief. He recited the rosary, slowly and deliberately, using his faith to calm the storm. But the moment he relaxed his vigilance it grew stronger again and tore at him with waves of castigation and self-pity and the bitter waters of loneliness, until at last the tears came again, and with them uncontrolled sobs that rendered him helpless.

When they finally stopped, he realized that the wagon had stopped as well, the oxen content to stand and chew their cuds unless prodded forward. It took the reins and the whip to get them moving again, but when they settled back into their steady gait, Goodfox knew he had made a mistake.

He should never have driven Rhondasue off like that. He should never have forced her to choose. She had been right and he had let pride keep him from accepting that. But what should he do? Should he try to go back for her? Should he stop and hope she had changed her mind? The crying had left him so washed out that he didn't know what to do, nor how to decide. It was as though something of himself had been lost in the process.

"Hello there," a woman's voice called.

Goodfox looked up, half-expecting to see Rhondasue. Instead he was greeted by five or six people on oxen, all armed, all smiling at him, a dark-haired woman kicking her ox closer to the wagon as his beasts came to a halt.

"You a priest?" she asked.

"I am," he answered without hesitation.

"Father Murray Goodfox?"

As soon as she said his name, he sent a sudden prayer for assistance to God. Rhondasue had been right.

CHAPTER 30

ONE | "And Azle?" Cody asked.

Morgan smiled. "She's going to be all right, Sarge—I mean—sir, but the medic said she's to take it easy for the next month or so. She was mad as hell not being able to come with us, but she said to tell you she's proud of you."

"Thanks, Morgan. I appreciate that." Morgan had the look of a boy pleased with himself, and for the first time since he'd met Morgan, Cody wondered what somebody so young was doing in the militia. "You go back and tell Sergeants Ensolita and Kolmer to make sure the troops are ready to load and that I'll be down there as soon as I can."

"Yes, sir." He gave Cody a sharp salute and quickly left the room.

"Bet you're glad to have some people you know on this thing," Sheriff York said with a smile.

"For sure, Aunt Bertha." He was startled to realize how much greyer she looked than the last time he had seen her, yet he wasn't surprised that none of the sparkle and fire had left her blue eyes. Seemed like everybody was looking either older or younger in the past few weeks. "The old squad's like kin, I guess. You go through a few hard fights with people and, well, somehow they mean something special to you. But enough of that. Where's that track supervisor, Mrs., uh—"

"Mrs. Millsap. She's waiting for us. Lewis," she said to a young deputy, "show Mrs. Millsap in."

Moments later a woman thin as a rail and weathered as a post entered the room with a large, rolled-up map. If she'd said she was forty years old or ninety, Cody would have believed her. It was impossible to guess her age.

"Althea, this is my nephew, Lieutenant Jeremiah Cody."

"Pleased to meet you, ma'am. What have you got for me?"

"Same here, boy. This is my working map," she said, unrolling it on the cleared desk. "Shows the whole system. I brought you a smaller one"—she patted her pocket—"to take with you, but I wanted you to see this one in as much detail as you could."

The map was marked TEXAS, N.E. scale 1:500,000, but he realized as soon as she got it flat that it was actually two old maps glued together—two pre-Shudderday maps.

"We're here," he said, jabbing her finger at a point an inch or so below Copper Breaks. "The border train has to be headed down the old Sante Fe line toward Truscott."

Cody leaned down beside her. "Why couldn't they just as well be headed down the Crowell-and-Weatherford?" he asked, tracing the hand-drawn tracks that ran from Crowell into Big Jack County.

"'Cause then they wouldn't have come through town," she said in a tone that implied the question was stupid. "'Sides, it was seen heading toward Foard City, and anyway, the C-and-W's been closed for a week so's we could fix the Beaver Creek bridge."

"I believe you. I believe you," Cody said with a defensive laugh. "So tell me about the track south of here."

"It's not the best track in the world," she said, "mostly because it's got a lot of bad ties that need replacing, but who's to do it is an argument ain't nobody won yet. Costs money, you know, and if Lubbock won't pay part of it, the Joint Rail and Roads Commission don't want to pay either."

"Just show him where it's bad, Althea," Sheriff York said.

"I'm getting to it, Bertha June. Don't rush me." Her smile deepened the wrinkles around her eyes. "From here to Foard City's fair track, boy. From there to Truscott is better, but not much. We been working on that section, but when that dam up the Middle Wichita broke last year we took a lot of damage on this bridge and we really need to rebuild it. If these recent quakes haven't weakened it too much, it'll hold a train going slow enough, but I wouldn't want to be near one trying to highball that way."

"Highball?"

"Run fast, open throttle. Don't they teach kids nothing nowadays?"

"Not about railroads," Cody said. "All right, so they'll have to slow down at the North Wichita Bridge. Then what?"

"Then it's slow all the way to the Brazos. After they cross that and get up the Benjamin incline, they can—"

"I'll tell you about Benjamin in a minute."

Mrs. Millsap frowned at the Sheriff. "Anyway, as I was saying, once they get up the incline, they can highball their asses all the way into Sweetwater if they want. They finished checking that track yesterday."

"Sweetwater? Why would they want to . . . Cody, you make any sense of this?"

"No, I don't. I can't figure out why they're going south instead of north, Aunt Bertha, much less where they wanta end up. Mrs. Millsap, is there anyplace else they could go?"

"Only with help. They could switch to the Knox City-Munday line here," she said poking her finger at Knox City, "but they'd end up heading north again that way because they're rebuilding the old Fort Worth-and-Denver track between Haskell and Munday, so they'd have to take it north toward Seymour. No sense in that if they want to go south."

"Except we don't know that's where they want to go."

Cody nodded, then grinned, suddenly feeling very foolish. "Seems to me like we're going about this all wrong. Why can't we just block the track somewhere down the line?"

"I sent a team in a truck down Hiway Six to do just that," Sheriff York said. "Told them to set up just north of Benjamin. Also called Aspermont and Seymour, and asked for help, but we don't know it's going to get there in time."

"Why can't Benjamin do it on its own?"

"Because Mayor Delagardo said if the government wasn't interested enough to send militia, he wasn't going to ask the townspeople to risk their lives to stop a train full of Nates. You see, Cody, Benjamin's at the corner of Districts Four and Seven and on the border of Five. They been left high and dry by the military districts more than once, and they ain't going to do anything they don't have to."

"I can read that. All right, you said you had a smaller map, Mrs. Millsap?"

She pulled it out of her pocket and handed it to him. "It's a copy of one of my section maps. Covers all the everything from Crowell to Knox City."

"Thank you—for this and all your help," he said, holding out his hand.

"You're welcome to it, boy." She shook his hand once then began rolling up her map.

Cody turned to his aunt. "Guess I've got everything I need to get started."

"Not quite, Jeremy. There's somebody else I think you ought to talk to before you set out."

"Who?"

"A healer, woman named Lucy Ilseng. I talked to her earlier. Best we can tell she was on that train, but they raped her and shot her and left her for dead just south of town."

"A Nate healer? Shot and raped? What the hell . . .?"

"Nope, not a Nate. One of ours. Her bag's got an address in Childress. Medic Leigh don't want her moved, so we'll have to go down there, but I think it'll be worth it to you."

"I'm not doubting that. I just don't understand why they'd have shot and raped a healer." He felt a flash of fear for Ann, but quickly suppressed it. "You ever hear of such a thing?"

"Goddammit, Cody! We're dealing with Nates, here, not with normal people. A Nate would eat his grandmother if he was hungry enough. You gotta remember that." She paused and let out a long sigh. "Didn't mean to shout at you, and I don't know what Terry's orders to you were, but I'll tell you this. If I got the chance you may get, I'd kill all those sons-of-bitches first and let God sort 'em out."

Cody frowned, the fear fighting back again. "There's something I haven't told you, Aunt Bertha. If these are the Nates I've been chasing, there's a good chance my wife is with them."

"Ann? With them? But how?"

"I don't know, how. I just know that she was with them when the main group split from the ones we captured. Unless somebody finds a pregnant woman sitting around Medicine Mound, there's a good chance—"

"Pregnant? My God, Cody, I'm so sorry."

"Don't know that there's anything to be sorry about. Just know that if she's with them, we can't just kill them all like you said. Might be other innocent people with them for all we know. Right?"

"All the more reason to talk to this Lucy Ilseng."

TWO | The two things Lucy was sure of were that she was alive and that she was in pain. Everything else drifted in and out of reality as freely as she drifted in and out of consciousness.

The medic—what was her name? Leigh? That was it. Medic Leigh said they couldn't give her too much morphine. Said it was dangerous with her kind of wound. Said it would slow her respiration too much.

The bed vibrated for a few seconds with a tiny quake. After it stopped she could hear the house creak and groan as it settled into some new alignment.

A weak smile twitched in the corners of Lucy's mouth. She remembered once when she'd fallen out of the big oak tree behind Mishla's house and when Lucy had complained about the pain after Mishla had set the arm, Mishla had said, "Think how bad it would be without the medicine I gave you." Maybe this was like that. How bad would she feel if Medic Leigh hadn't given her any morphine at all?

Besides, Mishla had always said that pain was instructive. The day after Lucy had broken her arm, Mishla had sent her to the library for a book called *Thorns*, then had told her to read it. The book had seemed pretty fantastic to Lucy and hard to understand. It was all about stuff that couldn't happen, about a man named Miner Burris going out in space and being captured by aliens who changed him inside so that he was always in pain, but he liked to squeeze cactus in his hand. It was also about a girl named Lona Kelvin who was the virgin mother of hundreds of babies, and a little crazy in the head because none of the babies were hers, and how Burris and Kelvin got together.

The one thing Lucy had been certain she understood was why Mishla had told her to read the book, because it was really a story about learning to live with pain. Somehow reading that book had helped her accept the pain of her broken arm.

Funny, but *Thorns* was the only book like that Mishla had ever encouraged her to read, and now, just the memory of it seemed to help her accept these new pains instead of fighting them.

"Miss Lucy? Miss Lucy? You have visitors."

Lucy forced her eyes open and found herself staring at a roughly handsome young man wearing a militia uniform.

"Miss Ilseng, I'm Lieutenant Cody, and I'd like to ask you some questions."

Cody. The name echoed in her mind. "Cody," she repeated aloud. Why was that name important? She knew there was a reason for it, but it was hidden from her.

"That's right, ma'am. Can you tell me where the Nates on that train were headed?"

"Cody," she whispered. Someone else had said that name.

"Yes, ma'am. Do you know where the train was going?"

"Away . . . south," she said, pleased that she remembered. "Mike Young . . . and . . . and, the . . ." She remembered their names, too, the brothers, the ones who—"Quentin!" The name came out in a growl.

Cody looked from the woman to the medic, who shook her head, and back to the woman. "Please, Miss Ilseng. It's important. We need to know where they're planning to go, and how many of them there are, and if they have any other hostages, and if"—he hesitated, afraid to know the answer—"and if there's a woman named Ann Cody with them."

That was it. Lucy understood. "Yes. Ann Johnson Cody. Pregnant. Soon." His face seemed to swim in front of her and she fought to focus. "Are you him?"

"Am I who, Miss Ilseng?"

"Ann's husband." She smiled, proud that she remembered and could answer so quickly. But what did he know? The smile faded.

"Yes, I am. Is she all right? Is Ann all right?"

"Yes," she repeated, liking the sound of the word. "Yes." It seemed so odd to tell things to strangers. Who were these people? What had they done to her? "No." It wasn't them. It was those others, those—

"Please, Miss Lucy. Is she all right or not?"

"Who?"

"My wife! Ann Cody, my wife!"

"Don't shout at her," the medic commanded. "She's still weak, and she's groggy with the morphine and the shock, and she doesn't need you or anyone else shouting at her. Bertha, get him out of here."

The medic sounded *so* stern. Lucy was glad.

"Can't, Leigh. He has a right to know about his wife, and

orders from Lubbock to stop those Nates she was with." She looked back at Cody. "Go easier, Jeremy."

"All right. I'm sorry, Miss Ilseng. I didn't mean to yell at you. I just need to know some things. Can you understand that? Can you help me, please?"

Lucy heard it all. She knew it made sense because it had made sense before, and it was no different than . . . than what? Before. No different than before. He wanted her help. The pain twisted suddenly in her chest and she moaned.

It was all so sharp now, like the pain had suddenly forced everything into focus. She could even hear them breathing. "Tell me again who you are," she said, surprised even as she spoke by what she said.

"My name is Jeremiah Cody. My wife's name is Ann. You said she was on the train. Is she all right?"

"Yes. She's all right, but the baby is due any time now." Her words sounded hard-edged and hollow as they echoed in her ears. "I don't know where the train is going, and I don't know—" She stopped, unable to remember what else he had asked.

"How many Nates are there? And do they have any other hostages?"

"No hostages," she said. "None. . . . Don't know how many of them there are. Lots. Twenty? Thirty? Maybe thirty." She paused again and turned her head as the pain twisted harder this time. Tears ran from the corners of her eyes. "It really hurts, Leigh. It really, really hurts." She blinked, then let her eyes close, feeling the tears squeezed out to run down her cheeks.

Someone patted her hand. Someone rubbed her arm. The needle bit into her flesh like the sting of a wasp far, far away and she wished and prayed it would come closer. And it did.

"No more, please," the woman said.

"Thank you for your help, Miss Ilseng," the man said.

"*You are very welcome,*" a voice said in her head, but it wasn't her voice. It was a voice she had never heard before, so she tried to turn to see who had spoken. Then she remembered Ann and opened her eyes. "The baby! It's coming soon. You have to help her."

Cody flinched and looked like he was on the edge of tears himself.

"Please," Lucy whispered as the warmth spread from her stinging arm through her aching chest, "please help her."

"I'll do my best, Miss," Cody answered. "Thank you, again."

Lucy closed her eyes. Footsteps faded away. Then except for the sound of her own breathing there was silence in the room, a silence that opened like the petals of a flower and took her in like a bee seeking nectar. Why had the wasp changed to a bee?

Suddenly it was all clear to her. She had talked to Ann's husband. He had said he would help her. He had said he would help Ann. She had talked to him, hadn't she?

Sleep was what she needed—sleep, and escape from all the questions and memories. But something else had to be settled first, something she just remembered, something she should have told Ann's husband because she knew it was important. She knew where Mike Young and the tonkaweya were going.

"Rhineland," she said aloud. "Rhineland," she repeated, waiting for a response that didn't come. Didn't he care? Didn't he want to know where they were going? "Rhineland," she said a third time, "to poison the water." Only the sound of her breathing and the creaking of the house came back to her.

She listened intently to that odd melody until it, too, disappeared into the silence.

THREE | If Murray Goodfox had known how, he would have prayed even harder than he was as he bounced around in the back of the wagon.

It had all been so easy. They had laughed when he had reached for his pistol and suddenly five guns had been pointed at him. Now he was tied up in the back of the wagon, going only-God-knew-where down a deserted gravel road. He could tell they were headed generally south, and that was all he could tell—but he guessed that they were going around Saint Jo on the back roads.

Did that mean his captors didn't want to meet with Nation authorities or DalWorth authorities—or neither? He tried to puzzle it out, tried to remember if they had said anything that would give him some clue. To the marker, they had said. At first he had thought it was *market*, but then they had repeated it and he was sure it was marker.

What marker? What did they mean? They had known who he was, had gotten the information, no doubt, from Vargin, and had asked where Nyllan was. When he'd said she had gone on ahead to make arrangements, they had laughed at him again.

"How you doing, Father?" a voice called from beside the wagon. "You comfortable back there? . . . Well, don't worry about it because we don't have far to go now."

The controller was between him and whoever was speaking, but he was sure it was the woman who was leading this gang. "What have I done to you that I should deserve this?" he asked, surprised to hear the hoarseness in his voice. "What in the name of Our Blessed Mother have I done to you?"

"Just that, Father. You have defamed Her name with your blasphemous teachings. But not to worry, it won't happen again."

"Who are you? Why won't you at least let me ride sitting up? This bumping around is bruising me."

She laughed. "Some call us the Willawalla Gang because they think we live on Willawalla Creek—and we let them because that's what we like them to think. But you know us by another name, the one H.S. gave us."

"You? No, you can't be . . . How did you . . ."

"Can't be the Ash Grove Boys? Why not, Father? Because we're not in Missouri? Because you flew away from us at Joplin? Did you think we were just a little group from a little town and that once you escaped us there you were home free? Father," she said in a soft, chastising tone heavy with sarcasm, "you should never underestimate old H.S. His reach is even longer than yours. Furthermore, there is nothing . . ."

The more she talked, the lower his spirit sank. If they were who she said, then all was lost. There would be no talking them out of whatever H.S. had ordered them to do.

". . . and so you see, you are in good hands, and soon will be facing justice in Missouri. There. You asked me, and like a good host, I told you. What more could you want?"

Back to Missouri? Back to face H.S. and the bishop? They'd put him in that prison in Springfield and let him rot the rest of his days away ministering to the insane. Wasn't that what H.S. had threatened him with? He had to escape. He had to find some way out of this, but . . . but how?

Blessed Mother, he prayed, *please intercede for me and help bring Rhondasue back to me. I know I was wrong in what I said to her and the way I acted. With your intercession, may God forgive me that, and forgive me, too, the pride which brought it to pass.*

In your name and in the name of Your Son, Our Lord, I pray, Our Father who art in Heaven, hallowed be Thy Name. Thy Kingdom come, Thy Will be done . . .

As he silently recited the prayer, he was surprised by the tears that filled his eyes. As he said the Amen, he automatically began the Twenty-third Psalm, wanting in some unspoken way to extend this moment of tender communion he felt, this touch of the Holy Spirit on his heart.

. . . and I will dwell in the house of The Lord forever, Amen.

Let them take him where they would. Let them turn him over to H.S. and the bishop. Let them lock him up in the Springfield jail. It didn't matter. He was the instrument of God and if that was what God wanted, then that was as it would be. His pride had brought him to this capture. His pride had bound him hand and foot and thrown him into the bed of this wagon. But it was the Spirit of The Lord that had touched him and filled his heart with—

"You falling asleep in there?" the woman asked. "Maybe we should make sure you're not so comfortable. Tommy, stop the wagon. Our friend's a little too quiet to suit me."

The wagon rolled to a gentle halt, and as it did, Goodfox struggled to sit up. Just as he did, the woman climbed over the side and kicked him in the chest, knocking him flat again.

He gasped for breath.

The woman grunted and fell beside him, followed by the report of a rifle. A loud wet *thwack* preceded another bang, then another. The driver screamed and fell forward.

People were shouting. The woman beside him moaned. Goodfox could see the blood running out of the side of her head and in a brief, still moment, wondered why she wasn't dead.

An ox bellowed in distress. Another sound followed it in the distance.

Shots were being fired all around him. Oxen were running. The wagon jerked about. The woman gurgled and fell silent.

Then he recognized the sound of a truck, its engine racing, its tires ripping through the gravel. Then another bang, louder, more hollow. Then the truck racing past. More shots, and then a long moment of silence.

Goodfox was not at all surprised to catch himself reciting the rosary.

He tried to ignore the dead woman as he forced himself to his knees. He desperately needed his hands free. There were confessions to be heard here, extreme unction to be administered. Goodfox heard a whimpering from below the wagon and assumed it was the driver. Another woman lay beside the road, her body arched in an unnatural pose, her back covered with a dark stain around a hole the size of her head.

Without warning Goodfox was sick. He vomited violently, sour bits of his breakfast in an acidic flood, first in the wagon, then over the side onto the road as wave after wave of spasms wrang his stomach dry. In the middle of it he heard the truck return, but couldn't look to see it.

When the spasms finally stopped, he heard Rhondasue's voice. "You're disgusting, Murray Goodfox, but I'm glad you're all right. I went a little crazy when I didn't see you. Thought they had killed you or something. Didn't even occur to me that they might have you tied up in here. I just wanted to kill them all, and I damn near did. Those two that got away are carrying some of my lead. You okay?"

"Untie me. And help me down. I have to give them extreme unction."

"These pigs?" she said as she climbed up in the wagon. "What do they deserve?"

"They are Catholics, just like us, doing what they were ordered by your uncle to do," he said as she cut his ropes. "They are still mortal souls deserving God's infinite mercy."

She wiped his face with her bandana. "You're the priest," she said in a voice that was part resignation and part pride. "What do you want me to do?"

CHAPTER 31

ONE | Cody and Kolmer rode with the engineer, a chunky young woman named Dennison whose hair stuck out from under her cap like a fringe of feathers, and her fireman, a skinny boy named Enrique. They were supposed to have been the relief crew for the border train. Behind the engine and a half-full coal tender were the boxcar and a cotton car, each containing twenty-five militia troops including Azle's old squad in the boxcar. In front of the engine was a short flatcar with five troopers behind a wooden barricade at its front, each of them armed with a sniper's rifle—a bolt-action .308 topped by a telescopic sight.

The snipers had been a pleasant surprise for Cody as had the three-man M-60 machine gun team that was riding in the boxcar. They had been flown in from Tampico in a two-engine plane, and had arrived right before the train was ready to leave Crowell. They provided the extra firepower he wanted, plus the plane that was scouting ahead for them, and now all he had to do was catch up with the Nates.

"Are we up to speed?" he asked Dennison.

"Not quite," she answered, never shifting her eyes from the track in front of them. "I've only driven this engine once, you know. Most of the line engines are diesel, although most of the yard engines are coalers. Have to get the feel of her, first, and the feel of the track, too."

"How is the track?"

"No worse than usual, but you see, this is a heavier engine than the two-oh-nine diesel pulling the border train, you know. On good track it can probably do seventy, maybe eighty miles an hour. We'll be lucky to hit sixty—with a tail wind."

"Not very damned encouraging, is she," Kolmer said.

"No. You stay here, though. I'm going back to see if they've heard from Crowell yet about the Benjamin blockade."

Going back was a dangerous process. First Cody made his way along the narrow walk on the side of the coal tender, holding on to the little shoulder-high rail. When he got to the end of the tender he gauged his distance carefully, then jumped to the ladder of the boxcar. After that it got easier. He climbed the ladder, crawled along the top of the rocking boxcar, and finally climbed down a rope ladder through the roof hatch. He did none of it very gracefully, but that didn't bother him as much as the thought of retracing his steps. He would have taken the radioman up to the engine with him, but Brisas had run a test and said there was too much interference from the iron engine itself and convinced him not to.

For some reason he felt like he had made that decision in a fog—not a fog, exactly, but rather like through a dirty window. It was like everything he'd said and done since his conversation with Lucy Ilseng had been happening at an unfocused distance—like there was something between him and the rest of the world. Only when he stepped off the ladder in the dim boxcar and saw Morgan's young face, did he realize what it was.

He'd been thinking about the baby, praying for the baby, hoping that somehow this would all turn out all right and the baby—his baby—would be saved.

"You okay, sir?"

"Yes, Morgan, I'm fine. Brisas, have we heard anything yet from Crowell?"

"Nothing, Cody—uh—Lieutenant."

He smiled at her. "Cody will do just fine, Juanita. You and I've been through too much to"—he thought of Melindo, and Roland Jessup, and before them, Shelia Emery, and his smile faded—"well, you know what I mean. Just call me Cody."

"Right . . . Cody. I've been trying to raise that plane that was supposed to check the track for us, but either one of us isn't on the right frequency, or he has his radio turned off, 'cause I'm getting nothing but static."

"And Crowell hasn't heard from him either?"

"Negatory. *Nada y pues nada.*"

"Keep trying. I'll go back up and—"

The train lurched. Brakes squealed. Cody fell to the floor with Brisas on top of him. People cursed.

The train lurched again and slid to a screaming halt.

Cody was on his feet as soon as Brisas climbed off of him. "Open the doors," he commanded, helping to push the left door open himself. He scanned the area quickly, then jumped to the ground. "Morgan, you, you, you, and Juanita, follow me."

He unslung his carbine as the five of them jumped to the ground, then they all made their way to the front of the train. Kolmer was already on the ground pointing west and shouting, "The plane! Over there!"

As Cody rounded the engine, he saw the pillar of smoke less than a mile to the west. Part of him relaxed with a strange relief that it wasn't the Nates. Part of him felt a sickening sense of loss. "Brisas, get your radioman on the horn. The rest of you go with Sergeant Kolmer to check it out." Even as he gave the orders he wondered if the Nates had shot the plane down. Were they that close?

"Sergeant Ensolita!" he shouted, seeing his new sergeant coming up from the cotton car. "Post a guard on the train—on the double! Get some up top." He spun around. "Two of you snipers get on top of the boxcar. Now! Now!"

In less than five minutes the guards were fully posted and Cody was sitting on top of the train following Kolmer and his team through his binoculars. They had almost reached the plane—or what was left of it, and Cody could see that if the pilot had ridden it to the ground, they weren't going to find him. For the third time since he climbed up there he shifted his gaze to the south, following the line of the tracks into the grey horizon.

At that moment he would have kissed an ox's ass for a little sunlight, because just at the horizon, just at the end of his visual range, there was a smudge over the tracks that might be the border train.

TWO | The sky was full of birds circling overhead, forming a vertical spiral of bodies, black against the high bright clouds like an upside down funnel that opened on a tiny patch of blue. Sunlight fell through the blue hole, a silver thread that followed the spirit of birds, twisting its way down, down, down, until it touched Lucy's chest as lightly as a feather.

Then a face appeared in the sky, a face she recognized but could not identify, a face radiant with peace and reassurance, a face bright with a smile of joy . . . but whose face? Whose?

"Lucy Ilseng? Listen to me. Can you hear me?"

Lucy nodded slowly, deliberately.

"I am Healer Jenny Augusta."

Again Lucy nodded. She remembered that name, but it didn't match the face in the sky.

"Are you the same Mishla's Lucy I met when she was but a child in Childress?"

With great effort Lucy opened her eyes, trying to remember where she was, trying to understand who was talking to her, trying to pull the wisps of reality together to form a picture she could recognize. The birds spiraled above her. "I am Mishla's Lucy," she said to the sky. "Where am I? What do you want of me?"

The woman looked away for a moment. "You have been injured," she said finally. "Do you remember anything?"

Lucy laughed, but when she did, it hurt so much that she cried, and Jenny Augusta patted away her tears with a handkerchief. "Yes, I remember Mishla. She is my mother-teacher. You are her sister, Jenny Augusta, who spent Christmas with us when I was ten years old. Why are you here, Jenny Augusta?"

The birds circled slower, then faster, then slower again, opening and closing the funnel, moving the familiar face back and forth until Lucy had to close her eyes again.

"I have come to take you home."

"I cannot go home. I have patients in Rhineland who must be cared for—a woman who is pregnant with no one to help her, and a boy with wounds who may have the radiation sickness described in my *Taber's*." It all seemed so simple, yet so complicated at the same time. Sweet bird songs filled her heart.

"Others will care for your patients," Jenny Augusta said.

"There are no others." There were no others. There would be no others. There could be no others. It was up to her, up to the face in the sky and the silver spiral of birds and her, Lucy Ilseng, because the others could not know what had to be done.

"Let me be," a voice cried inside her. *"Let the others do what they can. Let me rest."*

"You cannot rest," she said. "It is up to you and you alone to accept your duty and complete your task."

"I must rest," she said.

"You cannot," she said.

"I must, I must, I must."

"Shhh, Miss Lucy. Is the pain worse? Do you want another shot? I'll give you a little more, but that's all."

Who was that? What shot? What was she talking about? What happened to Jenny Augusta?

Something stung her arm. Now she remembered. It was the bee and the flower, the silence and the creaking house, the quakes and shakes, and Ann, poor pregnant Ann, and him . . . him, Tinker? No, Cody . . . Buffalo Bill Cody . . . No. That was a story. Ann's Cody. Him. He had been there. She had talked to him. She had told him about Ann, poor pregnant Ann, and about the tonkaweya. And had she? Had she told him about Mike Young and the spiraling birds and the tonkaweya and the thread of golden sunlight, woven sunlight through a patch of blue, and the face in the sky, the loving face in the sky? Had she told him about all of that?

She must. It was her duty. She must.

"Rest," a voice said. *"Rest now."*

THREE | "It just doesn't seem like a very satisfactory solution," Goodfox said, looking at the crude pyre he and Nyllan had built.

"It'll have to do, Murray. We don't have shovels to dig graves with, or rocks to pile on top of them—or time for much of anything else." She threw another little cedar on top of the stack. "Either we cremate them, or leave them for the buzzards. You're the priest. You decide."

Goodfox took a deep breath and let it out in a long sigh. "Very well. I will pray. You light the fire."

Nyllan took a fuel can from the truck and splashed a little gasoline on the downwind side of the pile. After closing the can and putting it back in the truck, she struck one of her waterproof matches and dropped it on the gas. It caught fire with a soft *whompf*, and within a minute the cedars began to burn hotly with a familiar popping sound.

Praying silently, Goodfox was startled and amazed by the fire. He had never seen anyone cremated, never witnessed a human body being consumed by flames, and as the fire spread quickly and the flames were leaping ten or fifteen feet in the air, he had to turn away from the heat and away from the sight. "Let's go," he said. "I cannot watch this."

"Whatever you say, Murray." Nyllan climbed behind the wheel of the truck, looking once in the bed as though to assure herself that the controller and radio they had transferred from the wagon were still there.

As soon as Goodfox climbed in the passenger side, she started the truck and headed them down the road. Only then did he realize that he had no idea where she had— "Where did you get this truck?"

She waited a long moment before answering him. "Don't you recognize it? It's Vargin's. And, I'm sorry to say, he didn't want to loan it to us," she said with a tight smile, "but he eventually came around to my way of thinking."

"You didn't . . . you didn't . . ."

"Kill him, Murray? No, I didn't kill him. But he'll be walking funny for the rest of his life."

God forgive her. God forgive us both. "And his wife?" He

hesitated, not sure he wanted to know any of this. "What did you do to her?"

"Not a thing. Oh, I tied her up, but I didn't hurt her, and besides, why are you so damned interested in Vargin and his wife? They're the ones who set us up for those New Feds."

"You don't know that for sure."

"The hell I don't," she said as she viciously shifted the truck into fourth gear. "Who else knew where we would be on that road? Who else was on the radio in the middle of the night? Dammit, Murray, sometimes you're so blind to what's happening that it's frightening. What would you have done if I hadn't pulled your ass out of there?" She jerked a thumb over her shoulder.

Again he hesitated, this time because he knew only too well that he had been helpless without her. But could he tell her that? Should he tell her? . . . How stupid! She already knew. His ineptness was painfully obvious to her. "I would have done whatever they had told me to do. I had no choice." The catch in his throat made his voice sound weak and pathetic in his ears.

"That's right—and the New Feds would have gotten rid of you in their own sweet way, and that would have been the end of you."

"But they weren't New Feds. You're wrong about that."

"Then who were they?"

"Ash Grove Boys." He said it almost with pleasure, as though it was a small triumph over her.

"Sheee-it! So old H.S. sent them this far, did he? I never would have guessed he'd risk that."

"They didn't come after us from Missouri. That is, my impression from what their leader said was that they were already here, that the Ash Grove Boys aren't just his enforcement gang in Missouri."

Nyllan looked genuinely puzzled and worried. "If that's true, Murray, then we really have big trouble. What's to stop them from being there in Rhineland waiting for you? Damn! I hope to hell you're wrong."

"I'm not. But surely you don't think they can be in the Republic, do you? H.S. doesn't have that much power."

"Maybe. Maybe not. I sure don't want to find out. Do you? We've got to assume that there are more of them around here, and that the two that got away can bring others after us, or at least warn others. Paved road coming up. We're taking it."

"But you don't know where it leads."

"South. Next chance we get we'll take one that heads west and keep favoring west until we get somewhere we can identify. If we don't know where we're going, it will be hard for them to guess."

He closed his eyes and leaned his head back against the rear window. The vibrations of the glass against his head made him straighten his neck out, but for the longest time he was content to listen to the sounds of the truck and the road, wondering how everything had gotten so confused in so short a time.

"If you're praying, Murray, tell God you'll talk to Him later. I need your eyes for a while."

Goodfox was surprised when he opened his eyes to see raindrops spattering on the windshield. "What do you want me to look for?"

"Anything that might give us some clue as to where we are. It's hard enough concentrating on missing the holes in this road and trying to watch for markers, and the rain's only going to make it worse."

"Like what?"

"I don't know. Mailboxes, cemetery signs, anything."

With a quiet sigh he peered through the windshield, looking for some physical thing that would help *them*, while his soul searched for something less tangible to help *him* in this greyest time of his life.

CHAPTER 32

ONE | They found the pilot's body near the plane, burned beyond recognition. Cody sent out a burial team while Kolmer's team searched all around the wreckage. They found nothing of interest except an unopened parachute that had apparently been blasted clear of the wreckage.

By the time the pilot was buried and Kolmer and his team returned from the crash sight, rain had started to fall and the grey sky, already dark in the east with the coming of night, turned black. Whatever Cody had seen on the horizon had disappeared into the glum weather.

As the train started moving there was something else to worry about. Could he pursue the border train during the night? Or would he just be setting them all up for a Nate ambush and a much greater loss of life? He didn't know the answer, but he had to decide. The engine's lone headlamp shone almost uselessly into the rain and he looked questioningly at Engineer Dennison when she took her eyes briefly from the window.

"Hate to say this, you know, but we're not going to make much progress like this, Lieutenant, and if them Nates are looking for us, we're going to stand out like a white heifer in a black herd, if you know what I mean."

"What if we turned out the light?"

She was looking out the window again and shook her head. "Then we'd have to stop. I mean, it's not like we can depend on the track being good under us."

"I understand. Crowell says the Nates haven't got to Benjamin, yet, so suppose we just keep going—as slow as you have to for safety—until we reach Truscott? Can we do that?"

"It's a good idea. There's some coal in Truscott we could take on, and water, too, and we're going to need both if we run long at slow speeds, you know. But it might take us three, four hours, Lieutenant."

"That's fine with me, Dennison. We've got no place else to go. Tell you what, stop us for a minute while I get the snipers off the flatcar and tell the others what we're going to do."

Even trying to make his instructions as short and straight-ahead as possible, it took Cody fifteen minutes to get everything and everyone squared away like he wanted them. He and Kolmer and Ensolita would alternate watches in the engine cab, and the command post would be the boxcar with a constant monitor on the radio, but with everyone else getting as much sleep as they could after eating. Cody didn't believe they would catch the Nates between here and Truscott, but he wanted to be ready if they did.

Hour after hour the train click-clacked its way slowly to the south, past a crossing sign that said Foard City, but where there were no buildings or lights visible in the darkness, down across the North Wichita, and back up to the plain where Cody, now on his second watch, expected to see some sign of Truscott. The train's headlamp seemed to be working backwards in the rain, presenting them with a well-lit wall of sparkling rain surrounded by hollow fields of darkness.

Faithful to her earlier warnings, Dennison was holding the train at a steady five miles per hour on the flat, and Cody knew from experience he could have marched his platoon faster than that, even in the rain—but he was glad he didn't have to, glad for the platoon and glad for himself. Patience, he told himself, was the thing he had to have at this moment, and as he stared out the window, he thought about patience and patients and Donna Melindo, wondering how she was doing in the Chillicothe Hospital, and that healer, Lucy Ilseng, wondering what had really happened between her and the Nates.

And, of course, Ann and the baby. No matter what turns his life took, now, everything seemed to hinge on the baby—on Ann, too, he guessed, but only because the baby needed her. Seeing as how she'd done what she'd done and he'd come to some kind of terms with it, Cody didn't wish her any harm, but he wondered just how she was going to accept it when he took the baby away from her.

She had no right to it any more, no claim on it, because of her desertion, and Cody had picked up enough about the law to believe that any court would back him, not her. If Ann wanted a baby, let her go find Kendrick Johnson in prison and get him to give her another one. Or any other man she wanted. What difference did it make?

Cody knew he must have failed her in some deep and terrible way, and despite his denials, he wanted her back, and wanted them both back on the farm with the baby beside them, and wanted everything to be right again. Was that too much to ask? Was that wrong? Was he being greedy? Or was he just feeling self-pity and looking for a way—

"Lieutenant," a voice said in the darkness as someone climbed into the cab from the tender, "Corporal Brisas said to tell you that the border train passed through Truscott less than an hour ago."

"Anything else, trooper?"

"Yes, sir. She said to tell you that they've called off the barricade at Benjamin."

"What! Are you sure?"

"Yessir, I'm sure. Corporal Brisas said, 'Tell Lieutenant Cody the barricade at Benjamin was called off by headquarters in Lubbock.'"

Cody stared at the trooper for a long second. "Very well, tell Corporal Brisas I appreciate the information and—"

"Truscott, sir," Dennison called out.

"And pass the word to Sergeant Kolmer that we'll be spending the rest of the night in Truscott."

TWO | *There were two of them, a tall, skinny one, and a short, fat one. Lucy chose the short one, liking the feel of the fat doll when she hugged it.*

"You're a good girl," Mishla said.

If she stayed a good girl, if she didn't break any of the rules, Lucy would get a special present on God Remember Day. But this was her birthday, and it was special, too, because it was the day Mishla had promised to read her a story from The Book of Memories.

That book had fascinated Lucy from the time she had first remembered seeing it on the shelf—maybe from the very time she understood that those things on the shelf were books, that they were full of stories for her. The Book of Memories *was the fattest book on the shelf, but when she had asked Mishla to read to her from that book, Mishla had told her she was too young.*

"When you are seven I shall read to you from that book," she had said.

Today Lucy was seven and today Mishla would read to her from that most special of all books.

"Once upon a time there was a little girl named Lucy whose parents could not take care of her."

"Why does she have my name, Mishla?"

"Let me read on, and you will see."

"Once upon a time there was a girl named Lucy who needed a place to live, a home she could call her own."

"Am I that little girl? Am I?"

"Once upon a time there was a woman named Mishla who wanted a little girl to come live with her."

"I am, I am!"

The doll laughed and so did Mishla. They all laughed so hard that they fell over and disappeared.

Lucy awakened with a start and opened her eyes. It was dark. Under her there was a bed, a wonderfully firm bed with soft sheets. Over her there were warm blankets—except over her left arm. Her arm was cold. As soon as she tried to move it she felt a prick of pain and the restraint of something that held her arm rigid.

Only then did she understand what was wrong. Like the slow pouring of corn syrup in winter, the memory of what had happened flowed into her brain. Ann, the train, the escape, the shooting, Quentin, the strange visitors, Jenny Augusta, and the doll. All of it came back to her.

Only part of it made sense. She had no idea of what time it was, or what day it was, or how long she had been in this bed, but she decided that however long it had been was too long. There was work to be done elsewhere.

Pushing herself up on her right elbow, she fought to focus in the darkness. She saw fuzzy shapes, furniture, a window, a door with a soft line of light underneath it, and a dark, open door—a closet? Were her clothes in there? Clothes? She rubbed herself. Something flannel, soft and warm.

Suddenly the air in the room was cold and she felt hot. She wanted her doll and she needed to cool off. But first she needed to free her left arm. It was so hard to see it, so hard to know what to do next, like her brain was slowing down in a strange dizzy fall with Mishla and the doll and herself, dizzy with laughter, falling, falling—

Lucy threw her body away from the fall, felt herself slip down the velvet way, felt the sharp, jerking pain against her arm, heard something clatter loudly to the floor and rattle in a ring, heard herself cry out, smelled the cool air that washed over her, all so slow and sweet in the distant embrace of the darkness, with voices calling to her through the column of light that changed the wall and spilled into the room like a soft, golden carpet spiked by a hard, blue pain in her chest.

"Oh, my God. The IV's ripped her arm open."

"It's all right. It's more blood than . . ."

"Get her up on the bed and we can . . ."

"Rhineland," Lucy said. "Have to take the doll to Rhineland. Please?"

"Shhh. Shhh, now. You just had an accident. You'll be all right. Just lie still."

"Jenny!"

"I'm here, Lucy."

"Jenny, take me to Rhineland."

"When you're better, dear."

Lucy saw the fire on the water and smelled the bitterness of Mike Young's heart, and knew his heart would make the waters turn dark with his poison. "I have to go. I have to warn them. Please, Jenny, please. I have to warn Rhineland."

Bites. First one arm. Then the other.

No. "No! Don't drug me, please? I have to . . . have to tell them about the baby and the radioactive poison in Rhineland."

"Who do you think she means? She talked about Rhineland before."

"I don't know, but I think we ought to tell Sheriff York."

"Tell the sheriff, tell the sheriff. Tell the sheriff."

"Yes, Lucy, we will tell her. You rest now."

"My knife! My MUST-Kit knife!"

"It's right here. We have it. Don't worry."

"I hope she's going to be all right. Is there anything else we can do for her?"

"Not now. Not until her fever breaks and she regains a little of her strength."

"Go, Lucy, go regain your strength, to tell the sheriff, to run to Rhineland . . . to run, to run and save your doll from the bitter Young and the hard water and the dark poison . . . of the bright swirling funnel, of the birds and the braves of the . . . of the . . . revenge when we get to Rhineland . . ."

THREE | There was just enough room for the two of them to lay side by side in the truck bed. The controller and the radio held up one side of the tarp to give them a little lean-to under which they had zipped their sleeping bags together.

"A silver dollar for your thoughts," Nyllan said as she curled up against him from behind.

"You don't want to know," Goodfox said.

"If I didn't want to know, Murray, I wouldn't have asked. What, are you mad at me again?"

"No, no, nothing like that. I was just, well . . ." Should he tell her, he wondered? "I was just feeling sorry for myself, I guess. I had expected everything to go so well for us, and instead it seems like everything that could go wrong has."

"Not really." She ran her fingers lightly over his chest. "The Ash Grove Boys could have killed you—or me. I could have missed the turnoff and never have found you. Vargin could have killed me. The plane could have crashed instead of having been stolen. The Ash Grove Boys could have caught us before—"

"Enough. Enough. You've made your point."

"Not mine, Murray. God's. You're the one who's always saying that His hand is in everything. If it is, that's why all those other things didn't go wrong. Right?"

Her hand had slipped under his shirt and was working its way in slow circles down toward his waist. He knew what she wanted and felt his body's response already tightening in his groin. As carefully as he could he turned to face her. "Yes," he said softly, aware that he was answering her question and also answering the request spoken only by her fingers. "Yes," he repeated, "everything is under His influence."

Kissing her softly on the nose and cheeks, his hand found the swell of her breast and began kneading gently, but firmly, alert for the hardening of her nipple.

She turned her head to kiss his neck, then began nibbling on his earlobe, darting her tongue around the edges of his ear, flicking it into his ear, as he responded by doing the same to her so that they twisted their bodies together in a brief struggle of passion.

When he relaxed, she relaxed. "I love you," he said softly.

"Don't talk. Don't say anything, Murray. Just make love to me. Make love to me now."

He wanted her. He needed her. God forgive him, he had to have her, now. Without saying anything he pulled her shirt up over her head. It was awkward under the tarp, but they each managed to undress the other quickly, slithering out of their clothes and into a warm, writhing embrace.

Her legs wrapped around one of his and as their mouths met in a rush of lips and tongues, their hips undulated under the press of flesh, each seeking some fuller melding.

Suddenly Rhondasue turned him on his back and straddled his body under the low tarp, pressing him into the warm depths of her, moving her knees up close to his armpits so that even the slightest movement of her hips sent sparks down the main cable of his senses. Goodfox brought his knees up slightly and slid even further into her.

She moaned and started moving up and down, stroking him, holding him, pulling him into her rhythm so that she was riding his hips faster and faster, each thrust bringing them closer to the edge of release.

Now he moaned, helping, sliding, straining until he felt that moment of purpose and knew nothing could keep him from the ecstasy.

They moved in urgent unison, panting, racing, reaching until low moans became cries of joy as Rhondasue peaked in a shuddering spasm and he followed her into the mindless, breathless moment of release, the quivering weight of her adding to the frenzy of his joy.

For several minutes neither of them said anything as they tried to bring their breathing back to normal. It was Rhondasue who spoke first. "Your body's so good. So good. And together we're dynamite." She kissed him softly.

"Amen," he whispered. "Praise the Lord."

CHAPTER 33

ONE | After Cody awoke and looked out of the boxcar, he saw a thin line of sunshine cutting under the pink clouds on the eastern horizon. Sergeant Ensolita brought him a cup of chicory brew and said, "What do you think, sir? Sunshine must be a good omen, wouldn't you think?"

"I don't know much about omens," Cody answered, "but I can tell you right now that I'll take all the sunshine Christodios wants to share with us. I'm tired of doing without."

"Me, too, sir." He took a sip of his own chicory, then said, "Can I ask you something about this mission, sir?"

He looked casually at Ensolita and realized that under the smooth olive skin and thick black hair was a man much older than he looked. "Whatever you want to, Sergeant."

"Well, sir, I understand that you got a field promotion for what happened before we joined up with you, but—"

Cody laughed with embarrassment at outranking this obviously senior man. "Two, Ensolita, neither one of them of my choosing. But I interrupted. I'm sorry. Please . . ."

Ensolita let a small smile curve his mouth. "It's not the promotions, sir, it's, well, if something's going on that's big enough to get your promoted twice in the field, then I'd really like to know what it is."

"How much did Lubbock tell you?"

"Nobody told us nothing much specific. They trucked us in from Quanah and said you were forming a strike platoon and we were part of it. Ed Kolmer filled me in on the Nates and the train, but he's kind of hard to dig information out of, and Brisas said I'd have to ask you."

"I'm sorry, Sarge. I didn't mean to keep you in the dark. It's just that this has all happened so damned fast that— Well, there's no sense making excuses. As soon as everyone's had breakfast, I'll brief you all. How's that?"

"Be fine with me, sir."

"Just one thing, Ensolita. Call me Cody. I may be a lieutenant on the books, but I'm Cody to me and mine, and since you're now one of mine, I'm Cody to you, too."

"Will do, s—uh, Cody, but it'll take some getting used to."

"Then do whatever it takes."

The people of Truscott seemed to be avoiding the train of militiamen sitting on their siding, and that was fine with Cody. His platoon deserved to know who they were up against and what the odds were, but he wasn't about to try to explain it to the civilians. That was Terry's job. Let him do it.

As he and the rest of the platoon were finishing breakfast, the lookout on the top of one of Truscott's grain silos called out, "Riders coming from the west southwest—lots of them."

"Cody, Foard Station's on the radio," Brisas said almost at the same time. "They want to talk to you, asap."

"Ensolita," he shouted, "get a couple of the snipers up on those silos. Kolmer, set up a perimeter. Lookout? How many riders? I want a count. Brisas, tell Foard Station to hold its britches." He watched his orders carried out with grim satisfaction while Brisas brought the radio to him.

"This is Bearcub Leader," he said quickly into the handset. "Please be brief and specific."

"You having problems, boy?" Sheriff York's voice asked in his ear.

"Don't know, Aunt Bertha. Unknown riders approaching from the southwest. Hold on." He covered the handset. "What's the count on those riders?"

"Hard to tell, sir," the lookout called back. "Looks like at least thirty."

"At least thirty riders, my lookout reports." He was startled when she laughed.

"Good. Those should be your reinforcements—least ways

that's what Terry called them. That's what I wanted to tell you about. They left Lubbock day before last—volunteers from the Free State of Utah called the Deseret Demons. Terry routed them from Finney last night to try to join you. And listen to this, Cody. Terry said they were riding *horses*—not mules, mind you, *horses*."

Cody let out a low whistle.

"You ain't heard the best of it. Terry said they gave the Republic three—count 'em—three stallions and ten mares. Can you believe that?"

"What's the catch?"

"I don't know. Terry said you should let them help if you could use them, but to keep an eye on them, too. It's an all-male outfit, and he's pretty sure they're looking for something they ain't told him about yet."

"So why are we taking them in?" He shook his head. "I don't understand. Why dump them on me?"

"I can't tell you everything"—her voice had dropped to a conspiratorial whisper in his ear—"but there's big stuff brewing, Cody. Big stuff. I think the Republic's about to grow real quick-like."

"So what's that have to do with us and the Nates?"

"Use your head, Jeremy. If I'm right about what's going on, the militia's going to be spread thinner than melted butter on a hot skillet. I think Terry's ready to take a chance with these Utah boys because they're basically free help that you'll have control over. That's the other part of it. They're entirely under your orders."

"Lieuten—ah—Cody, they're going to be in range pretty soon. What are your orders?"

"Just keep them in your sights," he shouted back to Ensolita, then to Sheriff York said, "I've got to go. Let you know what happens."

"Wait a second. There's something else. Doc Leigh says that healer we talked to is real concerned about Rhineland."

"What do you mean, real concerned?"

"Like maybe that's where the Nates are headed with their cargo."

Two | "How are you feeling this morning?"

"Better," Lucy said. "Much better than yesterday. Is it possible? Did all that happen only yesterday? My head's clear, but all the memories are fuzzy." That was a lie. Some of the memories were all too clear, but she didn't want to talk about them—at least not with this stranger.

"That's the morphine working."

"You're Jenny Augusta, aren't you?"

"Yes. I'm surprised you remember."

Lucy let that pass. "You were here yesterday . . . but that's all I'm sure of, that you were here. Can you help me?"

"That's why I came. As soon as you're strong enough to travel, I'm going to take you home."

"No," Lucy said firmly. It was time to find out if she could count on this woman or not. The need to know was so clear and simple in Lucy that she never questioned it. "You're going to take me to Rhineland."

Jenny Augusta's face fell into a frowning setpiece of wrinkles. "You mentioned Rhineland yesterday, but we thought you were just delirious. What's so important about Rhineland?"

"That's where my patient's going to be, and I *have* to be there with her."

"Just get that out of your head right now. You're not leaving here for at least a week. Then Mishla wants you back in Childress."

"Don't lecture me," Lucy said with a frown to match Jenny Augusta's. "You have no right. You do have two choices. Either you help me, or you get out of my way, because I am going to Rhineland."

Jenny Augusta hesitated before responding. "I'm sorry, Lucy, but Mishla was very explicit. You're—"

"Damn Mishla!" Lucy was startled and a little frightened by the anger that was boiling out of her, but she made no effort to control it. "I told you what I am going to do. Either you help, or you don't, but no one—not you, not Mishla, not Medic Leigh—no one is going to get in my way. Do you understand that?"

"I, uh, I . . . ." Jenny Augusta looked shocked.

"I have to go," Lucy said more quietly. "It's an obligation—a commitment I have to fulfill." To Ann—and for revenge, she thought. She was surprised by that, surprised by the wave of hatred for Max Quentin that followed the thought of revenge, and surprised most of all by how sure she was about what she had to do. Let Mishla take care of Mishla, and Jenny Augusta take care of who she would. It was time for Lucy to take care of herself.

"But you shouldn't travel, yet. Be reasonable, Lucy, and let others care for your patient. We can call Carol Downing in Munday. She can go up to . . ." Her words trailed off under the intensity of Lucy's gaze.

"The subject is closed," Lucy said with a firm, cold resolution that clung to the heat of her anger. Behind Jenny Augusta she could see her clothes hanging in the open closet. "You can go home, now, and wash your hands of me, and tell Mishla that you did your best. Tell her I refused to cooperate. Tell her I went crazy. Tell her whatever you please. Just stay out of my way, please?"

To emphasize her determination, Lucy shifted her weight and swung her legs around so that they dangled over the edge of the bed. A wave of dizziness threatened to knock her down, but she rode it out, then eased forward until her feet touched the floor.

"You're serious," Jenny Augusta whispered.

"Deadly serious." Leaning on her right side she slowly let her feet accept her weight. A fierce pounding in her head followed by another wave of dizziness threatened to topple her. A throbbing ache beat against the left side of her chest, and it took all her willpower to stand.

Max Quentin's face flashed through her mind, braced her knees, and stiffened her back. The dizziness passed. With Jenny Augusta watching in shocked disbelief, Lucy took her sure first step toward the closet—and toward Rhineland and revenge.

THREE | The road was in poor condition, full of potholes, covered in places by sand, and in several low spots almost completely washed out, but Nyllan drove the truck with confidence and an air of self-satisfaction that Goodfox found delightful and somehow amusing. "You're in a good mood this morning," he said with a smile.

"Course I am. We're on the road, headed in the right direction, and loaded for bear."

"Now that's a queer expression."

She laughed. "Everything's queer in this world, Murray, don't you think? I mean, look at us." She smiled at him. "Here we are driving through a country called DalWorth that used to be just part of a state called Texas, and part of a country called the United States, and part of a world that humankind was trying to tear apart until old Mother Earth did it for them. And what are we doing? We're on a mission to reunite what nature tore asunder and man divided further. Seems pretty damned queer to me." She slowed the truck to take a tight curve. "Doesn't it to you?"

"No. At least not in the way you mean it. We're doing God's work. If He separated us, it was for good reason, just as we are bringing people back together for good reason. I see nothing queer in that." There was an edge in his voice that he didn't mean there to be, and when he saw the muscles of her jaw tighten, he was sorry for it.

"Phew . . . You've got a body that drives me crazy, Murray, but sometimes I worry about you. It's like part of you is missing, or blind, or something. Why can't you see the humor in the world, the absurdity in our daily lives? Why do you have to take everything so damned seriously?"

"There's no need to keep cursing like that just to—"

"I know. I know. Look, I'm sorry my cussing bothers you, but I'm too set in my words to change much of it now. Just cut me some slack, and try to answer my question."

"Which question?"

"Shit. Never mind."

"You mean about why I take everything so seriously?"

"If you knew, why'd you ask?"

He let her new question hang as he sorted through his feelings, trying to find the right answer. "I don't know," he said finally. "Maybe it's because there is so much to be done and the sheer size of the task makes it necessary—"

"Maybe you just don't know how to see the humor."

"I beg your pardon."

The truck bounced erratically and she fought to control it. "You're stuck, Murray, stuck in a role you've taken on, a role you made up for yourself. But you forgot to leave room in it for anything funny—anything that would make you laugh first and wonder about it later. God, I don't understand you sometimes."

He hated discussions like this—especially when she made him realize some truth about himself that he hadn't recognized or accepted before. Changing the subject was his only escape. "Once we get home, how long will it take you to set up the controller?"

"A day, maybe two," she said without hesitation. "Then we'll have to check it out, of course."

"How?"

"Oh, I thought we'd take a shot at the Lake Catherine Dam, and see if it breaks. If it does"—she grinned when he gasped— "we know the satellite's working."

"I don't think that's funny."

"My point exactly. You don't think anything's funny."

"So? You have enough humor for both of us." He meant more than he said and hoped she understood that.

"Humor's better when it's shared. Fact is, sometimes that's the only time when things are funny—when they're shared."

"Then you'll have to teach me," he said quietly, "so we can share."

Her response was a puzzled look. "You're serious, aren't you?"

"Like you said, I'm always serious."

"Damn," she whispered. "How do you teach someone when things are funny? I don't know how, Murray."

There was a sadness in her voice that touched him, and he realized that she, too, was taking this very seriously. "Okay, start with the times you remember me laughing."

"No. I need to think about it for a while. Let's talk about the controller and your satellite. Do you actually know what this satellite will do?"

"Yes. Like I told you, it's armed with a solar-powered laser capable of penetrating five inches of titanium armor on a cloudy day."

"I read the book, too. What we need to know is if it was actually ever tested and proven."

"That's impossible to know. It didn't come with any documents about that."

"So we're back to square one. What the hell are you going to do if it doesn't work like it's supposed to?"

"That's where the Quentins' little project comes in. They're the backup, just in case."

"And you'd really do it? I have to know. Would you really poison the Brazos with plutonium?" There was a quiver of censure and disbelief in her voice.

"If that's what God wants," he said, "that's what we'll do."

She shook her head slowly, a grim look squeezing her face. "We'd better find you a sense of humor pretty soon, Murray, 'cause if things go wrong, you're going to be the butt of a great cosmic joke."

Goodfox didn't understand what she meant, but he didn't want to talk about it any more. Whatever happened was in God's hands.

CHAPTER 34

SISTER PAULA KATHRYN | St. Joseph Church in Rhineland sat atop a gentle hill on the northern side of town. Its tall middle spire, topped by a radio antenna with a cross at its peak, was visible from all the surrounding countryside. Despite its tan brick structure, St. Joseph looked like one of the faded prints of European churches that adorned the classrooms of the school next door.

To the south of St. Joseph, the town was laid out in neat blocks of white frame houses and large vegetable gardens. To the north, the open fields bordered by hedges and trees rolled gently down toward the Brazos River. Brick red indian paintbrushes and white-tipped bluebonnets crowded each other in large patches that transformed the fields into brilliant blankets trimmed in dark green. Along the hedgerow by the highway, nodding spiderworts towered over pink phlox and the yellow greenthread daisies. Warming southern breezes and occasional moments of sunshine encouraged ten or fifteen other varieties of flowers to fill every available piece of untended ground.

All the flowers trembled with the earth as Paula Kathryn waited on her hands and knees behind the church for the quakes to stop. If she thought about the quakes anymore, it was only to attend to a nuisance over which she had no control. In a way, she actually liked them, liked being reminded regularly that human beings were insignificant creatures on the face of God's creation. She liked as well the opportunity to pause in her daily chores and reflect in prayer the feelings of her heart. If there was peace to be found in this world, it could only be found in a life totally dedicated to God, with all trust and faith placed in His will and His love.

That was why she worried about Father Murray. His messages from Missouri had gotten stranger the longer he stayed there, and now he was bringing that electronics technician back with him, and Paula Kathryn was certain in her bones that he was attracted to more than Nyllan's knowledge and technical skills. How could he be so trusting of someone from the Old United States? Only once had Paula Kathryn met Rhondasue Nyllan, but that meeting was enough to convince her that Miss Nyllan was a sinful poison in a beautiful container waiting only to find the right victim. What Paula Kathryn feared most was that Father Murray had become that victim.

As the quaking stopped she stood up and wiped off her hands. She had known Murray Goodfox too long, from his days at Windthorst before he was ordained, and though she had never in all those years doubted the sincerity of his faith, neither had she ever allowed herself any illusions about his mortal vices and desires. Had she herself not shared with him . . . No, she wouldn't think about that. It was part of her sin, and she would do penance for it all the days of her life.

"Sister! Sister Paula?" Brother Jacob shouted to her from the vestry window, "there's a call for you on the radio."

"Coming," she called in return, gathering up her ankle-length brown dress and hurrying back to the church. She wondered if Father Murray had encountered more trouble along the way, or if the archbishop . . . Better not to guess about that. If the archbishop needed her services, she would find out soon enough.

"Thank you, Brother Jacob," she said as she entered the dimly-lit radio room and took her seat in front of the set.

"You are quite welcome, Sister," he said as he backed out of the room and closed the door.

Paula Kathryn was sure that sometimes Brother Jacob listened from the other side of the door, but she was also sure that his allegiance to Father Murray and the cause was unshakeable, and that Jacob only listened out of curiosity, and perhaps from a need to feel a part of what was happening.

"This is Sister Paula K., responding," she said in the deep voice she used only on the radio.

"Sister Paula K., please give our regards to His Holiness."

It took a full second for the message to register in her brain.

The caller wasn't talking about the Pope. He was telling her to prepare to send and receive scrambled signals. She took a rarely used key from the ring at her waist and inserted it in the scramble-board cover. "Transmitting your regards," she said before unlocking the board.

Moments later a sequence of colored lights flashed on the board. She typed in, "Faith of Our Fathers."

When the voice came back to her, it had a thin, tinny sound. "Our Father calls upon us to serve," he said.

"We serve at His pleasure," she replied.

"By the grace of Our Lord."

"By the love of Our Mother."

"Amen."

"Amen." She was surprised that she remembered the proper responses after not having used this special sequence for over a year, and she was pleased that she had recognized the voice of the archbishop before the coder went into effect. Something mighty important must be happening for the archbishop himself to be calling her.

"Sister Paula, I am speaking to you on behalf of His Eminence and the Conference of Cardinals. We believe that your pastor has deviated from the ways of God and the Church, and consequently, it is our duty to relieve him of his parish and call him back into the arms of the Church for a renewal of faith."

Nothing new here, she thought. Wonder what he's building up to? And what new trouble Father has managed to add to the list of grievances they have against him?

"Furthermore, we are disturbed to learn that a group of laymen setting out to assist your pastor have been waylaid and most cruelly roasted to death on an open fire."

Her stomach turned. Roasted to death? The words almost knocked her down. It was barbaric!

"Consequently, we must enlist your aid and assistance in helping Father Goodfox if you can. Have you followed our transmittal thus far?"

"I have, Your Grace," she said, "although I am shocked and saddened by what you have told me."

"We understand, and we are sure that Father Goodfox will share your feelings when he learns of what has happened. Therefore, if you can tell us where he is, or give us his radio code so that we may contact him directly, you will enable us to act in God's best interests."

Paula Kathryn rolled her eyes and hesitated for a long moment before answering. She had to be very careful here, or she was going to create problems rather than helping to solve them. "Say again, please," she whispered into the microphone. "We did not copy your last transmission."

"We want his radio code and his current location. Over."

She whistled hard into the microphone, drawing out the sound before answering. "Bad reception, here. Pastor's current location unknown. Last broadcast was night before last from a safe house somewhere near Saint Jo. He is traveling by oxen and wagon, so he cannot be too far away." At least she could be grateful for the fact that she didn't know what route he would be taking, or where he would be stopping along the way.

"And his radio code?" the voice asked impatiently.

Again she whistled, then scraped a fingernail lightly over the microphone. "That is set by the radios themselves at broadcast times and altered as the broadcast proceeds. Without one of these matching gizmos like we have on the radios, no one can follow the broadcasts or break the code. At least that's what their inventor claimed."

"Do you know his current route of travel?" the archbishop asked.

"No. He did not reveal that information to me."

"Very well, Sister Paula. When he next calls you, we expect you to ascertain his location, his route, his stopover plans, and his expected time of arrival. Is that understood?"

"Understood, Your Grace. Is there any other way I can serve?"

"Not at this time. Out." A roar of empty static followed his voice, and Paula Kathryn turned down the volume before switching the radio back to its monitoring status.

Her first instinct was to rush to the cloister chapel and pray for forgiveness for her lies to the archbishop, but she quickly repressed that urge. She would confess the lies with all her other sins tomorrow when Father Irving made his weekly visit. That would do. So long as she confessed and was truly sorry, God would understand. Yet as she left the radio room, she had to remind herself not to go to the chapel and consciously directed her steps back outdoors.

Deciding how she could best resolve the conflict that had been relentlessly growing within her was a problem not so easily dealt with. Her allegiances were strong to three aspects of her life—aspects she had assumed for years went hand-in-hand toward a multiply rewarding future. Now it was all too clear that her assumption was wrong.

First and foremost she was Paula Kathryn, sister of the Holy Catholic Order of Saint Geraldine, bride of Christ, keeper of the faith, and servant to the needy and afflicted. But she was still very much the woman she had been born, Margarita Maria Owen, daughter of devoutly Catholic, deeply political parents, heir to their fervor for reuniting the states, and a secret member of ASAP—the All States, All People party of the New Federalist League which they had helped found.

Ultimately, however, in ways that she dared not examine too closely, she was the devoted follower of Father Murray Goodfox, whose fervor for reunion and devotion to that belief served to enhance her love for this priest, who was both her spiritual father and her intimate friend.

How then could she answer the archbishop? she asked herself as she began walking through the flower-strewn field north of the church. How could she respond within the tenets of her faith, as she knew she must, without betraying Father Murray? And if the archbishop was truly the New Federalist he claimed to be, why was he so opposed to what Father was trying to do? It made no sense—except that it made all the sense in the world.

Father Murray was too aggressive for the archbishop, all too prepared to go to battle against the faithless for what he believed, and, it had to be admitted, all too ready to take the role of leadership offered in that battle with a pride that was surely as deadly a sin as any other he committed.

She blushed to think that she might be privy to his sins even as he was privy to hers. But that was different. When he heard her confession, he was the instrument of God, and it was God she was confessing to, not Father Murray. Still, she had no illusion that Father didn't hear and remember what she was telling God in the privacy of the confessional. After those times when she had confessed to an attraction of the flesh for an unnamed man, she felt an unspoken tension between Father Murray and herself that she could attribute to no other cause, no matter how hard she tried.

And he was a beautiful man. There was no denying that, and no sin in recognizing one of God's own, well wrought—no sin if recognition and admiration was all that happened. To dream about that beautiful creation, to open up to him in the dark unconscious, that was the sin.

As she shook her head, Paula Kathryn heard a goat bleating and suddenly realized that she had come full circle through the field and was back at her garden behind the church. Her thoughts had come full circle as well, only now they were clearer to her. Her first allegiance, whatever the cost, had to be to God and her order. Her second had to be to the archbishop. Only after she met her obligations to God and the church could she devote her energies to the reunification of America.

She picked up her shovel and started digging in the damp soil, turning it over, breaking up the heavy clods of dirt, trying to think of nothing else but the task itself—not the reason for it, not the goal to be accomplished, not the reward for a task well done, but rather, the doing of the work as an end in itself because it needed doing. She tried, but she failed, because the thorn under her best-seated resolutions was that she could not bring herself to betray Father Murray.

She would provide the archbishop with information, because that was her duty. She would be obedient in all ways to what His Grace demanded of her, provided that he neither asked her to break her vows nor to harm her priest and his church. Those things she could not and would not do, regardless of what the archbishop wanted. Those things, after all, were sacred.

Suddenly the digging went easier, the earth yielding to her shovel and breaking apart in preparation for the planting to come. There was a rhythm in it that was broken only when Brother Jacob shouted to her again from the vestry window.

"It's the father!" Excitement had raised his voice a full octave. "It's the father! Hurry, Sister, hurry!"

CHAPTER 35

ONE | The riders stopped fifty yards short of the tracks. "Hello, the train," shouted a man wearing a long, brown duster. "We're a-lookin' for a place called Truscott."

"You've found it," Cody answered. Never in his life had he seen so many men on horses. Horses! Broad-shouldered, long-maned, beautifully-formed animals immediately recognizable as different from mules. He counted thirty-two horses, three without riders, and took a quick breath. "You the Deseret Demons?"

"That's how we're known. We call ourselves the FURTs—the Free Utah Recon Troop. You the West Texas Militia?"

"We are," he called back. "Come on in." Turning, he said, "Ensolita, Kolmer, relax the troops, but keep the lookouts."

The closer the riders got, the more Cody realized how young they were. None of them looked to be more than twenty or so, yet they all had a look in their eyes and a set of their mouths that told him these were boys who had seen some hard times together. He didn't know what it was, exactly, but he knew for sure what it wasn't. It wasn't innocence. It wasn't carelessness. It wasn't uncertainty. And it wasn't fear. No, it was something that couldn't be spoken plain to someone who didn't know where to start talking about it.

"We were told to find a Lieutenant Jeremiah Cody." The man wore a scruffy blond beard under a hooked nose and eyes so dark they could have been black. Shoulder-length blond hair stuck out from under a dirty, sweat-stained grey hat.

"You got him," Cody said, trying to look at the man and not his beautiful horse.

"I'm Sam Ogden, elected leader of this recon troop. Understand you're in need of some help." The man climbed down from the saddle and the rest of his group did the same, all the while most of them seeming to keep their eyes moving around Cody's platoon.

"Not exactly." Cody noticed immediately how bowlegged the man was and wondered if that came from riding. "Attorney General Terry told me you volunteered to help if you were needed."

Ogden smiled for the first time and revealed straight yellow teeth. "That's a fair enough telling, I guess." He held out his hand and Cody shook it, then Ogden pulled a folded piece of paper out of his breast pocket and handed it to Cody. "But I'll tell you right now, Lieutenant, that you can use us whether you think you need us or not."

The paper was a free passage chit and a note recommending the FURTs to Cody. He handed it back. "You're pretty sure about that, aren't you, Mr. Ogden?"

"Sam. Everybody just calls me Sam, and yes, I am sure

about that. It ain't hard to tell that you people in this country are short on horses and mules, and heaven knows you can't make time on an ox's back."

"True enough, so far," Cody said. He didn't know if he liked the way this young man looked at him, or the tone in his voice, but he refused to make any judgements—yet. "But not having ticks don't make a dog lame."

Ogden shook his head with a rueful grin. "Shoot, we've never been compared to ticks on a dog before, but I think I see what you're sayin', Lieutenant. We can give you a lot of mobility—and that's better than ticks."

Cody allowed himself a smile in return. "Does that mean you're going to loan us your horses?"

Several of Ogden's men started to protest before he spoke. "Can't rightly do that, but you can use our mobility to help you find the people you're lookin' for. What did Terry call them?"

"Nates. But what do you get from us?"

"Women."

He said it so simply and quietly that Cody wasn't sure he had heard it. "Did you say, women?"

"Yep. One for each of us. That's what we're here for."

"Bet you didn't tell Attorney General Terry that, did you?"

"Nope," Ogden said with a smile that revealed even more teeth. "He seemed to have a lot on his mind, so we didn't want to burden him."

"And where do you expect to get these women?"

"Wherever they are. That one looks pretty good to me." He nodded toward Brisas with a broad wink.

Cody laughed. "She'd chew you up and spit you out before you got shuck of your clothes. How about it, Juanita? You think you could use any of these boys?" The sarcasm in his voice pleased him for no reason at all—or maybe because these boys were so cocky.

Brisas spat without changing her expression. "I'd take a team of four, Cody. They don't look like they could go more than once every six hours." Behind her the platoon laughed.

"I read you," Ogden said, winking at Brisas, "and I wouldn't bet against you. But don't you see? Where we come from there are too many free men and not enough free women, so you could probably work yourself a deal with two of us." He rolled his eyes. "Maybe even three if you give us a test run first."

His boys and the platoon whooped and hooted at that.

"Dibs on any three, Juanita? Sound like a deal to you?"

"Nope. Four or nothing. Maybe you'd better send them home, Cody, until they grow up."

"Well, Sam, since Juanita has always struck me as a real sharp woman, I'd have to agree with her that your deal's a little overrated. What else will you take for this mobility you're offering us?" This was getting them nowhere, but Cody sensed that it was allowing everyone to release a lot of tension, and there was nothing wrong with that. Besides, it was fun, and he was enjoying it, and right at this moment he couldn't remember the last time he'd done something just for the fun of it.

"We heard about you Texicans. Folks in New Mexico say you're hard and crazy. I'm beginning to believe 'em."

"As rightly you should," Ensolita said as he walked up beside Cody. "Tell you what, Lieutenant. Suppose they let us mount one of our troops for each four of theirs? That'd be, what—six of our people with twenty-four of theirs with two horses left over, right?"

"What's the advantage?"

Ensolita's mouth barely curled upward. "Well, if they can talk six of our women into riding with them, that'd get these boys out of our hair for three or four days."

Laughter and catcalls from both sides answered him.

"What do you say, Lieutenant?" Ogden asked. "Can you use us or not?"

The urgency to get moving had returned, and Cody was a little sorry that it had, but he knew it was time. "We'll use you for something," he said with a wink. "Let's have some chicory and talk about it."

TWO | Jenny Augusta had been true to her promise and had returned in less than an hour after Lucy convinced her that with or without help, she was going to Rhineland. Lucy hadn't realized how much the wound and the morphine had weakened her until she struggled to slip her head and right arm through the thong that held her MUST-Kit knife and settled it against her side under her armpit. But she refused—abolutely refused—to give in to physical weakness. She had been weak before and would be weak again. There was no time to indulge herself in it now.

"I can't believe I'm doing this," Jenny Augusta said as she laced up the second of Lucy's boots.

Lucy concentrated on putting her shirt on without aggravating her wound. "Uh-hunh."

Medic Leigh had told her she was literally taking her life into her own hands if she insisted on traveling. "It's my life," Lucy had replied, knowing that Medic Leigh was exaggerating. Lucy's wound wasn't that bad.

If her resolve started to slip, she would think about Max Quentin. To get even with him she could do anything. So long as she kept that thought in her head, the strength of her will would be more than enough to keep her going.

"There. Your boots are done," Jenny Augusta said as she stood up. "What do you want me to tell Mishla?"

"Nothing. She doesn't need to know anything about this." Lucy breathed slowly in and out as though she could suck strength straight from the air.

"But I have to tell her something."

"Then tell her the truth. I wouldn't lie to her. No need for you to lie on my behalf. Did you find me a driver?"

"Yes. One of my friends, Nancy Russell, said she would take us all the way to Rhineland in her covered surrey if that's where we wanted to go."

Lucy frowned, distrubed by a slight feeling of nausea as much as by Jenny Augusta's statement. "Us? We? What's that supposed to mean?"

"It means, young lady, that I'm going with you."

"You can't."

Jenny Augusta smiled with great patience and said, "I can— and I will. Who's going to stop me?"

"But this is no concern of yours."

"Yes, it is. Just as that pregnant woman is a concern of yours, you are a concern of mine. We all have obligations to our patients."

Lucy returned the smile as she felt a little wave of relief. "Thank you, Jenny Augusta. As much as I hate to admit it—to myself more than you—I'll need help on this trip."

"Of course you will, child. Do you want this?" She held out Lucy's pistol belt.

"Yes." She accepted it and automatically checked to see if her revolver was loaded. It wasn't, and there was no ammunition in the pouch.

"Medic Leigh put all the ammunition out in the shed. Said she wouldn't have it in the house. We'll get it as we leave."

"I have to thank her for what she did for me," Lucy said as she stood up very slowly and began putting on the belt. The weight of the pistol felt warm and reassuring to her, a strange counterbalance to the wound on her left side. Just having it on made her feel stronger.

"She left, Lucy. She didn't want to see you and didn't want to talk to you, or me either. Leigh doesn't have much use for healers—even if I was here in Crowell twenty years before her—and she thinks we're both reckless and foolish."

Lucy straightened up. "Then there's nothing more to do here, is there?"

"Just one thing."

"What's that?"

"I want to know your reason for doing this."

With a shake of her head Lucy said. "It's personal."

"You mean it's revenge, don't you?"

"It's that, too. But it's more than that. Maybe later I can explain it to you."

"If I'm going to help you all the way, Lucy, I need to know."

"I understand that." She took Jenny Augusta's arm. "And I'll tell you. I promise I will. Just as soon as I can." When he's finished, she thought. No one could help her with that except Max Quentin. She was going to give him a choice he wouldn't like.

THREE | "Goodfox, out," he said with resignation.

"Something's wrong with that woman," Nyllan said as she closed up the radio and began tying it down again.

"There's nothing wrong with Sister Paula Kathryn. She just must be tired because of all the responsibility she's been handling for me. Believe me, there's nothing wrong with her."

"Why are you so defensive about her?"

There was a hint of suggestiveness in Nyllan's voice that he didn't like. "Because she's my friend as well as my assistant, and I don't like you criticizing her."

"Oh, well, excuse me." She twisted the yucca rope tight. "I didn't realize Sister Paula was such a special friend that she couldn't do anything wrong. Not like me, is she? I do lots of things wrong—according to you, anyways."

"Now listen, Rhondasue, I don't want you acting like—"

"Dammit to hell, Murray, you listen. I don't give a shit about how you want me to act." She threw his side of the tarp at him. "I thought we'd settled this problem of yours, but I guess we haven't. Let me lay it—"

"What problem? What have I done now?" He was angry with her, and couldn't understand why she was always attacking him.

"It's simple. You can criticize me, right? Then I can criticize who I damn well please—including you and your precious nun. When you two move out of your little glass house, then we can have a real stone fight."

Goodfox concentrated on tying the tarp down, wondering how he could constantly keep overlooking the fact that Rhondasue was so sensitive. Maybe it was because she seemed so strong and independent. Or maybe it was the independence itself that made her so defensive.

"You ignoring me, now?" she asked as she opened the door to the cab. "Turning chicken on me, Murray?"

"No, to both questions. I was just trying to decide how to apologize to you."

"Just say you're sorry and mean it."

"All right. I'm sorry. I always assume I can treat you like an equal and be totally honest with you about—"

She climbed up into the truck and slammed the door. "You still don't understand, do you?" she shouted. "Equality's what I'm asking for—the right to an equal opinion whether you like it or not." Lowering her voice as he climbed in beside her, she stared straight at him, but he avoided her eyes. "Only I'm not asking you, Murray—I'm telling you that I won't settle for less than that. I've got no bitch with your honesty—only with your constant put-downs."

"That's a lie. If I'm honest, you call it a put-down. There's no way to win in that situation."

She laughed bitterly. "Are you telling me that you can't give me an honest opinion without either telling me what to do or attacking me?"

During the long pause before he answered her, he wondered if that was really what he did? Was that it? Was that why she flew off at him all the time? "I . . . I, uh, do I really do that?"

"All the time, Murray." Giving him a little smile, she

reached over and patted his hand. "I love you in spite of all that," she said, "but I could sure live without it."

He turned his hand over and clasped hers. "Then I am sorry, Rhondasue, and I do mean it, and I'll try—I promise I will try—not to do it again. I'll pray for God's help."

"That's why I love you. Because I know that you really do care about me and that you don't mean to hurt me."

"Thank you," he said softly, wondering why she averted her eyes and wanting more than anything to repeat their lovemaking of the night before. But there would be time enough for that later. "Maybe we'd better get going."

Nyllan laughed and started the truck. "Afraid I might jump your bones?"

"Nope. Afraid we might get caught by more of the Ash Grove Boys *in flagrante amori*."

"Does that mean what I think it does?"

He smiled. "Indeed, my most special friend, it means, in your vernacular, jumping each other's bones."

As she put the truck in gear, Nyllan looked almost disappointed. "Oh. I thought it had something to do with love."

"It has everything to do with love." He almost regretted saying that, sure that she would read more into his words than he meant her to. But maybe she needed something extra right now, and if he could give it to her this way, what was wrong with that?

"Then let's get some place where you can show me," she said with a sudden grin.

"To Rhineland, driver."

"To Newport across the border, first. We still have to get out of DalWorth."

FOUR | Instead of the cloister chapel where her sisters would be in afternoon prayer, Paula Kathryn went immediately from the radio room to the main sanctuary of St. Joseph and knelt before the altar.

Dearest Geraldine, saint of our order, blessed minister to the world's downtrodden, listen, I pray, to the troubles of my heart and speak to Our Lord God and Saviour for this unworthy bride of His church.

I have sinned by lies of omission against the archbishop whose leadership in all things temporal and holy I have sworn to obey. I have further sinned by omission against my pastor and friend whose temporal and holy works I have sworn to uphold. My heart is troubled, and my doubts are many. Grant me guidance, I pray, and reinforce my faith that I might live in the light of your beneficence and according to God's Holy Will. Amen.

Slowly she crossed herself, rose from her knees, and backed out the side door of the sanctuary. She felt better for having prayed, but felt no relief from the burden of her deeds. Soon it would be time to supervise the preparation of the guest room for Father Irving's arrival before supper, time to attend to the preparations for the morrow's mass, and time to ensure that she was ready for Father Murray's mystery guests. Tomorrow she could begin the preparations for Easter and Father Murray's homecoming.

As Paula Kathryn walked the narrow hall from the church to the kitchen and the dormitory wing, she felt a growing sense of trepidation about the arrival of strangers. Ordinarily she would be more than pleased to receive strangers, glad for the details of their travels and their comments about the greater world they had seen. However, there was something about the way Father had avoided giving her details about these unknown guests that hardened the edges of her heart against them.

If they were important guests, as they must be, why was he so secretive about them—especially when he knew she would want to have preparations exactly right for their arrival? It was not only that his actions made little sense to her. She quickly realized that she felt offended by his keeping such information a secret. What had she done or failed to do that he would treat her this way? Was she not his trusted assistant? Was she not the one person in whom—

She stopped with a smile. It was obvious. It was so obvious that she had missed it completely. The radio. Father had been afraid to tell her over the radio. Of course! How foolish of her to believe otherwise.

Opening the door to the kitchen, she was not overly surprised to see a stranger in dirty, weather-worn clothes sitting at the large worktable eating a bowl of Sister Joana's soup. St. Joseph's hospitality was well known in the region. "Greetings and welcome," she said.

"My thanks, Sister," he said, interrupting himself in mid-slurp to answer her.

"This is Sister Superior Paula Kathryn," Sister Joana said, "and this is Max Quentin, Sister, a friend of Father Murray's."

"Then doubly welcome," Paula Kathryn said looking more closely at Mr. Quentin for some sign of gentility under the dirt. Could this be one of those Father had told her— "I'm afraid Father Goodfox is not here, presently, Mr. Quentin."

He finished chewing, then said, "That's all right, Sister. I rode ahead just to let him know we're on our way. This is where he told all of us to meet him, so when the others get here, we'll just set up camp behind the church and wait for him."

Before she could respond, the room shook violently for a second or two. Paula Kathryn dropped to her hands and knees as the room vibrated in a long, fading tremor.

Soup sloshed out of the bowl. Pots and pans swung noisily on their hooks. The overhead light blinked. Dust sifted down from the high ceiling. Outside, mules brayed, goats bleated, and oxen bawled.

"Damn," Mr. Quentin said in a low voice.

Under ordinary circumstances, Paula Kathryn would have admonished him about cursing in God's kitchen, but she understood how the tension of the moment could have caused him to lose his sense of where he was, and held her tongue.

"Son-of-a-bitch."

That she couldn't ignore. "Please, Mr. Quentin," she said as she climbed slowly to her feet. "You are in God's house now."

His brief smile was hard and cold. "So what?"

She had never met anyone so arrogant in her life. "So, Mr. Quentin, if you cannot control your language, I must ask you to leave."

He pushed the soup bowl away and stood up. "I'll see what I can do about that. In the meantime, Sister Joana here said you had a hot-water shower, and I sure as hell could stand to be clean."

"You are most welcome to our facilities, of course," she said with less charity than she should have. "When will the rest of your party arrive?"

"Not for a day or two."

"Good. That will give us time to properly prepare for them. If you'll follow me, Mr. Quentin, I will show you the shower—and the laundry room," she added with the slightest hint of malice. The very thought of him sullying the shower with his filth gave her cold chills, and she prayed that he was not representative of the rest of his group.

CHAPTER 36

ONE | It took almost two hours for Cody to reach a compromise with Sam Ogden and his group. They would squeeze aboard the train with the militia, then as soon as the train either caught up with the Nates or reached Benjamin, the FURTs would give up half their horses to Cody and fourteen of his troops so that he had a mounted unit under his command.

In exchange for that, Cody agreed to help them in whatever way he could to find women willing to go with them once this current problem was solved. He wasn't at all sure what, if anything, he could do to help them. But once Ogden understood that Cody's assistance didn't guarantee anything, it seemed like an easy enough agreement to make. Through all the talk, Cody got the funny feeling that so long as some of the FURTs got to fight, and at least got the chance to look for women, that they wouldn't be too unhappy.

In less time than he would have expected, they were all aboard the train and Engineer Dennison soon had them rolling south at a respectable fifteen miles an hour. Only then did Cody see the lazy column of smoke rising against the grey sky and spreading out toward them under the clouds, and he had a bad feeling about what it might mean. Thirty-five minutes later as they headed down the incline to the South Wichita, they smelled what was burning and saw the border train sitting on the other side of the river.

"Damn," Cody said as Dennison applied her brakes and threw the engine into reverse. There was no railroad bridge across the river. The Nates had used their train to pull the supports out from under the bridge, then had set fire to the collapsed bridge and their train before abandoning it. Even from the opposite bank Cody could see fresh wagon tracks headed out of the bottom through the cedar brakes.

Dennison halted their train well short of the end of the tracks, and as soon as it stopped, Cody jumped off the engine and was quickly followed by his troops and the FURTs. A cloud of smoke rolled up the hill to greet them.

"Sure as hell somebody made a mess of that," Ogden said.

"Looks like this is where we divide up, Sam. Let's get your horses unloaded and decide who's going with who."

Sam's men drew straws. Cody asked for volunteers who had riding experience, then had to choose among them until he had his fourteen including Brisas, Kolmer, Morgan, and four more from Azle's squad, plus two of the snipers and the radioman. They spent an hour sorting everyone out and transferring equipment. "This machine gun scare your horses?" he asked Ogden.

"Probably. Far as I know, they've never heard automatic fire up close."

"The machine gun team will have to walk. Sergeant Ensolita, I'm going to ask you to lead the walking group into Benjamin. If I were you, I'd cross on the Six-bridge over there," he said, pointing to the highway bridge about a mile downstream, "and follow the highway on in. Shouldn't be more than about five miles on the road." The wind shifted, pushing the acrid smoke from the burning creosote-treated bridge away from them to the northwest.

"Yes, sir," Ensolita said with obvious disappointment.

"We're not much used to walking," one of the FURTs said reluctantly as he handed Cody the reins to a broad-shouldered paint with eyes that seemed intent on him.

"The sergeant will take care of you. Set an easy pace, Ensolita."

"Yes, sir."

"Jessup—" Cody could have kicked himself. Roland Jessup was dead, and the pain of that loss cut a thin layer of confidence out from under him. But something else replaced it. "Ed, Sam, let's get mounted and get after them." Despite the calmness in his voice, Cody had to fight the growing excitement he felt as he put his left foot in the stirrup and swung up on the paint.

"All right, Demons," Ogden said. "Mount up."

"I thought only other people called you the Deseret Demons."

Ogden grinned. "Well, I wouldn't deny that we've been known to encourage them a time or two."

Suddenly Cody understood. "So people just might think there are two groups, the FURTs and the Deseret Demons?"

"That wouldn't surprise me in the least, Lieutenant. Looks

like everybody's in the saddle—though some of them look more comfortable than others." As he spoke a soft rain began to fall.

"Sergeant Ensolita," Cody said, "if we make contact with the Nates, I suspect you'll hear the shooting. We'll send up a green flare it it looks like we'll need help, red if we don't. Green, you get to us as fast as you can. Red, you proceed to Benjamin and commandeer some transportation. The mayor there's named Delagardo. He may not want to cooperate, but you tell him you have full authority from Attorney General Terry, and take what you need to get back to us."

"Can do, Cody. But suppose you don't make contact?"

"If they've bypassed Benjamin, we'll send someone into town to get things ready for you and let you know what's happening."

"Gotcha. Good hunting," he said with a crisp salute.

"Thanks," Cody said, returning the salute. "With any luck we'll see you soon." Turning his horse, he lead the way down the slope toward the river, as full of amazement at being on a horse after so many years as he was at all that had happened this past week. The riverbed was wide at this point, but the water didn't look more than a foot or two deep, so without hesitation he set his horse to fording the South Wichita east of the burning bridge.

The whole group was across when mud splatted up beside one of the horses, followed by the distant crack of a rifle.

TWO | The back seat of the surrey was long enough for Lucy to lay down with her knees up, and she quickly found a way to brace herself so that she was fairly comfortable. They wrapped a blanket tightly around her and taped the IV needle and tube securely to her arm so that its bag swung hypnotically over her head from one of the roof supports. Jenny Augusta rode on the front seat with Nancy Russell, and once they had finally satisfied themselves that she was comfortable, they quit turning around every two minutes to check on her.

Lucy closed her eyes then woke with a start. It took her more than a few seconds to realize what had happened. She could tell by the change in the light that she had slept, but had no idea for how long. "Where are we?" she asked.

"A couple of miles from the Foard City cutoff. We've come about twelve miles since you fell asleep," Nancy said. "You even missed a hard little quake."

"Twelve miles? That far? What time is it?"

"Almost three-thirty. We'll be stopping soon just the other side of the cutoff at a friend of Nancy's. We can stay there tonight and get an early start in the morning."

Lucy didn't protest that decision. She would rather have kept going, to have gotten as close as possible to Rhineland, but if they couldn't do that, then they couldn't, and she would be content to get a good night's sleep before starting out in the morning. Already she felt stronger than when they'd started out. "If we stop there, will we reach Rhineland tomorrow?"

"That depends," Nancy said. "It's a good twenty-five miles or more from Foard City to Rhineland even if we take the Lake Catherine shortcut. We'd be better off spending tomorrow night in Benjamin and going to Rhineland the next day."

She groaned softly, partly out of frustration, partly from the pain spreading through her chest.

"Time for more morphine," Jenny Augusta said.

"I guess so," Lucy answered, lying still while Nancy stopped the surrey and Jenny Augusta gave her the shot.

Again she closed her eyes, waiting for the warm flush of the morphine to push the pain back, waiting for the tiny lizards to stop scurrying across her exposed brain, waiting for the gentle rain to turn colors again, waiting, waiting, a man waiting . . .

. . . for her, a smile on his lips, lights dancing in his eyes, but when he reached for her hand, his fingers burned her and she drew back, surprised and alarmed. Then the light in his eyes turned to fire, and the fire turned to rage when she struck him again and again and again, driving the stake in her hands deeper into his chest with each thrust that spouted blood and laughter against the pure white back wall of her mind.

I'm dreaming, she thought, but she knew it wasn't true, knew that dreams could be controlled and this couldn't, and knew most of all that if she stopped now, she would never get the revenge she needed and wanted while raising the hard, wooden stake clutched in both hands over her head, then plunging it over and over and over into his eyes and his mouth and his neck and his chest until blood ran like rivers of dawn through canyons of anger into the center of her heart and she awoke with a jolt as the wagon lurched then came level.

She contented herself with listening to the soft pat of rain on the roof, and the wet clops of the mules and the quiet voices she didn't recognize and couldn't understand, floating over her head where swirls of gold and silver birds opened whirlpools in the rain and the clouds that drew her up, up out of herself toward the smiling face of Cristodios alight in the sunshine that stood in the rain like a column of truth bedecked with flowers.

None of it made much sense, and she knew it didn't and wouldn't until she woke up—really woke up and could stop the pain without the morphine. Tomorrow, she thought. Tomorrow, no more shots, no more IV, no more sleeping the day away.

"But tomorrow will be the last day to sleep away."

Why?

"Because after that you will see him and meet him and catch him and kill him."

No. Better than kill. Much better than kill.

Tears fell from heaven. Something soft and forgiving inside her disappeared beneath their waters.

THREE | "This has to be the border," Nyllan said. "See here on the map where the road out of Crafton cuts due north? That's where it hits Eleven-twenty-five, which is what we're on. When Eleven-twenty-five turns due north, that's the border, and we're headed north now, so this should be it. The next town ought to be Newport in Big Jack, and from there we've got clean road to Vashti and on through Buffalo Springs to Windthorst."

Goodfox looked at where she pointed on the map and the cracked, floating compass fastened to the truck's dashboard. "Looks that way to me, too, but if we're both right, where are the border guards?"

"Maybe they don't have them on these back roads."

"Maybe not, but I don't think we should relax until we're positive that the border is behind us."

She patted his head. "You're learning, Murray. Slowly but surely you're getting the hang of survival."

He started to protest, then laughed. "Point to Rhondasue. Guess I can be dense about things like that sometimes, can't I?"

"You said it, I didn't." She put the truck in gear again and got them rolling. "We've got the guns ready, and a truck that's already proven it can go as fast as these lousy roads will allow. Let somebody try to stop us now."

"Don't sound so eager for trouble."

"I'm not. It just feels good to be ready if trouble comes."

They rode without speaking for a few minutes before Goodfox turned to her and said, "I think we ought to look for a concealed place to park the truck and camp."

"Why? We can make it to Newport before dark."

"I know, but, well, maybe you've made me paranoid, but I'm beginning to think that going to Newport isn't such a good idea."

"You think camping in the middle of nowhere is? Come on, Murray. Newport's a couple of miles inside the border. We've been really lucky, so far, but I wouldn't want to push it and end up getting caught out here. Would you?"

He shook his head. "I don't know. My gut tells me you're right, but I'm not too well known for good gut reactions when it comes to this. My head tells me we need to be wary, but you think we're safer in town than out here. How am I supposed to know what to do?" He hadn't meant to sound so pathetic, and when he realized what he sounded like, he laughed. "Listen to me."

"Town," she said. "We're better off surrounded by people than vulnerable to God-only-knows-what out here on the edge of DalWorth. Newport should be used to strangers and not pay us much attention." She paused and reached out to him without taking her eyes off the road. "But hey, this is a partnership, isn't it? We decide together what's best."

"I think you're right," he said, squeezing her hand gently before letting it go. "Newport it is."

They drove on talking about the orchards in bloom around them and the large number of active farms, and all the while Goodfox had a growing premonition that they had made the wrong choice. But he didn't say anything. Fatigue had colored his thinking, and he knew it. As they entered the outskirts of Newport, he saw a large sign that said NEWPORT: HOME TO EVERYONE. Underneath EVERYONE, someone had painted in, "EXCEPT NIGGERS AND CATHOLICS."

"Not too friendly, are they," Nyllan said more as a statement than a question.

"We can't judge a town by what some misguided person writes on a sign."

"No, but we can judge when they don't paint over that kind of obscenity. That tells us something about what the town's leaders think and feel. Even apathy can kill you."

"Whoa. Who said anything about killing?"

She shifted down and forced the engine to slow them as they

approached a stop sign. "Nobody said anything about real killing. You know that. I'm talking about killing your heart, your feelings."

A man in a dark hat and jacket stood under an awning on the near corner staring at them. When the truck stopped, he waved his left hand casually from side to side, and Murray returned the wave, surprised to catch himself using his left hand as well. "Wait a second," he said to Nyllan as he rolled down his window. "Can you tell us where we could find lodgings for the night?" he called to the man.

"Straight ahead," the man answered. "You'll see the sign."

"Thanks." Murray rolled up the window and waved again. "Straight ahead, he said."

Newport wasn't much to drive through, but just past the junction with Texas-Fifty-nine, a bright, red-and-white sign announced HILLTOP MOTEL. Nyllan drove the truck up the steep hill and pulled it under a roofed drive in front of the office. "Be careful," she said, pointing to a neatly lettered sign between the office door and the mirrored window that said,

HOUSE RULES:

NO KIDS UNDER 6 YEARS OLD.

NO PETS OF ANY KIND.

THAT MEANS NO CATS AND DOGS.

NO DRINKING ON THE PREMESIS.

NO PARTYS.

NO BUMS AND LOAFERS.

NO NIGGERS, METHOD-BABTISTS,
    NATES OR WHORES.

NO CHEKS—CASH ONLY

NO EXSEPTIONS.

    —THE MANAGEMANT—

"At least it doesn't say, 'No Catholics.'"

"You be careful anyway."

Goodfox got out and walked around the truck, feeling somehow conspicuous and intently watched, remembering a string of moments back through his life tied to this feeling, like uneven beads on a homemade rosary, each more than a memory, less than a prayer. As he opened the office door he smelled heavy sandalwood incense and saw the largest woman he'd ever seen in his life. Her washed-out eyes peered at him out of her bloated face.

"Harold! Got a customer! Get out here!"

A skinny boy no more than twelve or thirteen years old appeared through a curtained doorway wearing a yellow t-shirt with "Quaking Mothers" printed across it in oozing red letters. Goodfox heaved a small sigh of relief when he saw the St. Christopher's medal on a chain around the boy's neck, but caught the sigh when he realized the oozing letters on the boy's shirt were actually severed arms and legs, and in the center of the "o" in "Mothers" was a swastika.

"You want a room?" the boy asked, looking past Goodfox through the one-way window at the truck and Nyllan.

He said, "Yes," but he wasn't sure that was the right answer.

FOUR | Mr. Max Quentin didn't look quite so fearsome after he'd bathed and changed clothes, Paula Kathryn decided as she passed him the platter of fish. Having him share their dinner was Father Irving's idea, but she would probably have offered it in any case. Mr. Quentin was, after all, a friend of Father Murray's and according to his claim, there because of Father's request.

"Thank you, Sister," Quentin said flatly.

"I hope you like the fish," Sister Joana said. "It's catfish fresh from the river, and I fry it in a secret batter that Father Goodfox is particularly fond of."

"And I, as well," Father Irving said with a nod of his head and a wink of his good eye set deep in his mahogany face. "When I eat your catfish I must be vigilant against gluttony."

"You are too kind, Father."

"It is pretty good," Quentin said with his mouth still half-full. "Daa—darned near the best I ever ate." He followed his compliment with several noisy gulps from his wine.

The wine had also been Father Irving's idea. He would never ask for it for himself alone, but never missed the opportunity to have it served to a guest and thus to drink more than he ought. Paula Kathryn had no reason to begrudge him the wine, but part of her did not approve serving it to this rough stranger. *Tempt not the rough beast with the fruit of thy vines,* was a maxim she had learned as a novice and found useful ever since. Rough beasts and rough men rarely acted in an acceptable manner after partaking of the grape.

The rough beasts she had learned about when two of the parish boars had wandered into the winery and knocked down a precious barrel to get to the bunghole. There they'd gotten quite drunk and mean and had to be tied with ropes for a full day while they squealed in protest until they finally fell asleep. Paula Kathryn swore that the bacon and ham made from those pigs had a peculiar flavor she found distasteful even though no one agreed with her.

Rough men, hardened with drink, mean in their narrow drunkenness, she had known since her grandfather. She only had one memory of him when his breath didn't reek of spirits, and a thousand of him in rages of all sizes—large rages to rail against the cruelty of a God who would wreck an almost perfect world, and small rages if his dinner wasn't cooked to his liking.

The only time she had ever seen him when she knew he was sober was the day her grandmother was buried. All day and night he had sat alone in the tiny front room of the house going through picture albums, talking to himself, never asking for or getting anything to drink but chicory and water. The next morning after breakfast, he opened a fresh jug of liquor and drank it all, then started another before falling into a drunken stupor in the middle of the afternoon.

She kept on eye on Max Quentin as she ate, because she saw in his eyes the same dark light she had seen so many times in her grandfather's. It was the way rough men could be spotted by one who knew them even when there was no other evidence to single them out. Always, always it was something in their eyes that she recognized, something that repelled and fascinated her at the same time.

Had she been willing to admit it, she would have noted how Father Murray Goodfox sometimes had that same look in his eyes. But she didn't have to admit it, because she had never seen him drunk or even close to it, and the one time she had seen him let his emotions run wild, it had been she who had set him loose, not the craze of alcohol.

"And how long are you planning to stay?" Father Irving was asking.

"For as long as Father Goodfox needs us," Quentin answered.

"Might I inquire into the nature of your services?"

There was no hidden suggestion in the priest's voice, but Paula Kathryn was surprised to hear him ask such a question.

"That's between us and Good—Father Goodfox. If he wants you to know about it, he'll tell you." The edge in his voice carried a warning with it.

"Of course, of course," Father Irving said. "Here, have some more of this fine St. Joseph's wine."

Paula Kathryn winced and wondered where all this would lead.

CHAPTER 37

ONE | As soon as the shooting started, thirty-two riders scattered through the rainy bottoms—a whirling storm of shouting troops, neighing horses, and breaking saltcedar in the late grey afternoon. Behind them Sergeant Ensolita's troops fired two or three dozen shots across the river before someone realized that whoever was firing at the horsemen was well out of their carbine range.

The shooting stopped as suddenly as it started, and Cody began trying to get everyone back together. Surprisingly, no one was injured, but it took much longer than it should have to gather them all. An hour later they were still missing two people—Brisas and one of the Demons named Sertia—when Cody and Ogden decided to go with those they had. When they reached the top of the Benjamin incline they were joined by Brisas and Sertia. Those two had ridden upriver seeking another place where the incline was climbable in a vain attempt to out-flank the snipers.

"Their tracks are plain enough," Cody said, pointing to the darkened east. "Looks like they're bypassing Benjamin for sure." He took out his map, bending over it to keep the rain off, and studied it for a minute. "Morgan," he called over his shoulder, "I need a volunteer."

"Aw, Cody, why me?"

"Because I need you. We'll stay on their tracks. You cut across to the road and tell Sergeant Ensolita that it looks like the Nates are headed for the Lake Catherine cutoff. Tell him to get

his transportation in Benjamin and be ready to find us out on US-
Eighty-two when we call the Knox County Sheriff at first light
tomorrow. Got that?"

"Yes, sir, but couldn't you—"

"Just get going, Morgan"—he returned the map to his
pocket—"and get back to us as fast as you can. Now, go!"

Morgan took off at a gallop.

"We can't do that," Ogden said, jerking his head toward
Morgan. "These horses have been ridden almost daily for almost
three months. We'll kill them if we ride them too hard."

"Then you set the pace. We'll follow." Cody would have
galloped the horses if he could have, because the light was
deteriorating and the rain was coming down harder, and ahead of
them the Nates were taking his wife and child into the darkness
of another night.

Ogden set a pace faster than a walk, but slower than a
gallop, and once the horses sensed what it was, they all fell into
the rhythm of it. Cody stayed close behind Ogden, wishing there
were some way to know where the Nates were, hoping there were
no more snipers laying for them. He felt fairly safe on that count
because of the growing darkness, but that didn't do much to
brighten his mood. The only thing that made him feel better as
they rode and rode through the dim rain was that the wagon
tracks were clear in the red mud-and-gravel road, and he felt
sure they weren't going to lose the Nates now.

"Hold up," Ogden called.

Cody rode up beside him and saw why Ogden had stopped.
The tracks led across the blacktopped surface of Texas-Six to a
narrower paved road that headed toward the southeast. "This
should be the Lake Catherine cutoff," Cody said.

"That's what the sign says."

The sign was barely visible, white on a dark background.
"Lake Catherine, Davis Lake Dam."

"How do you feel about trailing these people at night?"
Ogden asked.

"Not very good—especially in the rain. God only knows what
they could have waiting for us."

"There's a little rise over there with some trees where we
could probably camp."

"Let's do it."

The fence carried a seal, but Cody had Pollard cut the wire
anyway. This was no time to be worrying about niceties. By the

time they all got to the grove of liveoaks on the rise Ogden had pointed out, it was fully dark. The Demons produced lanterns and soon had a fire going, much to Cody's surprise until they told him they'd used a little gas to encourage it.

As he warmed his hands, he thought for a minute about the Nates, but consciously decided not to worry. They were running. If the Nates sent someone back to spy on his platoon, let that someone see the fire and assume the obvious. That way the Nates just might stop and make camp themselves and stop the distance between them from growing.

Maybe that was wishful thinking, he didn't know. It was just that suddenly he was tired from his dripping wet hair down to the cold bones of his feet, and he thought of Ann pregnant, out in this rain, or worse, trying to take care of the baby out in this rain, and him not doing her any good at all, with little hope that he would ever be any good to her, and all he wanted to do was cry.

TWO | They made Lucy eat in bed and she didn't even think about protesting.

But when Jenny Augusta said, "I think you ought to give this idea up," her resolution hardened.

"With or without you, I'm going," Lucy said firmly.

"Now listen to me, Lucy Ilseng. You're not strong enough to go on alone. Why, if we told you to go on without us, you wouldn't make it a mile down the road."

Lucy threw back the covers, swung the IV tube out of the way, and carefully turned her body until her feet could drop to the floor.

"Don't you dare . . ."

"Then don't you," Lucy said through clenched teeth. "I have to do this thing. If you don't want to come any further with me, fine. But don't try to threaten me with your desertion. It won't change my mind about anything except your character."

"Just a minute. You have no right to make any judgements about my character."

"I do if you demand to come with me, then tell me you're going to desert me."

Jenny Augusta looked away. "That's neither what I said, nor what I meant. It's just that you—"

"I heard what you said—that I wouldn't make it a mile without you. Well, I would. If you don't believe me, get out of my way and I'll show you." With her free hand she reached for her undershirt which was neatly folded on the chair beside the bed. She didn't want to take the IV out, and she didn't want to get dressed, but if that was what was necessary, then so be it.

"Enough of that—from both of you," Nancy said from the doorway. "You'll not leave this room without us, Lucy Ilseng. And you, Jenny Augusta Van Zandt, will let this child alone so she can get some sleep. Tomorrow's going to be a long day."

Jenny Augusta sat on the bed beside Lucy, one slow tear running down her cheek. "It's *you* I'm worried about. I just don't want . . . can't stand to see you kill yourself because of some notion you have about revenge."

"It's more than that," Lucy said, putting her free arm around Jenny Augusta's shoulder. "There's no way to explain it to you, except to say that somehow I'm all tied in with these people, and I know as sure as we're sitting here that something . . . something important is going to happen in Rhineland. And I have to be there when it happens."

"What if you're wrong? What if they aren't going to Rhineland and nothing important is going to happen? Is that worth risking your life over?"

"I'm not wrong. Please believe me. It's what Mishla always calls my sixth sense. Sometimes I know things about people that I shouldn't have any way of knowing. But I do. When he—when Max Quentin shot and raped me, I learned something about him—and, well, the rest of it doesn't fit into words very well, but I know. I *know* I have to keep going."

"But we told Sheriff York about the radiation, and she said she would pass it on."

"I still have to go. Myself."

"All right," Jenny Augusta said. "Maybe I'm wrong. Maybe I shouldn't try to stop you. Going to Rhineland certainly won't kill you, but, but I pray to God . . ." She stood up and without saying anything else, rushed past Nancy out of the room.

Lucy grabbed the blankets, pulled her legs back in bed, and lay down, her head spinning with emotions and fatigue and the dull ache of her wound.

"Go to sleep now," Nancy said before she turned out the light and closed the door softly behind her.

Sleep. Lucy was almost afraid of it. But she adjusted the blankets and the IV tube and dutifully closed her eyes. Her body felt unusually heavy, her arms and legs, leaden, her head, like an immovable weight. The IV needle felt like it was slipping out, and the tape that held it made her whole arm itch. She smelled something faintly antiseptic as she began to lose touch with her body.

The wagon rolled down an endless hill. She couldn't see the bottom. There were no horses and no driver, but the wagon never went any faster, as though the hill wasn't real, and the sky wasn't brilliant blue, brighter than any summer sky she had ever seen, as though the clouds had parted for good, letting in the light of summer and warming her body until she was too hot and sweating and couldn't escape, and she thrashed against the restraints until one leg broke free into the cool air.

The bed. She was still in the bed. There was darkness instead of sunshine, and cold instead of heat, but her body was damp with perspiration. Lucy felt the side of her neck with the back of her fingers. No detectable fever. Had it broken? Or had she had one at all? Ask Jenny Augusta, she thought.

But Jenny Augusta was crying and it was Lucy's fault, but that was Max Quentin's fault, and when she caught him . . .

Blue sky again. White clouds—not grey—white like in the movies the Oldtimers liked so much. The Oldtimers. There were so few of them now, so few to remember skies like that and a land that didn't tremble like this, like now.

Lucy awoke to the trembling of her bed, and the rattling of the furniture and realized she was clutching the blankets and praying, praying for the quakes to subside so she could sleep, and she almost laughed because sleep had brought her the dreams that had kept her from sleeping.

Yet the quakes did stop, and she slipped once again into the shadows of nightmares.

THREE | They had been awakened by a small, almost gentle quake, and their quiet gestures of affection had quickly turned into urgent lovemaking. Then just as a series of stronger quakes started, Goodfox peaked into orgasm, followed immediately by Rhondasue.

He wanted to move, but couldn't, his body held fast by the intensity of his release. Rhondasue was locked against him, doubling that intensity with her own inner quakes.

They both gasped for breath.

A lamp rattled off a table. Distant people screamed. Dogs and oxen and mules cried in protest. Still the earth shook.

"Fire!" someone shouted. "Fire!"

Goodfox jerked himself out and off of her and reached blindly for the lamp. "Hurry," he said as he climbed out of bed on trembling legs. "Get dressed."

The lamp was gone, but a light shone around the edge of the drapes. He staggered weakly across the room and pulled them open. The light came from a fire on the other side of the U-shaped Hilltop Motel. For a long moment he stood there naked in the firelight before he turned and said, "It may not threaten us, but let's get everything out of here just in case."

She was half bent over putting her trousers on, but was still naked above the waist and the firelight played in warm colors on the curves of her breasts. As she straightened up, he said, "God, I love your body."

"I know. Didn't you say hurry up?"

"Hug me," he said, crossing to her with his arms open.

Rhondasue hugged him fiercely, her breasts pressed warmly against his chest. Then she let go with one hand and slapped his bare butt. "Get dressed. You want to burn up?"

"I already have," he said as he released her and reached for his underwear.

He laughed, but was suddenly embarrassed, as though making jokes about their sexual pleasure was worse than the sin it pertained to. *God,* he thought, pulling on his sweater, *if you planned for this pleasure, You must have planned for a sign to release me from the guilt it brings me. Please, God? Can You not give me a sign?*

As he put on his pants, something exploded very nearby. A woman screamed.

"Jesus, Murray," Nyllan said as she moved closer to the window, "it looks like somebody's car just blew up. There's burning gas running over half the parking lot."

Hardly a sign from God, Goodfox thought. "All the more reason to get out of here." He shoved his feet into his boots. "You close to being ready?"

"One sock, one boot, and my jacket to go."

"Did you put anything into these drawers?" he asked as he automatically checked them.

More screaming and shouting came from outside.

"No. But don't forget the ba

"Right." He stepped around t
bathroom where he gathered th
reasons he didn't understand, took
rack. His toilet kit and the towe
before Nyllan saw them, suddenly
the same time. The motel owed
night's sleep they were going to

"Ready," Nyllan announced.

"Me, too." Goodfox glanced
fifteen people running around, and
closer. "Let's go."

When they got outside, he saw
leaving. Half the other wing was i
with a pumper truck were fighting
looked like they were working aga
light rain that was falling. Goodfox
as he opened the tarp and put his ba
bed and tied the tarp back down.

She had backed the truck into the parking space, so as soon
as they were in, she started the engine, put it in gear, and rolled
out through the covered drive. The fat woman filled the office
doorway wearing a Mexican poncho. She was screaming for
Harold, but waved to them as they drove past.

Goodfox turned to look back and was startled to see how high
the flames were leaping into the air. Somehow they hadn't
seemed that bad up close. He crossed himself without thinking
and said, "God have mercy on them."

"And us, too, amen," Nyllan responded. She turned left and
the hill came between them and the flames, leaving only the
garish orange reflection flickering in the night clouds. "This is
the Vashti road—least according to the sign it is. I hope that's
what you wanted."

"Perfect," he said, still staring back, thinking of how even in
disaster there was evidence of God's perfection, surprised to see
so many other cars and trucks on the road at this time of night.

"You want to try to go all the way to Rhineland? Or you want
to keep an eye out for a place to pull over and get some sleep."

"I'm too agitated to sleep right now. You feel like driving that
far?"

"Sure, I'm fine." She gave the truck some gas as they
accelerated out of Newport.

He kept his eyes on the road behind them as though expecting any second to see flames leaping above the hilltop until— "Uh, Rhondasue, I don't want to worry you, but I think somebody's following us."

"Mmm, those lights?"

"They've been behind us since we left the motel."

FOUR | Paula Kathryn awoke to the sound of singing— a lone, baritone voice singing a slow sad song. She couldn't hear the words, but she knew the song was a sad one by the way it was sung.

And after a moment or two, she determined to her satisfaction that the singer was Mr. Quentin. Should she quiet him, or not? It was her duty as Sister Superior, but she secretly hoped that Father Irving would do it for her. It was he, after all, who had done so much to get Mr. Quentin drunk. He was the one who had tempted the rough beast. The image of the two of them as she had left them sitting in the kitchen with a pitcher of wine between them on the table filled her again with anger.

Where was Father Irving now? He should shut his rowdy friend up and let the rest of them get the rest God meant for them to. She looked at her bedside clock. 2:30. In three more hours it would be time for matins. That was no time to be groggy for want of sleep.

Reluctantly she got out of bed, lit her oil lamp, put on her nightrobe over her bedgown, and marched out of her room and down the hall, lamp in hand, ready to find Mr. Quentin—friend of the father's or not—and give him a full piece of her mind. At first she thought he was still in the kitchen, but before she reached the kitchen hall, she realized to her shock and dismay that his voice was coming from the cloister chapel.

Holding the lamp straight out in front of her as though its very brightness could dispel the shadows of his indecency, she entered the chapel prepared to do battle. Automatically she dipped her knee and crossed herself, but her eyes ranged the room like a hawk's looking for its dinner.

His singing stopped, and she couldn't see him, but a sudden movement near the front of the chapel made her swing around. He was sitting in the front pew, turned in her direction with an expression of perverse humor as outrageous—

My God! The man is naked.

As if reading her thoughts he suddenly stood up, then stepped onto the pew seat. Except for a bandage on one arm, he was totally naked.

She averted her eyes, but her anger heated the air between them. "Mr. Quentin! This is the most abominable sin and atrocity I have ever witnessed! You will dress yourself and leave the chapel at once. Do you hear me? At once!"

"And if I don't," he said with a drunken slur, "what are you gonna do, little sister? You gonna make me? Huh? Are you?"

Paula Kathryn turned the wrath of her gaze upon him, neither embarrassed nor intimidated by his nakedness. Walking very deliberately down the aisle, she spoke in a tone of barely controlled rage. "I certainly will make you, Mr. Quentin. I will make you leave this holy place, then I will make you sorrier than you have ever been in your life. I will take this lamp, and to use your vernacular, I will cram it up your ass!"

He stepped hesitantly down from the seat. "Now wait right there, Sister. You just stop and let me get my pants on and I'll be right out of here. Yes I will."

She paused then and might have stopped if she had not heard a second voice whispering behind him. The picture that voice drew in her mind destroyed what little control she had of her rage.

The sound that broke from her mouth was half-scream, half-roar as she charged the front of the chapel.

Quentin had his pants in one hand and his shirt held in front of him as he attempted to block her way saying, "Please, Sister, please, we're going, we're going."

Behind his dancing shadow a naked boy scurried toward the side door like a silent apparition, one frightened glance over his shoulder before he was gone.

Paula Kathryn hit Quentin with her free hand, hit him on the arm with the back of her hand, then balled it into a fist and hit him square in eye.

He howled in pain and backed away. She moaned and shook her hand, all the angrier now because she thought she had broken something. "Out!" she screamed. "Out, out, out! S-S-S-Satan take you back to his bosom, you b-b-b-bestial degradation of the name *man*."

Again she hit him, first with her open hand, then with the back of it, numbness and rage blotting out her own pain. "You filthy, buggering, faggot dung-heap. You slimy, excrementitious pit in the life of humanity. You disgusting, despicable pederast."

Hitting him again and again and again, she drove the cowering Quentin across the chapel and up the side aisle, castigating him the whole time until, when she paused for an instant to catch her breath, he turned and bolted down the hallway, disappearing into the night.

Suddenly she was surrounded by sisters who led her from the chapel to their common room where one of them bathed her bruised hand while they all strained to understand the torrent of words that she was powerless to stop rushing from her mouth.

CHAPTER 38

ONE | Cody awoke to a surprising dawn. Not only could he see the sun rising in the east, but he could see clear sky above it. That was a sight he knew he would never take for granted, so he just lay there and watched the sky change from pink to orange, thinking about nothing but the beauty of what he was seeing.

His enjoyment was spoiled when Ed Kolmer knelt down beside him. "Baylor Station's on the radio for you."

Forcing himself to his feet Cody saw that most of his platoon and the Deseret Demons were already up, and a mixed group of them were brushing down the horses and feeding them. The very sight of the horses made up for his loss of sunrise time and added unexpected cheer to his morning. As he walked over to where Brisas and Private Timothy Randon waited with the radio, he thought he smelled bacon frying, and suddenly he was very hungry.

"This is Bearcub Leader," he said after he took the handset from Brisas. "Come in Baylor Station."

"Jeremiah, you better set yourself down for what I got to tell you."

"Aunt Bertha? What are you doing in Seymour?"

"Never you mind. Just set yourself."

He squatted down. "Okay, I'm set. What's chewing at your worry knot?"

"Terry's called up thirty percent of the Farm Bureau, Tiga, Aqha, and God knows who else for active duty in the militia. Doc Brighton has sent out a general call for medics and healers. There's a war on, Jeremiah, a war you're not going to believe. The Republic's joined forces with Commanche, Texico, Wheatland, New Mexico, the Missouri Coalition, and—catch this—the Indian Nation in a war against—"

"The Indian Nation?"

"In a war," she continued, "against the True United States of America and something called N-A-T-O."

"The *what* United States?"

"The *True* United States of America. Terry thinks it's made up of most of the countries east of the Mississippi that survived Shudderday, plus some of those Frenchy Canucks."

Cody was totally confused. A war? Now? With the True United States? *And* the Canadians? A real war? The thought numbed his mind. "So what the hell does all that mean to us?" he asked finally. "Are we supposed to stop chasing these Nates?"

"No. Terry said it's even more important now that you catch them. And he said you'd better be on the watch for that loud-mouthed priest, Murray Goodfox, too. He's the one that's got that church and radio station in Rhineland."

"And you think he's mixed up in this war?"

"I'm not paid to think, boy, and neither are you, but anybody could tell from his radio show that Goodfox is a pretty radical Joiner, and his archbishop said he was over his pecker in revolution."

Despite Cody's confusion and the seriousness of what she was saying, Cody chuckled. "His archbishop said that, did he?" A burst of static filled his ear.

"—it from Terry. But that's the heart of it. How long will it take you to get to Rhineland?"

"Half a day or less, depending upon the horses, the weather, and iffen or not the Nates are laying for us."

"They'll be laying, all right. You be careful, Jeremy and—damn! I almost forgot. Terry wants to know if you still got those special suits he sent you."

He had to think for a second. "Three of them. We've got three of them." It had never occurred to him to retrieve the suits from Jessup's or Melindo's packs. "Just three."

"Well, he said you might need them, so you should be ready for that."

"You know what he's talking about, don't you, Aunt Bertha?"

"What I don't know, don't matter. You just be careful."

Cody waited for more from her before he finally said, "I suppose this means we're not getting any more reinforcements." A small group had gathered close around him, including Kolmer and Sam Ogden. He saw Ogden's eyebrows raise when he mentioned reinforcements.

"Shit, boy, haven't you been listening to me? Terry's not just *talking* about war. He's saying we're in one. The chances of you getting reinforcements—"

"Why? Did he say why we're in this war? Or what it's about?"

There was another long moment of hissing static. "Hell, no, he didn't say why."

As soon as she said no, Cody's thoughts jumped away from the sound of her voice, and though he heard and understood what she said after that, it was like she was talking to someone else, someone who would be more interested in it, someone who didn't feel so damned disconnected from the rest of the world, someone who didn't know how expendable he was.

"And you know what's funny?" she was saying, "I didn't ask him. I just figured it must be a damned good reason to get everybody to join together to fight it. Anyhow, war's been declared. That's all the reason you and me need to worry about."

"So what kind of new orders have you got for us?" He asked the question automatically, knowing she would have gotten off the radio if she didn't have more to tell him.

"None really. Terry just said to tell you that what you're doing is all the more important now, and that you should tell those boys from Utah that if they want out, they'd better head west as soon as they can, he's going to draft them into the militia."

"What about their horses?"

"You got some of their horses? You keep 'em."

"They're our horses," Ogden said as though he, too, had heard what she said.

Cody held up his hand. "We'll see about that, Aunt Bertha. You got anything else for me?"

"No, Jeremy, I guess that's it."

"Then I'm signing off. Bearcub Leader, out." He gave the handset back to Brisas and stood up. "Gather round," he called. "Sam, Ed, I want everyone to hear this."

"Can you tell us while we eat?" Kolmer asked. "Breakfast's almost ready, and these boys have donated three or four pounds of bacon to it."

"Fair enough," Cody said. He *had* smelled bacon. "Breakfast will get cold faster than this information I got. Let's eat." He turned to walk toward the cook fire.

"Why were you talking about our horses?" Ogden asked as he fell into step beside Cody.

"Let me tell this in my own way, Sam, and then you'll have the whole picture."

"I want to know now."

Cody heard the suspicion and hostility in Ogden's voice, but he refused to be put on the defensive. "I don't blame you, but it's not going to make twenty minutes' difference."

"Dammit, Lieutenant, I've got a right to know what's going on when it comes to us and our horses."

"He said we'd eat, first," Kolmer said, putting his well-muscled arm around Ogden's narrow shoulders. "Easier to listen on a full stomach, don't you think?"

Odgen started to protest when Brisas stepped up on the other side of him and took his arm, pressing it firmly against her side. He looked sharply down to where her breast flattened against his elbow.

"Ed's right," she said, smiling brightly. "Food first."

His frown turned into a sudden grin. "All right. We eat first, but"—he looked Brisas full in the face—"you'll have to sit next to me."

"Can do, Sam." She squeezed his arm. "Can do."

Cody was grateful for Kolmer and Brisas's intervention and was able to enjoy the breakfast of canned ration-eggs, fried and smothered in hot sauce, and four wide, thick, crisp pieces of bacon, the likes of which he hadn't eaten since joining the militia. He didn't even pay much heed to the little quakes that came and went for almost five minutes before the ground stilled again. If the quakes weren't strong enough to upset his stomach, he couldn't be bothered with them right now.

"This is great stuff," he said, waving the last bite of bacon to attract Ogden's attention before popping it in his mouth.

"Got it in a little town called Enochs, west of Lubbock, from a man said it was wild pig from the Muleshoe."

Brisas smiled. "The Muleshoe National Wildlife Refuge."

"You know it?"

"Sure. My mamacita took me hunting there a couple times before we moved down to Brownfield."

"You know an old geezer named Dinger, or Danger, or some—"

"Thanger. Louis Kleberg Thanger. Yeah, he'd be selling you bacon. Wonder he didn't want one of your horses for it."

Now Ogden smiled. "He did. Gave us two ounces of gold and thirty pounds of bacon for an old mare we had. Told him that mare hadn't dropped a colt in three years, but he didn't seem to care about that."

"Well, I'll tell you, there's something I care about," Cody said impulsively. "I care about all of you as well as the horses, and I care about what happens from here on, so you all pull up closer if you can't hear me, 'cause I'm not going to chew on this thing all day."

"Oh, Dios," Brisas said with a roll of her eyes. "Times must be bad for you to start getting folksy on us."

Cody shook his head. "I wouldn't know about that if I knew twice as much as I do now. You all ready to listen?" Quiet replies and nods answered him.

"Then here's the lay of it. Most of what I'm telling you was just told to me. Some of it I've known for a week. None of it adds up very well for any of us. Let me tell it all to you, then you can ask any questions you have, and I'm sure you're gonna have them." He paused, looking at the array of faces before he continued, wanting them to understand the seriousness of what he was about to say.

"First, there seem to be some big political changes taking place around us. Sheriff York told me that a group of countries this side of the Mississippi—including us and the Indian Nation—are now in a declared war with somebody calling themselves the True United States of America."

Low whistles and exchanged glances circled through the group accompanied by brief headshakes of disbelief.

"As far as I know, Utah isn't involved yet, so if you Demons don't want to get drafted into the West Texas Militia, you can head home just as soon as we meet the rest of our groups down on Eighty-two. I've got orders to keep your horses, but I don't think that's fair," he said before any of them could protest. "However, I would like to have the loan of four or five of them."

"Might be arranged," Ogden said with a worried frown on his face. "What else do you know about this war?"

"Just this. It's gonna be a mess. And it means that we—my

platoon, and you, if you decide to stay—are going to have to accomplish this crazy mission on our own. No reinforcements."

"What about us, Cody? Suppose we do catch those Nates? What happens then?" Morgan asked.

"We do our best to capture them and take the cargo—the radioactive cargo," he added, realizing that most of these troops didn't know about that, "away from them. We're pretty much on our own, which is why," he said, turning to Ogden, "I'd really appreciate the loan of those horses."

"Radioactives! What kind of radioactives?"

"Plutonium."

"Shit," Ogden said, "me and my boys'll have to talk about this."

"Sure. Of course."

Ogden led his Demons to where the horses were tied, and as Cody followed them with his eyes, he noticed that the clouds had blotted out the sunrise, but there appeared to be a break in the greyness way to the southeast, and he wondered if the sun was shining on Rhineland. He was surprised that none of the militia seemed too concerned about the plutonium.

"What do you think, Cody?" Brisas asked.

"I think if they're smart that they'll head home." He grinned. "Maybe they're dumber than they look."

"Not dumb, just horny."

He was momentarily surprised, but quickly realized that she might be on to something. "You mean you think . . ."

"I mean that four of them have already offered to marry me and take me back to Utah."

"They what? They did?"

"That's right . . . and they're just boys, Cody."

"All right," Ogden called as he and all but three of the other Demons headed back to them. "All of us but Milton, Dernier, and Calvert are going to stay. Not being stupid enough to mess with radioactives, they decided to go home."

"Then welcome." Cody held out his hand. "I think you're dumb to get tangled in this, but I'm real glad to have you all."

Ogden shook his hand. "Dumb, crazy, we don't care. A chance for good fighting and later, good women, that's all my boys seem to want."

Brisas held out her hand to Ogden. "I've heard that down in Weatherford on the Commanche-DalWorth border they got two women for every man."

"Then after we clean up this mess you got us into, maybe we'll head down that way. You can lead us, Juanita," he said with a lecherous grin.

Cody thought of Ann and his baby and hoped it would all be that easy.

CHAPTER 39

LUCY | As she settled herself in the back seat of the surrey with Jenny Augusta's help, Lucy realized she was feeling much stronger this morning. "I've changed my mind," she said. "Let's go do a simple IV."

"Glucose?"

"Yes. But no more morphine."

"It'll be rough to make this trip without it," Jenny Augusta said, tucking the blanket around Lucy's legs.

"Then that's what it will be." She rolled up her sleeve and bared her right arm. "If it gets to be more than I can stand, I'll tell you, all right?"

"Promise?"

"Yes." She lay patiently while Jenny Augusta searched for a vein and inserted the IV needle, thinking of how much her life had changed since leaving Mishla's house to warn the tonk-aweya, and more importantly, how her life would never be the same again. Then the tube was taped to her arm, her sleeve rolled down over it, and Jenny Augusta was climbing into the front seat.

"You all set back there?" Nancy asked over her shoulder.

"Ready."

"Then we're off." She smacked the mules with the reins and the surrey jolted to a start.

Almost immediately Lucy regretted her decision not to take the morphine. Her chest ached with each bump of the surrey until the pain settled into a constant throbbing ache.

But something stronger than the pain took hold of her, a fierce determination not to give in, so that she closed her eyes and counted silently to herself, *one thousand, two thousand . . . three thousand . . . four thousand,* counting to nine thousand as she had been taught, then starting over again, trying to use the meditation techniques to block the pain, trying to remember those wonderful, detached moments of peace she had experienced when she made her first Zen breakthrough—the breakthrough that good Baptist Mishla had found so disturbing—trying to focus on that which had to be done, on the counting itself, each number a singular thing, important in its own right until the numbers ran together in her mind where she could see them rise off the surface with a sudden quacking and rushing of wings, seeking the freedom of the bright blue sky.

Sunshine warmed her face.

"This is a good place to stop," Nancy was saying. "Should we wake her?"

"I'm awake. Why are we stopping?"

"Because both Jenny and I need to pee, and it wouldn't hurt to give the mules a little feed and water."

"Where are we?"

"Just past Truscott. At the cemetery, as a matter of fact."

Lucy suddenly felt cramped and stiff. "I'd like to walk around a little."

"You're sure?"

"Please, Jenny Augusta, I wouldn't be asking if—"

"I'm sorry. We can clip the IV bag to your cloak."

Five minutes later Lucy took in deep, slow breaths of the cool moist air as she walked slowly through the cemetery on Jenny Augusta's arm. She glanced from tombstone to marker with idle curiosity. Westbrook. Hayne. Westmoreland. Hitchcock. Berg. Ilseng.

"Ilseng!" She stopped so suddenly that Jenny Augusta almost stumbled.

"What?"

"There," Lucy said, pointing with her left hand. "On that headstone. Ilseng. Some of my relatives must be buried here."

"You can't be sure of that."

"Why not? How many Ilsengs have you run into? It's not the Republic's commonest name." She bent down to read more closely. "Stephanie Chowning Ilseng, born 1921, died 1963, beloved wife of Jonathan R. Ilseng. Let's see." She shifted her gaze to the other half of the stone. "He was born in 1919 and died in 1987. That was a long time ago."

"He barely missed Shudderday."

Lucy stood slowly and steadied herself on Jenny Augusta's

arm. As her focus sharpened a patch of filtered sunlight fell on the cemetery and she saw a tall stone marker carved like a tree trunk. "Look," she said, pulling Jenny Augusta with her. The name on the chiseled plaque was almost worn away. "Alfred C. Ilseng, born—what is that? Eighteen eighty something?"

"1884 it looks like."

"Died, uh, 1913. February 7, 1913. He was twenty-nine when he died. I wonder what life was like for him back then."

"And I wonder who 'Woodmen of the World' were," she replied, running her fingers over the disk above the plaque.

"I'm glad we stopped," Lucy said. "This makes me feel like I really have roots in this part of the country."

"I still don't think you can be sure of that."

"Maybe not, but I'd like to think so, and the odds of there being unrelated Ilsengs living all over the place seem worse than having related ones." She let her eyes linger for a few long minutes on the Alfred's stone tree before saying, "We can go now if Nancy's ready."

She wasn't, so they stayed a little longer at the Truscott cemetery eating sandwiches Nancy's friend had packed for them, drinking cold water from a thermos, and enjoying the sunlight—however weak it was. All the time Lucy marveled over her discovery, wondering most about Jonathan Ilseng who had lived somewhere near this place for sixty-eight years—almost to the brink of Shudderday. Had he been happy? Did he like the old state of Texas? Was it a good place to live? The red dirt around the cemetery seemed fertile enough, showing signs of cultivation across the road, and she wondered if Jonathan and his Stephanie had worked that same dirt, and what they had grown.

She wondered, too, if her father had known of this place, had known that there was a connection here that linked him and her directly to the very soil of this place. But she quickly sheltered that thought about her father and tucked it away, not wanting to deal with it at this moment. Somehow it was more comforting to think of her ancestors without him in between. And by now she had convinced herself that this cemetery indeed held some of those ancestors. For all she knew, she could be a direct descendant of Jonathan and Stephanie. Or all of them could even be descended from young Alfred. The very notion of that possibility lifted her heart and made her feel stronger. She should make notes. She should—

"Truck coming," Nancy announced.

"Fast," Lucy added as she looked up the road. Her right hand moved involuntarily, but was stopped by the pain of the IV needle, so her left hand reached inside of her cloak for her revolver.

Nancy pulled a short-barreled pump shotgun from under the surrey seat, and an automatic pistol had appeared in Jenny Augusta's hand.

The Crosby truck slowed as it approached, then pulled off the road behind the wagon. The glare on the windshield made it impossible to see who was in it.

Lucy leaned against the surrey, cocked her revolver, and took awkward aim with her left hand. "You! Driver! Climb out real slow," she shouted, not surprised by the force of her command.

"Would you shoot your own teacher?" Mishla asked as she climbed from the cab.

Lucy was so startled that it took her a second to lower the gun. "Mishla? What are you doing here?"

"Better to ask what you're doing here," she said as she walked quickly to Lucy and gave her a gentle hug.

Jenny Augusta smiled. "It's good to see you, sister. This is my friend, Nancy Russell."

"Pleased to meet you," Mishla said as she turned to give Jenny Augusta a hug. "Now, what do you mean by hauling my Lucy out into the countryside like this?"

"Talk to me," Lucy said. "I'm the one who hauled *her* out into the countryside."

"Well, at least you are all right. As soon as I get you home, we can make sure—"

"I'm not going home," Lucy said as flatly as she could. Conflicting emotions were churning inside her, and for perhaps the first time ever she realized how hard it was going to be to go against Mishla. Her body felt like it was strung as taut as a new clothesline.

"Of course you are, child." Her eyes flashed darkly. "The matter isn't even open to discussion."

Shocking herself, as well as the rest of them, Lucy fired her pistol into the ground. Then she automatically cocked it and raised it to waist level pointing at Mishla. "You, you have two choices," she said in a voice that trembled with every syllable. "You can get in that truck and take me to Rhineland, or you can get out of my way and I'll drive myself."

Mishla's jaw hung slightly open for a long moment before she spoke. When she did, her voice trembled, also. "I do not understand, Lucy. Why would you threaten me? What is so important about Rhineland that you would point a gun at me, your mother?" Tears ran from her eyes.

The ache of Lucy's wound burned under her left breast. She glanced quickly at Jenny Augusta, then back to Mishla. "You know exactly what is going on," she said, not surprised by the look on Jenny Augusta's face. "So don't cry on me, Mishla. I love you. I love you like a daughter loves her mother, but, but"—the words fought spasms in her throat—"but that's not going to stop me from going to Rhineland. You have to understand that."

"Then let me drive for you," Mishla said softly.

"You promise to take me there?" Lucy's arm trembled with the weight of the pistol.

"Didn't I just say that?"

"No! Promise me. Say, 'I swear on everything I hold sacred to take Lucy to Rhineland and to help her in any way I can.'" Her whole body trembled now, and she tried to shift more of her weight against the surrey, but instead, her knees buckled and she slid down to the damp ground.

The image of Mishla hovered over her, touching, holding, comforting. Then as Lucy's eyes fell shut, Mishla's voice spoke into the grey swirls of her consciousness. "I promise to take you to Rhineland. I promise to help you in any way I can. I promise to love you all the days of my life, dear, dearest Lucy. I promise. I promise."

Tears fell on Lucy's face—Mishla's tears.

That damp feeling was the sensation of consciousness that Lucy clung to. She refused to let go, refused to relax her grip and fall into the waiting, peaceful darkness. But with all her efforts focused on staying awake, she had no energy left to reply. She wanted to tell Mishla that she was sorry, that she hadn't meant to make her cry, that she was sorry she had pointed the gun at her, sorry that it had happened, but it was all his fault, because it was he who drove her.

"Quentin," she said aloud. "Max Quentin." She wanted to explain, but the thoughts refused to form. All she chould do was rest in Mishla's arms and repeat the name. "Quentin. Quentin."

"The man who shot and raped her," Jenny Augusta's voice said like a knife stabbing the ache in her chest.

"Mother of God be merciful," Mishla whispered.

"She's set on revenge. She says it's more than that, and

maybe it is, but she's determined to go to Rhineland. I couldn't stop her, and I don't think you should try." The voice echoed strangely.

Lucy tried to agree, tried to make her tongue and mouth work for her, but again only one word escaped her lips. "Quentin."

"How bad is the wound?"

"It's weakened her, but she's not going to die from it. If she rests, she'll be all right."

"What do you think?"

I'm all right, Lucy wanted to say. *Trust me, I'll be all right. I will. I will.* But no words left her.

"I think if we are both there to help her, she'll be just fine because she won't have to do it all herself."

Again tears fell on Lucy's face.

Mishla sighed heavily. "Then we'll both have to go with her. But if I find this Quentin before she does, I'll kill him myself."

"No! Don't kill him!"

"Don't kill him," Lucy whispered, and somehow she knew that they heard her.

CHAPTER 40

GOODFOX | Father Murray Goodfox shared a secret with God that he dared share with no mortal soul until the day of revelation. He was waiting for a personal sign, waiting to feel the power of the Lord within him that would tell him God was ready. Then he, Murray Goodfox, would announce on the radio to the soon-to-be-reunited states that God was displeased with them, and as proof of His displeasure with their unnatural division, all the sinners in DalWorth would be struck down.

Regardless of whether Rhondasue could make the controller operate the Space Command satellite as an instrument of Almighty Power, God had decided that Goodfox should use the plutonium to turn the waters bitter—in the Brazos, and in DalWorth's reservoirs. Goodfox would instruct Wendel Quentin to fly over DalWorth and hit the three lakes that mattered—Lewisville, Lavon, and Ray Hubbard.

Then the people of DalWorth would begin to die and would

cry with the prophet, *The Lord our God has put us to silence, and given us water of gall to drink, because we have sinned against the Lord.* And the people of the separate states would know that God's wrath was to be feared, and that God spoke to them through His Good and Faithful Servant, Murray Goodfox.

For God had told him in a vision, *Behold, I will lift My hand above the nations and raise My signal to the peoples of the earth and they will bow down before you, calling My name, and they will know that I am the Lord and that I honor those who serve My will.*

Yes, God would triumph. There would be no one who could then resist the edicts from their heavenly Father.

But why DalWorth? he had asked God in prayer. The answer had been slow in coming, but when it came, it was clear and pure with the certainty of Truth. For all its diminutive size, DalWorth was a communications center, in touch with all of the Americas and most of Europe and Asia. Through DalWorth passed the lightwave cables that distributed vital information about the state of the world. DalWorth controlled those cables and the dispersal of all that information.

Thus, when DalWorth began to die, the world would be made aware of their plight immediately and take heed. They would learn the inevitability of God's will and be forced to accept Murray Goodfox's ascendancy to the leadership of the One True Church.

No longer could the Collegium Dominica and those heretics of the Society of Jesus ridicule his call from God. No longer would the bishop and H.S., the so-called secret archbishop, be able to smother him with their prescriptions and their proscriptions. God's instrument would strike all of them down and bring them to their spiritual knees begging for forgiveness.

That was a scene Goodfox imagined with great satisfaction as he thought of those pompous officials groveling in repentance. He knew that through the Charity of Christian Love and through the Grace of the Saviour, the wayward would be forgiven their sins and their false beliefs, and perhaps, even, be allotted small roles to play in the grand pageant of reunification. Thus would they learn the humility of true and faithful service, and perhaps one day step up to Glory in the sight of God.

All this God had laid out for him. All this God had shown him in visions and in dreams and in the daily answers to his prayers when God spoke directly to him. All this had consumed more and more of Goodfox's energies until God led Rhondasue Nyllan to his side.

Now God had opened an even greater plan before him—not just the old United States, but the whole world could be unified. And as God had chosen Nyllan for his helpmeet, so God, through His servant Murray Goodfox, would begin to choose helpmeets for all the leaders of the church, spiritual and physical partners striving always to continue the work of God's tender mercies.

Goodfox knew there would be great rejoicing among the clergy when he made known this part of God's plan. Oh, some would rebel against it, he was sure—mostly old prelates who had lived past their prime. But the vast majority of priests would welcome the brilliance of God's change for their lives with arms as open as when they had lain prostrate on the floor and taken their vows.

There would be new vows, of course, vows demanding allegiance to God and the Church above all things, vows that would be required not only of all priests and nuns, but also all lay workers, and all those who aspired to political office. How else could a candidate's faithfulness to duty be guaranteed? God first. Then Church. Then country and world—and both would soon be synonymous with Church in a democracy of faith.

The simplicity of that plan, the clarity of his understanding, and the necessity he felt to bring all of mankind into the drama of that vision, swelled Goodfox's heart with joy. God had chosen a glorious duty for him to perform, and he could do no less than his absolute best in—

"Murray, wake up."

"What?" Goodfox looked at her for a full second before the truck and the road and Nyllan fell into their proper places for him and brought him back to the realities of the moment. Must have been daydreaming, he thought. "What is it?"

"There's somebody following us again."

He looked over his shoulder and saw a dark-colored Crosby pickup hanging behind them at about the same speed they were traveling. "Now what? Same thing we did last night?"

Slowing the truck, she made a sharp corner as the road turned north. "That'll only work in the dark, remember? Listen, I figure we're about five or six miles from Windthorst. I'm going to see how fast this truck will go between here and there. You get the rifle and shotgun ready, okay?" She accompanied her question with an increase in speed.

"Of course. I think you're right." He smiled as he checked the rifle in the bouncing truck. The sun broke through a large hole in the clouds and lit the road ahead of them like a sign of confirmation.

"Damn!"

"Now what?"

"This sunshine. That's the last thing we need right now. Makes us that much easier a target."

"Don't curse a blessing, Rhondasue. The good light makes them an easier target,too," he said, loading the shotgun and closing it firmly. Again he looked back. The dark truck seemed to be losing ground. "Besides, I'm not sure they can keep up with us."

"Good." Her eyes were intent on the broken pavement, but she flashed him a quick smile. "What's the border station like in Windthorst? Gate? Guards? Militia?"

He grabbed the chicken-bar and braced himself for the broken stretch of road coming up. "A rolling gate manned by militia."

"Any way to crash it?"

"You don't have to. By the time you get to the gate itself, we'll be in West Texas, so if that truck is still following us, it will have to contend with the militia as well."

The truck bounced heavily then skidded as Nyllan dodged a large hole. "Any way around it?" she asked as she slowed even more to make a ninety-degree turn back to the west.

"No, but I don't think they'll give us any trouble. They're mostly on the lookout for DalWorth Rangers and migrating Nates."

Nyllan slammed the truck into fourth gear as they rolled downhill on a straight section of smooth asphalt. "And you don't think they'll care about a renegade priest carrying an illegal radio and a satellite controller?"

"No." He glanced through the rear window just in time to see the Crosby top the hill. "I think that truck's gaining on us again."

"We're doing forty-five. If the tires don't blow and the axle doesn't break and the road holds good—"

Skronk-eeeng!

The sound jumped from the truck roof with the metallic whine of a ricochet.

Goodfox looked up, then jerked his head around.

"They're shooting at us, Murray!"

Someone was standing in the bed of the Crosby shooting over the top of the cab. Goodfox pulled the rifle up, barrel first, then pushed it out the side window followed by his head and arms. He hadn't practiced shooting left-handed as much as he now wished he had, but it was too late to worry about that.

He braced his body in the window and steadied himself as best he could. Holding the bouncing sight on the middle of the Crosby, he squeezed off the first round. His automatic jack of the rifle's lever ejected the spent shell past his cheek and reloaded and cocked the rifle.

The truck jumped as Nyllan put it into third gear to climb the hill. The engine moaned in protest. Goodfox fired again.

"Hold on!" Nyllan yelled.

The truck careened through a right-hand downhill turn, and Goodfox pulled himself back inside as Nyllan gave it full throttle. "Don't think I hit them," he said sitting sideways in the seat and watching the road behind them for the reappearance of the Crosby.

"Another turn coming up."

"You should be able to see St. Mary's and Windthorst from there. Our tail still hasn't made the corner."

"Don't complain about a blessing, someone once said." Nyllan geared down through the corner then accelerated toward the silhouette of St. Mary's Church and Seminary standing dark against the grey skies over Windthorst.

"Slow down," Goodfox said. "Rushing up on the border isn't going to endear us to the militia, and our tail seems to have given up along with the sunshine."

She eased off the accelerator. "Ash Grove Boys."

"You think so?"

"Who else?"

"Bandits, highwaymen—human refuse scrabbling for survival."

"They can scrabble somewheres else for all I care. Better clear the rifle. Here comes the border gate. And straighten your collar."

He left the rifle as it was, but straightened his collar and brushed at the dirt on his jacket. Nyllan brought the truck to a gentle, coasting stop in front of the gate where three men and a woman in militia uniforms sat on a bench in front of a small rusted metal building.

The woman stood, hitched up her pants, then walked slowly over to them with her right hand on the butt of her holstered pistol, and her eyes carefully examining the truck. Then she leaned down and crossed her arms on the windowsill, almost poking her head into the cab. "Y'all come to join us?"

"Beg your pardon?" Goodfox said.

"To join us, you know. To join the militia for the war."

"War?" Nyllan shook her head. "What war? Are the Nates really at it this time?"

"Bigger than that," the woman said, her face breaking into a smile full of crooked brown teeth. "Us and the Nates have joined together, so we hear, to fight those yankees east of the Mississippi River. What about you, Father? You got anything against fighting?"

Goodfox was stunned. "No," he managed to say, suddenly aware of the rotten smell of her breath. "We're just heading home to Benjamin"—the lie came without thinking—"after serving a revival down in Jermyn. Thought we'd come this way to visit my old seminary. You sure this war isn't just a rumor?" How could there be the kind of war she spoke of?

"No rumor, Father. Fact. So, y'all go on. But be careful, and think about joining us for the fight."

"Thank you," Nyllan said as the woman stood and waved at one of the other guards.

The guard rolled the gate back and Nyllan drove the truck through as Goodfox waved to the woman and the other militiamen. He still couldn't believe there was a war going on or that the Republic and the Nation had joined together. Was this part of God's plan to assist the reunification? He prayed that this was God's work, and not Satan's.

"I don't think we ought to stop here for very long," Nyllan said as they drove to the intersection of US-Two-eighty-one and Twenty-five.

"Why? Because of this war talk?" Surely what the militia woman told them had only been a rumor.

"That and more," she said, pointing to a crude banner strung across the road from Osterman's Store to a telephone pole.

KILL A YANKEE FOR CHRIST, it said. JOIN THE MILITIA NOW.

Somehow this war, this new conflict had never entered his visions. Had he misunderstood something God had told him? Or was this part of a new message? "Maybe you're right. I think it's time to make a flat-out run for Rhineland." The tone of his voice reinforced the turmoil building in him.

"Don't worry, Murray. The hard part's behind us. I'll get you home, now."

CHAPTER 41

PAULA KATHRYN | After her sisters calmed her down, and after hours of fluctuating between explosive rage and prayers for inner peace, then prayers for understanding and charity, Paula Kathryn had finally awakened Father Irving and told him what happened. When she asked him what he was going to do about it, he asked her what had happened to Quentin and the boy, and all her prayers went for naught. Her rage won out.

"Let the devil worry about those beasts! And thanks to the devil for taking their souls!"

"Sister!" Father Irving had said with horror.

There was something in his eyes she hadn't liked and something missing she wished were there, and she had known then that Father Irving would be of no use to her in this matter. Without further word she had left him standing in the guest room looking puzzled and confused, and went to the sanctuary, unable to face the cloister chapel. There she had knelt in prayer until Father Irving had come in to lead the special Good Friday mass. Then she had turned her back on him again in anger, and left him and her sisters to think what they would.

Now as she worked in her garden behind the church under the warmth of a sun that was almost breaking through the clouds, she accepted the gentle trembling of the earth as counterpoint for her own emotional trembling. There she prayed not for herself, nor for Quentin and his soulmate, Father Irving, but only for Father Murray and his quick return.

Chopping steadily and automatically with her hoe, she began to truly understand how much she needed Father's presence— not only for St. Joseph, but as much for herself. She also realized that when he returned, she would have to endure the Nyllan slut's proximity until Father recognized the evil in Nyllan and sent her back to the sons of hell where she belonged. And in Paula Kathryn's own heart she knew that it was her natural self, Margarita Maria Owen—not the holy sister, Paula Kathryn—who understood these things with a special kind of instinct.

That instinct also told her there was a fast way to make Father realize Nyllan's evil—a way to bring him fully back into the arms of the church, a way Paula Kathryn trembled to think about, but one which might eventually be necessary. Yet, hadn't Archbishop Truman said he wanted Father Goodfox to return to the bosom of the church? Wasn't it her duty and obligation to help him do that? Was one of her holy vows really more important than service to God through the whole church, or service to the future of all mankind?

The more those questions infiltrated her thoughts, the harder she chopped at the clods in the garden, as though her body was intuitively seeking physical relief for the tension in her soul. She could not, must not let herself come close to the specifics of that intuition, dared not dwell on the meaning of her reactions.

The details she brushed aside in hurried mental sweeps before they came into focus. The flashes of imagination she dimmed with the practiced discipline of stern resolve. The memories of another time she forced firmly back into the closets of her subconscious. But despite all her well-trained avoidance, and despite all her denials of where her most intimate impulses led, there in the garden she was suddenly frozen in place by a knowledge of two things about herself she would never have allowed herself to accept or believe before this day.

She knew that if it was necessary, she would personally take Murray Goodfox away from the Nyllan slut by using every resource God had given her. She also knew with a surety beyond all denial that part of her longed for just such a necessity.

Slowly, ever so slowly, she pulled herself from her frozen posture and drew herself up to her full height, holding the hoe as though it were a scepter of power—for that was what she felt rising through her, a power and a rapture that almost took her breath away. Her eyes followed the sweep of the flower-laden fields down to the river then up again into the bright grey northern horizon, and Sister Paula Kathryn knew that what she beheld was beautiful and perfect in the sight of God.

But now, for the first time in her life, she herself felt totally pure and beautiful in the sight of God, because only now did she understand that God wanted *all* of her in His service.

Nothing else had ever made her feel this way—not her novitiate, not her final vows, not her prayers, not her work. Nothing else had ever filled her with such a conviction of total purpose. Nothing else had ever confirmed that she was *wholly* acceptable and *wholly* worthy in her service to God.

How long her rapture lasted, she did not know, but gradually she became aware of movement in the distance, and when she forced her eyes to focus, she saw a caravan of wagons coming south on the road. She immediately assumed that they must be Father Murray's guests—and Mr. Quentin's friends.

A tiny shiver of disgust ran through her. The peace and glory of her moment was disturbed—but only briefly. There were people to be notified and work to be done and it was her duty to see to both. That is as it should be, she thought as she walked back to the church. Anyone seeing her would have thought she hadn't a care in the world.

The first one who did see her was Sister Joana. "Are you well, Paula?" she asked, her voice implying more than she would ever put into words.

"I am quite well," Paula Kathryn said cheerfully. "Has Father Irving left yet?"

"No, Sister. He is still hearing confessions."

"Good. Have someone tell him that as soon as he is finished he must prepare for a group of visitors who may also wish to confess. Then you had best put on extra soup and breads for I believe your kitchen will have twenty or thirty extra mouths to feed this noonday."

Sister Joana looked at her quizzically. "I do not mean to pry, but your eyes sparkle with a special joy, and well, after this morning's events, I mean, it would please me if you could share it."

"I wish I could, Joana. I wish I could share it with all the world." But only the joy, not the cause of it, she thought selfishly. "Let it be sufficient to say that God has blessed me this day in a way that scours my soul clean of the curse from the devil's nasty trick this morning. My joy this Good Friday is the joy of the Resurrection."

"God be praised," Sister Joana said, crossing herself.

"In the highest," Paula Kathryn responded, feeling another surge of self-satisfaction as she, too, crossed herself. She smiled as Sister Joana hurried away, and then went to find Mr. Simmons, the parish stabler, to tell him about the guests.

As she entered the stables she stifled a surge of anger when she saw Mr. Quentin there. He was handing something to Mr. Simmons who immediately said, "Good morning, Sister Paula," as he hurriedly put whatever Quentin had given him into his pocket.

Quentin frowned at her, but said nothing. She forced herself to give him a smile in return and said. "Good morning, Mr. Simmons, and to you, too, Mr. Quentin. I suppose you both know about the arrival of our guests?"

"Max here was just telling me, Sister, and I was fixing to come talk to you about it. I don't think we have enough grain and hay for as many oxen and mules as he says is coming." All the time he spoke he kept his eyes averted as though he was afraid to look at her.

"If you have enough for a day or two, I'm sure you can find more tomorrow. God will provide."

"We have some in the wagons," Quentin said grudgingly, then quickly added, "but we'll need about like as much for the trip home."

"Then that takes care of it," she said, suddenly wanting to get away from both of them. "By the time our guests are ready to leave, I'm sure Mr. Simmons will have found fodder enough for you to go home on." She knew Simmons could always find what they needed if given enough time to do so. Father Murray had told her not to question Simmons's resources, and consequently, she had never felt at ease with him.

"Oh, there's another thing we'll need," Quentin said, as though suddenly remembering a minor detail. "Got us a woman about to have a baby with us—that is if she didn't have it after I left them—so she'll be needing some help, I guess."

"A mother about to deliver? That means an Easter baby. How wonderful! Well, we will certainly attend to her, Mr. Quentin. Perhaps you should ride up to meet them and check on her."

"I'll send my boy, Billy, with you," Mr. Simmons said.

Suddenly Paula Kathryn saw the face of the boy in the chapel this morning and realized who it had been. Then she remembered that Quentin had handed Simmons something when she entered the stables—something Simmons hadn't wanted her to see.

"D-d-don't you d-dare!" she stuttered in the rush of her anger. "Y-you tell your Billy that I want to see him before lunch.

And if you've d-done what I think you've done, Father Goodfox will hear about this!"

Quentin was already backing away as she turned toward him. "And you!" she screamed, now in full control of her voice again. "I don't want to see you near that boy again—never! Do you hear me? Never, never, never!"

He paused for a moment as though he were going to stand his ground, then said, "Get the hell off my back," as he turned toward the door. "I don't need any crap from a lezzie-nun cunt."

"Mr. Quentin!" she roared as she charged after him. "You will leave the church grounds immediately! You are no longer welcome here!"

With a dismissive shake of his head and shrug of his shoulders, he walked out of the back door of the stable without answering her. Paula Kathryn stopped in the doorway, unsure of what to do next while Quentin mounted a bay mule and started riding out toward the road. She wanted to scream something else at him, to put him once and for all in the lowly place he deserved, but all she could do was struggle to calm her anger while she watched him go.

Finally she turned and looked back into the stable for Mr. Simmons, but he was no longer in sight, and she didn't really care. She left the stable and walked around it back to the church, determined to call Father on the radio and find out when he would be home.

Brother Jacob greeted her with a mechanical smile. "How can I help you, Sister Paula?"

"Are you scheduled for a radio check with Father Goodfox?"

"Yes, this evening at eight."

She didn't want to wait that long. "Do you think you can reach him before then?"

"I can try, Sister, but since he is traveling, we don't know if he is monitoring his radio."

"Try him anyway, please." Stilling her impatience, she waited calmly for Brother Jacob to set up the code sequence, then listened to his monotonous repetition of calls. He glanced at her occasionally, but when she didn't say anything, he continued calling. Finally she accepted that they would have to wait and turned to leave. "Eight o'clock, you say?"

"Yes, Sister."

"Very well, I will join you then."

"Sister, there's something going on out there, but I'm still not sure what it is."

"Like what?" she asked as she turned back to him.

"Like radio traffic ten times normal—almost all of it in one kind of code or another—but several of the clear broadcasts have been talking about war."

"What's the Republic doing now—getting ready to attack the Nates?"

He shook his head and looked at her with a kind of sadness in his eyes she had never seen before.

"It's bigger than that. Much bigger. I've still only picked up fragments, but it sounds to me like it's going to be a real war—a war for control of North America."

She refused to believe that. Father would have told her. But she didn't want to belittle Brother Jacob. "Well, keep listening," she said with a smile, "and if you get more definite information, perhaps we can make sense of all this."

"Yes. Of course," he said, looking away from her.

Paula Kathryn knew she had hurt his feelings, but there was nothing to be done about that. "I'm sorry, Brother Jacob. I don't mean to doubt you. It's just that—"

"No. It is my fault." He looked up at her with a forced grin. "I got excited about something that may not mean a thing. And I can see now that you have important things on your mind. As you said, if I get more definite information, I will tell you."

She almost reached out to touch him, but didn't. "Thank you. I will see you later."

"Yes, Sister, later."

After closing the door softly behind her, she started for the kitchen, then abruptly changed her mind and went to her room. There she knelt before the cross over her bed and prayed silently to Saint Geraldine for patience and forbearance, and as she prayed, she felt better and stronger. She remembered what had happened earlier in the garden, and a gentle warmth seemed to spread within her until she felt again that sense of peace that had been broken by her anger and the interruptions of events.

Tonight she would talk to Father. Perhaps in a day or two he would be home. Then God would lead her through what she had to do.

CHAPTER 42

ONE | Cody's combined force of militiamen and Demons followed the Lake Catherine cutoff to US-Eighty-two without sighting any of the Nates. But Ensolita was waiting for them at the intersection with his troops loaded on mule-drawn freight wagons.

"They were waiting for us in Benjamin, Lieuten——ah, Cody," Ensolita said. "Must have hidden every truck and car they had. Would have hid the mules, too, I 'spect, 'cept they were in a barn near us and started braying to beat all in one of the quakes and Harold found them. That Mayor Delagardo wanted to sell us oxen for *fifty* dollars a head."

"What did you give him?"

"IOU's for eight mules at one hundred dollars a head and four wagons at eighty dollars each. He was madder than hell. Said the mules were worth four times that, but I told him what you said about Attorney General Terry, and he quit yelling at me and said he knew whose ass to chew."

"Ya done good, Ensolita."

"Also found out from somebody a little friendlier that this cutoff won't get us to Rhineland. We'll have to keep going on over Eighty-two, then down Texas-Two-sixty-seven."

"I know," Cody said. "Now y'all listen up." As quickly as he could, he told all of Ensolita's group about the war, and let Ogden go into pow-wow with the Demons who had come with Ensolita. After twenty minutes of busy talking and hand-waving, five more of Ogden's Demons decided to leave.

"Y'all be careful," Cody said as the five swapped their gear out with the troops who had ridden their horses. "Mostly you better keep a hawk's eye out for militia groups. Lubbock will probably be looking to conscript anyone they can find, so stay away from there, and go easy around the towns, you understand?" No matter how much he would have liked them to stay, he didn't blame them a bit for leaving.

"Thanks for the advice, Lieutenant. And good luck to you, too. Bye, Sam, guys," the spokesman for the five said. With brief farewells and a few waves they headed up the Lake Catherine cutoff toward where the troop had left the other three who had decided to go home.

"So now what?" Ogden asked as he rode up beside Cody.

"Now we go after the Nates. Sergeant Ensolita," he called, "Mr. Ogden and me and ten riders will proceed to Two-sixty-seven as fast as we can. If we haven't made contact by then, we'll leave someone to wait for you there, and we'll keep heading for Rhineland. You come quick as you can behind us. And drive those mules."

"Can do, Cody. Anything else?"

"No, that'll do 'er. See you later." He pointed at Kolmer. "Ed, you, Brisas, Hermosa, Morgan, and the radioman. Sam, pick five of yours to come with us, then lead us out as fast as you think these horses of yours can stand."

Ogden's trotting pace turned out to be faster than Cody expected it to be and they'd been riding less than an hour when they reached the intersection where Two-sixty-seven came in from the north. Cody pulled up beside Ogden and reached for his map, but Ogden laid a hand on his arm.

"Look."

A quarter of a mile or so ahead of them, a wagon sat at right angles to the road with several people visible around it. "That oughta be about where Two-sixty-seven cuts south," Cody said.

"That's what I figured. And who do you suppose that party is? Your Nates?"

"I wouldn't be surprised. Rifles ready, lock and load," he called over his shoulder as he pulled his own rifle out of its saddle scabbard. "And keep your eyes and ears open. You got any suggestions on how we ought to approach these folks on horseback, Sam?"

"Slowly, well-spaced, staggered double file."

Ogden had barely spoken when the first shot zinged over their heads. Without thinking, Cody brought his rifle to his shoulder and fired three quick rounds at the wagon.

It was moving now, picking up speed as it headed south. Cody fired again and heard others firing as well. But they were all too excited. "Cease fire!" he yelled. "Cease fire and get after them."

He kicked his horse into a trot, then forced it into a gallop along the soft shoulder of the road. It was hard to keep the Nate wagon in sight as he bent low over the horse's neck. It was

impossible to shoot from there. On instinct he reined in a little as
he made the turn onto Two-sixty-seven.

A bullet tore up the gravel beside him. Another whistled by
his ear. With a hard pull of the reins he brought his horse to a
stop. He slammed the butt of his rifle into his shoulder before the
horse stopped trembling, and fired again at the wagon. Once.
Twice. But before he could stop pulling the trigger the third time,
the wagon dipped out of sight.

Ogden rode up beside him. "I left one of my boys back at the
intersection."

"Good. Let's try to keep ahold of their shadow without getting
close enough to get shot at."

They did exactly that until they got within sight of the
Rhineland bridge. On a hill about four miles to the south they
could see a church topped by a radio antenna tower standing tall
against a darkening sky.

"Rain," Ogden declared.

"And plenty of it," Cody added. "What'll you bet they have
that bridge guarded tight?"

"I'd bet a hot meal if we camp up here."

"We'll stop at least," Cody said grimly, "and wait for
Sergeant Ensolita's group. Then we'll decide what to do."

TWO | "How far?" Lucy asked as she opened her eyes.
The noisy truck bounced along at a steady twenty miles per hour.

"We just turned onto the Lake Catherine cutoff," Jenny
Augusta said with a frown. "Horsemen coming, sister."

"I see them. Get your gun out." Mishla pulled her revolver
out of its holster under her arm and laid it in her lap. "I'm ready
if they are."

"Me, too," Lucy said.

"You just sit still."

Lucy nodded and knew she was stronger than she sounded.
Strapped tightly into the seat between Mishla and Jenny
Augusta, she felt a sense of assurance that she had chosen the
right thing to do. She took her own pistol from its holster at her
waist, but kept it under her cloak so as not to worry Mishla.

"I'm not going to stop unless they make us," Mishla said,
"and maybe not even then. Hang on." As the truck got to within

a hundred feet of the first of the five riders, she shoved the truck into second gear and hit the accelerator.

Much to Lucy's surprise, the riders moved farther off the road and waved as the truck roared past them. "Who do you think they are?" she asked, turning in the seat so she could look at them out the back window.

"Strangers," Jenny Augusta said. "Probably one of those gangs from Big Jack or Commanche."

"Their horses are beautiful."

"Tired-looking if you ask me," Mishla said.

Lucy turned back in the seat and squirmed a little to find the most comfortable position. She was aware of the dull ache of her wound, but she'd come to accept that pain as part of living and breathing—and she was learning just how much about her body she had always taken for granted, like moving and breathing and just taking a pee without hurting. Miner Burris in that book made more and more sense to her now. Pain could be instructive.

"That's a funny smile on your face."

Lucy looked at Mishla and let the smile grow. "I was just appreciating being alive."

"As well you should. It's not like you've done much to aid your own cause."

"Dammit, Jenny Augusta!" Lucy's smile disappeared in the fire of her pain-shortened temper. "Don't start in on me again. I'm doing what I have to do, and you're—"

"Easy, child, easy. No sense in getting mad at Jenny just because she's worrying about you." Large raindrops spattered on the windshield, and Mishla turned on the wipers.

"I'm not a child. But that's what's wrong. That's why I get mad at both of you. You think a child could do the kind of missions you send me on, Mishla? You think you can just—"

"Easy, chi—Lucy. Easy. We both know you're a grown woman with the right to do what you have to. If we didn't, we wouldn't be here. We'd be hauling you back to Childress."

"You might be trying," Lucy said quickly, the frustration building in her again, "but I'd be fighting you scapel and saw. Sometimes I just want to scream at you. I've had it, Mishla! I've had it! Up to here!" Lucy was as startled by her shouting as they were, but it was like an artery had popped inside her and she couldn't stop the spurting anger.

"When are you going to give me control of my own life? When I'm thirty? Or forty? Or . . . never?" She paused only for a second, then asked, "I do get to have my own life one day, don't I?" She felt the tears in her eyes and wanted Mishla to see them, too. "Will you stop and answer me that?"

Only the sound of the truck and the wind filled the cab for a long moment before Mishla spoke. "You can leave me any time you're ready to."

"That's not fair. I didn't say I wanted to leave you. I just said I wanted to have control of my own life. Are you saying I can't have that as long as I live with you?"

Again there was a long pause. "Yes. If you're in such an all-fired hurry to be on your own, then do it. But you'll not call my house home again."

Jenny Augusta gasped.

The shock of Mishla's words hit Lucy so hard that her tears stopped. Never would she have expected Mishla to say that to her. Never could she have imagined herself being told she no longer had a home. "I don't understand," she said softly. "If you love me, why—"

"Of course I love you," Mishla snapped with a sharp glance at her before turning back to the road and letting the truck slow down. The rain battered the truck in hard, gusting waves that sent stinging spray through cracks where the windows didn't close properly.

"Then why would you tell me to leave? Because I won't be your unquestioning errand-girl any more?"

"No. That's not it at all. It's because you obviously don't appreciate what I've done for you."

"Oh, Mishla! I appreciate everything you've done for me. Everything. But I'm a woman now, not a little girl." Lucy's eyes burned dryly now. "I love you. You're my mother. But I need to begin . . . begin making my own decisions and trying to find my own life. Why is that so wrong?"

"This is US-Eighty-two," Mishla said, swinging the truck onto a wider paved road. "If this rain doesn't slow us down too much, we ought to reach Rhineland in an hour or so. And no, it's not wrong to want your own life. But I think you're damned ungrateful."

Lucy watched Mishla clench her jaws tight and knew there was nothing for her to say, nothing that could explain to Mishla what she meant or how she felt. When Mishla got that look of determination on her face, there was nothing anyone could say to change her mind. With a deep sigh of fatigue and resignation

Lucy closed her eyes and leaned back against the seat. Maybe it was just as well to accept Mishla's rigidity now and move on. Lucy's life had already changed too much in this past week to ever go back to what it had been.

The noise of the truck and the wind and the rain blended into a white wall of sound that blotted out the rest of the world. But much to her surprise and pleasure, she felt Jenny Augusta take her right hand in her own and give it a gentle squeeze. Lucy took that as a small sign of hope and let her mind drift into light sleep.

THREE | Nyllan had driven them quickly and skillfully over the eleven miles of rough road from Windthorst to Archer City where the square was congested with wagons, trucks, and cars. Under the sagging awnings of decrepit buildings, small groups of people were talking excitedly. A sign stuck in the courthouse lawn said, WAR MEETING AND ENLISTMENT 1:00 PM TODAY.

"This is really getting exciting," she said as she maneuvered away from the square and headed them west again.

"Wars are always exciting in the beginning . . . until people find out how deadly serious they are. When God said—"

"Don't be pompous, Murray. If this is going to be a real war—like in the history books—then it's scary. But it's exciting, too."

"When God said," he continued, ignoring her sarcasm, "that men would come to the altars of war sooner than the altars of love, He only pointed out how weak and corruptible we poor humans are."

"You really are in a preachy mood."

He frowned. "Why must you always be so ready to—"

"Oh, shut up. Can we just follow the signs to Seymour?"

Goodfox bit back a rejoinder that would have put her in her place. Slowly and deliberately he dug out his copy of Eagil's map. "Yes. We take Two-ten at the first Y and Four-twenty-two"—he squinted at the numbers—"I think it is at the next Y, and that will take us straight into Seymour."

"With all this war recruiting going on, do you think we'll have any trouble getting through Seymour?"

"We shouldn't. Besides, we'll avoid the square. If Archer City was that busy, Seymour will be mobbed."

Compared to most of what they had been traveling on, the road was in very good condition, and two hours later they circled south of Seymour's square and picked up US-Eighty-two heading west into the black heart of a thunderstorm on a road that quickly deteriorated, forcing Nyllan to shift repeatedly from first to second and back to first again.

"We'll go into Rhineland the back way," Goodfox shouted above a roll of thunder.

"Why?"

"Call it caution. About five miles past a wide spot in the road called Red Springs we'll come to FR-Two-sixty-six. That's the old Hefner road. Course, Hefner isn't there any more—maybe never was. But there's a well and a sign there, and a road that will take us into Rhineland's back door. The only problem may be the bridge. Old one collapsed Shudderday. New one isn't so new or so well built, so I'll probably have to walk you across it."

"In this rain?"

"If that's God's will. Don't worry. Once we make it home, everything's going to fall right into place." When he said that he began to realize how eager he was, as though they were already climbing the hill to St. Joseph. He couldn't wait to see Sister Paula Kathryn's face, and Brother Jacob, and Sister Joana, and maybe even his old friend Father Irving.

"I'm not sure how much farther we can go, Murray."

"What's the matter?"

"This rain. I can barely see."

Goodfox realized in a brief flash of chagrin that once again he had taken Rhondasue and her talents for granted. It just didn't occur to him that she would have any problem getting them through the worst of weather. "Maybe we should pull over and give it a chance to pass."

"As dark as it's getting, I think I will," she said, driving off onto the shoulder.

He was disappointed, but knew that it would be foolish to take unnecessary risks this close to home.

Lightning cracked up the hill. Thunder rocked the truck. Ozone filled the air.

"Jeee-sus," Nyllan said. "You all right?"

"Yes, praise be to God. That was close."

"You think maybe He's trying to tell us something?"

"Keep moving."

"I'm for that." She hunched over the wheel, peering through the sheeting rain, and eased the truck back onto the broken roadbed.

"Rhondasue?" he said suddenly.

"What?"

He didn't know why he had said her name, so he reached over and tenderly patted her arm. "Nothing. Except, thanks, maybe. I ought to say that more often."

She smiled, but never took her eyes off the wet pool of light in front of her as she shifted down again. "You only have to say when you feel like. There's no quota you have to fill."

"Thanks for that, too." He wanted to say more, wanted to say, Rhondasue, I love you, but the words wouldn't come out of his mouth, and the warm, glowing image that dominated his mental eye was not of Rhondasue. It was of Sister Paula Kathryn. "I love you," he whispered compulsively, but his words and confusion were lost under the noise of the storm.

FOUR | By the time Mrs. Quentin and the braves got Ann Johnson into the guest room in the sisters' dormitory, she had gone into labor.

"Is this your first child?" Paula Kathryn asked as she began helping the woman take off her wet clothes.

"Yes, Sister."

"Then you may be at this a while. We will make you as comfortable as possible, but you must realize that there is little we can do to ease your pain. Sister Angelica will show you how to breathe more easily, but that is really all we can do until delivery starts."

"I understand and thank you for your help."

"You are more than welcome, Mrs. Johnson."

"Mrs. Cody," the woman said flatly. "Ann."

Paula Kathryn was confused and looked at Mrs. Quentin who took that moment to turn away.

"My name is Mrs. Ann Johnson Cody," the woman said. "Please call me Ann."

"Yes, of course, Ann. Here, put this on," she said, handing her a long flannel nightgown. "It should be quite big enough and will help keep at least part of you warm when delivery finally starts."

Ann took the gown and awkwardly pulled it over her head with help, then let it fall over her huge abdomen with a smile. "Thank you, Sister."

"You're quite welcome. Now, to bed with you. Mrs. Quentin, can you stay here with her until one of my sisters gets here?"

"Certainly."

"Good," Paula Kathryn said as she walked to the door. "I will check on you later." Later came sooner than she expected as she saw to the church's guests for supper, made sure that Simmons was taking care of their livestock, and repeated in the presence of Mr. Young, the group's leader, that Mr. Quentin was not to be allowed within the church buildings. She paused only to listen to the clock chimes, and suddenly realized it was almost time for the radio check with Father Murray.

As she entered the dimly lit radio room, Paula Kathryn heard someone saying, "Come in, St. Joseph. Come in, please." Then she saw Brother Jacob, hunched over the transceiver.

"Brother Jacob," she said sternly. "Brother Jacob, wake up. There's a call coming in." She turned up the overhead lights and immediately knew something was wrong. One hand went to her rosary beads, the other to the carved wooden cross hanging between her breasts.

"Brother Jacob?" Still he didn't answer her, and only then did she notice the dark, wet stain in the middle of his back. In five quick steps she reached his side and laid a hand lightly on his shoulder to shake him. "Please, Brother Jacob. What is the matter with . . ."

The stain was blood. Why? How? Who? A low, moaning protest escaped her lips. "No-o-o. No-o-o."

Laying her shaking fingers on his throat, she felt for a pulse. There was none. Brother Jacob was dead.

"Barton's Chapel calling St. Joseph Church," the voice droned on the radio. "Come in, St. Joseph."

She picked up the microphone with a trembling hand and heard her voice saying, "This is St. Joseph. Come in, Barton's Chapel."

"We have the rest of the alert message for Father Goodfox."

"He's not here," she said dully. "Call back tomorrow. St. Joseph, out."

"No!" the voice shouted. "You must accept this transmission

and relay to St. Michael's in Dickens. This will complete the message."

She wanted to scream, to tell them she was standing next to a dead friend—who had been murdered! But the radio voice sounded so desperate that she automatically said, "Preparing to receive alert message." Taking the key from the ring at her waist, she unlocked the scramble-board cover and tapped the alert sequence. "Transmit."

The message came in a burst, and as soon as it ended, she said, "St. Joseph, out," and turned off her microphone. The printer whined at her from behind the board, then rolled out a short piece of paper with the unscrambled message on it.

Part Two: All pastors will coordinate with the diocese before taking or approving any military actions during this conflict. Do not forget that some of our brothers struggle for the other side. More specific directives will follow when appropriate.

There was more, but none of it made much sense to her, so she folded it neatly and put it in her pocket. Only as she went to find Father Irving did it occur to her that there was no first part to the message—unless that was what someone had killed Brother Jacob for.

CHAPTER 43

ONE | With the help of some gas, the Demons started a fire and kept it going under a lean-to affair. The fire was big enough to cook on, so that by the time Sergeant Ensolita and the rest of the troops arrived, there was hot food and steaming chicory enough for everyone. For that Cody was grateful.

There was little else to be grateful for. The radio wouldn't pick up anything but lightning static no matter how much Brisas fiddled with it. The rain fell in an unending deluge that had long before turned the saturated ground into a bog and made the chances of sleeping dry seem pretty unlikely. Beneath Cody's feet the earth twitched with jerky little quakes that threatened to get worse. And in the dark distance, the blue beacon light on the radio tower atop the Catholic church steeple broke through the swirling clouds of rain every now and again to remind Cody that the Nates were all probably sitting in Rhineland warm and dry.

Well, maybe not all of them. Some of them were bound to be guarding the bridge, and he sure hoped they were even more miserable than he was. But what bothered him most was not the thought of the dry, comfortable Nates, and not the radio, and not the weather, and not even the quakes. What bothered Cody most was the bad case of the now-which-aways he had got, because now that they'd caught up the Nates, he didn't know which way to turn or what to do next.

Should he get his troops ready and try to take control of the bridge? How would they do it? And when? Tonight? Or in the morning? If they did someways manage to capture the bridge, should they attack the town? And what if Terry was right? What if that priest, Goodfox, was involved in this? Should they raid the church to find out?

Raid a church? The idea was disgusting. Even someone with as little use for churches and what they stood for as Cody had a hard time with the idea of attacking a church. But what if he had to? What if that church was the center of all this trouble? What was he going to do then?

Cody didn't have trusty answers to any of those questions and part of him—a deep and frightened part of him—felt like he hadn't come any ways at all since that morning in the draw below the caprock where Shelia Emery had been killed. No matter what he did, somebody was sure to get hurt and maybe even killed because of it—maybe even a lot of innocent somebodies.

Then what?

Shelia Emery was dead. Roland Jessup was dead. Donna Melindo was close enough to dying last he'd heard.

Who else had to die for these damn Nates? Weren't there enough dead already? Wouldn't it be better if he just went by himself—snuck across the river and tried to find Ann and his baby? Wouldn't that be the best thing he could do? Rain trickled steadily off his jacket collar and down the back of his neck.

Going alone after Ann would be the most selfish thing he could do, not the best.

He had to remind himself that out beyond his reckoning there was a war starting up. What the hell that was going to mean, he didn't know, but it sure enough didn't matter if he felt bad and sorry about what was going on. Feelings didn't count for anything, not now. They couldn't. All he was supposed to worry about was his job—capturing these Nates and their radioactive booty—and getting his troops through it all so they could help fight this new war some group of fools had dreamed up.

Yet, there was the trouble. Getting them through was going to be the toughest part of all. And if there was—

"Can we talk, Cody?" Brisas asked from close behind him.

It took him a moment to react. "Sure, Juanita," he answered. "Pull up a log." It took another moment to register that Brisas wasn't alone. Kolmer, Ensolita, and Ogden sat down with her by the sputtering fire. "Y'all got something on your minds?"

"We'd like to know what your plans are," she said.

They all sat very still for thirty or forty seconds as the earth trembled beneath them. Finally Cody chuckled. "Me, too. I've just been fretting over that very thing. Seems to me we've got to attack those Nates, but the questions are where, when, and how."

"Seems to us like if we did it now, we'd sure enough surprise them," Ensolita said.

"But if we wait until morning, they might be laying for us," Ogden added as he put another split log on the fire.

Cody looked from face to face, each under a rain-soaked hat. He couldn't tell much from their expressions, but he had the feeling that none of them was too happy with their own plan.

"On the other hand," he said with a tone of authority he didn't feel, "if we attack with full forces right at dawn, we're less liable to be all confused about what's going on. It's not like any of us have ever practiced a night attack across a bridge with horses now, is it?"

"You're right on that account," Ogden said. "Me and my boys have never done nothing like that."

"And neither have we." Cody let that hang for a second. "The Nates might be expecting us in the morning, but we can at least make ready for that, and maybe even surprise them by not doing what they think we're fixing to do."

"Like what?"

"Oh, I don't know—like backing the wagons across the bridge with the machine guns on them," he said off the top of his head. "And the horses could carry the rest of us double across the river around that bend to the east."

"You think we could get away with that?" Ensolita asked.

"I think the whole thing's open for discussion, but I think we have to set up a plan for dawn, not for tonight."

"My boys got a big tarp set up," Ogden said. "Let's get out of this rain and talk about it."

Cody stood up. "Sounds good." What he wanted was a plan they could all live with, and maybe the five of them could come up with just that. "Lead the way, Sam."

TWO | Several minutes after Lucy awoke in the bouncing truck, she was pleased with the strength she felt in herself. On her left, Jenny Augusta worked the wheel and the pedals and the shift lever with her eyes glued to the pale splotches of light hanging in the rain before them. On her right, Mishla sat almost rigid, seemingly just as intent on guiding the truck as Jenny Augusta. Neither of them had seemed to notice that Lucy was awake. "Are we getting close to Rhineland?"

"Yes," Mishla said as she turned and put her arm around Lucy's shoulders. "But I do wish you'd change your mind."

"I can't." Resting her head against Mishla, Lucy wanted to say more, but the memory of Mishla's words hardened her reaction. "We each do what we have to. You taught me that."

"I thought I also taught you the meaning of prudence and— Jenny, why are you stopping?"

The truck shook and rattled. Lights vibrated in the darkness in front of them. Rain whipped the windshield. The earth trembled again and again and again as the quakes passed underneath them with irregular shocks.

The three women braced themselves against each other to ride it out.

"Bad, bad," Mishla finally whispered. It sounded like she was chastising the earth for shaking.

"They're getting worse," Jenny Augusta said when the tremors finally stopped.

"The day after tomorrow is Easter," Lucy said softly.

"And this is Good Friday. So what?"

Lucy had no idea why Easter had suddenly popped into her head and out of her mouth, but for no reason she felt like it had some significance. "I don't know. I just realized it, I guess."

"I don't believe in it," Jenny Augusta said as she started the truck forward again. The rain was pounding them now.

"Believe in what? In Easter?"

"Exactly." She shook her head. "It doesn't make any sense. How could they kill God? He was always alive, wasn't he? That's what Mother taught us."

Mishla laughed. "So she did," she shouted above the drumming of the rain. "But you'll never get me to argue religion with you."

Lucy only smiled, her thoughts already drifting past what they were saying. She believed, of course, because of what Mishla had taught her. She believed Cristodios had indeed come down to earth in the body of a man, and that the Romans had crucified that body, and on the third day it had been resurrected from the dead and walked in the garden and ascended to the right hand of God the Father Almighty. The difference between herself and Jenny Augusta was that Lucy believed all of the story. She just wasn't impressed by it.

How could one be impressed by a deity that had changed from God to God to God and died without death? And if eternity was all Mishla had said it was, Lucy thought God's brief stay of thirty years on earth was an infinitesimal drop in the ocean of time—hardly enough to warrant all the praise preachers and priests wanted to give Him for the whole thing. Even taken symbolically it didn't amount to much.

No, for her Cristodios wasn't some carnival phony trying to impress the world with the illusion of sacrifice. He was not a God who struggled for her soul, but rather was a universal spirit of good against the forces of darkness and evil. If in the process of His fighting, Lucy found benefit, it was not because He loved her as an individual. Because He loved the whole world, His love was the greatest force against evil. Thus her intent when she prayed was always to help Cristodios in His fight so that when He won, she could share in the peace that followed.

"Lights ahead," Mishla announced.

"I see them. We better stop."

No sooner had the truck stopped than a woman appeared wearing a green poncho that covered most of her and all but the barrel of her rifle. At the same instant, someone tapped the driver's window. "Open up."

Jenny Augusta rolled her window partway down. A young man's eyes appeared under the dripping brim of a militiaman's hat. "Sorry, ladies," he said, "this road is closed. You'll have to—"

"But I have to get to Rhineland," Lucy said quickly. "We are healers and I have a patient there about to give birth."

The man seemed unsure of himself, and Lucy knew she had to press him. "What harm could it do to let us through? Like I said, we're just healers trying to reach our patient." As she spoke, the rain suddenly slackened off to a blowing drizzle.

"What's the trouble, Morgan?" the woman in the headlights called.

"Healers. They're healers, they say, and they need to get to a patient in Rhineland. What do you think?"

"Let Cody decide. I'll stay here."

Cody! That was the name in her dreams. Or had he been real? Could this be Ann's Cody? Yes. No. The rush of thoughts all jumbled in Lucy's head.

The man leaned back down to the window. "Okay, follow me. I'm going to take you to our lieutenant and you can talk to him." He walked to the front of the truck and waved.

Lucy glanced at Jenny Augusta as she put the truck in gear. "Didn't a man named Cody visit me when I was . . ."

"Yes," she said easing the truck forward behind the militiaman. "If I've figured all this out right, he's the father of your patient's baby."

THREE | After turning onto Two-sixty-six they stopped and climbed in the back of the truck under the tarp to make their radio check with Sister Paula Kathryn. Because of all the lightning around, they dared not raise the antenna above the top of the truck. Goodfox tried from eight until eight-twenty, and finally gave up, only slightly concerned that they hadn't gotten through.

Four miles south they reached the Brazos above Hefner. "There's the bridge," Goodfox said as Nyllan stopped the truck and he struggled to get his poncho over his head in the close confines of the cab. The rain had slackened considerably, and the headlights lit almost half the narrow wooden span.

"Sheee-it," Nyllan said softly, pointing into the darkness beyond the bridge. "You see how high that river is?"

"Actually, it's not the river being high so much as the bridge being too low. Folks that built it didn't go anywhere near high enough. I'll get out and walk you across. From the looks of it, it shouldn't be too bad."

"Just you be careful."

Goodfox climbed quickly out of the truck and walked in front of it to the beginning of the bridge. With a wave over his shoulder he began walking on the right hand plank of the pair of worn planks laid across the railroad ties. The thin warp of the wood told him that the bridge was in worse shape than he remembered it. But the rushing river was still three or four feet below the planks and as far as he could see, the bridge still looked reasonably sturdy. The headlights cast his shadow into the darkness as behind him Nyllan inched the truck forward.

Step by step, yard by yard, Goodfox walked toward the middle of the bridge, feeling more and more confident even as the rain began to get heavier again.

Suddenly the plank gave way beneath him. His foot sank through rotting wood. The river roared up at him. He threw himself forward, jerking his leg spasmodically as he skidded on the slick surface.

"You all right?" Nyllan called from the truck.

"Yes," he managed to call back as he shakily raised himself to his knees and turned around. The hole in the plank wasn't much bigger than his foot. "Come on," he said with a wave as he stood up. Pain stabbed through his left ankle, but he forced himself to stand straight, and the pain quickly subsided to an ache. "Come on," he repeated.

Nyllan started the truck forward again, and Goodfox walked carefully backward, watching first over his shoulder, then pausing to watch the wheels as they approached the hole. The front wheel bounced gently down then back up onto the plank again.

"Hold it," he called as he signaled her with his hands and walked back to the cab. "I think you're going to have to go a little faster with the back wheels past the hole, Rhondasue."

"All right. You check as far ahead as you can see, then I'll come on." She poked the end of a stick out the window. "Take this."

"What is it?"

"A walking stick, I guess. It was just hanging in here on the gun rack. Maybe it will help."

It did help, not only for testing the planking as he walked along, but also for helping to bear his weight. The ache in his ankle was worse now. The rain pounded harder as the wind picked up and shoved at his poncho as though it were a sail and he fought to keep his balance.

Once he had waved Nyllan past the hole, he kept waving until the front of the truck got within ten feet of him. Turning and probing with his stick, he moved forward, and probed again, testing not the planks so much as the ties underneath them, all the time fighting the wind, resisting the sounds of blowing rain and rushing water that threatened to engulf him.

Every few minutes he looked back as though to assure himself that the truck was still behind him, that he wasn't standing in the middle of purgatory in some unholy light. His prayers as he worked his way deliberately across the bridge were wordless and mindless, silent beckonings from the center of his faith for God's vigilant protection.

Yet his thoughts floated above his perilous trek, and he wondered if this war between the old states was the sign from God that he had been waiting for. Was this the sanction of his plans, a continent alert and waiting, people and governments on the brink of change, ready at last for the holy proclamation of unity? Of course. It was so obvious. God had awakened them for him and prepared the way. If only he knew how—

Awwwnk!

The horn startled him. Then he realized that he was off the bridge and so was the truck.

"What the hell's the matter with you?" Nyllan asked as he climbed back into the cab.

"Nothing." He smiled with a sense of inner peace and pushed the dripping hood back off his head. "Absolutely nothing."

She switched on the interior light and moaned. "Oh, God. You've got that look on your face. Dammit, Murray," she said with sudden anger, "you could have—fallen off the bridge!"

Goodfox could only smile at her concern. "No. God was with me, as He is with us now, Rhondasue." He was talking to her, but his mind was still on the wonder of the revelation. "This war between the old states is His *sign*."

Giving him a very strange look, she turned off the light and shoved the truck into first gear. "Whatever you say, Murray. I just wish you'd remember what you tell me about God helping those who help themselves."

"But I never forget that. Never."

"Just make sure you don't." The truck jumped forward.

The tone of her voice broke the tranquillity within him. He stared across the cab through the glow of the instrument panel at the intensity on her face and had the odd impression that he was seeing her for the first time. A chill raced up his spine.

FOUR | Father Irving had administered extreme unction, then Simmons and Father Irving had carried Brother Jacob to his room and laid him on the narrow cot. After swearing Simmons to silence Paula Kathryn had shooed him off to the stables to count the guests. She wanted to know if any of them had left.

When he was gone, she had turned to Father Irving, sure already that because of his unsuspicious nature that he would be of little use to her, but bound by the rules to consult with him, and asked, "What are you going to do about this?"

"What is there to do, Sister? We must pray, of course, and in the morning we must report this to your local sheriff's deputy."

"I mean, what are you going to do about it now? One of these *guests* of ours is responsible for this."

"You have no way of knowing that, Sister. With so many strangers"—he paused and closed his eyes for a second—"I understand your suspicion. But there is nothing we can do. This is a matter for the sheriff's office, not for the church."

"Very well, Father. Why not send someone immediately to get Deputy Whitten? Why wait until morning?"

He must have heard the anger and impatience in her voice, because he blushed before he spoke. "Yes, of course, I suppose we should do it that way." His hands clutched each other before him. "Oh, this is a terrible thing, Sister."

"Indeed it is, Father," she said with one last glance at Brother Jacob before indicating that they should leave his room. He did not look at all peaceful, and even though her voice betrayed nothing, her heart was pounding with anxiety. "But it will be far more terrible if the murderer gets away."

Father Irving nodded silently as she closed the door, then crossed himself and paused for a moment of silent prayer. Her instinct was to join him, but her mind was racing too furiously over what she should do next. She could send Sister Benedict to get Deputy Whitten. That would be good, because Sister

Benedict was always calm in a crisis. But should she tell Father Irving about the alert message? Or should she save that until—

Suddenly she realized that she had missed the scheduled radio check with Father Murray. Save my soul, she thought, how can I reach him now? And when will he be here?

Turning quickly she walked away, leaving Father Irving still at his prayers before the door. First she found Sister Benedict, and with minimal explanation sent her to get Deputy Whitten. Then without hesitation she made straight for the radio room, and after making sure no one else was in it, locked the door behind her and stationed herself at the transceiver console. After setting up the coded call to Father Murray, she began the standard procedures and for the next thirty minutes tried to raise a response. All she got for her efforts was crackling static and fifteen or twenty seconds of a skip from BBC News in London, New Anglia.

As she was shutting down the board, she was surprised to see that it was already after ten o'clock. She felt tired, and frightened, and angry, and wasn't at all sure what to do next until she remembered the message from Barton's Chapel and the instructions with it. No, she decided, there was no need for Father Irving to know about this.

First she would try to raise Barton's Chapel and get a repeat of the beginning of the message. Failing that, she would try to relay the part of the message she had to St. Michael's and tell them what little she knew.

Then, she thought with a sad, nervous shake of her head, I must confront Mr. Young and our guests, for surely as I sit here, one of them killed Brother Jacob.

CHAPTER 44

ONE | "Lieutenant? Cody? Wake up."
Cody recognized the voice. He'd heard it before. But it took several seconds to remember that it was Morgan's voice. Then the damp smells of the earth and the popping of the fire brought him fully awake as he sat up under the Demons' lean-to. The rain had stopped again. "What? What's the matter, Morgan?"

"We got somebody here needs to talk to you—three healers who say they gotta get to Rhineland."

Cody looked around and saw the three women standing on the other side of the fire. He was awake now and after a long second recognized all three of them. "Come sit over here, ladies," he said with a smile. "It's a little drier and warmer. Morgan, you hang close." As they stepped around the fire, Morgan moved to where they had been standing and squatted on his heels.

Lucy let Jenny Augusta and Mishla steady her as they walked through the mud around the fire, but she pulled free of them to sit under the edge of the big tarp facing this man who kept appearing in her life. "You're Ann's husband," she said, holding out her hand. "I am Lucy Ilseng."

He took her hand and shook it. "Jeremiah Cody," he said.

"This is my mother, Mishla. And this is her sister, and my friend, Jenny Augusta. Mr. Cody, we have to get down to Rhineland. Ann's going to deliver any time now, I'm sure of it."

"I know who all of you are," he said slowly, pointing to them one at a time. "You are the healer who was at that meeting at Patricia Brighton's house—the one who left with the Nate commissioner."

"Correct, young man," Mishla said.

"And you are the one who was helping take care of Miss Lucy up in Crowell. Aunt Bertha—Sheriff York—introduced us when she brought me to see her."

"Yes, it is good to see you again."

"And you," he said, turning back to Lucy, "you are the one the Nates shot and threw off the train." And raped you, too, he thought, but he couldn't bring himself to say it. "What makes you so sure Ann hasn't had our baby already?"

"I'm not sure," Lucy said. "But I can't take that chance. I have to be with her if I can."

He laughed bitterly, wanting to tell her to grow up, to face the fact that Ann was in with the Nates where she wanted to be. Of a sudden he wanted to shake her and make her understand that the three of them couldn't just drive on in to Rhineland like everything in the world was ready-made for her to smoke without having to roll it. His laugh stopped abruptly as he decided not to tell her anything—yet—and he started digging in his pack for a cigarette. "'Scuse me a second."

As the three women sat patiently waiting for him to find what he was looking for, something about Cody was bothering Lucy, something back behind all the connections they'd already drawn. She felt like she'd known him even before all this had happened. Then a brief gust of wind carried the answer to her.

This was the man whose guilt she had smelled so strongly back below the caprock. It had to be. The odor was very distinctive. Yet it wasn't nearly as strong now. There was only a trace of that guilt that burns like sulphur from the soul, and more of something else, a grief that was just as distinctive in its own way. He showed remarkable signs of healing on his own and she was glad for him.

"There," he said, lighting the cigarette and taking a long, deep drag. The smoke caught in his throat. He coughed violently several times and looked at the cigarette oddly as though startled that such a thing could happen. "Well, that's disappointing. And I'm afraid I'll have to disappoint you ladies as well." He coughed again.

"Mr. Cody, I have to get to Rhineland."

"Even if I let you go across the bridge, there are Nates on the other side who might shoot at you first and ask who you are and what you want later. So even if I was of a mind to, I couldn't let you go. You see that, don't you?" He took another, easier drag from the cigarette. When that, too, caught in his throat, he flicked the cigarette impulsively into the fire.

"I insist." Lucy stared at him, wanting him to see her determination, demanding that he bend to her will.

He smiled. "Insist all you want. You're not going past this camp. Morgan, confiscate their transportation."

"Right, Cody. It's a truck." He stood immediately and walked away.

"Mr. Cody, you have absolutely no—"

"It's Lieutenant Cody to you, ma'am." Annoyance edged his voice as another fact slipped into place for him. This Mishla was the one who had helped Kendrick Johnson. "There's a war on, lady. Or hadn't you all heard?" They looked so surprised that he continued. "The Republic's joined up with the Nation and some others to fight all the countries east of the Mississippi. I got every right to take what I need to get this job done. You don't like it? Call Winslow Terry and complain."

Lucy's spirits slumped, and her body slumped with them, but even as Mishla steadied her, Lucy forced herself to sit up straight again, wincing with the pain. "When are you going to attack,

Lieutenant? You are going to attack Rhineland and try to capture the plutonium, aren't you?"

Cody did a double take. "What do you know about their cargo? How do you know it's plutonium?"

"Because their leader, Mike Young, told me it was. And you are going to attack, aren't you?"

Cody looked away from her and into the fire, liking her for the way she talked, but suspicious of all three of them. "I suspect we will move on into Rhineland tomorrow, but that's got nothing to do with you."

She had to convince him, for Ann's sake and for her own. No militia lieutenant was going to keep her from the revenge she deserved against Max Quentin. "It has everything to do with me—and Ann and your baby, Lieutenant." She added his rank, hoping it would feed his ego. "I have to be with her if I can. It's her first and she's going to need a lot of help."

There was something else in Lucy Ilseng's voice, and when Cody recognized it, he liked her even more. "You think the people in Rhineland won't help her?"

"We don't know that they're qualified to." She was grateful that Mishla and Jenny Augusta seemed willing to hold their tongues for the moment.

He didn't want to give in, but her open and hidden reasons added up pretty strong. Besides, if she was right, he couldn't deny help to Ann and the baby. But how was he going to handle it? He couldn't take them with him in the morning, and he could hardly afford anyone to guard them, yet he wasn't willing to trust them, either. However . . .

"All right," he said very deliberately, "here's my one and only offer. We are going to move against Rhineland at dawn. It won't be an attack unless they try to stop us. If you each give me your promise not to cross the river before I send for you, I'll send for you as soon as it's safe—or if we find Ann before then. Promise?"

The three of them exchanged glances. "Promise him," Mishla said. "It's a fair offer, and I think you ought—"

"No. I want to go with the attack. Please, Lieutenant, I owe Ann something."

"And you want your revenge," Cody said with a grim smile. What with her being shot and raped, he understood her need and why she had a bad case of it. Because of that and maybe because old Mishla didn't want her to go and because of an unexpected special sympathy he had for her—

"You can beg my pardon, Lieutenant Cody." She stared at him. How had he guessed about the revenge? How could he know? "I don't see that my feelings are—"

"Okay."

"—any business of . . . What did you say?"

"I said, yes, you can come with us at dawn. If you're set enough on risking your life over this, I'm not the one who's gonna hold you back. Now, since you can't sleep in your truck, I suggest you get your bedrolls and squeeze in under this tarp."

"One of us will have to come with her," Mishla said.

"Then you're both crazy. Now are you going to let me get some sleep, or not?" Cody felt suddenly rude and angry and upset and he didn't have a reason for any of it. And scared, too, and that was why the other feelings bothered him so much.

"You sit still," Jenny Augusta said, patting Lucy on the shoulder. "I'll get your bedroll, and you can sleep here."

"Thank you." Lucy's words were for Jenny Augusta, but her eyes were on Jeremiah Cody as he lay back down and settled his poncho around him. There was a gentle, sensitive quality about this man that she liked and she wondered how Ann could have left him.

TWO | "There's the church light," Nyllan said.

"Praise God. I wonder if the Quentins have arrived."

"I still don't understand what you see in that family. The brothers are scoundrels—especially Max—and that Suzanne doesn't have the brains of a diode."

"They, too, are God's faithful servants. We must learn to accept them as they are."

"Bullshit. If Max Quentin is God's faithful servant, then you're Saint Peter."

Goodfox clenched his teeth. The Quentin brothers might be crude tools, but so long as they aided in God's work, there was no reason to criticize their human failings. "We all live in glass houses," he said without looking at her.

"Don't give me that clichéd pap, Murray. You're the priest. You ought to be able to see that they only help you because they think there's profit in it for them."

"A profit for their souls."

"A profit for their pockets is more like it. I swear I don't understand how you can be so blind. Aren't you paying them?"

"The church is meeting their expenses," he said defensively, "but that doesn't mean that they are—"

"Their expenses? Who's checking them? You?"

"Yes—that is, I will be when they present their account."

"Then you'd better check them damn carefully, because they're going to take you for every penny they think you'll pay."

He sat angry and silent, unwilling to discuss the subject any further, yet reluctantly accepting her warning. He knew there was probably some justification in her suspicions, but he was willing to give the Quentins the benefit of faith until there was solid evidence to do otherwise. That was the only fair choice open to him.

Nyllan turned north on Rhineland Road and drove the truck up to the large graveled lot in front of St. Joseph Church before she spoke again. "Where are we going to sleep?"

"Separately, as before," he said without thinking. Whatever resolution he had made to be more open about their relationship dissolved in the blue light of the church beacon.

"Shit. I guess that tells me where I stand."

Before he could respond she got out of the truck and slammed the door. By the time he got out, she had jerked her bag out from under the canvas covering the truck bed, and the glare on her face kept him from saying anything.

"You're a goddamned hypocrite, Murray. I hope that keeps you warm tonight." She turned and marched through the gate in the hedge toward the dormitory wing.

Goodfox watched her with churning emotions—wanting to call out to her, needing to ask for her understanding, unwilling to risk further argument, and hating the anger she roused in him. Then out of the corner of his eye he saw someone coming from the church and turned in time to realize it was Sister Paula Kathryn.

Paula Kathryn had seen him staring toward the dormitory with an odd look of anguish on his face, and knew intuitively that he and the Nyllan bitch had argued. So much the better, she thought. When he turned toward her, her step quickened and she called out, "Oh, Murray, Father Murray, I'm so glad you're home!"

The stress he heard in her voice startled him. "What is the

matter, Sister?" he asked as he limped toward her and held out his hands to accept hers.

"A great deal, I am afraid," she said, squeezing his hands in her own, accepting his kiss on her forehead, giving way to her impulse and hugging him.

Again he was startled, but he gently wrapped his arms around her and felt the trembling of her body. "Tell me," he said. "Why are you so troubled?"

"Brother Jacob is dead," she whispered. The comfort of Father's presence was almost overwhelming.

"Dead?" Brother Jacob? He couldn't believe it.

"Murdered, Father . . . by one of those people who came to meet you here, I'm afraid." As she spoke, a light mist began to fall.

"I don't understand. When did this happen, and why do you think one of . . . Who is here to meet me?" A slight quake shuddered through the ground underneath them.

"A tonkaweya from the Nation led by a man named Mike Young, who looks like he's a druggie on hangers, and three brutish brothers named Quentin, and I didn't even know they were coming." An image of the naked Max Quentin flashed through her mind as a second shudder followed the first. "One of them violated our chapel, but there's also a woman in labor, and we received some kind of alert message, only half of one, actually, and I think that's why they killed Brother Jacob." The words just rushed out of her, and she knew she must sound foolish to him, but for the moment she didn't care.

"Easy, easy," he said as he stroked her back and tried to calm her. "Tell it to me again, slowly."

As the quaking stopped she reluctantly released her grip on him and stepped back a little. The mist was increasing to a drizzle. "Inside. Let's get you out of this rain. I'm sorry I sounded so . . . but it has been hard here the last few days." She offered him her hand and he took it. Together they began walking up to the church. "You're hurt!"

"Just twisted my ankle. I should have told you they were coming," he said as they entered the sanctuary foyer and turned toward the hall that led to his office and room. "I'm sorry." When they got to the office he poured each of them a large glass of Palo Pinto sherry. He drank his very quickly, and much to his surprise, so did she, so he poured them each another large glass. "Now, tell me what is going on around here."

In as much detail as she thought necessary Paula Kathryn told him what had happened since he'd left three weeks before, dwelling longest on the events of the last few days. As she told him about Max Quentin and Billy Simmons she stopped and took two or three long swallows of the wine, then held out her glass, which he filled again before she continued.

Everything Goodfox heard disturbed him: the drunkenness of Father Irving with Max Quentin, the abomination of sodomy—in the cloister chapel of all places—and the apparent murder of Brother Jacob. She had barely finished telling him about Father Irving's unwillingness to deal with the problem when Sister Benedict and Deputy Whitten appeared at the office door, both of them soaking wet.

"I have just told Father Goodfox what happened," Paula Kathryn said.

"Good." Deputy Whitten's dark eyes flashed under his heavy brows. "I'd like to see the body, first."

"So would I," Goodfox said. For the next hour he and Sister Paula Kathryn accompanied Whitten while he inspected the body, then the radio room, and finally questioned Paula Kathryn about the exact events leading up to her discovery of the body.

"I'll talk to the others in the morning," Whitten said.

"But what if the murderer gets away?" Goodfox didn't like Whitten's seeming lack of real concern.

"Don't worry about that, Father. There's a militia patrol just north of the bridge, and a Farm Bureau platoon coming up from Munday." He paused and put his hat on. "They won't get away."

Goodfox was surprised and frightened by that news, but he tried to look unconcerned.

"What does a Bureau platoon want here?" Paula Kathryn asked.

"Don't rightly know, Sister. Just know they're coming." He looked away from them as he spoke. "I'll see you folks later in the morning. Good-bye."

After he left, Goodfox said, "We'd both better try to get some sleep." What he was thinking was that if both the militia and the Farm Bureau were headed for Rhineland, Lubbock must know far too much about what he planned to do.

"Certainly, Father." Paula Kathryn watched him limp down the hall to his rooms, then turned toward her own filled like a boiling-over pot with thoughts and emotions she couldn't seem to cool. After dressing for bed and saying her prayers she suddenly remembered that she hadn't told Father Murray about the message from Barton's Chapel. She decided it was too important to wait, so she took the copy of the message from her dress, put on her robe, and headed for his rooms.

Goodfox was in his pajamas, kneeling in prayer when he heard the soft knock at the office door. Fully expecting to find Nyllan asking to join him, he opened the door with his thoughts cocked to send her away and was completely disarmed to find Sister Paula Kathryn standing before him in her robe.

"May I come in, Father?" she asked as she entered the room. "I'm sorry to bother you, but there is something I forget to tell you that couldn't wait."

"Yes, of course. Sit down," he said, waving to the one chair in the room while he sat on the wide bed. "Please tell me what is so important."

When she leaned forward to speak, her robe fell open ever so slightly, and he was surprised to feel the arousal fill his pajamas.

"It's the message—the one from Barton's Chapel. I never could raise them to get the first part." She took it from her pocket and handed it to him, watching him read with a sudden awareness of the muscles in his neck, and his broad shoulders, and the strength in his hands.

The message from the bishop didn't surprise him, but he was puzzled about what the first part could have said that was worth killing for, and arched an eyebrow as he looked up at her.

"I'm frightened, Father," she said, standing up suddenly and taking a step toward him. "I don't know what's going on, and I'm frightened."

He stood up also, and in a moment of unexplained emotion pulled her into his arms. The thrill that raced through him was like the caressing love of God, and Goodfox eagerly gave himself over to it, his thoughts surrendering to his emotions.

Paula Kathryn freed her hands and undid the belt of her robe as he pressed himself gently but firmly against her, and she knew that this was her moment to steal him away from that Nyllan whore. Without hesitation she pulled him even closer and started kissing his shoulders and neck. When he began returning her kisses, she knew the night and the victory were hers.

CHAPTER 45

Cody awoke to quakes and the sound of voices and discovered Lucy Ilseng sitting beside him staring toward the east.

"I don't remember a time when we had so many quakes," she said as he sat up and rubbed his eyes. She hadn't slept much, but she felt an almost euphoric kind of strength within herself.

"Neither do I."

"They worry me, Mr. Cody. I fear another Shudderday."

Shaking his head Cody said, "Seisers say it'll take fifty thousand years or more for the old teck plates to store up enough energy to cause another Shudderday. Least ways, that's what they taught me in school." When she didn't reply, he crawled out from under the lean-to and stood up. Only then did he see Juanita Brisas squatting by the fire watching a chicory pot percolating.

"Must have a clock in your head."

"Quakes woke me."

"That Ogden fella's up, too. Went off in the brush there to do his business, but said he was ready for adventure. Cody, you figure a boy like that would be good for me?"

"Are you serious?" he asked in surprise.

"Of course she is," Lucy said before Brisas could reply.

"I was telling Miss Ilseng here that Sam said he'd make me his queen. Ain't never been queen of nothing."

Cody didn't know what to say. "Well, if that's gonna make you happy, who am I to tell you not to?"

Brisas fought to suppress a giggle and flashed Lucy a look that said, *I'm gonna do it*. Lucy felt her own sense of delight in the decision and gave her a positive smile in return.

"Bad news," Ogden's voice said from beyond the firelight.

"What?" Cody asked.

"I think the damn river's too high for us to ford it. Oh, we could do it, I guess, but it'd have to be all experienced horsemen."

"Meaning mostly your men?"

"Meaning *all* my men—except for Juanita. She sits a pretty nice saddle."

Lucy watched Juanita Brisas's face as the two men talked, and she could almost see the signs of approval flashing through her eyes. Boy or man, Sam Ogden had Juanita's full attention.

Cody nodded. He knew he didn't have to ask Brisas to know she'd be willing to go with Ogden. The look on her face was enough. "Well, Sam, we could do it that way, or we could use the truck Miss Lucy and her friends brought last night by putting our machine gunners in it and making a run across the bridge—then follow with the horses and bring the wagons last. Nates probably won't be expecting a truck. And I'll bet anything they won't be expecting machine guns."

Lucy listened as they talked about the various options, but her thoughts gradually shifted across the river to Rhineland. She hoped and prayed that Ann was all right. More than that, she hoped that Max Quentin was waiting there . . .

"I said, what do you think, Miss Lucy?"

"Pardon? I'm sorry. I think the tonkaweya has a machine gun, too. I guess my mind—"

"Do you think you're strong enough to ride with me?" Cody asked again, wondering because of the concentrated look on her face what she was thinking.

"You mean double? Yes, certainly."

"No, she isn't," Mishla said from beneath a patched poncho.

"I didn't ask your opinion." He had no idea why he was making Lucy Ilseng this offer, but he wasn't about to let Mishla-the-Nate-helper interfere.

Lucy smiled. "Thanks."

"Then get yourself organized, woman," Cody said, returning her smile, "because when we're ready to go, you'd better be, too. Now, Sam, if they do have their own machine gun . . ."

The next hour passed very quickly as everyone was awakened and the final preparations were made for the move into Rhineland. They notified Baylor Station on the radio of what they were about to do, but Cody wasn't surprised that no one there had new orders for him. This was his little sideshow all the way.

Despite Mishla's protests, Cody decided to put two of the machine gunners and four of his troops into the truck along with the driver, with Ed Kolmer as the shotgunner and team leader. Once the truck cleared the south end of the bridge, Ogden and half the mounted troops would make the charge across the bridge to be followed by Cody with the rest of the mounted troops and finally the wagons containing the remainder of the militia and the Demons, and Mishla and Jenny Augusta. Also against Mishla's protests, Lucy would ride double with Cody. When everyone was ready, they sat in the predawn greyness and waited.

As soon as it was light enough to see across the river, Cody gave Kolmer the signal and the truck started down the hill. They hit the bridge doing forty or fifty miles an hour and passed the middle of it before the Nate machine gun opened fire. By then it was too late for the Nate guards. Cody felt a rush of energy and fear. This was it, and he prayed to Christodios it would work.

The machine guns chattered in long violent bursts. Carbines barked in two directions. Suddenly Ogden's group of riders was charging down the road after the truck, yelling and screaming like wildmen in an Oldtimer's movie.

"Get ready," Cody shouted.

Lucy tightened her grip around his waist. Over his shoulder she could see Ogden's group crossing the bridge at a dead run— a dark string of horses outlined by muzzle flashes. The machine guns had stopped firing, but she couldn't see the truck.

"At the gallop!" Cody screamed. "Charge!"

One moment they were standing still and the next they were racing through the wind, the horse pounding the pavement beneath them—three bodies locked together in one rhythm followed close behind by twelve clattering horses and yelling riders. Lucy was clinging desperately to Cody, momentarily frightened by the thought of falling off, but quickly overcome by the sheer physical thrill of the charge itself.

Cody caught himself leaning over as far as Lucy Ilseng's grip would allow, breathing with the horse, bursting with an exhilaration that he almost couldn't stand but didn't want to end. Then he realized that he, too, was yelling, screaming for the frightful joy of it, and Lucy was screaming with him.

Above the noise of the horses, the machine guns fired again. Lucy saw the truck a hundred yards beyond the bridge, Ogden's troops fanned out behind it close to trees beside the road, all of them firing up the hill.

Then as if by magic she and Cody were galloping off the bridge past mangled bodies lying behind a heavy machine gun in a smashed wagon. The thrill left her for an instant and was replaced by revulsion. Just as suddenly it returned as bullets whined over their heads. Someone was shooting at them!

Only when they were almost on top of Ogden's group did Cody bring his horse to a stop. "Get down," he said, holding out his arm for her and freeing his left foot from the stirrup.

Without thinking she started to do as she was told, but a sharp flash of pain in her wound made her pause. "Are you getting down?"

"No."

"Then neither am I."

He twisted in the saddle as if to grab her and force her off the horse, but she twisted with him. "You have to get down," he shouted.

"Cody! Over here!" Kolmer shouted.

There was no time to argue, so he turned the horse and galloped to the truck. The firing had slowed, and only occasional shots zinged past them, all seemingly too high.

"They're in the church. See those dormers in the roof? They must have a gun in every one of them."

"Pull back with us. You're too vulnerable out here."

The truck backed up and Cody and Lucy followed back to the tree line where everyone else had gathered. The wagons were coming across the bridge, but the Nates apparently decided they were all out of range because the firing stopped. This time when Cody told Lucy to climb down, she did because it was obvious that they were going to have to regroup and develop a new plan and she suddenly felt exhausted.

"We may have a better chance on foot," Brisas was saying. "We can creep along the tree lines and behind the hedges, but they'd see the horses for sure."

"I think you're right," Cody said as he followed Lucy to the ground. "Ensolita, get the snipers working on those dormers. I want that fire suppressed when we start to move."

Lucy sat with her back to a tree, breathing slowly and deeply, trying to calm herself and get her energy back while Cody and the others worked out what they were going to do. As soon as the wagons arrived, Mishla hurried over to her with a deep frown on her face.

"Don't look at me like that," Lucy said. "Just give me a little morphine and a couple of those amphetamines you always carry with you, and I'll be all right." Much to Lucy's surprise, Mishla did exactly that. Behind them snipers fired one slow shot after another up the hill at the church.

"Can you walk, Lucy?" Brisas asked.

Lucy quickly swallowed the second amphetamine capsule. "Of course, Juanita."

"Good, then Cody says you can come with my group. We're going to circle the long way around to the east and try to get to the church, but we should draw the least fire unless the Nates are laying for us." She held out her hand and Lucy took it and Mishla's and pulled herself to her feet.

"I'm coming with you," Mishla said following them as Brisas and Lucy headed east behind the trees with fifteen militiamen.

Cody smiled after them, admiring Lucy Ilseng's grit and Brisas's leadership. He half expected Sam Ogden to volunteer to go with them, but he didn't.

"I know this town, sir," Ensolita was saying. "Stopped here once coming through with a convoy, and the only two places I remember that the Nates could use to hole up are the church and the gin—and I'd bet they're not at the gin. Too flimsy."

"So you think they might all be at the church?"

"I'd say that's our best bet. We know we're catching fire from there, and it wouldn't surprise me none to find out most of those Nates are holed up in or around it."

"Sounds right to me. Sam?"

"No quarrel from here, but what are we going to do about the horses?"

"Leave them here with ten riders as our reserve along with the truck. Ed, that'll be your command—and the snipers. We'll shoot red flares off if we're in trouble and need you, green if we've cleared the way, yellow for everybody meaning time to attack. Ensolita, you can lead the first group up that hedge on the west side of the road. If it goes far enough, maybe you can get to the front of that church. Sam and I will take who's left up the east side of the road. Any questions?"

There were none, so Cody quickly divided the troops and sent Ensolita's team on its way. Then he and his team started up the bar ditch on the east side of the road, crawling on their hands and knees and hoping that the Nates couldn't see any of them.

To the east Brisas found a narrow cart path bordered on each side by tall, thick hedges. She led her group to the east side of the second hedge so that both hedges were between her and the church, then led them quickly through thick wildflowers up the long slope until the hedge ended abruptly.

"There's a door," Lucy panted, pointing to a low wooden door on the side of the church.

"Looks like a cellar door. Can't believe we haven't seen any Nates yet."

"Shall we run for it? Not much more . . . than thirty yards from here."

"You don't sound like you could run five yards, much less thirty. We may have to drag you over there."

"Whatever it takes," Lucy said with a halfhearted grin.

"Then I'll go first. Morgan, you follow me. Then you, Lucy—and Mishla. Then the rest of you, one at a time. Ready?"

When Lucy nodded, Brisas ducked from behind the hedge and ran in a low crouch until she reached the side of the church. Lucy could hear shots as Morgan followed Brisas, but the shots were coming from the direction of the road. Now Morgan was standing in the concrete well in front of the door and waving to her.

Lucy ran as best she could. With a great deal of panting she made it to Morgan's side.

Mishla came next and was only three or four steps away when a shot rang out and she twisted and fell forward.

CHAPTER 46

Distant sounds of gunfire woke Goodfox and he reached out to touch Rhondasue. No, not Rhondasue. The images flooded back to him and it was Paula Kathryn who filled them. Only then did he open his eyes and see that the other side of the bed was empty, and wonder, dear God, what had they done last night?

The gunfire quickly grew louder and closer, and it finally dawned on his sleep-drugged brain that St. Joseph was under attack. Goodfox sat up just as the bed trembled in a little quake. The church was under attack! What godless fools would risk their souls by firing on a house of the Lord?

Someone was pounding on his office door. As he got out of bed and put on his robe to answer it, Sister Paula Kathryn came out of the bathroom wearing only her sleeping gown. The smile she gave him was as beatific as any he had ever seen.

Her smile broke as she heard the pounding on the door and the sounds of gunfire and she rushed to get her robe. Then she stepped out of sight so that whoever was seeking Father wouldn't be able to see her. Standing close to the wall, she felt it vibrate as another little quake passed under them.

"Get the hell up, Murray," Nyllan said, storming into his office as soon as he opened the door. "There I was, up before dawn busting my fingers to set up the controller for you, when bang-o, we're under attack, and there's a woman in the dorm screaming her head off trying to have a baby, and here you are sleeping your life away."

He saw her glance into the bedroom—her eyes hooded with suspicion—but he dared not follow her gaze. "Who's doing all the shooting from here?"

"Sister Joana said the Quentin brothers and the tonkaweya are holding off a bunch of militiamen just south of the bridge. How'd you sleep last night?"

"He slept very well, thank you," Paula Kathryn said with great confidence as she stepped into the doorway between the bedroom and the office.

At that instant Goodfox wanted to curse them both. Nyllan's face and body went rigid with anger, and for a moment he thought she might attack Paula Kathryn, but instead, she turned to him. "You better get your ass in the right gear," she said through clenched teeth, "or maybe it's already too damned late for you, Murray." She glared at him a second longer, then spun around and stormed out the door.

"Rhondasue," he said, limping a few steps after her. It was a halfhearted attempt to call her, and he knew it, but he also knew she wouldn't have stopped no matter what he'd said. With a sigh of resignation he turned back to the bedroom. God, how the plan got upset sometimes. As if in response, the ground trembled again.

"You don't need her," Paula Kathryn said, blocking the doorway.

"She's the only one who can work the controller." He put his hands on Paula Kathryn's shoulders and turned her gently so he could get into his room. "And this is no time for either of you to be giving me problems. I need you both." Stepping past her he went immediately to his closet. The firing outside seemed to have stopped, and that worried him almost as much as its continuing had.

Paula Kathryn felt her confidence rapidly slipping away, but she refused to accept any kind of setback. "You'll have to choose, you know that, don't you?"

Goodfox turned and fixed her with a cold stare. "Go get dressed and meet me in the kitchen."

"You can't avoid it . . . Murray." She forced herself not to say Father, but felt unjustifiably wrong in doing so.

"Please, go get dressed."

"All right, Father. For now. But you might as well understand that neither of us is going to let go of you. You're going to have to choose one and reject the other." She spun around the same way Nyllan had and tried to make her exit equally dramatic by slamming the door behind her.

Goodfox shook his head as he hurried into his clothes and wrapped his sore ankle. Here the church was under attack from the militia, and those two women wanted to fight over him. Of course I'll have to choose, he thought, pulling on his boots, and Rhondasue will be it. He had escaped from Paula Kathryn's lustful clutches once before and he would do it again, because he knew that he could find a way to justify Rhondasue to his followers, but never could he justify marrying a nun.

God! Marriage. How strange his world had become.

Grabbing his antique M-16 from its rack in his closet and the bandolier of ammunition that hung beside it, he left his rooms and limped through the halls to the kitchen. From the dormitory wing he could hear the pregnant woman screaming, and his heart went out to her, but he had no time to cope with childbirth at the moment. Father Irving was in the kitchen along with Max Quentin.

"Got here just in time for the fight, Father," Quentin said. "Seems the militia don't much care about your church." His expression was hard and grim.

"Praise God, you're back," Father Irving added.

"Thank you, Father. Would you please see if you can help that poor woman? Max," he said as Father Irving left shaking his head, "fill me in on what's going on." He listened carefully as Quentin told him about the militia charging the bridge with a machine gun truck and how Mike Young's tonkaweya had held them to the tree line down at the curve.

"They're probably going to circle around us," Quentin said, "'cause apparently they don't know there's help for them coming up the Munday road."

"The Farm Bureau," Goodfox said, remembering what

Deputy Whitten had told them. Another gentle quake made him pause for a second as dust sifted down from the ceiling beams, and from the dormitory he heard the woman screaming even louder. "Did you get what I sent you for?"

"We did. Four twenty-gram containers. It's in the church, behind the altar like you said to."

"Good. Now what about the Bureau? How close are they?"

"Two hours, three at the most. Hector said they were in ox wagons, but seeming to make good time. You want to know about Kendrick? We left him behind."

"I assumed you would. He didn't want to cooperate, did he?"

"Not hardly. What happens now, Father? We going to dump that plutonium in the river? And what's this war business we heard?"

"The war business is just that. West Texas has joined up with the Nation to fight part of the old United States. One container of plutonium will go into the river below the Hefner bridge. I'll make my broadcast tonight, then I want Wendel to dump the other three in DalWorth's lakes."

Quentin looked skeptical. "Don't know how Wendel will feel about that, but I'll talk to him. You got him a plane?"

"There's a three-seater down at the gin field he can use, but do you think we can hold off the militia?"

"Of course we can. We got the high ground and all the advantages. How do you figure Wendel should do it?"

"What do you mean?"

"You know, Father. How do you figure he should drop them? You got some dynamite or something?"

Goodfox was confused, but another brief quake gave him a moment to think. "What would you need dynamite for?"

"To open the damn containers, Father. It's not like they'll unscrew themselves falling out of the plane."

Suddenly Goodfox realized that he'd never thought about how they were going to disperse the plutonium. It wasn't like he could ask somebody to unscrew the tops and pour them out of the plane like they were emptying a jar. "You think dynamite will blow the containers open?"

"If we got enough of it."

"All right." He put his hand on Quentin's shoulders and pointed. "See that door at the end of the pantry hall? That leads down into the cellar. There's a dry box down there with about a case and a half of dynamite that the parish used for blowing stumps. Go down and check it, but don't bring it up until we're ready to use it. When you get back up here we'll decide what to do about the militia and the Bureau."

After dressing, Sister Paula Kathryn had gone first to the dormitory where Ann Cody was in labor and had been surprised to find only Suzanne Quentin and Father Irving taking care of the woman. Now, already angered by what Mrs. Quentin had told her, she entered the kitchen from the other direction and saw that pervert Max Quentin. "Get him out of here!" she shouted. "He's the one who defiled our chapel."

"Go on," Goodfox said. "I'll deal with the sister."

"I want him out of my church!"

"Calm yourself, Paula," Goodfox said, holding out his hand to her. "He is doing something for me."

So taken was she by his informality and hint of intimacy that she dismissed Quentin with the touch of Father Murray's fingers. She would not, could not press him for another night like the last, but some of the confidence that had slipped away from her earlier was returning. With that confidence came the need for action. "Our sisters have deserted us," she said, emphasizing the "us." "They've run with Sister Joana and Mr. Simmons to get away from the fighting."

Goodfox shook his head. "We can't worry about them now. What about that woman?"

"Father Irving and Mrs. Quentin are with her. I don't understand what's happening. This isn't what you planned, Murray. Why are we being attacked?" As soon as she said his name, his expression changed and he dropped her hand.

"Don't worry about it. A war's started and we're already in the middle of it."

"And you don't want me to worry? How dare you treat me like that! I'm not some whore—like your precious Rhondasue."

He was startled by the bitterness in her words—even though he knew he shouldn't have been—but he didn't have time to cope with her jealousy at the moment. He had to make sure someone got the plane ready and to find out if Rhondasue had the controller working yet.

Pots rattled. Dishes clattered. The floor shook.

Both of them went to their knees as the whole building vibrated from below. Someone screamed.

Without thinking Paula Kathryn threw herself into his arms. Instinctively they held each other as the whole world shook and swayed.

"Our Father, who art in heaven, hallowed be thy name. Thy kingdom come. Thy will be done," Goodfox whispered.

Paula Kathryn automatically joined him. "On earth as it is in heaven. Give us this day—"

The floor jumped. A cabinet crashed to the floor. Wood cracked loudly over their heads sending a cloud of dirt and dust down on the kitchen. Screams echoed from the dormitory.

Suddenly everything was still.

Paula Kathryn heard her own breathing and felt Murray's heartbeat against her trembling breast. His arms were wrapped tightly around her, and she clung to him. Was it over? Had it stopped?

With a long sigh he released his grip on her and eased himself out of her embrace.

"It's a sign from God," she said softly, knowing in her heart that this was a warning because of what they had done last night.

He stood carefully and helped her to her feet, refusing even to consider the idea that she might be right.

"They've never been like this. Never."

Yes, they were, he thought, on Shudderday. As quickly as that idea came to him he shoved it aside. "Go see if that woman's all right. She may have had her baby already."

"Murray," she said, fighting the tremble in her voice, "if anything happens . . . I mean if . . . well, I just want you to know that I . . ."

"I understand. Now go check on that woman."

She couldn't say what she felt, but she gave him a quick kiss on the lips and ran for the dormitory.

Goodfox watched her go for a brief moment, then turned toward the radio room to find Nyllan.

CHAPTER 47

ONE | The quaking stopped, but Cody still shook as he crawled up the bar ditch to where Ogden waited by the end of the hedge. He was surprised to see the man smile. "What's so damned funny?"

"Funny?" Ogden shook his head. "Nothing's funny, Cody.

Just that quake reminded me of home, and then I thought about how really far from home we are."

"You mean you have them this bad all the time?"

"Of course. Don't you?"

"Never. That's the worse quake I've felt in my whole life."

"Then you're spoiled rotten. No wonder you people can keep electricity going and stuff like that. Back home the quakes mess it up too much. And down in Nevada and California it's even worse. Most people there live in domes or fancy tents 'cause they can't count on anything else standing up to the shakes. You people been living the good life and didn't know it. And would you believe that a healthy woman will bring three horses in California?"

"What do you mean?"

"I mean that Mormons will sell their extra daughters to the Shakers for three horses apiece—four if she's really good-looking and already proved she can have children."

Cody was stunned. "Is that why you're looking for women?"

Ogden grinned. "Hell, no. We don't want to sell 'em. We want to marry 'em. Problem for us was that none of us could afford to buy a wife, so's we came looking for some that might be cheaper."

The ground trembled quietly for a second or two before Cody spoke. "Well, I guess things really are different all over. You got any ideas what we should do next?"

"This ditch is deep enough. I think we ought to keep on crawling. Your Sergeant Ensolita's obviously pinned down, so I guess it's up to us to break through. You want to lead the way?"

"It's my job. Listen up," he called to the troops behind them, "we're gonna keep going up this ditch. Keep your muzzles out of the mud and your butts out of the air. And no talking. Got that?"

A series of nods and grunts answered him. "Let's go then." He lay his carbine across the crooks of his elbows and began crawling up the ditch, trying to keep his body flat against the muddy bottom, ignoring the cold water soaking through his clothes, thinking only about not getting seen and shot at.

Down the hill Kolmer's snipers had begun firing again, one slow shot following another, and Cody imagined he could hear them hitting the church.

Two | Lucy was sure whoever was at the other end of the cellar could hear the ten of them breathing in the stillness—especially Mishla. She had bandaged Mishla's head and given her some of her own morphine, but Lucy was frightened for her and for all of them. Mishla's loud ragged breathing was sure to give them away. Fortunately the man was talking to himself as he prowled among the boxes and old furniture stacked against the walls, and perhaps his own noise would protect them.

Suddenly she recognized the voice.

She started and Brisas put a hand on her arm. The man stopped talking. Lucy slipped a bandage over Mishla's face to muffle her breathing. But it wasn't necessary. Mishla had stopped breathing. The silence echoed off itself.

"Anybody back there?" the man called.

Cold anger filled Lucy. It was Max Quentin. She eased herself out from under Mishla's dead weight as he repeated his question. Putting a finger to her lips and her face close to Brisas's in the dim light, she shook her head. Then she stood up and drew her pistol.

"Just me," she said in a falsetto while stepping around a stack of wooden crates—moving like a character in an Oldtimer's movie, seeing herself from above and behind, knowing exactly what she was going to do. "You see, I was so frightened by the earthquake that I—"

"Who are you?" Quentin called.

She could see him, finally, a dark shape against the light of a weak lantern, and brought the pistol up in front of her, wrapping her left hand around her right. "Why, it's me," she said in the same high-pitched voice. "Who are you?"

"Never you mind that, wench," he said putting both hands on his hips. "You just come over here where I can see you."

The tone of his voice made her tremble. She knew what it meant. "Of course I'm coming. I have to go upstairs and help."

"You ain't one of the nuns," he said as she got within twenty feet of him.

"No," she answered, cocking the pistol and leveling it at him, "I'm not one of the nuns, Mr. Quentin." This time she spoke in her own angry voice. If it hadn't been for him, Mishla would still be alive back in Childress.

"Well, I'll be goddamned. If it isn't Miss Lucy herself. You bring your soft-stuff for me?" He stepped toward her.

She lowered her aim to his crotch. "You take one more step and I'll blow your balls off."

He stopped immediately. "Shit fire."

"Drop your pants." Her voice was steady now, cold and hard, the anger settling into her trigger finger.

"What?"

"Drop your pants. And don't put your hands anywhere near that pistol you're wearing. Juanita, come on up," she called, never taking her eyes off of Quentin.

Very slowly he unbuckled his belt and let his pants and holster fall to the floor. "What do you want from me?" he asked as Juanita and the others came up behind her.

"This one's mine," she said. "He's the one who shot and raped me and left me for dead. I'm going to give him a choice. You like choices, don't you, Max? Step out of those pants and kick them toward me."

"Goddammit. What d'you want?"

"Your balls, Max—and your pecker. That's all. Not even a whole pound of flesh." She felt pleased and angry and ugly all at the same time.

"Take it easy," Juanita said. "There's no need to—"

"You ever been raped? No? Then stay out of this. You got a knife, Max?"

He hesitated.

"I asked you a question, Mr. Quentin. You answer it or I'll pull the trigger now."

"Yeah, I got a knife—in my pants pocket." Now there was a quaver in his voice.

"Then here's your choice, Max. You can take out your knife and cut off your own balls and pecker, or you can stand right there and I'll shoot 'em off."

"Hey, that's no way to treat a man," one of the militiamen complained before Juanita spun around and said, "Shut up! All of you bite your tongues. This is Miss Lucy's affair, not ours. You, you, find the stairs and see if it's clear up there."

Lucy was trembling again, but she felt stronger inside. "Which will it be, Max?"

He lunged at her and she pulled the trigger. Clutching his groin, he collapsed in a howl of pain.

Something inside her refused to let him suffer, and she knew right then that his death was all the revenge she could stand. Very deliberately she pulled the trigger again and again, stopping only when his body stopped moving and the pistol quit firing. Suddenly she bent over and vomited until the dry heaves forced her to her knees and wrenched the tears out of her.

Through her spasms of pain and nausea she heard someone say, "There's some woman screaming her head off up there."

THREE | Goodfox pounded on the radio room door. "Rhondasue! Rhondasue! Let me in."

"Go away, Murray. I'm working."

"I need to talk to you."

"No, you don't. If you want this controller to work, leave me alone."

"When will it be ready?"

"Never, if you don't leave me the hell alone."

He started to turn away from the door when he heard a radio voice say, "Come in, Texas."

Even pressing his ear against the door, he couldn't hear Rhondasue's reply, but he could tell that she was talking to someone on the radio. "Rhondasue! You open this door immediately or so help me God I'll break it down."

When she didn't reply, he realized how empty his threat was. At his request Brother Jacob had reinforced that door, and Goodfox knew it would take more than one person to break it down—unless he had an ax. The cellar, he thought.

He limped as fast as he could down the hall, intent on taking the pantry stairs down to the cellar. Just as he turned the corner, the cellar door opened and two Texian militiamen jumped out.

He ducked back instinctively and held himself against the wall, as still as possible. How had they gotten in? What had happened to Max Quentin? Only then did he remember that he'd left his rifle in the kitchen.

After a long moment's wait he crept back to the radio room. "Rhondasue," he called softly, "listen to me. There are militiamen in the church. Let me in."

A few seconds later she unbolted the door and jerked him

into the room. "What's the matter with you, you idiot? Do I always have to pamper you?"

"Who were you talking to?"

She looked at him darkly and shook her head as she bolted the door again. "No one. Now sit down and shut up and stay out of my way."

"Don't lie to me. You don't lie very well."

Nyllan sat down where the controller was patched into the radio with colored wires and cable and laughed. "Shows how much you know, Murray. This whole trip with you's been a lie."

"What? What are you talking about?"

"Oh, never mind. If you want this thing to work, just leave me alone."

He crossed the room and stood in front of her. A feeling was churning through his gut that he didn't like at all. "Tell me what you mean. What's been a lie?"

Without answering she dug into a tool bag and pulled out her revolver, aiming it right at his stomach. "I said, sit down and shut up, and I meant it."

Goodfox was so startled that he backed up and sat in the empty chair at the end of the radio table. "Rhondasue, what is going on here?"

Using her free hand she pulled a pair of handcuffs out of the tool bag and tossed them to him. "Put one of those on your left wrist, then put the other on your right ankle."

"No." He stood up and tossed the cuffs back to her.

The pistol roared and bucked in her hand. The bullet buried itself in the wall beside him. "Next one's for you if you don't do what I told you," she said softly. "Don't make me shoot you, Murray."

There was a hard certainty in her voice that told him she would do it. He swallowed with great difficulty and sat down, catching the handcuffs again. "But why?" he asked as he snapped one cuff around his left wrist. "Did good old Uncle H.S. put you up to this? Is that it? Have you been working for him all the time?"

"Would you believe me if I said no?"

"Then why? Who?" As soon as he cuffed his wrist to the opposite ankle, his back muscles complained. "Is this torture really necessary?"

She put her pistol on the table in front of the transceiver. "You're a great lay, Murray," she said, picking up a pair of pliers and going back to work. "I wish I could thank your dead wife for all the bed tricks she taught you, because I sure enjoyed them. I'm gonna miss that. 'Cause you see, Murray, you didn't find me by accident. I found you. I was sent to find you and help you— and to keep you from polluting the world." She grinned at him. "Getting well-laid regular was just a bonus."

His heart sank with every word she spoke. "H.S. sent you."

"Yeah, I'm sure gonna miss your body. Hope Sister Self-Righteous had a good time with you last night, 'cause she's not getting any more. Not a lick, not a stroke. Zip, zero, nothing. It's over for you, Murray."

"Ready for the second check, Texas," a male voice said from the radio.

"Wait ten," she replied. "Will call."

"Roger, Texas. We'll wait ten for your call."

Goodfox couldn't believe that this was the same woman who had made love to him so many times and killed those Ash Grove Boys to save him. But none of it made any sense. Why would she have killed them if she was working for H.S.? "Who in the name of all that's holy are you?" he asked.

Her only response was to laugh.

FOUR | As the scream died on her lips, Ann Cody slumped back on the bed, her mouth slack, her eyes closed, her breathing ragged.

"I've got two pots of water on to boil and clean rags in one of them. Either of you have any idea what else we need to do?" Paula Kathryn asked.

"No, Sister," Suzanne Quentin said. "I've never done this before."

Father Irving looked away and blushed. "Neither have I. Perhaps I should go find help."

Paula Kathryn shook her head in dismay. "Go on. See if you can find my brave sisters who are hiding somewhere in town— preferably Sister Angelica or Sister Benedict. The shooting's stopped. Go find them."

Father Irving stood and automatically signed the cross over Ann Cody before hurrying from the room.

"Fat lot of help he's been."

Ann moaned and stirred, her swollen body writhing slowly

under the sheets. Her puffy eyes opened in narrow slits. "Please help me," she whimpered. "Oh, God, Suzanne, please make them help me." Without warning she shrieked in pain and tried to sit up.

"We have to hold her down, I know that much," Mrs. Quentin said. "I seen it once in an Oldtimer movie."

Stepping quickly to the other side of Ann's bed, Paula Kathryn helped hold her down as Ann's body bucked and she screamed again.

"Down here," a voice called from the hall.

At first Paula Kathryn thought help was coming, but when she looked up she saw first one, then three militiamen crowding in the doorway. "She's going to have a baby," Paula Kathryn said.

Suzanne Quentin reached down beside the bed and came up holding a pistol. Two shots knocked her out of the chair and onto the floor before she had a chance to aim.

Paula Kathryn was so stunned that for a second she wasn't sure what had happened. Ann was screaming. She was trying to hold her down. And the militiamen had guns pointed at her.

"Let me through, let me through," Lucy said as she pushed through the doorway. The first thing she saw was Ann Cody bucking against a nun. The second thing she saw was Suzanne Quentin lying very still on the floor in a spreading pool of blood.

Much to Paula Kathryn's surprise, the woman who had forced her way into the room gasped Ann's name and pushed Paula Kathryn away from the bed.

CHAPTER 48

ONE | An unexpected explosion to the south was followed by a rash of distant gunfire. Palmer fired a yellow flare that burst high over their heads below the thin grey overcast.

"Charge!" Cody yelled. He felt foolish, stupid, and very vulnerable as he stood up with his rifle at the hip and began running and firing at the same time.

To his relief, his whole group came right behind him. To his surprise, Ensolita's group rose from the ditch on the other side of the road, and suddenly they had a large force charging the Nates.

The ground trembled.

From down the hill he heard the whine of the truck and the spitting of the machine guns. Kolmer must have been lying in wait for the signal.

The Nates seemed caught by surprise. Return fire was light, and Cody and seven or eight of his group managed to get to the closest outbuilding without getting hit or pinned down. The truck was roaring up the road now, chattering fire over their heads.

Taking advantage of the machine gun fire, Cody moved around the building and caught two Nates running from it to the church. Cody and someone beside him fired at the same time. The Nates fell. Only then did he look to see that it was Ogden.

"Ready?" Again Cody led the charge, Ogden by his side, Ensolita's group sweeping up on his left, and now from the south the machine gun was firing in sporadic bursts as the truck worked its way around the church. Brisas must be south of town, he thought, when an explosion blew a dark cloud over the trees. God bless her.

The ground trembled again. Rifles spat in a deafening roar. Return fire chewed up the wet ground around them. Troops screamed and fell.

Cody lunged forward and lost his balance, tumbling into the mud. Animals cried. The ground shook. Church bells clanged. Cody twisted around to shoot at three Nates dug in at the corner of the building. The ground jumped, then vibrated violently.

"Nimenim!" a Nate wailed.

Fire burned Cody's butt. The earth beneath him moved so much, he couldn't steady his aim. Pointing his carbine at the corner, he just kept pulling the trigger until it stopped firing.

As he reloaded he heard a great cracking, rending sound—the sound of tearing metal and snapping wires. He looked up in time to see the radio tower atop the church steeple twist and lean to the north until it paused, hanging over the church itself. Then with an awful crash it collapsed onto the church roof.

"Nimenim!" a Nate screamed again. A swarm of bullets filled the air.

Then suddenly the firing stopped. Cody crawled as fast as he could to the corner of the building. He saw one of the Nates ducking through the cedar hedge in the direction of the old part of the church, but he didn't see any more. Palmer and several members of Cody's group crawled up to join him.

"There's a door around the corner. I want to get in this building. It's connected to the church. Cover me." He rolled right, crawled left, and brought himself up next to the building beside the door. Raising himself on his hands and knees, he signaled for the others to join him.

Only when there were two of them on each side of the door did he reach up and try the handle. It turned easily and the door swung inward. Flattening himself on the ground, Cody carefully eased his head into the doorway.

What he saw was a dim, empty hall. Then he heard a woman scream like she was being tortured to death. He started to crawl in when someone stepped from one of the doorways. He had all but pulled the trigger when he realized it was Brisas.

"Juanita!" he called, scrambling to his feet. "I thought you were south of us blowing things up."

"And I thought that must be you," she answered. "You better get down here. We found your wife."

Only then did he connect the screaming woman with Ann. "Guard the door," he shouted as he ran down the hall.

"Morgan, you stay here," Brisas said. "The rest of you come with me."

Lucy looked up to see Cody stumbling in the door. "She's having a bad time of it. I think her pelvis is too narrow."

Cody stared at the bed, hardly recognizing the bloated woman as Ann—her copper-colored hair matted and dirty, her blue eyes dull in their sockets, her face distorted by pain. Was this really Ann, the woman he had loved? Was this what he had driven her to? "Can't you do something for her?"

"I'm doing everything I know how. Can you get Jenny Augusta up here?"

"I think so. Let me send someone for her."

"On my way," Morgan volunteered from the doorway.

"What else?" he asked, feeling very out of place.

She saw the look of helplessness on his face and the weak slump of his shoulders, but had little energy to give him. "If these quakes continue, we may have to get her out of here. I'd hate to be delivering a baby and have the roof coming down on top of me."

"That I can do something about." He glanced around the

room and saw a large bloodstain on the floor. Pointing to it he said, "That's not . . ." The rest of the words wouldn't come.

"No. Your men shot Suzanne Quentin."

The name didn't mean anything to him. "There must have been a reason. I guess we can move Ann in the bed she's in. I think it'll fit through the doorway."

"They did have a reason. She drew her pistol on them. That's what the sister said."

"I'll go get some help." He left quickly, not wanting to look at Ann any more, unable to accept what had happened to her—and to them—since he had seen her last. He quickly found four men to carry the bed and led them back to Ann's room. Ogden and Brisas were waiting for him in the hall when the men, trailed by a tired-looking Lucy Ilseng, began carrying Ann outside.

"They're holed up in the main part of the church—least ways most of them, we think," Brisas said.

"And the rest of them are boarded up in the stables."

"Any sign of their radioactive cargo?"

"Not that we've seen." Brisas looked at him with a strange expression. "You still have your suit, don't you?"

"That and the geiger counter. Maybe we should scout with that—but not yet. How hard would it be to take the church?"

"God only knows," Brisas said, "and that's not a joke. Big old Catholic churches like this are full of hallways and hidden rooms and secret passageways, and we'd play the devil's own getting them out of there."

"All right. For the time being, let's just keep all the exits well covered. I'm surprised that radio tower didn't crash through the roof."

"Where is she?" Paula Kathryn asked when she saw the militiamen in the hall. "What have you done with Mrs. Cody?" It was bad enough that these people were desecrating the church with their weapons and bloodshed, but to have taken a pregnant woman?

"She's outside," Cody said, seeing an attractive woman under the shabby brown dress and dirt-smeared face. "Who are you?"

"I am Sister Paula Kathryn, Sister Superior of St. Joseph Parish. Who are you?" she asked with a sniff.

"I'm Ann's husband."

"Not a very good husband, I suspect. Why did you remove her from our dormitory?"

"Sister, I don't want her in here when the roof comes down, and I don't have time for your stupid games. Just get your butt out there and help Lucy Ilseng and my wife."

Paula Kathryn hesitated, then headed for the door, wanting more than anything else to know what had happened to Father Murray—and Father Irving—but accepting her obligation to Ann Cody and her baby, and fighting off the craziness in her head brought on by the gunfire and explosions. This was all insane, but she didn't know how to make it stop.

TWO | Nyllan closed the peephole and turned around to face him. "The hall's full of your Nates."

"I could scream and get their attention, I guess," Goodfox said. This had all turned into a nightmare, and he was sure that any second he would awaken in his own bed with everything under control again. God wouldn't do something this cruel to him, he was sure of it.

"You could die, too, but I've decided that would be a waste, Murray. Don't get me wrong. I don't need your body, but Little Miss Communion Britches might want to screw you again, so I've decided you can live. But if I'm going to let you keep your life, you'll have to give me something in return."

His back ached, his arm ached, his ankles ached, and his patience was strained to the point that he almost didn't care what happened next. "Like what?"

"How about my life? The transceiver's worthless without the antenna. So's the controller. And some miserable son-of-a-bitch has cut us off from the antenna. It's a shame, too. This is one of the nicest private rigs west of the Mississippi. But, since I can't use them, I'll have to destroy them, and I've got a little plastic explosive we can do that with"—she held up a six-by-six-inch blue-grey slab—"but we both need a way out of here. You have any ideas?"

No, he thought, she can't destroy the controller. Not now. Not after all he had gone through to get it—and get it here. He had to stop her, but how? "There is a way out, but you'll have to get me out of these stupid handcuffs." The floor trembled.

"You tell me first."

"No. Just kill me. I'm sure that's what your people want, a martyr for our cause."

"Go to hell, Murray. You want out of here alive? You tell me how we get past the Nates. You don't want out of here alive? Fine," she said, pressing the explosives against the front of the controller. "I'll just blow this room to smithereens, and no one will ever know you were a martyr."

Again the floor trembled. "You can't blow this room up."

"I sure as hell can."

"Then this whole area will be radioactive."

"You mean your precious plutonium's in here?"

"Might as well be." For the first time in his life he felt like he could kill someone with his bare hands. Rhondasue had betrayed him, and now she wanted to destroy everything he had worked for. Anything was fair now. "Under the transceiver table," he continued, "there's a small door that opens onto a secret storage area behind the altar, which is where Max hid the plutonium."

"So why are you telling me this?"

He looked down at the floor, tired of straining his neck to see her when he talked and not wanting her to see the thoughts behind his words or the fear he felt for his own safety. She just might be willing to kill him. "Because I suspect that whoever you are working for, whether it's H.S. or somebody else, only wants me out of the way. They won't be very happy if you create a radioactive hot spot out of Rhineland."

"Damn, Murray. You've got enough ego for ten priests—with some left over. You know that? The United States government doesn't give a rat's ass about you. They wanted—"

"The United States government? Who in the name of—"

"They wanted the controller—if it worked—to do a few jobs for them, but after that it was going to get destroyed anyway. You were never more than a loud-mouthed nuisance to them."

His anger dissolved into confusion and anxiety. "You mean there is still a United States government?"

"Of course, stupid. Even Shudderday couldn't totally destroy a good bureaucracy. The True United States is back in business—been working its way quietly back into business for years—from Maine to Illinois and Ontario to the New Tennessee coast. The capitol in Springfield, D.C. is almost finished and you squabbling little countries out here in the boonies are in deep shit."

"But why attack me? I wanted the states reunited more than

anyone." He heard the whine in his voice, but couldn't stop it. "And what about us, you and me?"

"There was no us—not out of the sack. I told you, your body was just an unexpected bonus for doing my job. There was never anything more than that."

He thought she was lying, hoped she was lying, but when he twisted up to look at her, she was facing away from him working on the front of the transceiver.

"The government couldn't let you keep going the way you were, because you wanted to be pope of America, Murray, and what we want is our country back the way it was—a reunited democracy, not a religious dictatorship."

The floor bucked. A beam splintered. Dirt and mortar fell on their heads.

"Get me out of these," Murray shouted as the floor jumped again and again.

CHAPTER 49

ONE | A light drizzle fell. Some of Ogden's Demons had hung a tarp between two trees to form a large shelter, and under it Jenny Augusta sat beside Ann Cody on the bed and held her down by the shoulders. On the ground next to the bed, Lucy taped a bandage over Lieutenant Cody's wound. Just outside the tarp a fire was beginning to crackle, and Lucy thought briefly of last night and this morning and how she couldn't have envisioned this moment.

"Didn't even know I was hit," he said, embarrassed about the wound in his butt, and even more embarrassed to have her working on it. The earth hummed beneath him, and for the first time in his life he was completely aware of what earthquakes could do to him.

She smiled slightly. Her strength had been washed down to the bare rocks of her determination. "Well, if you hadn't been rolling in the mud, it wouldn't have been anything to worry about until you climbed into the saddle." The horses were tied to a picket line just down the slope, and Lucy thought they might be

the most beautiful things she had ever seen. If only Mishla—
She cut that thought off as tears sprang to her eyes.

Ann grunted fiercely, then moaned as her body slumped
heavily down on the bed. Jenny Augusta said, "She can't go
through much more of this, I don't think. She's worn out and the
baby's nowhere near coming. We're gonna have to help it."

Hearing a tone in her voice that frightened him, Cody asked,
"What does that mean?"

"It means doing a C-section," Lucy said. She patted his
unbandaged cheek as the earth quivered a little. "You're
finished."

After squirming into his pants, he stood up and buttoned
them with his back to the women. "What's a C-section?"

"It means cutting her open to save her and the baby," Jenny
Augusta said.

He was startled. "Can you do that? Then what do you do?
Stitch Ann up?"

"Yes."

Cody turned around and knew that under the flat rock of her
words was a rattlesnake. "That will kill her, won't it?"

"No."

"But it might?" He was surprised to feel the lump in his
throat. "Or is it even more sure than that?"

Lucy stood and put a hand on his arm, pulling him out from
under the tarp. She had heard stories about C-sections from
medwives, and Jenny Augusta had taken one look under Ann's
dress and told her she thought they would probably have to do
one. "Please, Lieutenant Cody. You've got to understand. If Ann
can't deliver the baby naturally, they both might die. If we do a
C-section, we might be able to save both of them."

"Jeremy?" Ann called weakly.

Pushing past Lucy, Cody knelt beside the bed. "Yes, Ann,
it's me."

"He made me do it," she said, her face swollen and twisted.
"Kendrick did. Said he'd tell you . . . tell you . . . couldn't
let him. Make them help me, Jeremy. Please make them help
me."

"They're doing all they can," he said, taking her hand in his.
"What did Kendrick make you do?" The earth shook again.
Tears ran freely down his face, and all at once he knew that he'd
never really stopped loving her, that he'd only told himself that
so he could live with her being gone.

Lucy glanced at Jenny Augusta who slowly shook her head.

"My brother . . . said he'd tell you . . . if I didn't come with him. . . . I swore . . . Oh, oh!" she whimpered. "Jeremy, I'm sorry. Aaaaa!" She clutched his hand.

"What? Tell me! Oh, dear God, Ann, it doesn't matter. Nothing matters but you and the baby. Nothing."

"Lucy knows." Ann opened her eyes wide for a second and seemed to stare straight through Lucy. "It hurts bad." She closed her eyes again and groaned through clenched teeth.

"I think you'd better go now," Jenny Augusta said. "Send somebody to find that nun. We're going to need that hot water and soon."

Cody pried his hand from Ann's and stood, not wanting to leave, not caring about the tears, not knowing what to do except what he'd been told as Lucy pulled him away from the bed. "I'll get you all the hot water in the world." Part of his mind told him that was a stupid thing to say, but he didn't care about that either. Turning quickly he rushed out from under the tarp and straight into Brisas's arms.

"We need you, Cody. Come on."

"Hot water," he said angrily.

"I'm coming," Paula Kathryn said from behind the tarp. The pot of steaming water sloshed between her and the soldier who held the other handle as a little shock swept under them. One glance at Mr. Cody's face told her that things were bad. She began a silent Hail Mary as they carried the pot into the tent, and even as she said it, her heart cried for Father Murray.

"Go on, Lieutenant," Lucy said, wanting to comfort him, but not knowing how. "You take care of what you have to, and we'll take care of Ann." She gave Brisas a pleading look.

"It's the Farm Bureau," Brisas said, "reinforcements Sheriff York drummed up for us. They killed some Nates down at the south end of town, and Ed cleared the stables, and Ogden thinks the only ones we have to worry about are in the church."

All the time she was talking to him, she was pulling him away from the rude tent where Jenny Augusta had dumped a handful of shiny medical instruments into the pot of water. A great numbness had settled onto his mind and he was barely aware of the little quakes running under his feet. "Nates in the church. Right. I want to see Ogden, Kolmer, Ensolita, and whoever's running the Bureau. And get the radio cranked up."

TWO | "If I uncuff you, Murray, you have to promise to do what I tell you, and nothing else. I don't want to have to kill you because you did something stupid." She had finished molding the explosive around the transceiver and was setting the detonators.

His back muscles screamed in protest against the awful position she had locked him in. His arm ached. His neck hurt to the base of his brain. Yet he knew he could endure the pain if he had to. He also knew that if he broke one more commandment, if he lied to her, he could free himself from the pain and have the chance to stop her. Not for himself, of course—for God.

In betraying him, Rhondasue had betrayed God, had become the instrument of the devil—whatever name she gave that devil—and as such, she had to be punished. It was his job to mete out that punishment, and he understood now that Satan had used Rhondasue's body against his mind and despoiled the vision God had given him.

"I'm waiting, Murray. Promise or not?"

"Promise," he said slowly, unwilling to force his neck through the pain of looking up at her. "I'll do what you say."

"In God's name? Do you swear in God's name to do only what I tell you and nothing more?"

Goodfox hesitated only for a second. "I swear in the name of my Lord and Saviour Jesus Christ."

"Finish it."

He guessed that her demolitions were all set when she stood up and walked over to him. "Finish what?" he asked, knowing the answer and knowing he would give in.

"Say the whole thing. Say, I swear in the name of our Lord and Saviour Jesus Christ to do exactly what Rhondasue tells me and absolutely nothing more."

With an anger at himself that he fought to keep under control, he repeated her words verbatim.

The floor trembled as she knelt down beside him and unlocked the cuff around his ankle. Then she helped him straighten up and before he knew what she was doing had cuffed his left hand to his right in front of him. "I don't trust you, Murray."

"But I swore!"

"And you swore not to commit adultery, but that didn't keep you from screwing me or Sister Holy-hole, did it? And how many others after you took your vows?" she asked as she rubbed his back. "I'll bet you met a lot of willing women what with all the traveling you did."

"Hundreds," he said in disgust, hating her for thinking that, much less saying it, despising himself for the sins that had led him to this point, and wishing for one brief instant that it were true, that he had known more than three women in his life—his wife and Paula Kathryn and Rhondasue. A sickening wave of revulsion swept through him and a long, shuddering sigh escaped uncontrollably from the depths of his despair. He had brought himself to this point, and he knew it. God had cast him out, but the fact that tomorrow was Easter reminded him there was a way back to redemption.

"Now," Nyllan said, "how the hell do we get out of here?"

"Through that storage area I told you about."

"But you said that leads to the altar."

"It also has a trapdoor down to the basement."

"Stand up. Test your legs. Can you move?"

He stood slowly and the pain was a little more bearable now that he had a purpose. Silently he began his confession, the sins piling one on top of the other in their rush to illustrate his unworthiness. Whatever pride he had foolishly enjoyed as God's special servant dissolved in the acid of his failure to that very service.

"When I hit the timer, we'll have ten minutes to get through your trapdoors and out of here. You ready?"

"Yes, I'm ready," but for more than you will ever guess, he added to himself.

She switched on the timer. "Then let's go."

CHAPTER 50

ONE | Cody stood in the trees on the south side of the open lot staring at the beautiful old brick church with the broken antenna on its roof. Never in his life had he felt so helpless and uncertain—not even when Deborah was giving birth. At least then he had been doing something, fighting to save her, doing what had to be done as best he knew how to do it.

Now he didn't know what had to be done. Lucy Ilseng and the others were taking care of Ann and the wounded. The townspeople, who were furious about the attack on their church, were under Bureau guard down by the gin. The Nates were trapped in the church, and it was all-about surrounded inside and out—not only by the militia and the Demons, but also by the forty Bureau volunteers who had come up from Munday. No Nate was going to bust through Cody's little army very easily.

But Brisas still hadn't been able to raise anyone on the radio, and Cody had no idea where the Nates' plutonium was, and he felt like he was standing on a hill waiting for the wind to blow him one way or another. Should he risk more lives by attacking the church? That Sister Joana had told Ensolita there was plenty of food and water in the church basement, so they weren't likely to starve the Nates out any time soon. Yet he couldn't just sit there, could he? Something told him that was more dangerous than attacking or—

A hard quake broke his thoughts and jerked his legs out from under him. He landed with a yelp on his sore butt. Rolling over he looked around in panic. Everyone was down on the ground. Trees vibrated in an awful rattling of branches.

The quake kept coming, bucking the ground, thrashing the trees, shaking the buildings. Dogs howled. Horses screamed. People cried out in fear.

With a crunching rumble the steeple collapsed over the front of the church, dragging the broken antenna with it. The antenna slammed down in the open lot like the slap of an angry god.

Cody cursed as he flattened himself on his stomach and clutched the earth like a baby opossum clutching its mother. His bladder released, urine momentarily warming the moving wet earth beneath him. Choking sobs escaped him as he prayed to Cristodios like he'd never prayed before.

West of the church under the flapping tarp, Lucy cried and threw her body across Ann's to hold her against the bouncing bed as Jenny Augusta reached inside the long incision for the baby. Ann moaned and tried to twist away, the pentobarbital obviously not controlling her pain.

Oxen bawled and goats bleated in terror. The ground shook violently again and again. Paula Kathryn lunged toward the shelter of the tarp as though that flimsy thing could protect her. But her feet moved out from under her and she slammed head first into a tree and darkness.

Jenny Augusta struggled to pull the baby free. She lost her grip, cursed, and reached again into the bloody gash that opened onto Ann's womb.

"Hold her, dammit. Hold her!"

"I'm trying! Hurry!"

The bed bucked against both of them. The ground fought to slide away. Ann screamed and screamed and screamed—then stopped with a deep rasping cry, her body rigid with agony.

Jenny Augusta jerked the slimy infant feet first out of Ann's womb and it, too, screamed as though protesting the violent world it was entering. It was a girl.

"There!" Jenny Augusta shouted triumphantly. She flopped the wailing infant high on Ann's stomach and plunged a bloody hand back into Ann's body to remove the placenta.

Even in her fear and desperation Lucy felt a huge wave of relief flood through her. They'd saved the baby! She eased her grip on Ann's shoulders, holding the bed for what little security it offered, and used the piece of yucca thread they had boiled to tie off the baby's umbilical cord. With her MUST-Kit knife she cut the girl-child free.

The earth moved like it would never be still again, as though once it had started it couldn't stop shaking. Lucy realized it was Shudderday all over again—only worse, worse than anything the Oldtimers had ever described. What a day to come into the world!

She wadded a damp, boiled cloth and used it clean the baby's eyes, then to wipe her face and body as best she could with the earth quaking constantly underneath them, finally wrapping her in one of the dry blankets Sister Paula had brought from the church. Only then did she wonder what had happened to the nun and look outside.

Sister Paula lay still against the trembling earth, her head on the exposed root of the tree. The rain had stopped, and a bright sun broke through the clouds, dappling Sister Paula's body with light and shadow from the limbs above her. Lucy felt suddenly lightheaded.

"I've got to start sewing Ann up," Jenny Augusta said, "but I can't until these damn quakes stop." Tears ran down her face. "Can you believe this insanity?"

Lucy couldn't. It was a nightmare she'd never had. "We just have to hold on until it stops," she said in a voice that betrayed how tired she was. She wondered what had happened to Lieutenant Cody and all the others and why Ann was so still and why Jenny Augusta was taking the baby from her and why the world was spinning around before she fell heavily back across Ann's body.

Against a wall in the basement of the church, Father Murray Goodfox and Rhondasue Nyllan held each other for what little comfort there was in a world falling apart. Close by their feet, Max Quentin's body lay surrounded by the dark stain of his own blood. In the distance above them they heard rumble and crash of the church collapsing.

"We have to get out of here, Murray!" Nyllan screamed above the noise. "We're almost out of time!"

Around them boxes, crates, shelves, and stacks of furniture tumbled into shifting piles of debris.

"We can't until it stops!" They had only gotten this far by luck, and he knew it was the safest place in the building. He prayed they would escape, prayed for a miracle that would let him live a life of penance. "God forgive us all our sins as we forgive each other, for Thine is the kingdom and the power and the glory forever and—"

An explosion roared above them. Timbers shrieked then splintered. The ceiling sagged, paused, then crashed down on top of them under the weight of tons of debris as St. Joseph Church fell in on itself.

Father Murray Goodfox's last thought was of Paula Kathryn and where they would conduct Easter Mass.

TWO | Sister Paula Kathryn stood with a sore and aching head in the bright afternoon sunshine staring at the ruins of the church, unable to believe her eyes.

Thirty or forty people—including one in a strange white suit carrying a Geiger counter—were working in the wreckage trying to rescue those who had been buried alive whose cries for help could be heard coming weakly from under the rubble. The quakes had stopped hours before, but the timbers and bricks and pieces of wall that had once been her beautiful church continued to shift and settle noisily causing the diggers to jump clear and wait to see what would happen next. There was still fear in everyone's eyes, fear that more quakes would shake the ground from underneath them.

Deep in her heart she knew with terrible certainty that Father Murray would not be found alive. She didn't want to be the one to discover his body—especially if he was with that whore of his—but she had to help with the digging. If there was any chance at all that he had lived through that destruction, she couldn't give up hope. Joining St. Joseph's faithful parishioners and the other workers, she would dig until she knew for sure. This act would be the beginning of her penance.

With a slow, measured tread, paced by the silent recitation of her rosary, she walked toward the rubble and a future stripped to a single assurance—that God would go with her.

Cradling his daughter in his arms, Cody stood beside Lucy Ilseng and watched Sister Paula Kathryn as she joined the diggers. "Is that all it was?" he asked. "That Ann was a Nate?"

"A Nimenim," Lucy said. "That's important." She thought sadly of Tinker Oberly whose body had been one of the first pulled from the church ruins and how he should be listening to the Bridgeport Ramblers on the radio instead of lying under a blanket waiting to be buried.

"But she wasn't a religious fanatic. Why? Why would she be so afraid because of that?"

"I don't know, Lieutenant Cody. I just don't—"

"Call me Jeremy, please?" Only family and close friends had ever called him Jeremy, but for some reason he wanted her to.

"All right, Jeremy. All I know is what Ann told me, that Kendrick was her stepbrother and she owed him because he had killed his own father to save her life." Lucy refused to tell him that both Kendrick and his father had forced Ann sexually. There was no need for that. "Now I have a question for you. Are you going to raise your daughter by yourself?"

"Well, what else can I do?"

"You'll need a goat for milk. I heard some around here before the big quake, so you might be able to buy one, but they have to be milked every four or five hours—around the clock. You're going to need help."

"Jennifer Lucy," he said. "I think I'll name her Jennifer Lucy after the two of you, and call her Jennifer."

Despite his smile she could tell how lost he felt. "Thank you. I'm sure Jenny Augusta will be pleased. Ann would have liked it, too."

"I'm glad you think so." Ann was dead, but Cody felt no guilt, only grief and a deep, aching sadness. Kolmer already had a crew digging graves, and soon they would be seeing other people into the ground with Ann—Pollard, Hermosa, six other militia men, five Demons, and Nates, lots of Nates.

"Maybe I could help you for a while." She hadn't planned to make such an offer, but she remembered her promise to Ann and was glad the offer had popped out of her before she worried about it. "Would you like that?"

He didn't understand. "You mean come home with me and help take care of her? Why would you do that?"

"Because I want to. Because I told Ann I would. Because I like you and I think you're going to need all the help you can get. I'm not very strong, yet, but I'd bet Jennifer's diapers that I know more about babies than you do. You ever taken care of a baby before?"

He blinked and shook his head to clear his eyes, seeing for the first time the size of this new task. Jennifer squirmed in her blanket and smacked her tiny lips. "Miss Lucy, if you'd do that, I'd be more grateful than you could know."

"Excuse me," Brisas said, walking up to them, "but I got some news you might want to hear. We just listened in on a radio call from a seiser down in Abilene to some guy in DalWorth." She paused to peek under the blanket corner at Jennifer. "The seiser said his instruments picked up quakes four times as bad as those on Shudderday and that they were worse from Missouri eastward—something about the New Madrid Fault. The guy in DalWorth said the first shortwave messages coming from the east reported lots of damage and casualties. Anyway, seems like there ain't gonna be a war after all."

"Thanks, Juanita," Cody said, "but somehow none of that surprises me."

"Me, neither, but I thought you'd want to know." She looked over at the diggers. "What are we going to do if Morgan finds the plutonium?"

"Bury it and let Terry worry about it."

Brisas nodded and smiled at Jennifer. "She's beautiful, Cody. Maybe Sam and I will have one that pretty."

"I hope you do." After Brisas headed back to where Ogden and several Demons sat under a tree, he turned to Lucy and asked, "What do we do now? Find a goat?"

"It's a little early yet, I think, to feed her. But it wouldn't hurt to have a meal lined up. May I hold her for a while?" As he handed Jennifer to her, Lucy felt comfortable in Jeremy's presence and thought she was going to enjoy the next few months. She would miss Mishla terribly, but she felt sure this child of Shudderday would help relieve her grief.

The way she held the baby made Cody smile. He thought Lucy Ilseng looked like a natural mother. "Goat time," he said.

"Goat time," Lucy responded. Together they headed for the animal pens behind the church ruins.

IN THE BEGINNING | April. West Texas. The Republic of West Texas.

Wind. Today, warm wind from the south. Yesterday, cooler wind from the north. But always wind. And always quakes. Wind and quakes with their new rhythms reshaping lives after the second Sudderday.

Today, sunshine spilled brightly over the land, lighting full fields of bluebonnets and red paintbrush, splashing white primrose and crimson clover and yellow flax along the roadsides, touching the edges of shadows with fuchsia winecups and orange mallows, and everywhere, daisies.

Today, a man, a woman, a week-old baby, and a goat rode north in an oxen-drawn wagon with two horses trailing behind. Today they didn't know that the New Madrid Fault in Missouri had rattled everything east of the Rocky Mountains, or that the ring of fire around the Pacific had erupted in new volcanoes and quakes, or that ninety percent of the earth's surface had felt the new tremors. Today they did not know about those things, nor did they care.

Tomorrow the sun and blue skies might be hidden again, and the earth might continue to shake. Tomorrow they would face the tasks ahead, of building toward the future with what Sudderday had left them, of living their lives as best they could for themselves and for each other. Tomorrow, with luck and compassion, they would also share the joys of those tasks as well as the pains.

But today, riding through the sunshine with flowers before them, a gentle breeze following, and their dead blessed and buried behind, they had put their concerns about a shaking earth and political turmoil and tomorrow's worries aside. Today they were intent only on enjoying each other's company.

Cody looked over at his daughter. "Jennifer's smiling."

"It's just gas," Lucy said, but she smiled, too.

-The End-

ABOUT THE AUTHOR

Warren C. Norwood began writing when he was nine and got hooked on science fiction when he was eleven reading Tom Swift and Tom Swift, Jr., books. At seventeen he made a serious commitment to becoming a writer. College, marriage, the Viet Nam War, and eleven years in the selling end of the book business intervened before he saw the publication of his first novel, *The Windhover Tapes: An Image of Voices*, which was followed by three other volumes in that series. He also wrote *The Seren Cenacles* with Ralph Mylius. His last series, *The Double-Spiral War*, was completed early in 1986 with the publication of *Final Command*. *Shudderchild* is his ninth novel, and he swears it will never become a series.

Warren was twice–nominated for the John W. Campbell Award as one of the best new writers of 1982–83. He lives in a little house in the country outside of Weatherford, Texas, on three acres filled with spectacular wildflowers.

In addition to writing, Warren teaches several writing courses at Tarrant County Junior College in Fort Worth. He has recently completed *SHIFT!*, a novel set in the near present which is either about people who appear to have been driven crazy by quantum physics, or about alternate realities. He is currently working on a novel in which a modern man is forced to battle the Mayan underworld.

> "AN ABSOLUTE DELIGHT ... FAR AND
> AWAY HER BEST."
> —Morgan Llywelyn, author of
> LION OF IRELAND

R.A. MacAVOY
THE GREY HORSE

From a time when Ireland strained against the reins of English rule, comes a saga lush with enchantment. It begins of an afternoon when the wind blows wet from Galway Bay and a magnificent grey stallion appears in the Irish town of Carraroe. With the horse comes magic, for in its noble shape stands Ruairi MacEibhir, who has come in a time of great peril to win the heart of the woman he loves.

Buy THE GREY HORSE, on sale wherever Bantam Spectra Books are sold, or use the handy coupon below for ordering:

Special Offer
Buy a Bantam Book
for only 50¢.

Now you can have Bantam's catalog filled with hundreds of titles plus take advantage of our unique and exciting bonus book offer. A special offer which gives you the opportunity to purchase a Bantam book for only 50¢. Here's how!

By ordering any five books at the regular price per order, you can also choose any other single book listed (up to a $4.95 value) for just 50¢. Some restrictions do apply, but for further details why not send for Bantam's catalog of titles today!

Just send us your name and address and we will send you a catalog!

THE UNFORGETTABLE FANTASY NOVELS OF
R. A. MacAvoy

```
  190              1750
  130
   70              800
   80              443
   10            ──────
  149             1243
   25
 ─────            1190
  654      8         6
           15
           36
          17.50   12 43
          90.00      90
        ────────   ───
        158.50      3
                   13
                    9

   2              3

  25     Blower
4 55     open     7 24
  149    Boing    158
   10    Dave    ─────
  130    Tim      882
  190    Seatcoat
   70    whitey —  96 = 166 – month
   15    Broom
   80    Paint                 800 00
 ────                          443
 7 24          80            ──────
                               12 43
                               74 0
                             ──────
                               5 03
```